THE BOOK THE MILLIONS
OF READERS OF *RICH MAN, POOR MAN*
HAVE AWAITED IS HERE!

"A BETTER BOOK,
A GOOD DEAL MORE SUSPENSE . . .
CONSIDERABLE ENJOYMENT."
—*The New York Times*

THESE WERE THE JORDACHES . . .
and theirs was a tumultuous passage from generation to generation . . . a turbulent story of a young
man's quest for vengeance and self-discovery . . .
of love and violence on two continents . . . of people caught in the inexorable pull of limitless wealth,
bloody terrorism, and sexual depravity.

This is the tale of a passionate, lustful, ruthless
family—driven by dark forces deep within their
blood to live life like a powerful and magnificent
obsession.

IRWIN SHAW'S
*BEGGARMAN, THIEF*

"IT STANDS ALONE AS A FICTIONAL CREA-
TION. . . . Polished prose, authentic dialogue,
well-realized characters . . . Shaw's expertise is
evident on every page . . . SOMETHING FOR
EVERYONE!"
—*Los Angeles Times*

## Books by Irwin Shaw

### NOVELS

\* *Voices of a Summer Day*
\* *The Young Lions*
\* *The Troubled Air*
\* *Lucy Crown*
\* *Two Weeks in Another Town*
\* *Rich Man, Poor Man*
\* *Evening in Byzantium*
\* *Nightwork*
\* *Beggarman, Thief*

### SHORT STORY COLLECTIONS

*Sailor off the Bremen*
*Welcome to the City*
*Act of Faith*
*Mixed Company*
*Tip on a Dead Jockey*
\* *Love on a Dark Street*
\* *God Was Here, but He Left Early*

### PLAYS

*Bury the Dead*
*The Gentle People*
*Sons and Soldiers*
*The Assassin*
*Children from Their Games*

### NONFICTION

*In the Company of Dolphins*
\* *Paris! Paris!*

\* Available in Dell Editions

# IRWIN SHAW

# Beggar-man, Thief

**A Dell Book**

# To Jim and Gloria

Published by
DELL PUBLISHING CO., INC.
1 Dag Hammarskjold Plaza
New York, N.Y. 10017

Portions of this work have been
previously published in *Playboy* and *Family Circle*
in somewhat different form.

Dell ® TM 681510, Dell Publishing Co., Inc.

ISBN: 0-440-10701-6

Reprinted by arrangement with
Delacorte Press

Printed in the United States of America

First Dell printing—August 1978
Second Dell printing—September 1978
Third Dell printing—September 1978
Fourth Dell printing—September 1978

*Author's Note*

Ordinarily there is no need for a preface for a novel, but because of the television presentation of "Rich Man, Poor Man" (Part I and Part II), I believe the readers of *Beggarman, Thief* should know that the new book is a sequel to the *printed* version of *Rich Man, Poor Man,* not the televised one, and any similarities to the Part II television offering are purely coincidental.

I hope this note helps clear up any confusion in the mind of the reader of this book who has also viewed either or both of the two television series.

# VOLUME
## ONE

# CHAPTER 1

*From Billy Abbott's notebook—*

I am worthless, Monika says. She says it
only half-seriously. Monika, on the
other hand, is not demonstrably
worthless. Being in love with her
undoubtedly clouds my vision of her.
More about that later.

She asked me once what I write in this
notebook. I told her that the Colonel
keeps saying we here in NATO are on the
firing line of civilization. It is
important for future generations, I told
her, to know what it was like to be on
the firing line of civilization in
Brussels in the second half of the
twentieth century. Maybe some dusty,
irradiated scholar will dig around in
the ruins of the city and come upon
this notebook, charred a little around
the edges and perhaps stiff with the
rusty stains of my blood, and be
grateful to Wm. Abbott, Junior, for his

forethought in jotting down his
observations of how the simple American
soldier lived while defending
civilization on the edge of Europe.
What the price of oysters was, the shape
and dimensions of his beloved's breasts,
his simple pleasures, like fucking and
stealing gasoline from the army, things
like that.

Monika said, Did I always have to be
frivolous? And I said, what else is
there to be?

Don't you believe in anything? She
asked me.

I believe in not bucking the tide, I
told her. If there's a parade going
down the street I fall in line and keep
step, waving to the populace, friend and
foe alike.

Go back to your scribbling, she said.
Write down that you're not a true
representative of your generation.

Scribbling perhaps is the word for
what I'm doing. I come from a literary
family. Both my mother and father are—
or were—writers. Of a sort. My father
was a public relations man, a member
of a profession not held in particularly
high esteem in the halls of Academe or
in publishers' offices. Still
whatever the merits or failures that can
be put to his account, he achieved them
at a typewriter. He lives in Chicago now
and writes me often, especially when he
is drunk. I reply dutifully. We are
great friends when we are four thousand
miles apart.

My mother used to write criticism for
nasty little magazines. Our com-

<br/>

munications are minimal. She does
something for the movies now. I grew up
to the music of typewriters and it seems
normal for me to put my thoughts, such
as they are, on paper. The amusements
are limited here, although it's better
than Nam, as the Colonel keeps saying.

I play tennis with the Colonel and
praise his feeble backhand, which is one
way of getting ahead in the army.

If the preemptive Russian strike
doesn't hit NATO, as the Colonel warns
it will, I'll keep scribbling. It gives
me something to do when things get slow
at the motor pool, where I am called
the Truckmaster.

I wonder what the guy in charge of the
motor pool at the headquarters of the
Warsaw Pact Forces is doing tonight as
I write this.

———

Alexander Hubbell was a newspaperman. Or at least
he worked for *Time* Magazine in Paris. He was not supposed to be a newspaperman this week because he was
on holiday with his wife. His wife was taking a siesta in
the hotel at the base of the cape and Alexander Hubbell
was approaching the *préfecture* of police in Antibes. He
had been puzzling over a name that he had read in
*Nice-Matin* three days ago, Jordache. An American
named Jordache had been murdered in the port of Antibes just five days after his wedding. The murderer or
murderers were being sought. For the time being no
motive for the crime had been found. The victim who
had been the owner of a yacht called the *Clothilde,*
berthed in the harbor of Antibes, had been clubbed to
death on the deck of his own ship.

Hubbell prided himself on his newspaperman's memory and it had annoyed him that a name he felt he should have recognized and classified played only at the edges of his consciousness. He was relieved when he remembered. When he was still working in New York, there had been an issue of *Life* Magazine with the photographs of ten promising young politicians throughout the United States and one of the pictures had been of somebody called Jordache, he couldn't recall the Christian name, who was the mayor of a small town about a hundred miles from New York City called Whitby. Then he remembered more. After the piece in *Life* there had been a scandal at the college in Whitby when rioting students had demonstrated in front of the mayor's home and the mayor's wife had appeared at the doorway drunk and naked. Somebody had taken a photograph and the print had gone around the office.

Still, a man whose wife had exposed herself bare-assed in front of a howling mob of students might well have gotten rid of her and married somebody with less flamboyant habits.

Of course, it might be somebody entirely different with the same name, Hubbell thought, as he waited for a light to change. A yacht in Antibes was a long way from Whitby, New York. Anyway, it was worth looking into. If it turned out to be the same promising young politician it would make a useful little story, vacation or no vacation. He had been on holiday five days already and was beginning to get bored.

The single policeman in the paint-flaked empty anteroom was dozing behind his desk, but brightened, glad for company, when Hubbell told him, in his good French, that he was a newspaperman and that he had come to make inquiries about the murder. The policeman went into another room and came out a moment later to tell him that the *chef* could see him now. Crime, it seemed, was not rife in Antibes that afternoon.

The *chef* was a sleepy-eyed, small, dark man in a blue T-shirt and rumpled cotton pants. A gold front tooth gleamed when he spoke: "What can I do for you, *monsieur?*"

Hubbell explained that the details of the murder of an American in France, especially if this was the Jordache he thought it was, a man of considerable importance back home, would be of interest to the American public. He and his editors would be most grateful to the *chef* for any light he could shed on the affair.

The *chef* was used to French newspapermen, who had treated the murder as a routine settling of waterfront accounts. This shrewd-looking American, representative of a prestigious magazine, investigating the death of a fellow countryman in a holiday resort that attracted many Americans, was a different matter. The *chef* would have been happier if the arrest had already been made and the culprit behind bars, but there was no help for that at the moment.

"Are there any clues," the man was saying, "as to who might have done it or what the motives were?"

"We are working on the case with diligence," the *chef* said. "Twenty-four hours a day."

"Do you have any leads?"

The *chef* hesitated for a moment. In the movies reporters were always finding clues the police overlooked. The American seemed like an intelligent man and there was the possibility that he might come up with something useful. "On the night of his wedding," the *chef* said, "*Monsieur* Jordache was involved in an argument—a brutal argument, I have been told by his sister-in-law—in a bar in Cannes called La Porte Rose—with a man who is known to the police. A foreigner. Yugoslav. By name Danovic. We have interrogated him. He has a perfect alibi, but we would like to question him again. Unfortunately, he seems to have disappeared. We are at the moment looking for him."

"A brutal argument," Hubbell said. "You mean a fight."

The *chef* nodded. "Of extreme brutality, I have been told by the sister-in-law."

"Do you know what it was about?"

"The sister-in-law claims that the foreigner was about to commit rape on her when *Monsieur* Jordache intervened."

"I see," Hubbell said. "Was Jordache in the habit of getting into fights in bars?"

"Not to my knowledge," the *chef* said. "I knew *Monsieur* Jordache. In fact, we occasionally had a glass together. It was with great sorrow that I learned of his death. I knew him as a peaceful man. He was very well liked. He had no known enemies. However—I cannot believe that he was a man of some importance in America, as you have said."

"*Nice-Matin* says he owned a yacht," Hubbell said. He laughed lightly. "That's pretty important."

"He worked the yacht," the *chef* said. "He was a charter captain. It was his means of livelihood."

"I see," Hubbell said. He couldn't imagine one of the ten most promising young politicians in America making his living out of ferrying boating parties around the Mediterranean, no matter how many times his wife had displayed herself naked back home. The story was becoming less interesting. "Perhaps the murder was political?" he asked hopefully.

"I don't believe so. He was not a political man at all. We tend to accumulate information on political people."

"Smuggling?"

"I hardly think so. In that field, too, we have our information. Or at least suspicions."

"How would you describe him, then?" Hubbell persisted, out of force of habit.

The *chef* shrugged. "A decent workingman. A good type." *Brave type* in French. Measured praise, slightly patronizing from a French cop. "Honest, as far as anyone knew," the *chef* went on. "We were not really intimate. He spoke very little French. Not like you, *monsieur*." Hubbell nodded recognition of the compliment. "And my English, I regret to say, is most rudimentary." The *chef* smiled at his disability. "We did not discuss our private philosophies."

"What did he do before he came here? Do you know?"

"He was a merchant seaman." The *chef* hesitated. Jordache had told him over a glass of wine, after the *chef* had commented on the broken nose, the scar tissue, that he had been a boxer. But he had asked the *chef* to keep quiet about it. In waterfront cafés boxers were likely targets for large men made belligerent by drink. "I didn't come to France to fight," Jordache had said. "It isn't my lucky country for fighting. I had one bout in Paris and got my brains knocked out." He'd laughed as he said it. From the look of the body the fight he'd been in before he died hadn't been a lucky one, either.

Well, the *chef* thought, why not tell the newspaperman? It couldn't do any harm anymore to Jordache, who wasn't going to be doing much drinking in waterfront cafés from now on. "It appears," said the *chef*, "that he was a professional pugilist. He even fought in Paris. Once. In the main event. He was knocked out."

"A fighter?" Hubbell's interest was aroused once more. The sports section might run a couple of hundred words. If the man had fought a main event in Paris he must have had some sort of reputation. People would be curious about an American fighter being killed in France. He would telex into the office as much of the story as he could dig up here and tell it to get the background dope out of the morgue. They rewrote all of his stories in New York anyway. "Jordache?" Hubbell said. "I don't remember any fighter by that name."

"He fought under an assumed name," the *chef* said, making a mental note for himself to look into that part of Jordache's history. Professional boxing was a business that gangsters were always mixed up in. There might be a lead there—a promise broken, a deal gone sour. He should have thought of it sooner. "He fought under the name of Tommy Jordan."

"Ah," the newspaperman said. "That helps. Certainly. I remember some stories in the papers about him. That he was promising."

"I know nothing about that," the *chef* said. "Just the fight in Paris. I looked it up in *l'Equipe*. He was a great disappointment, *l'Equipe* said." Now he wanted to call a promoter in Marseilles who had connections with the *milieu*. He stood up. "I'm afraid I have to go back to work now," he said. "If you want more information perhaps you could speak to the members of his family. His wife, his brother, his son."

"His brother? He's here?"

"The entire family," the *chef* said. "They had been on a cruise together."

"Would you happen to know the brother's first name?"

"Rudolph. The family was originally German."

Rudolph, Hubbell thought, remembering, Rudolph Jordache, that was the name in *Life*. "So," he said, "he wasn't the one who was married here?"

"No," the *chef* said impatiently.

"And his wife is here, too?"

"Yes, and under the circumstances she, the sister-in-law, might be able to help you more than I can . . ."

"The sister-in-law?" Hubbell said, standing too. "The one in the bar?"

"Yes. I suggest you ask her," the *chef* said. "If you find out anything that might assist me I would be grateful if you visited me again. Now, I'm afraid I . . ."

"Where can I find her?"

"She is at the Hôtel du Cap at present." He had ordered Jean Jordache to remain in Antibes for the time being, and had taken her passport. He would need Jean Jordache for help in the case when he found Danovic. *If* he ever found him again. He had interviewed the woman, but she had been hysterical and drunk and he had gotten only a confused and disjointed story from her. And now the idiot of a doctor had put her under sedation. The doctor had said she was unstable, a confirmed alcoholic, and that he wouldn't be responsible for her sanity if the *chef* kept after her with questions. "The others," the *chef* said, "I believe can be found on the *Clothilde* in the harbor. Thank you for your interest, *monsieur*. I trust I haven't wasted your time." He put out his hand.

Hubbell said, *"Merci bien, monsieur."* He had gotten all the information he was going to get, and left.

The *chef* sat down at his desk and picked up the phone to dial Marseilles.

The small white ship moved slowly in the afternoon sunlight across the Mediterranean swell. On the far-off coast, the buildings along the shore and back in the hills made a pink and white pattern against the green background of pine and olive and palm. Dwyer stood in the bow, the name of the ship, *Clothilde,* printed on his clean white jersey. He was a short, tight-muscled man and he had been crying. Because of his protruding long

front teeth he had always been called Bunny, as far
back as he could remember. Despite his muscles and his
workingman's clothes, there was something ineradicably
girlish about him. "I'm not a fag," he had said the first
time he had had any kind of conversation with the dead
man, whose ashes had just been strewn over the sea. He
stared at the pretty coast through tear-blurred, soft
black eyes. *Rich man's weather,* the murdered man had
said.

*You could say that again,* Dwyer thought. *Not his
weather, nor mine either. We fooled ourselves. We
came to the wrong place.*

Alone in the pilothouse, dressed like Dwyer in chinos
and white jersey, his hand on a spoke of the polished
oak and brass wheel, stood Wesley Jordache, his eyes
fixed on the point of land on which stood the citadel of
Antibes. He was tall for his age, a lanky, powerful, raw-
boned boy, tanned, his blond hair bleached in streaks
by sun and salt. Like Dwyer, he was thinking of the
man whose ashes he had consigned to the sea, the man
who had been his father. "Poor, stupid, crazy son of a
bitch," the boy said aloud, bitterly. He remembered the
day his father, whom he hadn't seen for years, had
come to take him out of the military school on the Hudson, where he had fought half the students, all ages, all
classes, all sizes, in blind, incomprehensible, meaning-
less fury.

"You've had your last fight," his father had said.

Then the silence. And the rough man saying, "Did
you hear me?"

"Yes, sir."

"Don't call me sir," the man had said. "I'm your father."

*His father had laid down the rules for the wrong
member of the family,* the boy thought, his eyes on the

citadel where, he had been told, Napoleon had been imprisoned one night on his return from Elba.

At the rail aft, dressed in incongruous black, stood
the boy's uncle, Rudolph Jordache, and his aunt,
Gretchen Burke, brother and sister of the murdered
man. City people, unaccustomed to the sea, accustomed
to tragedy; stiff figures of death against the sunny horizon. They did not touch or speak or look at each other.
What was left unsaid on this azure summer afternoon
would not have to be explained or mourned or apologized for later.

The woman was in her early forties, tall, slender and
straight, her black hair blowing a little in the offshore
breeze, framing a luminously pale face, the signs of age
just omens now, hints of things to come. She had been
beautiful as a girl and was beautiful in a different way
now, her face stern, marked by sorrow and a troubled
sensuality that was not temporary or fleeting but a permanent habit. Her eyes, squinting against the glare,
were a deep blue that in some lights shaded down to
violet. There was no damage of tears.

*It had to happen,* she thought. *Of course. We should
have known. He probably knew. Maybe not consciously, but known just the same. All that violence
could not have a nonviolent end. True son of his father,
the blond stranger in the family, alien to the dark
brother and the dark girl, although all from the same
bed.*

———

The man was slim, too, a well-cared-for, aristocratic
Yankee slimness, inherited from no parent, acquired by
an act of will, now accentuated by the neatly cut, almost
ambassadorial dark American suit. He was younger by

two years than his sister and looked younger than that, a false, gentle echo of youth in the face and bearing of a man whose speech and movements were always deliberate and considered, a man who had known great authority, had struggled all his life, had won and lost, had taken on responsibility in all situations, had come up from penury and want to amass a considerable fortune, who had been ruthless when necessary, cunning when it was useful to be cunning, harsh with himself and others, generous, by his lights, when it was possible to be generous. The resignation that had been forced upon him was there in the thin, controlled mouth, the watchful eyes, was there to be discovered or guessed at. It was a face that could have been that of a youthful air force general whose command had been taken away from him for a failure in the ranks below him that might or might not have been his fault.

*He went alone,* Rudolph Jordache was thinking; *he came into the cabin where I was sleeping and closed the door softly and left alone. Left for what was to become his death, disdaining my help, disdaining me, disdaining my manhood or what he would think of it, if he ever thought, as my lack of manhood, in a situation that required a man.*

Down below, Kate Jordache was packing her bag. It didn't take long. On top of her other things she first put the white jersey with the ship's name on it that had made Thomas laugh when he saw what her full bosom had done to the lettering, then the bright dress he had bought her for their wedding just eight days ago.

*She had nagged Thomas into marrying her. That was the word—nagged. They had been perfectly happy before, but then when she knew she was pregnant— Proper, bloody little well-brought-up, lower-class, obedient, English working girl . . . Here comes the bride. If there had been no wedding, that awful, twittery, smart-talking woman, that fancy wife of Rudolph's, would never have had the excuse to get drunk, would not have gone off with a Yugoslav pimp, would have kept her expensive pink pants on her, would not have needed rescuing or a man fighting for her, and a man a lot better than her husband would be alive today.*

*Enough of that,* Kate thought. *Enough. Enough.*

She closed the bag with a snap and sat down on the edge of the bunk, her solid brown body just beginning to show the swell of the child within her, her capable, quick hands folded quietly in her lap as she looked around her, for the last time, she had decided, at the cramped cabin with the familiar noise of the sea swishing past the open porthole.

*Thomas,* she thought, *Thomas, Thomas.*

"Who was Clothilde?" she had asked once.

"She was a queen of France. She was somebody I knew as a boy. She smelled like you."

Absent from the small company of mourners on the vessel heading for the coast of France was Jean, Rudolph Jordache's wife. She sat on a bench in the park of the hotel watching her daughter playing with the young girl Rudolph had hired to take care of the child until, as Rudolph had put it, she was in condition to handle Enid again herself. How long would that be? Jean had asked herself. Two days, ten years, never?

She was dressed in slacks and a sweater. She had not brought along clothes suitable for a funeral. Rudolph had been relieved when she said she wouldn't go. She could not bear the thought of stepping aboard the *Clothilde* again, of facing the silent, accusing stares of the wife, the son, the beloved friend.

When she had looked at herself in the mirror in the

morning she was shocked at what the last days had done to the small, pretty, girlish face.

The skin of her face, her entire body, seemed to be stretched unbearably on some invisible rack. She felt as though at any moment her body would explode and her nerves erupt through the skin, snapping and crackling like wild lines of wire, crackling under fatal electrical charges.

The doctor had given her some Valium, but she was past Valium. If it weren't for the child, she thought, she would go down to the sea and throw herself off the rocks into it.

As she sat there in the shadow of a tree, in the spicy fragrance of pine and sun-warmed lavender, she said to herself, *Everything I touch I destroy.*

———

Hubbell sat over a coffee on the *terrasse* of a café in the main square, thinking over what the policeman had told him. The policeman obviously knew more than he was telling, but you had to expect that from the police, especially with an embarrassing unsolved murder on their hands. The sister-in-law might be able to help you more than I can, the cop had said. The sister-in-law. The naked lady, the wife of the promising young mayor. Definitely worth a couple of hundred words. The harbor could wait.

He paid for his coffee and walked over to a parked taxi and got in and said, "The Hôtel du Cap."

Madame Jordache was not in her room, the concierge said, but he had seen her go out into the park with her child and the child's nurse. Hubbell asked the concierge if there was a telex in the hotel and was told that there was one. He asked if he might use it that evening and after a moment's hesitation the concierge said he thought that could be arranged. The hesitation Hubbell rightly interpreted to mean that a tip would be involved. No matter. *Time* Magazine could afford it. He thanked the concierge and went out to the terrace and the steps leading to the long avenue through the noble park down to the bathing pavilion and restaurant and the sea. He suffered a moment of envy as he thought of the small room in the noisy little hotel on the highway in which his wife was taking her siesta. *Time* Magazine paid well, but not well enough for the Hôtel du Cap.

He went down the steps and into the fragrant park. A minute later he saw a little girl in a white bathing suit throwing a beach ball back and forth with a young girl. Seated on a bench nearby was a woman in slacks and a sweater. It was not the sort of scene that you would ordinarily associate with a murder.

He approached the group slowly, stopping for a moment as if to admire a bed of flowers, then smiling at the child as he neared the group. *"Bonjour,"* he said. "Good afternoon."

The girl said, *"Bonjour,"* but the woman on the bench said nothing. Hubbell noticed that she was very pretty, with a trim, athletic figure, that her face was drained and pale, with dark circles under the eyes. "Mrs. Jordache?" he said.

"Yes?" Her voice was flat and toneless. She looked up at him dully.

"I'm from *Time* Magazine." He was an honorable man and would not pretend to be a friend of her husband's or of the murdered man or an American tourist who had heard about her trouble and wished, in his frank American way, to offer his sympathy. Leave the tricks for the young fellows fighting for by-lines. "I've been sent down to do a story on your brother-in-law."

A white lie, but permissible within his code. If people thought you were assigned to do a job, they often felt some small obligation to help.

Still the woman said nothing, just stared at him with those lifeless eyes.

"The chief of police said you might be able to give me some information about the affair. Background information." The "background" had an innocuous ring to it, with its assumption that what would be said would not actually be published, but merely used as a guide for a responsible journalist who wanted to avoid errors in writing his story.

"Have you talked to my husband?" Jean asked.

"I haven't met him yet."

"Haven't met him yet," Jean repeated. "I wish I hadn't. And I bet *he* wishes I hadn't."

Hubbell was taken aback, as much by the intensity with which the woman had spoken as by what she had said.

"Did the policeman tell you why I could give you information?" the woman demanded, her voice harsh and rasping now.

"No," Hubbell lied.

Jean stood up abruptly. "Ask my husband," she said, "ask the whole goddamn family. Just leave me alone."

"Just one question, Mrs Jordache, if I may," Hubbell said, his throat constricted. "Would you be prepared to lay criminal charges against the man who attacked you?"

"What difference would it make?" she said dully. She sat heavily on the bench, stared at her child, running after the beach ball in the sunshine. "Go away. Go away. Please."

Hubbell got out of the taxi and walked along the port. Not a fitting place to die, he thought as he went toward the port captain's shack to find out where the

*Clothilde* was berthed. The port captain was a weathered old man, sitting outside his shack, smoking a pipe, his chair tilted against the wall as he took the afternoon sun.

The port captain gestured with his pipe toward the mouth of the port, where a white boat was slowly coming in. "There she is. They'll be here for a while," the old man said. "They chewed up their starboard propeller and shaft. You American?"

"I am."

"It's a shame what happened, isn't it?"

"Terrible," Hubbell said.

"They just buried his ashes in the sea," the old man volunteered. "As good a place to be buried as anywhere else for a sailor. I wouldn't mind it myself." Even in midseason, the port captain had plenty of time for conversation.

Hubbell thanked the man and walked around the port and sat down on an upturned dory near the place on the quay into which the *Clothilde* was being maneuvered. He saw the two figures in black at the stern, with the American flag rippling in the breeze behind them. He saw a short, tight-muscled man working on the chain forward and a tall blond boy spinning the wheel in the pilothouse as the ship slowly came in, stern first, with the engine now off and the blond boy running aft to throw a line to a sailor on the quay, as the man ran to the stern and jumped nimbly to the quay to catch a second line that the boy threw to him. When the two lines were secure, the man leaped back onto the deck and he and the boy manhandled the gangplank into place, practiced and skillful, no word between them. The two people in black had moved from the stern, out of the way, superfluous.

Hubbell got up from where he was sitting on the dory, feeling clumsy and heavy after the display of sea-going agility, and started up the gangplank. The boy looked at him sullenly.

"I'm looking for Mr. Jordache," Hubbell said.

"My name is Jordache," the boy said. He had a deep, non-adolescent voice.

"I believe I mean that gentleman over there," Hubbell said, gesturing toward Rudolph.

"Yes?" Rudolph came over to the head of the gangplank.

"Mr. Rudolph Jordache?"

"Yes." The tone was short.

"I'm from *Time* Magazine . . ." Hubbell saw the man's face set. "I'm very sorry about what happened. . . ."

"Yes?" Impatiently, questioning.

"I don't like to intrude on you at a moment like this . . ." Hubbell felt foolish, talking at a distance, blocked off by the invisible wall of the boy's hostility, and now the man's. "But I wonder if I could ask you a few questions about . . ."

"Talk to the chief of police. It's his business now."

"I have talked to him."

"Then you know as much as I do, sir," Rudolph said and turned away. There was a cold, small smile on the boy's face.

Hubbell stood there another moment, feeling that perhaps he had been wrong in his choice of a profession, then said, "I'm sorry," to nobody in particular because he couldn't think of anything else to say or do and turned around and walked toward the entrance to the port.

When he got back to his hotel, his wife was sitting on the small balcony outside their room in a bikini, working on her tan. He loved her deeply, but he couldn't help noticing that she looked absurd in a bikini. "Where've you been all afternoon?" she asked.

"Working on a story," he said.

"I thought this was going to be a vacation," she said.

"So did I," he said.

He got out his portable typewriter, took off his jacket and began to work.

---

# CHAPTER 2

*From Billy Abbott's notebook—*

The telegram from my mother came to my
APO number. Your Uncle Tom has been
murdered, the telegram read. Suggest
you try to come to Antibes for funeral.
Your Uncle Rudolph and I are at the
Hotel du Cap Antibes. Love, Mother.

I had seen my Uncle Tom once, the time
I had flown from California to Whitby
for my grandmother's funeral when I was
a boy. Funerals are great occasions for
families to get to know each other
again. I was sorry my Uncle Tom was
dead. I had liked him the night we had
spent together in my Uncle Rudolph's
guest room. I was impressed by the fact
that he carried a gun. He thought I was
sleeping when he took the gun out of
his pocket and put it away in a drawer.
It gave me something to think about
during the funeral the next day.

If an uncle had to be murdered, I
would have preferred it to be Rudolph.
We were never friendly and as I grew
older he showed me, very politely, that
he disapproved of me and my views on
society. My views have not changed
radically. Jelled, my uncle would
probably say, if he took the trouble to
examine them. But he is rich and there
might have been some mention of me in
his will, if not out of any fondness for
me then out of brotherly love for my
mother. Thomas Jordache was not the type
of man to leave a fortune behind him.

I showed the telegram to the Colonel
and he gave me ten days compassionate
leave to go to Antibes. I didn't go to
Antibes, but I sent a telegram of
condolence to the hotel and said that
the army wouldn't let me off for the
funeral.

Monika got time off her job, too, and
we went to Paris. We had a marvelous
time. Monika is exactly the sort of girl
you want to have with you in Paris.

---

"I'm afraid the time has come," Rudolph said, "to
discuss a few things we've avoided up to now. We have
to talk about what we're going to do next. The legacy.
Painful as it is, we're going to have to talk about
money."

They were all in the saloon of the *Clothilde*, Kate in
a dark dress that was obviously old and now too tight
for her, with her scuffed, imitation-leather suitcase on
the floor next to her chair. The saloon was painted
white, with blue trim and blue curtains at the portholes

and on the bulkhead old prints of sailing ships that
Thomas had picked up in Venice. Everybody kept looking at Kate's suitcase, although no one had said anything about it yet.

"Kate, Bunny," Rudolph went on, "do you know if
Tom left a will?"

"He never said anything to me about a will," Kate
said.

"Me, neither," said Dwyer.

"Wesley?"

Wesley shook his head.

Rudolph sighed. Same old Tom, he thought, consis-
tent to the end. Married, with a son and a pregnant wife,
and never took an afternoon off to write a will. He himself had drawn up his first will in a lawyer's office when
he was twenty-one years old and five or six later ones
since then, the last one when his daughter Enid was
born. And now that Jean was spending more and more
time in drying-out clinics he was working on a new one.
"How about a safe-deposit box?" he asked.

"Not that I know of," Kate said.

"Bunny?"

"I'm pretty sure not," Dwyer said.

"Did he have any securities?"

Kate and Dwyer looked at each other, puzzled. "Securities?" Dwyer asked. "What's that?"

"Stocks, bonds." Where have these people been all
their lives? Rudolph wondered.

"Oh, that," Dwyer said. "He used to say that was just
another way they'd figured out to screw the workingman." He had also said, "Leave stuff like that to my
goddamn brother," but that was before the final reconciliation between the two men and Dwyer didn't think
this was the time for that particular quotation.

"Okay, no securities," Rudolph said. "Then what did
he do with his money?" He tried not to sound irritated.

"He had two accounts," Kate said. "A checking account in francs at the Crédit Lyonnais here in Antibes and a dollar savings account in Crédit Suisse in Geneva. He preferred being paid in dollars. That account is illegal, because we're French residents, but I wouldn't worry about that. Nobody ever asked."

Rudolph nodded. At least his brother hadn't been *totally* devoid of financial sense.

"The bankbook and the last statements from the Crédit Lyonnais and the checkbook are in the drawer under the bunk in the cabin," Kate said. "Wesley, if you'll go in there . . ."

Wesley went forward toward the captain's cabin.

"If I may ask, Bunny," Rudolph said, "how did Thomas pay you?"

"He didn't," Dwyer said. "We were partners. At the end of the year, we split up what was left over."

"Did you have any kind of papers—a contract, some kind of formal agreement?"

"Christ, no," Dwyer said. "What would we need a contract for?"

"Is the boat in his name or in your joint names, Bunny? Or perhaps in his and Kate's name?"

"We were only married five days, Rudy," Kate said. "We didn't have any time for anything like that. The *Clothilde* is in his name. The papers are in the drawer with the bankbooks. With the insurance policy for the ship and the other papers."

Rudolph sighed again. "I've been to a lawyer . . ."

Of course, Gretchen thought. She had been standing at the doorway, looking aft. She had been brooding over Billy's telegram. It had been a brief message from a polite stranger, with no feeling of grief or attempt at consolation. She didn't know the army all that well, but she knew that soldiers got leave, if they wanted it, to attend funerals. She had written Billy, too, about com-

ing to the wedding, but he had written back saying he
was too busy dispatching half-tons and command cars
through the streets and roads that led through Belgium
to Armageddon to dance at half-forgotten relatives'
weddings. She, too, she thought bitterly, was included
among the half-forgotten relatives. Let him wallow in
Brussels. Worthy son of his father. She focused her attention on her brother, patiently trying to disentangle
tangled lives. Of course, Rudy would have gone immediately to a lawyer. Death, after all, was a legal matter.

"A French lawyer," Rudolph went on, "who luckily
speaks good English; the manager of the hotel gave me
his name. He seems like a reliable man. He told me that
although you're all French residents, since you live on
the boat and have no home on land and by French law
the boat is technically American territory, it would be
best to ignore the French and accept the jurisdiction of
the American consul in Nice. Do either of you have
any objection to that?"

"Whatever you say, Rudolph," Kate said. "Whatever
you think best."

"If you can get away with it, okay with me," Dwyer
said. He sounded bored, like a small boy in school during an arithmetic lesson, wishing he was outside playing
baseball.

"I'll try to talk to the consul this afternoon," Rudolph
said, "and see what he advises."

Wesley came in with the Crédit Suisse passbook and
the Crédit Lyonnais checkbook and the last three
monthly bank statements.

"Do you mind if I look at these?" Rudolph asked
Kate.

"He was your brother."

As usual, thought Gretchen, at the door, her back to
the saloon, nobody lets Rudy off any hook.

Rudolph took the books and papers from Wesley. He

looked at the last statement from the Crédit Lyonnais. There was a balance of a little over ten thousand francs. About two thousand dollars, Rudolph calculated as he read the figure aloud. Then he opened the passbook. "Eleven thousand, six hundred and twenty-two dollars," he said. He was surprised that Thomas had saved that much.

"If you ask me," Kate said, "that's the whole thing. The whole kit and caboodle."

"Of course, there's the ship," said Rudolph. "What's to be done with it?"

For a moment there was silence in the cabin.

"I know what *I'm* going to do with the ship," Kate said mildly, without emotion, standing up. "I'm going to leave it. Right now." The outdated, too-tight dress pulled up over her plump, dimpled, brown knees.

"Kate," Rudolph protested, "something has to be decided."

"Whatever you decide is all right with me," Kate said. "I'm not going to stay aboard another night."

Dear, normal, down-to-earth woman, Gretchen thought, waiting to say a last good-bye to her man and then leaving, not looking for profit or advantage from the object that had been her home, her livelihood, the source of her happiness.

"Where are you going?" Rudolph asked Kate.

"For the time being to a hotel in town," Kate said. "After that, I'll see. Wesley, will you carry my bag for me to a taxi?"

Silently, Wesley picked up the bag in his big hand.

"I'll call you at your hotel when I feel I can talk, Rudy," Kate said. "Thank you for everything. You're a good man." She kissed him on the cheek, the kiss a benediction, a tacit gesture of exoneration, and followed Wesley past Gretchen out the saloon door to the deck.

Rudolph sank into the chair she had been sitting on

and rubbed his eyes wearily. Gretchen came over to him and touched his shoulder affectionately. Affection, she had learned, could be mixed with criticism, even with scorn. "Take it easy, Brother," she said. "You can't settle everybody's lives in one afternoon."

"I've been talking to Wesley," Dwyer said. "He knew Kate was leaving. He wants to stay on the *Clothilde* with me. At least for a while. At least until the screw and the shaft're fixed. Don't worry about him. I'll take care of him."

"Yes," Rudolph said. He stood up, hunched over a little, his shoulders burdened. "It's getting late. I'd better try to get to Nice before the consulate closes. Gretchen, do you want me to drive you to the hotel?"

"Thanks, no," Gretchen said. "I think I'll stay on here a few minutes and have a drink with Bunny. Maybe two drinks." This was no afternoon to leave Dwyer alone.

"As you say," Rudolph said. He put the bankbooks and the statements he had been holding in his hand on the table. "If you see Jean, tell her I won't be back for dinner."

"I'll do that," Gretchen said.

It was no afternoon, she thought, to be forced to speak to Jean Jordache, either.


"I think it might be nicer on deck," Gretchen said to Dwyer after Rudolph had gone. The saloon, which had until now seemed like a welcoming, cosy room, had been darkened for her into a sinister countinghouse, where lives were entered in ledgers, became symbols, credits and debits, not flesh and blood.

She had gone through it before. When her husband had been killed in the automobile accident there hadn't been a will, either. Perhaps Colin Burke, who had never hit a man in his life, who had lived surrounded by books, play scripts, screenplays, who had dealt gently and diplomatically with the writers and actors whom he had directed, and often enough hated, had more in common than was apparent on the surface with her barely literate, ruffian brother.

Without a will, there had been confusion about the disposal of Colin's property. There was an ex-wife who lived on alimony, a mortgaged house, royalties. The lawyers had moved in, the estate tied up for more than a year. Rudy had handled everything then, as he was doing now, as he always did.

"I'll bring the drinks," Dwyer was saying. "It's nice of you to visit with me. The hardest part is being alone. After everything we been through, Tom and me. And now Kate's gone. Most women would have made trouble aboard. Between two men been friends and partners for so long. Not Kate." Dwyer's mouth was quivering, almost imperceptibly. "She's all right, old Kate, isn't she?"

"A lot better than all right," Gretchen said. "Make it a stiff one, Bunny."

"Whiskey, isn't it?"

"Plenty of ice, please." She went forward where the saloon cabin and wheelhouse would hide them from passersby on the quay. She had had enough of friends of Tom and Dwyer and Kate from the other boats in the harbor coming on board with doleful faces to mumble their condolences. Their grief was plain. She was not as sure of her own.

In the bow, with the neat coiled spirals of lines and the polished brass and the bleached, immaculate teak deck, she looked out at the now familiar scene of the crowded harbor which had enchanted her when she saw it the first day: the bobbing masts, the men working slowly and carefully at the million small tasks that seemed to make up the daily routine of those who took

their living from the sea. Even now, after all that had
happened, she could not help but be affected by its
quiet beauty.

Dwyer came up behind her, barefooted, the ice tin-
kling in the glasses in his hands. He gave her her glass.
She raised it to him, smiling ruefully. She hadn't had
anything to eat or drink all day and the first mouthful
tingled on her tongue. "I don't usually drink hard
stuff," Dwyer said, "but maybe I ought to learn." He
drank in small sips, thoughtfully savoring the taste and
effect. "I tell you," he said, "your brother Rudy is one
hell of a man. A take-hold guy."

"Yes," Gretchen said. That was one way of describing
him.

"We'd've been in a stink of a mess without him. . . ."

Or no mess at all, Gretchen thought, if he'd kept his
wife at home and stayed on the other continent.

"We'd've been stolen blind without him," Dwyer said.

"By whom?"

"Lawyers," Dwyer said vaguely. "Ships' brokers, the
law. Everybody."

Here was a man, Gretchen thought, who had been
caught at sea in hurricanes, had done his job at the ex-
tremity of physical endurance, when a failure would
have sent him and those who depended upon him to the
bottom, who had survived the company of violent and
brutal men, but who felt reduced to helplessness by a
slip of paper, a mention of land-based authority. Another race, thought Gretchen, who all her adult life had
been surrounded by men who moved among paper, in
and out of offices, as surefooted and confident as an
Indian in the forest. Her dead brother had belonged to
another race, perhaps from birth.

"The one I'm worried about," Dwyer said, "is Wesley."

Worried, not for himself, she thought, who saw no

need for contracts, who just split up what was left over at the end of the year, who had no legal right, even, at this moment, to be standing on the scrubbed deck of the pretty boat on which he had earned his living for years. "Wesley will be all right," she said. "Rudy'll take care of him."

"He won't want that," Dwyer said, drinking. "Wesley. He wanted to be like his father. Sometimes it was funny, watching him, trying to move like his father, talk like his father, live up to his father." He took a gulp of his drink, made a little grimace, looked thoughtfully at the glass in his hand as if trying to decide whether it contained a friend or an enemy. He sighed, uncertain, then went on. "They used to stand up in the pilothouse all hours of the night; at sea or in port, you could hear them talking below, Wesley asking a question, Tom taking his time answering, long answers. I asked Tom once what the hell they had to talk about so much. Tom laughed. 'The kid asks me questions about my life and I tell him. I guess he wants to catch up on the years he missed. I guess he wants to know what his old man is all about. I was the same about my father, only he didn't give me any answers, he gave me a kick in the ass.' From what Tom let drop," Dwyer said, careful, understated, "I guess there wasn't no love lost between them, was there?"

"No," Gretchen said, "he wasn't a lovable man, our father. There wasn't much love in him. If there was, he reserved it for Rudolph."

Dwyer sighed. "Families," he said.

"Families," Gretchen repeated.

"I asked Tom what sort of questions Wesley asked him about him," Dwyer went on. " 'The usual,' Tom told me. 'What I was like when I was a kid in school, what my brother and sister'—that's you and Rudy— 'were like. How come I became a fighter, then a merchant seaman. When I had my first girl. What the other women I'd had were like, his goddamn mother. . . .' I asked Tom if he told the kid the truth. 'Nothing but,' Tom said. 'I'm a modern father. Tell the kids where babies come from, everything.' He had his own kind of sense of humor, Tom."

"Those must have been some conversations," Gretchen said.

" 'Spare the truth and spoil the child,' Tom said to me once. Every once in a while he sounded as though he'd picked up a little education here and there. Though he wasn't big on education. Tom had a deep suspicion of education. Maybe I shouldn't be saying this to you," Dwyer said earnestly, swishing the last of the ice around in his glass, "but he used your brother Rudy as an example. He'd say, 'Look at Rudy, he had all the education a man's brain could stand and look where he wound up, dry as an old raisin, a laughingstock after what his drunk wife did in his hometown, out on his ass, sitting there wondering what he was going to do with the rest of his life.' "

"I believe I could use another drink, Bunny," Gretchen said.

"Me, too," Dwyer said. "I'm beginning to like the taste." He took her glass and went aft and into the saloon.

Gretchen reflected on what Dwyer had said. It told more about Dwyer than it told about either Tom or Wesley. Tom had been the center of Dwyer's life, she realized; he probably could reproduce word for word everything that Tom had said to him from beginning to end. If Dwyer were a woman, you'd say he'd been in love with Tom. Even as a man . . . That girlish mouth, that little peculiarity in the way he used his hands. . . . Poor Dwyer, she thought, maybe he's finally going to be the one who's going to suffer most.

She had no real fix on Wesley. He had seemed like a mannerly, healthy boy when they had first come aboard. After his father's death, he had fallen silent, his face giving nothing away, avoiding them all. Rudy would take care of him, she had told Dwyer. She wondered if Rudy or anybody else would be capable of it.

Dwyer came back with the whiskey. The first drink was beginning to take effect. She felt dreamy, remote, all problems misty, removed. It was a better way to feel than the way she had been feeling recently. Maybe Jean, with her hidden bottles, knew something useful to know. Gratefully, she took a sip from the new glass.

Dwyer looked different, somehow troubled as he stood there, leaning against the rail, in his clean white jersey and chino pants, the comical protruding teeth that had burdened him with his nickname, chewing on his lip. It was as though he had decided something, something difficult, while he was alone in the saloon pouring the drinks. "Maybe I oughtn't to say this, Mrs. Burke . . ."

"Gretchen."

"Thank you, ma'am. But I feel like I can talk to you. Rudy's a fine man, I admire him, you couldn't ask for a better man to have on your side in the kind of situation we're in now—but he's not the sort of a man a guy like myself can talk to, I mean *really* talk to—you understand what I mean?"

"Yes," she said, "I understand."

"He's a fine man, like I said," Dwyer went on, uncomfortable, his mouth fidgeting, "but he's not like Tom."

"No, he's not," Gretchen said.

"Wesley's talked to me. He don't want to have nothing to do with Rudy. Or with his wife. That's just natural human nature, wouldn't you say, considering what's happened?"

"I'd say," Gretchen said. "Considering what's happened."

"If Rudy moves in on the kid—with the best intentions in the world, which I'm sure Rudy has—there's going to be trouble. Awful trouble. There's no telling what the kid will do."

"I agree with you," Gretchen said. She hadn't thought about it before but the moment the words had passed Dwyer's lips she had seen the truth of it. "But what's to be done? Kate's not his mother and she has her own problems. You?"

Dwyer laughed sadly. "Me? I don't know where I'll be twenty-four hours from now. The only thing I know is ships. Next week I may be sailing to Singapore. A month later to Valparaiso. Anyway, I ain't made to be anybody's father."

"So?"

"I been watching you real careful," Dwyer said. "Even though you didn't take no more notice of me than a piece of furniture . . ."

"Oh, come on now, Bunny," Gretchen said, guilty because almost the same thought had passed through her mind just a few minutes ago.

"I'm not sore about it and I'm not making any judgments, ma'am . . ."

"Gretchen," she said automatically.

"Gretchen," he repeated dutifully. "But since it happened—and now, staying here with me and letting me gab on—I see a real human being. I'm not saying Rudy ain't a human being," Dwyer added hastily, "only he's not Wesley's kind of human being. And his wife—" Dwyer stopped.

"Let's not talk about his wife."

"If *you* went up to Wesley and said, fair and square, right out in the open, 'You come along with me . . .'

he'd recognize it. He'd see you're the kind of woman he could take as a mother."

A new idea in the process of natural conception, Gretchen thought, sons choosing mothers. Would evolution never cease? "I'm not what you might call a model mother," she said dryly. The thought of being responsible in any way for the lanky, sullen-faced, silent boy with Tom's wild genes in him frightened her. "No, Bunny, I'm afraid it wouldn't work out."

"I thought I'd give it a try," Dwyer said listlessly. "I just don't want to see Wesley left on his own. He's not old enough to be left on his own, no matter what he thinks. There's an awful lot of commotion ahead for Wesley Jordache."

She couldn't help smiling a little at the word "commotion."

"Pinky Kimball, that's the engineer on the *Vega*," Bunny went on, "he's the one who saw Mrs. Jordache in the nightclub with the Yugoslav, he tells me Wesley's been pestering him. He wants Pinky to help find the guy, point him out to him. . . . I may be wrong, but what I believe, what Pinky thinks, too, is that Wesley wants to get revenge for his father."

"Oh, God," Gretchen said.

"You look around you here"—Dwyer made a gesture to take in the quiet harbor, the green hills, the useless fort and the picturesque, obsolete military walls—"and you think, what a nice, peaceful place this is. But the truth is, from Nice to Marseilles you got just about as many thugs as anyplace in the world. What with whores and drugs and smuggling and gambling there's an awful lot of gun and knife toting in this neighborhood and plenty of guys who'd kill their mother for ten thousand francs, or for nothing, if it came to that. And from what Pinky Kimball's told me, the fella Tom had the fight with is right in with them. If Wesley goes looking for the fella and finds him there's no telling what'll happen to him. At that military school Wesley was at, they had to tear him off other kids in fights, it wasn't just sparring in a gym, he would've killed them if there'd been nobody else around. If he wants Pinky Kimball to point out somebody it's because there's a good chance he wants to kill him."

"Oh, Christ," Gretchen said. "What're you trying to say, Bunny?"

"I'm trying to say that no matter what happens you got to get the kid out of here, out of the country. And Rudolph Jordache ain't the man to do it. Now," he said, "I'm drunk. I wouldn't've talked like this if I wasn't drunk. But I mean it. Drunk or sober. I mean every word of it."

"Bunny," Gretchen said, "thank you for telling me all this." But she was sorry she had decided to stay on with him when the others had gone. The problem was not hers, she thought resentfully, and the solution was beyond her grasp. "I'll talk to my brother," she said; "see what we can figure out. Do you think it would be a good idea if I waited until Wesley came back and we all three had dinner together?"

"You want me to be honest?"

"Of course."

"I believe Wesley likes you. In fact I know he does, he's told me as much," Dwyer said. "But tonight I don't think he wants to see any Jordache for dinner. I'll take him out myself. We got some things to talk about together, private, him and me."

"Thanks for the drinks," Gretchen said.

"On the house."

"Drop me a postcard. From Singapore or Valparaiso or wherever."

"Sure." Dwyer laughed, a dry little laugh.

She nursed her drink. She had the feeling that if she

left Dwyer alone, he would break down, sit on the deck and weep. She didn't want Wesley to find him like that when he got back. "I'll just finish my drink and . . ."

"You want another one? I'll go get you one."

"This'll do, thanks."

"I've become a whiskey drinker," Dwyer said. "What do you know about that?" He shook his head. "Do you believe in dreams?" he asked abruptly.

"Sometimes." She wondered if Dwyer had ever heard of Freud.

"I had a dream last night," Dwyer said. "I dreamed Tom was laying on a floor—I don't know where it was—he was just laying on the floor looking dead. I picked him up and I knew I had to carry him someplace. I wasn't big enough in the dream to carry him in my arms so I laid him across my back. He's a lot taller than me, so his legs were dragging on the floor, and I put his arms around my neck so I could get a strong hold on him and I began to walk, I don't know where, someplace I just knew I had to take him. You know how it is in a dream, I was sweating, he was heavy, he was a deadweight around my neck, on my back. Then, all of a sudden, I felt he was getting a hard-on against my ass. I kept on walking. I wanted to say something to him, but I didn't know what to say to a dead man with a hard-on. The hard-on kept getting bigger and bigger. And I felt warm all over. And even in my dream I was ashamed. You know why I was ashamed? Because I *wanted* it." He shook his head. He had been talking dreamily, compulsively. He shook his head angrily. "I had to tell someone," he said harshly. "Excuse me."

"That's all right, Bunny," Gretchen said softly. "We're not responsible for our dreams."

"*You* can say that, Mrs. Burke," he said.

This time she did not correct him and tell him to call her Gretchen. She could not bear to look at Dwyer, because she was afraid she could not control what her face would tell him. The best she might manage would be pity and she feared what her pity might do to the man.

She reached out and touched his hand. He gripped it hard, in his tough seaman's fingers, then in a swift, instinctive movement, brought her hand to his lips and kissed it. He let her hand go and turned away from her. "I'm sorry," he said brokenly. "It was just . . . I don't know . . . I . . ."

"You don't have to say anything, Bunny," she said gently. Silence now would heal wounds, staunch blood. She felt confused, helpless. What if she said, Take me down to your cabin, make love to me? Womanly thought, the central act. Would her body be a consolation or a rebuke? What would it mean to her? An act of charity, a confirmation of continuing life or a last, unworthy cry of despair? She looked at the neat, muscular back of the small man who had kissed her hand and turned away from her. She almost took a step toward him, then pulled back, a psychic retreat rather than a physical one.

The hand with which she still held the whiskey glass was cold from the melting ice. She put the glass down. "I've got to be getting on," she said. "There are so many things to decide. Tell Wesley to call me if he needs anything."

"I'll tell him," Dwyer said. He wasn't looking at her, was staring, his mouth quivering, toward the entrance to the port. "Do you want me to go to the café and call a taxi?"

"No, thank you. I think I'll walk; I could stand a little walk."

She left him there in the bow of the *Clothilde,* barefooted and neat in his white jersey, with the two empty glasses.

She walked slowly away from the ships, into the town, up the narrow street, the night looming threatening ahead of her. She looked into the window of an antique shop. There was a brass ship's lamp there that attracted her. She would have liked to buy it, take it home with her; it would brighten the corner of a room. Then she remembered she had no real home, had come from an apartment rented for six months in New York; there was no room of hers for a lamp to brighten.

She went deeper into the town, thronged with people buying and selling, reading newspapers at café tables, scolding children, offering them ice-cream sandwiches, no one concerned with death. She saw the advertisement for a movie house, saw that an American picture, dubbed into French, was playing that night, resolved to have dinner in town alone and see it.

She passed in front of the cathedral, stopped for a moment to look at it, almost went in. If she had, she would have found Wesley on a bench, far back in the empty nave, his lips moving in a prayer he had never learned.

# CHAPTER 3

*1968*

*From Billy Abbott's notebook—*

My father was in Paris once, when they
let him out of the hospital just after
the war. He had not yet met my mother.
He said he was too drunk for the three
days he was there to remember anything
about it. He said he wouldn't know the
difference between Paris and Dayton,
Ohio. He didn't talk much about the war,
which made him a lot better company than
some of the other veterans I've been
exposed to. But on some of the weekends
that I spent with him under the terms of
the divorce, when he had had enough
to drink, which usually was early on,
he'd make fun of what he did as a
soldier. I was mostly concerned with Red
Cross girls and my personal safety, he'd
say; I was in the air force and flew a
tight desk, tapping out stories for
hometown newspapers about the brave boys
who flew the missions.

Still, he <u>did</u> enlist, he <u>did</u> get
wounded, or anyway hurt, on the way back
from a mission. I wonder if I would
have done as much. The army, as I see it
from here and from what I read in the
papers about Vietnam, is a macabre
practical joke. Of course, as everyone
says, that was a different war. With the
Colonel I assume an extreme military
pose, but if war in Europe did break
out, I'd probably desert the first time
I heard a shot fired.

NATO is full of Germans, all very
palsy and comrades-in-arms, and they're
not much different from the other
animals. Monika, who is German, is
another story.

-----

It was almost dark when Rudolph left the consulate.
The consul had been an agreeable man, had listened
thoughtfully, made notes, called in an aide, promised he
would do everything he could to help, but it would take
time, he would have to call Paris, get legal advice, he
was not convinced that the lawyer in Antibes had been
on sure ground when he had told Rudolph to ignore the
French, there would have to be a determination from
higher authorities as to what documents would be
needed to transfer the ownership of the *Clothilde* and
free the bank accounts. The death of an American in a
foreign country always presented knotty problems, the
consul had said, his tone hinting that it bordered on
treason to commit an act of such importance on alien
soil. That day, Rudolph thought, hundreds of Americans had died in Vietnam, which might be considered a

foreign country, but the deaths had not produced knotty problems for consuls anywhere.

The demise of Thomas Jordache was going to be even more complicated than usual, the consul warned; it could not be solved overnight. Rudolph had gone out into the gathering dusk feeling hopeless, trapped in a dark web of legalisms which would entangle him ever more tightly with every move he made to free himself. Trapped once more, he thought, self-pityingly, in other people's necessities.

What did they do, Rudolph wondered as he left the consulate behind him, in the old days in the American wilderness when the leader of the tribe was killed in battle? Who got the wampum, the wives, custody of the children, the tepee, the warbonnets, the eagle feathers, the lances and arrowheads? What clever nonwarrior, what shaman or medicine man, took the role of administrator and justifier?

He had left his car along the shore, in front of the Hôtel Negresco on the Promenade des Anglais because he hadn't wanted to risk getting lost in the streets of the unfamiliar city and had taken a taxi to the consulate. On foot now, not knowing exactly where he was going, not caring, he went in the general direction of the Negresco, not paying attention to the people around him hurrying home to dinner. Suddenly he stopped. His cheeks were wet. He put his hand to his eyes. He was crying. He had been crying without knowing it as he walked blindly toward the sea. Oh God, he thought, I had to come all the way from the Hudson River to Nice to cry for the first time since I was a boy. None of the passersby seemed to notice his tears; there were no curious stares. It could be that the French were used to seeing grown men walking weeping through their streets; maybe it was a national custom. Perhaps, he thought, after what their country had gone through since Louis the Sixteenth, there was plenty to cry about.

When he reached his car it was already dark. He had wandered through back streets, changed direction aimlessly. *Bella Nizza*, he remembered. The Italians had taken it back in the Second World War. Briefly. In the Italian equivalent of the Pentagon there probably was a plan for recapturing it at some belligerent future date. Good neighbors. They were growing jasmine and roses for the moment on all battlefields, waiting for the next war to come along. Poor, hopeful, doomed Italian generals. Not worth the trouble, not worth the bones of a single Calabrian peasant. It wasn't *Bella Nizza* anymore, it was a modern, junked-up commercial city, a peeling jumble of tenements, with rock music blaring from the loudspeakers of music shops, promoting its past loveliness in fake tourist brochures. All things became worse.

The lamps of the Promenade des Anglais were lit, reflecting off the roofs of the endless stream of cars, twinkling in the polluted sea murmuring against the meager strip of gravelly beach. In his conversation with the consul the man had said that Nice was a good post in the Foreign Service. The consul must know something about Nice that was not evident to the naked eye. Or perhaps he had been stationed in the Congo or Washington and even Nice would look good after that. Rudolph wondered if he had passed his brother's murderer somewhere between the consulate and the sea. Entirely possible. Murderers were constantly being arrested by the police in Nice. He speculated about what he would do if a man sat down next to him in a café and recognized him and said, calmly, *"Bonjour, monsieur,* you may be interested to know that I am the one who did it."

He opened the door to his car, then stood there, not getting in, thinking of the night ahead of him, going back to the hotel in Antibes, having to explain to Jean

that they would have to plan on staying on in the place
that had become a horror for them, having to explain to
Kate and Wesley and Dwyer that nothing was settled,
that everything was in abeyance, that they were tied in-
definitely to death, that there was no way of knowing
when they could get on with the business of living.

He closed the door of the car. He could not face
what was ahead of him in Antibes. As unattractive as
Nice was it was better this evening than Antibes. At
least he had stopped crying.

Careful in the traffic, his nostrils assailed by the
fumes the scientists of his country had assured him were
deadly to the human race, he crossed to the other side
of the Promenade des Anglais, bright with illuminated
storefronts and the lights of cafés. He went into a café,
seated himself at a table on the *terrasse,* ordered a whiskey and soda. Time-hallowed cure, palliative, nepenthe,
transient unraveler of knotty problems. When the whiskey came, he drank slowly, glad that Jean was not with
him, since he could not drink in her presence. Sometimes he felt he could not breathe in her presence—a
condition to be dealt with at another time. He took another sip of his drink.

Suddenly, he was ravenously hungry. He hadn't eaten
since breakfast and then only a croissant and coffee.
The body had its own rhythms, made its own uncomplicated, imperative claims. His hunger drove all other
thoughts from his mind. He sat back in his chair sipping
his whiskey, luxuriously composing the menu for the
evening meal. Melon with a dash of port to begin with,
then fish soup, he decided, specialty of the region, with
garlicked croutons and a sprinkling of grated cheese,
steak and salad, slab of Brie, strawberries for dessert. A
half bottle of *blanc de blancs* with the soup and a half
bottle of heavy red wine of Provence with the steak and
cheese. The evening stretched out ahead of him in glut-

tonous splendor. He never had to worry about getting fat, but he knew that he would have been ashamed to order so self-indulgent a meal at a time like this if he were not alone. But he knew nobody in Nice. The mourners were in another town. He paid for his whiskey and went along the promenade to the Negresco and asked the concierge for the name of the best restaurant in Nice. He walked to the address he was given, striding out briskly, his eyes dry.

The best restaurant in Nice was lit by candles, decorated with glowing bouquets of pink roses, with just the right faint aroma of good cooking from the kitchen. There were not many diners, but they looked prosperous and well-fed. The room was quiet, the atmosphere fittingly serious, the headwaiter a smiling Italian gentleman with brilliant teeth who spoke English. Perhaps, Rudolph thought, he is a spy for the Italian Army, goes home every night to draw up plans of the harbor to be microfilmed by an accomplice. *Bella Nizza.*

Seated at a table with a gleaming white tablecloth, breaking a crisp roll and spreading butter over it, Rudolph felt that perhaps he had been wrong in thinking that the town was not worth the bones of a single Calabrian peasant. He knew no one in Calabria.

To put an even keener edge to his appetite he ordered a martini. The martini came to the table, pale and icy cold. He fished out the olive and nibbled at it. It tasted of juniper and Mediterranean sunlight. He waved away the menu that the headwaiter offered him. "I know what I want," he said.

The meal, when it came, did justice to the concierge's estimate of the restaurant's cuisine. Rudolph ate and drank slowly, feeling newly restored with every bite of the food, every drop of the wines. Sometimes, he thought, the best of holidays can be fitted into only two hours of your life.

When he had finished with the strawberries he asked for the check. He wanted to take a stroll, replete, nameless, unencumbered, sit at a café table and watch the evening traffic on the promenade while having his coffee and a brandy. He tipped the maitre d'hôtel and the waiters grandly and sauntered out into the balmy night air. He walked the few minutes to the beach. Oldest sea. Ulysses had survived it. Strapped to the mast, his sailors' ears stopped by wax against the songs. Many brave men asleep in the deep. Tom now among them. Rudolph stood on the stony strand a few yards from where the gentle waves slid into France in a small lace of foam. It was a moonless night, but the stars were brilliant, and along the curve of the dark coast thousands of pinpoints of light made jeweled strings against the hills.

He breathed deeply of the salt air. Even though there was the mumble of traffic behind his back he felt beautifully alone, the beach deserted except for him, with nothing before him but the dark expanse of water. Tomorrow, he knew, would be a day of guilt and turmoil, but that was tomorrow. He leaned down and picked up a smooth round stone and threw it, skipping, along the surface of the sea. It skipped three times. He chuckled. If he had been a younger man, a boy, he would have sprinted like a halfback down the beach, along the water's edge, dodging the irregular ebb and flow of the waves. But at his age, in his black suit, it did not seem advisable, even in his mellow after-dinner state, to draw attention to himself from the strollers on the walk above the beach.

He went back to the promenade and entered a brightly lit café, seating himself so that he could watch the crowded pavement, the sauntering men and women, their day's work done or their tourists' duties performed, now just enjoying the climate, the momentary exchange of glances, the opportunity to walk, unhurried in the soft night, arm in arm with a loved one.

The café was not crowded. At a table, just one removed from his, a woman was reading a magazine, her head bent so that he could not see her face. She had looked up when he came in, then quickly gone back to her magazine. She had a half-full glass of white wine on the table in front of her. She had dark hair, nice legs, he noticed, was wearing a light blue dress.

He was conscious of another, unspecific hunger.

Don't spoil the evening, he warned himself.

He ordered a brandy and coffee from the waiter, in English. The woman, he noted, looked up again when he spoke. He detected, or thought he detected, a momentary glimmer of a smile on her face. She was not young, in her late thirties, he would have said, somewhere around his age, carefully made up, eye shadow. A little old for a prostitute, but attractive just the same.

The waiter put down his coffee and brandy and the little stamped check and went back toward the bar inside. Rudolph took a sip of the coffee, strong and black. Then he lifted the small glass of brandy and sniffed it. Just as he was about to drink, the woman raised her glass of wine to him. This time there was no doubt about it. She was smiling. She had a full red mouth, dark gray eyes, black hair. Politely, Rudolph raised his glass a little higher in salute, drank a little.

"You're American, aren't you?" She had only a slight accent.

"Yes."

"I knew as soon as you came in," she said. "The clothes. Are you here on a pleasure trip?"

"In a way," he said. He didn't know whether he wanted to continue the conversation or not. He was not easy with strangers, especially strange women. She didn't look like the prostitutes he had seen prowling the streets of New York, but he was in a foreign country and he wasn't sure how French prostitutes dressed and spoke. He was not used to being accosted by women. There was something forbidding about him, his friend and lawyer Johnny Heath had said, austere. Johnny Heath was accosted wherever he went, on the street, in bars, at parties. There was nothing austere about Johnny Heath.

From adolescence Rudolph had developed an aloof, cool manner, believing that it gave him the air of belonging to another class than that of the boys and men he had grown up among, with their easy comradeship, their loud, plebeian conviviality. Perhaps, he thought, looking at the woman at the other table, I have overdone the act.

"Are you enjoying yourself?" the woman asked. Her voice was husky, with a certain harshness in it that was not displeasing.

"Moderately," he said.

"Are you in a hotel here in Nice?"

"No," he said. He supposed that there was a certain set routine ladies such as this one went through. He guessed that she was one of the higher paid members of her profession, who did not get to the point immediately but flattered a man by pretending that she was interested in him, putting the eventual transaction on a level that was not merely physical and commercial. "I'm just passing through," he said. He was beginning to think, Why not? Once in my life, he thought, why not see what it's like? Besides, he had been continent for a long time. Too long. He had not slept in the same room with Jean since she had had her miscarriage. More than a year. Sometimes, he thought, you must remember you are a man. Bare, forked animal. Even he. He smiled at the woman. It felt good to smile. "May I offer you a drink?"

He had never offered a drink to a stranger before, man or woman. About time to begin. What have I been saving myself for, what have I been proving? In the one city of Nice itself, at this moment, there were probably thousands of men tumbling with women in joyous beds, regretting nothing, grasping the pleasure their bodies were conceived for, forgetting the day's labors, the day's fears. What put him above common humanity? "I'm alone," he said daringly. "I don't really speak French. I would enjoy some company. Somebody who speaks English." Always the saving, modifying hypocritical clause, he thought.

The woman looked at her watch, pretended at decision. "Well," she said, "that would be very nice." She smiled at him. She was pretty when she smiled, he thought, even white teeth and nice little wrinkles around the dark gray eyes. She folded her magazine and picked up her handbag and stood up and took the three steps to his table. He stood up and held the chair for her and she said, "Thank you," as she sat down. "I like to talk to Americans whenever I get a chance. I was in Washington for three years and I learned to like Americans."

Gambit, Rudolph thought, but keeping his face agreeable. If I were Swedish or Greek, she'd say she liked Swedes and Greeks. He speculated on how she had spent her three years in Washington. Entertaining lobbyists, subverting congressmen in the bedrooms of motels for pay?

"I like some Americans myself," he said.

She chuckled, a small, ladylike chuckle. She was definitely not a sister to the prowling, gaudy savages of the streets of New York, regardless of the bond of their profession. He had heard that there were well-mannered whores in America, too, who charged a hundred dollars or more for an hour's visit, and who could only be ordered by telephone, out-of-work actresses and models, elegant housewives working on a mink coat, but he had never met any of them. In fact, he had never spoken more than three words to any prostitute: "Thank you, no."

"And the French," the woman was saying. "Do you like them?"

"Moderately," he said. "Do you?"

"Some of them." She chuckled again.

The waiter appeared, his face stolid, accustomed to movements from table to table. *"La même chose? Un vin blanc?"* Rudolph asked the woman.

"Ah," she said, "you speak French."

*"Un petit peu,"* Rudolph said. He felt playful, tipsy. It was a night for games, masks, pretty French toys. Whatever happened that night, the lady was going to see that she didn't have just another ordinary American tourist on her hands. *"Je l'ai étudié à l'école."* High school. What's that in French?"

*"Collège? Lycée."*

*"Lycée,"* he said, with a sense of triumph.

The waiter shuffled his feet, a small reminder that he didn't have all night to stand around listening to an American trying to remember his high-school French to impress a lady who had just picked him up. *"Monsieur?"* the waiter said. *"Encore un cognac?"*

*"S'il vous plaît,"* Rudolph said with dignity.

After that, they spoke in a mixture of the two languages, both of them laughing at the kind of French Rudolph managed to dredge up from his memory, as he told her about the bosomy French teacher he had had as a teenaged boy at home, about how he had believed he was in love with her, had written her ardent letters in French, had once drawn a picture of her, naked, which she had confiscated. For her part, the woman had seemed to be pleased to listen to him, to correct his mistakes in her language, to praise him when he got out more than three words in a row. If this was what French whores were like, Rudolph thought drunkenly, after a bottle of champagne, he understood why prostitution was such a respected fixture of French civilization.

Then, the woman—he had asked her name, which was Jeanne—had looked at her watch and become serious. "It's getting late," she said in English, gathering in her bag and magazine, "I must be getting on."

"I'm sorry if I've wasted your time," he said. His voice was thick and he was having difficulty getting the words out.

She stood up. "I've enjoyed it very much, Jimmy," she said. He had told her that was his name. One more mask. He would not be traced. "But I expect an important call . . ."

He stood up to say good-bye, half relieved, half sorry that he wasn't going to make love to her. His chair fell back and he teetered a little as he rose. "It's been sharm—charming," he said.

She frowned at him. "Where is your hotel?" she asked.

Where was his hotel? For a moment the map of France was blotted from his consciousness. "Where's my—my hotel . . ." he said, his voice blurred. "Oh. Antibes."

"Do you have a car?"

"Yes."

She thought for a moment. "You are in no condition to drive, you know."

He hung his head, abashed. Americans, he felt she was saying, scornfully, arrived in France in no condition to drive. In no condition to do anything. "I'm not really a drinking man," he said, making it sound like an excuse. "I've had a bad day."

"The roads are dangerous, especially at night," she said.

"Especially at night," he agreed.

"Would you like to come with me?" she asked.

At last, he thought. It would not be a sin now, merely a safety measure. As a businessman, he really should ask her what it would cost, but after the drinks together and the friendly conversation it would sound crass. Later would do just as well. Whatever the price turned out to be, he certainly could afford one night in Europe with a courtesan. He was proud of himself for thinking of the word—courtesan. Suddenly he felt his head clearing. *"Volontiers,"* he said, using her language to show her he wasn't as far gone as she thought. He called loudly for the waiter: *"Garçon,"* and got out his wallet. He covered his wallet with his hands so that she couldn't see how many bills he had in it. In situations like this, even though he was not used to them, he knew one had to be careful.

The waiter came over and told him, in French, how much he owed. He couldn't understand the man and turned helplessly, ashamed, to the woman. "What did he say?"

"Two hundred and fifteen francs," she said.

He took three hundred-franc bills out of his wallet and waved away the waiter's fumbling effort to make change.

"You shouldn't have tipped him that much," she whispered as she took his arm and guided him out of the restaurant.

"Americans," he said. "A noble and generous race."

She laughed, held his arm more tightly.

They found a taxi and he admired the grace with which she raised her arm to hail the driver, the shapeliness of her legs, the warm curve of her bosom.

She held his hand in the taxi, no more. It was a short

ride. The taxi now smelled of perfume, musky, just the
hint of flowers in its past. The taxi stopped in front of a
small apartment house on a dark street. She paid the
driver, then took his arm again and led him into the
house. He followed her up one flight of stairs, admiring
her from below now. She opened the door with a key,
guided him along a dark hallway and through a doorway and switched on a lamp. He was surprised at how
large the room was and how tastefully furnished, although he couldn't make out too many details in the
shaded light of the single lamp. She must have a generous clientele, he thought, Arabs, Italian industrialists,
German steel barons.

"Now . . ." she began to say, when the telephone
rang.

She wasn't lying, he thought, she *was* expecting a
call. She hesitated, as though she didn't want to pick up
the phone. "Would you mind . . . ?" she said. She
gestured toward another doorway. "I think it would be
better if I was alone for this."

"Of course." He went into the next room and
switched on a light. It was a small bedroom, with a double bed, already made up. He heard her voice through
the door that he had closed behind him. He got the impression that she was angry with whomever she was
talking to, although he couldn't make out what she was
saying. He looked thoughtfully at the big bed. Last
chance to leave. The hell with it, he thought and undressed, dropping his clothes carelessly on a chair and
switching his wallet to a different pocket from the one
he had been carrying it in. He got into bed and pulled
the covers over him.

He must have fallen asleep because the next thing he
knew a warm perfumed body was in bed beside him,
the room was dark, there was a satiny, firm leg thrown
across him, a soft, exploring hand on his belly, a mouth

against his ear, murmuring words he could not understand.

He did not know what time it was when, all nerves quiescent, his body glowingly at rest, he finally lay still, his fingertips just touching the now familiar body that had given him so much pleasure. Fragrant, accidental humanity lying in the bed beside him. All praise to the animal hidden in the black suit. Disregarded, gloriously disregarded the deprived Puritan. He raised his head, leaned on one elbow over the woman, kissed her gently on the cheek. "It must be late," he whispered. "I have to go now."

"Drive carefully, *chéri*," the woman said, dreamy, replete. His doing.

"I'm all right now," he said. "I'm not drunk anymore."

The woman twisted and reached out and lit a lamp on the bedside table. He got out of bed, proud of his nakedness. Adolescent vainglory, he admitted wryly to himself, and dressed. The woman rose, too, strong, supple body, breasts full, haunches muscled, and covered herself in a gown, sat in a chair watching him with a little smile as he put on his clothes. He wished she hadn't put on the light, had not wakened. Then he could have left a hundred francs, maybe a thousand francs, on the mantelpiece, darkness and sleep concealing his provincial American ignorance of such matters; he could have slipped out of the apartment and out of the house, all connections broken. But the light was on, the woman was watching him, smiling. Waiting?

There was no avoiding the moment. He took out his wallet. "Is a thousand francs enough?" he asked, stumbling a little over the "enough."

She looked at him curiously, the smile vanishing. Then she began to laugh. The laugh was low at first, then became raucous. She bent over, put her head in her hands, her thick, gleaming hair falling in a dark cascade, hiding her face, the laugh continuing. He watched her, feeling his nerves twitching, regretting that he had been in her bed, that he had offered her a drink, that he was in Nice, regretting that he had ever set foot in France.

"I'm sorry," he said inanely. "It's just that I'm not accustomed . . ."

She raised her head, her face still distorted by laughter. She stood up and came over to him and kissed his cheek. "Poor dear," she said, the laughter still there, at the back of her throat. "I didn't know I was worth that much."

"If you want more . . ." he said stiffly.

"Much more," she said. "I want nothing. The most exorbitant price. Dear man. Thinking all this time that I was professional. And being so polite and gentle, too. If all customers were like you, I think we'd all become whores. I liked Americans before, but I like them even better now."

"Christ, Jeanne," he said. It was the first time he had spoken her name. "It never occurred to me that anybody would pick me out, take me home with her and . . . I don't know what to say."

"Don't say anything. You're too modest, my charming American, too modest by half."

"Well," he said, "it never happened to me before." He was afraid she was going to start laughing again.

She shook her head wonderingly. "What's wrong with American women?" she said. She moved over to the bed and sat on the edge. She patted it. "Come, sit down, please," she said.

He sat down next to her. She took his hand, sisterly now. "If it will make you feel any better, *chéri,*" she said, "it never happened to me before, either. But I have been so lonely—starved—Couldn't you tell?"

"No," he admitted. "I'm not really a ladies' man."

"Not a ladies' man," she said, gently mocking. "Not a drinking man. Just the sort of man I needed tonight. Let me tell you a little about myself. I'm married. To a major in the army. He was an aide to the military attaché in Washington."

That's where the English came from, he thought, no lobbyists, no congressmen, no motels.

"Now he is stationed temporarily in Paris. At the Ecole Militaire," she said. "Temporarily." She laughed shortly, harshly. "He's been there three months now. I have two children in school here in Nice. They are visiting their grandmother tonight."

"You weren't wearing a wedding ring," he said. "I looked."

"Not tonight." Her face grew grim. "I didn't want to be married tonight. When I got my husband's telegram this afternoon telling me he was going to call, I knew what he was going to say. He was going to say that once again he would be too busy with his work to come to Nice. He has been too busy for three months. They must be preparing a terrible war at the Ecole Militaire when a poor little major can't get off for even one day to fly to Nice to see his wife once in three months. I have a very good idea of what kind of war my major is preparing in Paris. You heard me on the telephone . . . ?"

"Yes." Rudolph said. "I couldn't hear what you were saying. . . . You sounded angry."

"It wasn't a friendly conversation," Jeanne said. "No, not friendly at all. So now you are beginning to have some idea of why I was sitting at a café table, not wearing a wedding ring?"

"More or less," Rudolph said.

"I was on the point of quitting and going home when you came into the café and sat down," she said quietly.

"Two men had approached me before. Posing, stuffy men, experts, connoisseurs of—what's the American phrase—one-night . . . ?"

"One-night stands," Rudolph said.

"That's it."

"At least they didn't think you were a whore," he said ruefully. "Forgive me."

She patted his hand. "There's nothing to forgive," she said. "It added just the right note of comedy to the evening. When you came in and sat down, with your decent, bony, respectable American face, I decided not to go home." She smiled. "Not just then. It turns out I didn't make a mistake. You must never be modest again." Another sisterly pat of the hand. "Now, it's late. You said you had to go. . . . Do you want my telephone number? Can I see you again?"

"I suppose I ought to tell you a little about myself, too," Rudolph said. "First of all, my name isn't Jimmy. I don't know why I . . ." He shrugged. "I guess I was ashamed of what I was doing." He smiled. "What I *thought* I was doing. Maybe I half believed if it wasn't my own name it wasn't me who was really doing it. More likely, if we ever met and I was with somebody else and you said hello, Jimmy, I could say, I'm sorry, madam, you must be thinking of somebody else."

"I wish I could dare keep a diary," Jeanne said. "I would write down all that happened tonight in detail. In great detail. It would give my children something to laugh at when they discovered it after my death. What do you know, dear, old, sensible *Maman?*"

"My name is Rudolph," he said. "I was never fond of the name. When I was a boy I thought it sounded un-American, though it's hard to tell what sounds American anymore and what doesn't. And why anybody should care. But when you're a boy in his teens, your head full of books, with heroes with names like Huckleberry Finn, Daniel Boone, Studs Lonigan . . . Well, it seemed to me that Rudolph sounded like . . . like heavy German cooking. Especially during the war." He had never told anyone how he felt about his Christian name, had never formulated it clearly for himself even, and now found that it was with a sense of relief, mixed with wry amusement, that he could speak about it openly to this handsome stranger, or almost stranger. Also, sitting in the muted lamplight on the bed which had been the furniture of exquisite pleasure, he wanted to make a further offering of himself to the woman, find reasons for delaying leave-taking, join her in the pretense that the dawn was not near, departure inevitable.

"Rudolph," Jeanne said. "Neither good nor bad. Think of it as Rodolfo. That has a better sound, doesn't it?"

"Much better."

"Good," she said teasingly. "From now on I will call you Rodolfo."

"Rodolfo Jordache," he said. It gave him a new, more dashing view of himself. "Jordache. That's my family name. I'm at the Hôtel du Cap." All defenses down now. Names and addresses. Each at the other's mercy. "One more thing. I'm married."

"I expected as much," Jeanne said. "Your affair. Just as my marriage is my affair."

"My wife is with me in Antibes." He didn't feel he had to tell her that they were not on the best of terms, either. "Give me your telephone number."

She got up and went over to a little desk where there was a pen and some paper and wrote down her telephone number. She gave him the slip of paper and he folded it carefully and put it in his pocket.

"Other times," she said, "you will have to rent a hotel room. The children will be here."

Other times. . . .

"Now," she said, "I'll call you a taxi." They went into the salon and she dialed a number, spoke quickly for a moment, waited a little while, said, *"Très bien,"* hung up. "The taxi will be here in five minutes," she said. Before she opened the front door for him they kissed, a long, grateful, healing kiss. "Good night, Rodolfo," she said. She smiled, a smile he knew he would remember for a long time.

———

The taxi was waiting for him when he got down to the street, its diesel motor making it sound like a launch waiting to put out to sea. Voyages.

*"L'hôtel Negresco,"* Rudolph said as he got in. When the taxi started, he looked back at the house. It was imperative for him to be able to find it again, to recognize it in his dreams. When they got to the Negresco he made sure he was not run down as he crossed to where his car was parked. Then, at the wheel of his rented car, he drove slowly and very carefully on the deserted road along the sea to Antibes.

When he reached the port he slowed down even more, then abruptly swung the car into the parking lot and got out and walked along the quay to where the *Clothilde* was berthed in the silent harbor. There were no lights to be seen on the *Clothilde*. He didn't want to wake Wesley or Bunny. He took off his shoes and climbed down from the deck into the dory lying alongside, slipped the line, sat amidships and noiselessly put the oars through the locks. He rowed almost soundlessly away from the ship toward the middle of the harbor, then, pulling more strongly, toward the harbor entrance, the tarry smell of the water strong in his nostrils, mixed with the flowery fragrance from shore.

He had acted almost automatically, not asking himself why he was doing this. The pull of the oars against his shoulders and arms gave him a sober pleasure, and the sigh of the small bow wave against the sides of the dory seemed a fitting music with which to end the night.

The city of Antibes, looming shadows, with a light here and there, receded slowly as he headed toward the red and green lights that marked the channel into the sea. The rhythm of his body as he bent forward, then leaned back, satisfied him. How many times had these same oars moved in the hands of his brother. His own hands were soft against the smooth wood, polished by the strong hands of his brother. The thought that perhaps in the morning his palms would be blistered pleased him.

Being alone on the dark surface of the water was a benediction to him and the blinking lights of the harbor entrance comforted him, with their promise of safe anchorages. Grief was possible here, but also hope. "Thomas, Thomas," he said softly as he went out into the sea and felt its gentle swell lift the dory. He remembered, as he rowed, all the times they had failed each other, and the end, when they had forgotten the failures or at least forgiven them.

He felt tireless and serene, alone in the dark night, but then he heard the coughing of a small fishing boat putting out to sea behind him, one small acetylene lamp at its bow. The fishing boat passed near him and he could see two men in it staring curiously at him. He was conscious of how strange it must look to them, a man in a dark business suit, alone, headed out to sea at that hour. He kept on rowing until they were out of sight, then let the oars dangle and stared up at the starlit sky.

He thought of his father, that enraged and pitiful old man, who had also rowed in darkness, who had picked a night of storm for his last voyage. Suicide had been

possible for his father, who had found the peace in
death he had never achieved in life. It was not possible
for him. He was a different man, with different claims
upon him. He took one long, deep breath, then turned
the dory around and rowed back to the *Clothilde,* his
hands burning.

Quietly, he tied up to the *Clothilde*'s stern, climbed
the ladder and went ashore. He put on his shoes, a rite
observed, a ceremony celebrated, and got into his car
and started the engine.

It was past three in the morning when he got to the
hotel. The lobby was deserted, the night concierge
yawning behind the desk. He asked for his key and was
turning toward the elevator when the concierge called
after him. "Oh, Mr. Jordache. Mrs. Burke left a message
for you. You are to call her whenever you get in. She
said it was urgent."

"Thank you," Rudolph said wearily. Whatever it
was, Gretchen would have to wait until morning.

"Mrs. Burke told me to call her when you got in. No
matter what time." She had guessed he would try to
avoid her, had taken steps to make sure he couldn't.

"I see," said Rudolph. He sighed. "Call her, please.
Tell her I'll come to her room as soon as I look in on
my wife." He should have stayed the night in Nice. Or
rowed till dawn. Faced everything in daylight.

"One more thing," said the concierge. "There was a
gentleman here asking for you. A Mr. Hubbell. He said
he was from *Time* Magazine. He used the telex."

"If he comes here and asks for me again, tell him I'm
not in."

"I understand. *Bonne nuit, monsieur.*"

Rudolph rang for the elevator. He had planned to
telephone Jeanne, say good night to her, try to tell her
what she had done for him, listen to the husky voice,

with its rough, sensual shading, fall off to sleep with the memory of the night to take the weight from his dreams. He could forget that now. He shuffled into the elevator, feeling old, got off at his floor, opened the door to the suite as silently as he could. The lights were on, both in the salon and in the bedroom in which Jean slept. Since the murder she refused to sleep in the dark. As he approached her doorway she called out, "Rudolph?"

"Yes, dear." He sighed. He had hoped she was asleep. He went into her room. She was sitting up in bed, staring at him. Automatically he looked for a glass or a bottle. There was no glass or bottle and he could tell from her face she hadn't been drinking. She looks old, he thought, old. The drawn face, the dull eyes over the lacy nightgown made her look like a malicious sketch of the woman she would be forty years from now.

"What time is it?" she asked harshly.

"After three. You'd better go to sleep."

"After three. The consulate in Nice keeps odd hours, doesn't it?"

"I took the night off," he said.

"From what?"

"From everything," he said.

"From me," she said bitterly. "That's become quite a habit, hasn't it? A way of life with you, wouldn't you say?"

"Let's discuss it in the morning, shall we?" he said.

She sniffed. "You stink of perfume," she said. "Shall we discuss that in the morning, too?"

"If you wish," he said. "Good night."

He started out of the room. "Leave the door open," she called. "I have to keep all avenues of escape open."

He left the door open. He wished he could pity her. He went into his bedroom through the salon, closing

his own door behind him. Then he unlocked the door
that led from his room into the corridor and went out.
He didn't want to have to explain to Jean that he had to
see Gretchen about something that his sister thought
was urgent.

Gretchen's room was down the corridor. He went
past the pairs of shoes left out by the guests to be shined
while they slept. Europe was on the brink of Communism, he thought, but shoes were still shined by future
commissars, budding Trotskies, between midnight and
six each morning.

He knocked on Gretchen's door. She opened it immediately, as though she had been standing there,
alerted by the concierge's call, as though she couldn't
bear to wait the extra second or two it would have
taken her to cross the room and confront her brother.
She was in a terry cloth bathrobe, light blue, the blue
almost identical with the blue of the dress Jeanne had
been wearing in the café. With her small pale face, dark
hair and strong, graceful body, she bore a striking resemblance to Jeanne, he thought. Echoes everywhere.
The idea hadn't occurred to him before.

"Come in," she said. "I've been so worried. God,
where've you been?"

"It's a long story," he said. "Can't it wait till morning?"

"It can't wait until morning," she said, closing the
door. She sniffed. "You smell heavenly, Brother," she
said sarcastically. "And you look as though you've just
been laid."

"I'm a gentleman," Rudolph said, trying to make
light of the accusation. "Gentlemen don't discuss matters like that."

"Ladies do," she said. She had her vulgar side,
Gretchen.

"Let's drop it, please," he said. "I need some sleep. What's so damned urgent?"

Gretchen fell back into a big armchair, sprawling, as though she were too tried to stand anymore. "Bunny Dwyer called an hour ago," she said flatly. "Wesley's in jail."

"What?"

"Wesley's in jail in Cannes. He got into a fight in a bar and nearly killed a man with a beer bottle. He hit a cop and the police had to subdue him. Is that urgent enough for you, Brother?"

# CHAPTER 4

*From Billy Abbott's notebook—*

There've been riots in Brussels today
and bombs exploded. It's all about
whether kids from Flemish-speaking
families should be taught in their own
language or in French and having the
street signs in both languages. And the
blacks in the units here are talking
about mutiny if they aren't allowed to
have Afros. People are ready to tear
each other apart about <u>anything.</u> Which,
sad to relate, is why I'm in uniform
although I haven't the faintest desire
to do the least bit of harm to anybody
and as far as I'm concerned anybody who
wants to can speak Flemish or Basque or
Serbo-Croat or Sanskrit and all I'd do
would be to say, It sounds great to me.
   Is there something lacking in my
character?
   I suppose so. If you're strong you

want to dominate everything and
everybody around you. It's hard to
dominate people if they don't speak your
language and being strong you react
angrily, like American tourists in
restaurants in Europe who begin to shout
when a waiter can't understand what it
is they're ordering. In political terms
this is translated into riot police and
tear gas.

Monika speaks German, English, French,
Flemish and Spanish and she says she
can read Gaelic. As far as I can tell
she is as pacific as myself but because
of her job as translator for NATO she
gets to hurl the most awesome threats,
composed by belligerent old men, at
other belligerent old men in the
opposite wing of the great lunatic
asylum we all inhabit.

I spent the day in bed with her.
We do that occasionally.

---

Dwyer was waiting outside the Cannes *préfecture*
when Rudolph's taxi drove up to it. The taxi, Rudolph
had decided, was a wiser choice than his own car. He
didn't want to go charging into a French police station
to demand his nephew's freedom, only to be forced to
take a breathalator test. Even in his heavy, dark blue
seaman's sweater, Dwyer was shivering as he leaned
against the wall and his face was pale, greenish, in the
watery light from the *préfecture*'s lamps. Rudolph
looked at his watch as he got out of the taxi. Past 4:00
A.M. The streets of Cannes were deserted, all errands
but his completed for the night or postponed until
morning.

"God," Dwyer said, "I'm glad to see you. What a night! Shit, what a night."

"Where is he?" Rudolph asked, trying to keep his voice calm to take the edge off the hysteria that was showing in Dwyer's face, in the way he was rubbing the knuckles of one hand against his other palm.

"Inside somewhere. In a cell, I guess. They wouldn't let me see him. I can't go in there. They said they'd throw me into the can, too, if I showed my face in there once more. French police," he said bitterly. "You might as well talk to Hitler."

"How is he?" Rudolph asked. Looking at Dwyer, hunched against the cold night air, he felt small shivers run down his spine, too. He was dressed for the day's warmth, had neglected to grab a coat at the hotel.

"I don't know how he is *now*," Dwyer said. "He wasn't too bad when they dragged him in. But he hit a cop and God knows what they've done to him since they got him in there."

Rudolph wished that there was a café open, a lighted place with at least the semblance of warmth. But the street stretched away on both sides, narrow and dark except for the weak glow of lampposts. "All right, Bunny," he said soothingly. "I'm here. I'll see what I can do. But you have to fill me in. What happened?"

"I took him out to dinner in Antibes," Bunny said. He said it defensively, as though Rudolph was accusing him, as though his innocence had to be claimed and confirmed before anything else was said or done. "I couldn't leave the kid alone on a night like this, could I?"

"Of course not."

"We drank some wine. Wesley drank wine with all of us, in front of his father, his father would pour it out of the bottle for him as though he was a grown-up, you forget that he's just a kid . . . You know, in

France . . ." His voice trailed off, as though the shared
bottle of wine between the boy and himself in the restaurant in Antibes was another unjust charge against him.

"I know," Rudolph said, trying not to sound impatient. "Then what?"

"Then the kid wanted a brandy. Two brandies. I
thought, why not? After all, the day you bury your father . . . Even if he got drunk, we were right near the
port, I could get him back to the ship with no trouble.
Only he wouldn't go back to the ship. All of a sudden
he got up from the table and he said, 'I'm going to
Cannes.' 'What the hell do you want to go to Cannes
for, this time of night?' I said. 'I'm going to visit a nightclub,' he said. His exact words. Visit. 'I'm going to visit
the Porte Rose.' God knows what the brandy, the day,
everything, was doing to that kid's head. I tried to reason with him, I swear to God I did. 'Fuck you, Bunny,'
he said. He never swore at me before. He had a funny
dead look on his face. You couldn't budge him with a
bulldozer. 'Nobody's asking you to come with me,' he
said. 'Go get your beauty sleep.' He was half out of the
restaurant before I could get to him, grab his arm, at
least. I couldn't let him go to that goddamn place alone,
could I?"

"No," Rudolph said wearily. "You did the right
thing." He wondered if he would have done better or
worse in Dwyer's place. Worse, he thought.

"So we got a taxi and we went to the Porte Rose,"
Dwyer rattled on, made garrulous by grief or fear or
impotence. "He never said a word in the taxi. Not word
one. Just sat there looking out of the window, like a
tourist. Who the hell knew what he had in his mind?
I'm not a psychologist, I never had kids, who knows
what crazy things they think of?" The tone of innocence, not expecting the innocence to be believed or recognized was in the voice again. "So," Dwyer went on,

"I thought, Okay, he's disturbed. Who isn't today, a day like this one, he has some crazy notion maybe that he owes it to his old man to go and see the place where it all began. He saw the end, with the ashes floating out to sea, maybe he had to see the beginning, too."

The beginning, Rudolph thought, thinking of the ferocious brother he had slept with in the same bed over the bakery store, the beginning was not in a nightclub in Cannes. You'd have to go back further than that. A lot further.

"Maybe even it was a good idea, I thought," Dwyer said. "Anyway, one sure thing, the Yugoslav Tom had the fight with wasn't going to be there—the police've been hunting for him ever since they talked to him the day after the murder and they ain't found any trace of him yet. And I never saw the guy, anyway, and neither did Wesley, we wouldn't know him from Adam, even if he was standing along the bar right next to us with a spotlight on him. It wouldn't be a pleasant experience for me, but what's the harm, a couple of drinks and then home to bed and a hangover tomorrow and that's it?"

"I understand, Bunny," Rudolph said, shivering. "You couldn't do anything else, given the circumstances."

Dwyer nodded vigorously. "Given the circumstances," he said.

"How did the fight start?" Rudolph asked. Dwyer's excuses for himself could wait until another day. It was four in the morning and he was cold and Wesley was inside the police station and maybe the cops were working him over. "Was it Wesley's fault?"

"Fault? Who ever knows whose fault it is when something like that happens?" Dwyer's mouth quivered. "We were standing at the bar, not saying anything to each other, maybe after two, maybe three whiskeys, we were on Scotch now, Wesley wanted Scotch—he didn't seem drunk—that kid must have a head like iron—and there was a big Englishman next to him, and he was drinking beer and talking loud. He was off some ship in the harbor, you could tell he was a seaman, he was saying something about Americans in English to the girl, I guess it wasn't very complimentary because all of a sudden Wesley turned to him and said, quiet-like, 'Shut your big trap about Americans, limey.' "

Oh God, Rudolph thought, what a time and place for patriotism.

"It was something about how the Americans let the English fight their war for them—Wesley wasn't even *born* then, what the hell did he care? Christ, his own father would never've had a fight in a bar if *ten* Englishmen said Americans were all yellow pimps and whoremongers. But Wesley was spoiling for a fight. I never saw him fight before—but Tom told me about him and I could see the signs and I grabbed his arm and said, 'Come on, kid, time to go.' But the Englishman, Christ, he must've weighed two hundred pounds, thirty, thirty-two years old, drinking all that beer, he said, 'Would you repeat that, please, sonny?' So, nice and calm, Wesley said, 'Shut your big trap about Americans, limey.'

"Even then, it could've been avoided, because the girl kept tugging at the Englishman's sleeve and saying, 'Let's go home, Arnold.' But he shook her off and said to Wesley, 'What ship you off, mate?' and I could see him reaching, slow, toward the beer bottle on the bar. 'The *Clothilde,*' Wesley said, and I could feel all his muscles tensing up in his arm. The Englishman laughed. 'You better be looking for another berth, sonny,' he said. 'I don't believe the *Clothilde* is going to be a popular ship from now on.' It was the laugh that got Wesley, I think. He reached out sudden and grabbed the beer bottle first and cracked it across the man's face. The

Englishman went down, blood all over him and everybody screaming all around and Wesley started stomping
him, with the craziest expression you ever saw on a
boy's face. Where he ever learned to fight like that nobody'll ever know. Stomping, for Christ's sake. And
laughing, crazy as a bedbug, with me hanging on him to
pull him back and making no more impression on him
than if I was a mosquito buzzing around his neck.

"It didn't take long. There were two cops in plain-
clothes at a table and they jumped him, but he got one
good punch in on one of the cops and the cop went
down to his knees. But the other cop got out a billy and
clouted him on the neck and that was the end of the
match right there. They hauled Wesley away and into a
police car outside and they wouldn't let me come with
them, so I just ran to the police station and an ambu-
lance went by full speed with the lights full on and the
siren going and God knows what short of shape that
Englishman is in right now." Dwyer sighed. "That's
about it," he said breathlessly. "Just about it. Now you
know what it's all about, why I called your hotel."

Rudolph sighed, too. "I'm glad you called," he said.
"Wait here. I'll see what I can do."

"I'd go in with you," Dwyer said, "but they hate the
sight of my face."

Rudolph settled his shoulders into the jacket of his
suit and went into the police station, the sudden light
glaring in his eyes, but the warmth, even on this errand,
welcome. He was conscious that he needed a shave, that
his clothes were rumpled. He would have felt more confident if, in Gretchen's words, he didn't look as if he
had just been laid. He was still conscious, too, of the
musky fragrance of perfume that still clung to him. You
are not dressed or properly deodorized for the occasion,
he told himself as he went toward the high desk behind

which sat a fat policeman with blue jaws, scowling at him.

Travel, he thought, as he smiled, or hoped he smiled, at the policeman, travel broadens one's horizons; one visits cathedrals, the beds of the wives of continental military men, one sails over the hulks of ships sunk in many wars, one becomes familiar with foreign customs, strange foods, police stations, crematories . . .

"My name," he said to the policeman behind the desk, in slow French, "is Jordache. I am American . . ." Did the policeman know of Lafayette, the Marshall Plan, D day? Take a chance on gratitude. A long chance. "I believe you have my nephew Wesley Jordache here."

The policeman said something rapidly in French which Rudolph couldn't understand.

"Speak slowly, please," he said. "I am not good in French."

"Come back at eight o'clock in the morning," the policeman said slowly enough so that Rudolph could understand him.

"I would like to see him now," Rudolph said.

"You heard what I said." The policeman spoke with exaggerated slowness and held up his two hands, with eight fingers extended.

Rudolph decided that the policeman had not heard of Lafayette or D day. "He may need medical attention," he said.

Again, with mocking slowness, the policeman said, "He is getting excellent medical attention. Eight o'clock in the morning. French time." He laughed.

"Does anybody here speak English?"

"This is a police station, *monsieur,*" the policeman said. "You are not at the Sorbonne."

Rudolph would have liked to ask about bail but he didn't know the word for bail. There must be fifty thou-

sand American and English tourists each year in
Cannes, you'd think at least one of the bastards could
take the trouble to learn English. "I'd like to talk to
your superior officer," he said stubbornly.

"He is not here at the present time."

"Somebody."

"I am somebody." Again the policeman laughed.
Then he scowled. The scowl was more natural to him
than laughter. "You are invited to leave, *monsieur*," he
said harshly. "This room must be kept clear."

For a moment, Rudolph thought of offering a bribe.
But he had made the mistake once that night of offering
money in the wrong place. Here it would be considerably more dangerous.

"Get out, get out, *monsieur*." The policeman waved a
thick hand impatiently. "I have work to do."

Beaten, Rudolph left the room. Dwyer was still hitting the knuckles of one hand against the palm of his
other hand outside. "Well?" Dwyer asked.

"Nothing doing," Rudolph said flatly. "Not until
eight o'clock in the morning. We might as well go to a
hotel here. There's no sense in going back to Antibes
for just a couple of hours."

"I don't like to leave the *Clothilde* alone," Dwyer
said. "There's no telling, what with the way things are
. . ." He left the thought unfinished. "I'll be back in the
morning."

"Whatever you say," Rudolph said. He felt as though
he had run for hours. In the morning, early, he would
call the lawyer in Antibes. He remembered old Teddy
Boylan, whose family owned the brickworks in Port
Philip, where Rudolph was born, and who had be-
friended him, if that was the word, and had, in a way,
educated him. Teddy Boylan, who had advised him to
go to law school. "Lawyers run the world," Boylan had
said. Good advice perhaps for men who wanted to run

the world. He had once been one of them. No longer
was. If he had taken the advice, been admitted to the
bar, would the blue-jowled policeman inside have
laughed at him and kicked him out? Would Wesley be
behind bars now, at the mercy of a cop he had knocked
down in a brawl? Would Tom be alive or at least have
had a neater death? Four-o'clock-in-the-morning
thoughts.

He trudged through the empty streets, cleared now of
whores and gamblers and ambulances, toward the Hotel
Carlton, where he could get a room for a few hours'
sleep and Dwyer could find a taxi to take him back to
the *Clothilde.*

———

This is the way my father must have felt a hundred
times in his life, beat up and aching, not wanting much
to move, Wesley thought as he lay on the bare board
that pulled down from the wall of the cell into which he
had been thrown. The thought somehow comforted
him, made him feel closer to his father, as the prayer
the afternoon before had not. He felt quiet now, relaxed, not caring about anything, at least not just yet.
He was glad they'd pulled him off the Englishman and
he hoped he hadn't killed the son of a bitch.

If the son of a bitch didn't die, his Uncle Rudy would
get him off. Little old Mr. Fixit, Rudy Jordache. He had
to smile, even though it hurt to smile, when he thought
this.

The smile didn't last long. He hadn't known his father long enough. He didn't know how long was
enough, but he knew that the time he'd had wasn't it.
There wouldn't be any more of those long conversations
in the darkened wheelhouse. Makeup time, his father
used to call it, filling in the blanks, making up for the

years when his mother had run away with him, had shuffled him off to one miserable school after another, telling him his father had deserted him, had run off with a cheap tart, was probably dead, the life he led, drinking, whoring, gambling, fighting, throwing his money away, everybody's enemy. His mother had a lot to answer for.

For that matter, he had a lot to answer for himself. If he had been a little more alert, had seen or sensed the sunken log they'd hit, and they hadn't had to come back to Antibes for repairs, they'd all be along the coast of Italy now, Portofino, Elba, Sicily, his father talking in that low, rough voice with everybody sleeping below, telling him about Clothilde Deveraux, the woman the boat was named for, the servant in Tom's fat, German Uncle Harold's house, scrubbing him down naked in the bathtub, feeding him gigantic meals, making love to him. His first real love, his father had said sadly, there for a while and then gone.

Or if he hadn't been sleeping like a baby, he'd have heard the footsteps on the deck, the way his father always did, no matter how tired he was or how deep in sleep, and come up to see his father on the way to rescue Jean Jordache, alone. He could have gone with him, maybe had the sense to make him call the police, at least be with him so that the Yugoslav would have realized there was no sense in fighting.

Who'm I kidding? Wesley thought. One night it would have happened in Portofino or Elba or Sicily. There was no stopping Jean Jordache from getting into trouble and dragging everybody along with her. He hadn't liked her from the beginning and he'd told his father so. His father had said, "I admit she has her problems. *I* wouldn't've married her, but Rudy is a different kind of man. She's rich, she was pretty and smart . . ." Tom had shrugged. "Maybe you got to

pay for rich, pretty and smart." Only it was his father
who'd paid. Too brave for his own good, too sure of
himself. "I've had plenty of woman troubles myself."
He'd smiled a little sadly in the dark as he'd said that,
and told his son about the twins they said he'd knocked
up in Elysium, Ohio, when they jailed him on the
charge of statutory rape. "Looking back," Tom had
said philosophically, "maybe it was worth it, though I
didn't think so at the time. I suppose I could tell you to
be careful, but I don't suppose it'd do any good, would
it, Wesley?"

"I'm half careful," Wesley had said. He'd screwed
two married ladies on two different voyages, taking
chances, with their husbands on board, and he knew his
father knew about it.

"I noticed you like the stuff," Tom said dryly.

"About like average, I guess," Wesley said. "I
wouldn't know."

"I did, too," Tom said. "There was a wild English
girl by the name of . . . let me see if I can remember
her name . . . Betty, Betty Something—Betty Johns—
that nearly got me killed in Paris because I spent two
weeks with her down in Cannes, squandering my money
and blowing up on wine and fancy meals before a fight.
By the time the fight was over in Paris, with that Frenchman hitting me with everything but the water bucket,
I was ready to take orders and become a monk." He
chuckled.

There were other names that came up in his remi-
niscences of his past for his son's benefit, names he did
not chuckle over: the boy with whom he had set fire to
the cross on Boylan's lawn and who had turned him in;
Schultzy, his manager; the man he had blackmailed at
the Revere Club for five thousand dollars; Falconetti,
whom he had shamed before twenty-seven other members of a ship's crew and caused to commit suicide. It

was as though he felt the boy, starved for a father, now that he had finally found one, might get a false, noble impression of him that Tom could not live up to and had to correct to save the boy from inevitable and bitter disillusionment.

What advice he gave was practical. "You like the sea. Follow it. It's a good life, at least if you get lucky, like me. It's a nice mixture of laziness and work and variety and you're out in the open air. In the end, you'll have the *Clothilde* or maybe a better boat. Know what it's all about. Give it loving care, like Dwyer and me. And I'd advise not screwing the lady guests." He grinned. Father or no father, he couldn't be holy about a young man's overpowering interest in sex. "Be your own boss, because working for anybody else is the big trap. Learn everything. Above deck and below deck. You got a good chance with me and Bunny and Kate here to watch. Don't skimp on equipment. If you don't like anybody you hire on, for whatever reason, put him off at the next port. If you catch a guest with drugs, throw the drugs overboard without any conversation about it. If possible, don't booze with them. You'll be able to afford your own booze. Don't be greedy. The word gets around. Fast. If you don't like the looks of the sea, make for port, regardless of what some fat cat on board tells you about having to get to Rome or Cannes or Athens for an important business conference or to pick up a girlfriend. Don't volunteer for any wars. Don't back down, but don't pick fights. . . ."

He should've put that on tape, Wesley thought, remembering, and played it before he went to sleep every night.

"Keep a gun on board. Just in case. Locked up. It can come in handy." His father's legacy—Don't skimp on the equipment and keep a gun handy.

Wesley didn't know where the gun on the *Clothilde*

was locked away. Probably Bunny knew, but he was sure Bunny wouldn't tell. It hadn't been handy when it was needed.

His father talked on in the barred darkness, the voice calm, slightly amused, but the words incomprehensible.

The ache in the back of his head throbbed, the memory of his father's voice dwindled away, like the sound of a buoy left to stern in a fog, and he slept.

# CHAPTER 5

*From Billy Abbott's notebook—*

I have a weakness for my father, who is
a weak man. I forgave him. I have no
weakness for my mother, who is a strong
woman, and whom I do not forgive. Let
the scholar who sifts through the ruins
of Brussels in the next century figure
this out. We are all haunted by our
parents, one way or another. I am
haunted by two fathers. William Abbott,
who sired me, was, and I suppose still
is, small and delightful, charming and
useless.

Colin Burke, second husband of my
mother, was a glittering, selfish,
talented man, who could make actors
perform like angels and the screen light
up like a bonfire. I loved him and
admired him and wished I could grow up
to be like him. I did not. I grew up,
I'm afraid, like Willie Abbott, although

without some of his essential attractive
qualities. I loved him, too.

  I have put him to bed, drunk, fifty
times.

  I played five sets of tennis today for
side bets, and won them all.

———————

He had been to the consulate in Nice again, to the
jail in Grasse, to which Wesley had been moved, twice
during the week and three times to the lawyer's office.
The consul had been vague and apologetic about being
vague, the lawyer had been helpful, up to a point, Wesley not helpful, just silent, unrepentant, physically no
worse for wear and less interested in his own fate than
that of the men imprisoned along with him, among them
a jewel thief, a passer of stolen checks and an art forger.
He hadn't shaved since his arrest and the blondish thick
stubble gave him an unkempt and wolfish look, at home
among criminals. When he came into the small room in
which Rudolph was permitted to speak to him, there
was a rank, feral smell, a hunting beast caged in an un-
sanitary zoo. The smell transported Rudolph uncomfortably back to the room above the family bakery, the
bed he shared with his brother Tom when they were in
their teens, when Tom would come back late at night
after a night of brawling in the town. He took out his
handkerchief and pretended to be blowing his nose as
Wesley sat down, grinning a little, opposite him across
the small, unpainted, scarred table, guaranteed Provençal antique, provided by courtesy of the police of the
floral city of Grasse.

  Rudolph put on a solemn face, to indicate that this
was no laughing matter. The police, through the lawyer,
had let Rudolph know that the case was grave—a beer
bottle might be construed to be a dangerous weapon—

and that Wesley was not going to be let out of jail for some weeks, if then.

Rudolph had also spoken several times to his lawyer, Johnny Heath, in New York, who had told him that if he could extricate himself from the French, in all probability the estate would have to be settled in New York, as the last known residence in the United States of the murdered man, and that it would take time.

We will all be drowned in paper, Rudolph thought. He could see the *Clothilde* going down with all aboard in a sea of writs, court orders and legal foolscap, as he listened to Johnny Heath saying he guessed that the judge would almost certainly appoint Kate Jordache, the wife, even though she was a British subject, as executrix of the estate, which would probably be divided one-third to her and two-thirds to the son, although the child she was bearing was a complicating factor. The son, being a minor, would have to have a guardian until he reached the age of eighteen, and he didn't see any reason why Rudolph, as the oldest and nearest male relative, couldn't have the job. The estate would most probably have to be liquidated and taxes paid, which would mean selling the *Clothilde* within the year. But, Heath warned, he could not say definitely as yet—he would have to get other opinions.

He said nothing to Wesley of the problems that Heath had discussed. He merely asked if he were being treated well, if there was anything he wanted. Carelessly, the boy said that he was being treated like everybody else, wanted nothing. Baffling, unrewarding young man, Rudolph thought resentfully, immutably hostile. He cut the visits as short as possible.

When he returned wearily to the hotel, it was no better. Worse, in fact. The scenes with Jean were becoming more violent. She wanted to go home, get out of her

prison, as she called it, probably the only time in its
history that the Hôtel du Cap had been so described.
Somehow, she had gotten it into her head that it was
Rudolph's fault that she couldn't leave and his telling
her that it was the policeman who was holding her passport and not himself could not stem the flood of her
hysteria. "God damn it," she had said, during their lat-
est argument, "your idiotic brother should have minded
his own business. So I'd've been fucked. Big deal. It
wouldn't've been the first time an American lady got
fucked in France and I'd've been on my way home by
now."

As the shrill voice battered at his ears, he had a quick
vision of Jean as she had been when they had first married, a quick, lovely girl, passionate in the warm, afternoon lovemaking in the room overlooking the sea (was
it the same room in which she slept now?—he couldn't
remember), offering to buy him a yacht on that surpris-
ing afternoon when she confessed that she, who he had
believed before their marriage was a poor working girl,
was wealthier by far than he was. Better not think of
those days. . . .

The fact that Wesley had nearly killed a man Jean
took as proof that it was the Jordaches' inherent lust for
violence, not her drunkenness or emotional instability,
that had been at the root of the tragedy. "One way or
another," she had screamed at her husband, "with or
without me, with their characters, those two men, that
man and that boy, were doomed from the beginning.
It's in the blood." Gretchen, he remembered, had said
much the same thing and he damned her for it. He had
seen Wesley in jail. It was not only Jordache blood in
Wesley's veins. He remembered the pouting, hard-eyed,
curvaceous mother—Teresa. Who knew what Sicilian
bandits had contributed to that rank smell, that wolfish
grin? Guilt, if it *was* guilt, had to be fairly apportioned.

"I know about your crazy father," Jean ranted on, accusing him, his crime-stained German ancestors. "I don't know how you and your holy sister escaped it this long. And look at your sister—how did her husband die? Killed, killed, killed. . . ."

"In an automobile accident." Rudolph tried to break through her high-pitched, intoning chant. "Fifty thousand people a year . . ."

"Killed," Jean repeated stubbornly. "I'm frightened to think of what kind of life our child is going to have with you as the father. . . ."

Rudolph felt helpless before her attacks. He felt confident of himself, able to solve rational problems, but irrationality frightened him, confused him, left him unarmed. When he left the room Jean had thrown herself facedown on a couch, beating her hands against the pillows like a child, sobbing, "I want to go home, I want to go home. . . ."

Gretchen, too, although she didn't say anything, was growing restive. She had work to go back to, a man kept telephoning her from New York, the attractions of the Côte d'Azur had long since lost their charm for her, and Rudolph realized that she was only staying on out of loyalty to him. Another debt.

Once, during the week, when they were alone together, she asked quietly, "Rudy, has it ever occurred to you to just pull out?"

"What do you mean?"

"I mean quit. It isn't your mess after all. Just pick up and leave. One way or another, they'll all survive."

"No," he said shortly, "it's never occurred to me."

"I admire you, Brother," Gretchen said, although there was no admiration in the manner in which she said it. "I admire you and I wonder at you."

"*You* don't have to stay, you know."

"I know," she said. "And I don't intend to stay forever. I suppose you will, if necessary."

"If necessary." He had no job to go back to, nobody
was calling him from New York.

"Add pity to what I just said, Brother," Gretchen
said. "I am now going to go down to the sea and bask in
the sunshine."


Kate had not yet called from her hotel and he was
thankful to her for that. But he dreaded the moment
when he would have to go to her and tell her what had
to be done and what it would mean for her.

Poor Bunny Dwyer, he thought, as he walked slowly
once again through the narrow streets of the old city
toward the lawyer's office—old companion, old partner, unprovided for by law or custom, friendship and
the work of years not bearing the weight of a feather in
any legal balance.

The only thing that had kept him sane was the two
afternoons in a hotel in Nice with Jeanne. No complications, no iron cables of love or duty to consider, only
the unthinking satisfactions of the flesh to make forget-
fulness possible for an hour or two in a darkened room
rented in a strange town.

Was that really the reason he was willing to stay, for
those precious afternoons in Nice? For the selfish sport
of double adultery? Was he being admired and pitied
for a lie?


His steps were heavy as he approached the lawyer's
office and the bright sunlight made him sweat uncomfortably.

The lawyer had his office in his own house along the
ramparts, in two of the old humble stone buildings now
turned into a single exquisite mansion, where once the
fishermen who sailed out of Antibes had lived, but

which, converted and modernized, now were owned by people who had never cast a net, had never pulled an oar or survived a squall. Contrary to established economic doctrine, Rudolph thought, the rich follow the poor, not the other way around. At least to the good spots the poor have accidentally found, where they in times past had been the first citizens of the town exposed to pirates, enemy fire and the erosion of storms.

The lawyer's office was impressive, the walls lined with calf-bound legal books, the furniture elegant, dark, eighteenth-century pieces, gleaming with wax, the wide window opening on a view of the sea that lapped at the rampart walls. The lawyer was an old man, but straight and as impressive as his surroundings, beautifully dressed, with large, well-kept hands, sprinkled with liver spots. He had a shining bald pate over a large-nosed, sharp face, and sad eyes. Why shouldn't he be sad, Rudolph thought, as he shook the old man's hand, think of what he must have been through to arrive in this room.

"I have considerable news for you," the lawyer said when Rudolph had seated himself across the great polished desk from him. He spoke English slowly but with care. He had let Rudolph know from the beginning that he had spent the war years in England. His voice was juicy. "First, about your wife. I have her passport here." He opened a drawer, bent a little, produced the passport and pushed it gently across the desk toward Rudolph. "The police have found Danovic, the man they wished to question further. They assure me their interrogation was—er—vigorous. Unfortunately, while he has a police record of previous arrests for various crimes, he has been discharged each time without going to trial. Besides, his alibi has stood up. He was in Lyon all day, having his teeth fixed. The dentist's records are irrefutable."

"That means what?"

The lawyer shrugged. "That means that unless the

police can prove that the dentist lied or that Danovic had accomplices whom he directed or ordered or conspired with to commit the murder they cannot arrest him. So far, there is no evidence that he knew anything about it. The police would like to continue to question him, of course, but there is no way at the present time that they can hold him. Unless . . ." He paused.

"Unless what?"

"Unless your wife wishes to place a charge of attempted rape against him."

Rudolph groaned. He knew that it would be impossible to get Jean to do anything of the kind. "All my wife wants," he said, "is to go home."

The lawyer nodded. "I quite understand that. And of course, there are no witnesses."

"The only witness was my brother," Rudolph said, "and he's dead."

"In that case, I think the best thing your wife could do would be to leave for home as soon as possible. I can imagine the ordeal . . ."

No, you can't, old man, Rudolph thought, not for a minute. He was thinking of himself more than of his wife.

"In any case, rape cases are most difficult to sustain," the old man said. "Especially in France."

"They're not so easy in America, either," Rudolph said.

"It's a crime in which the law finds itself in an uncomfortable position," the lawyer said. He smiled, aged and used to injustice.

"She'll be on the plane tomorrow," Rudolph said.

"Now—" The lawyer smoothed the shining surface of his desk with a loving gesture, his white hand reflecting palely off the wood, one problem neatly disposed of. "About your nephew." He looked obliquely, pale eyes in yellowing pouches of wrinkled skin, at Rudolph. "He is not a communicative boy. At least to me. Or to the police, either, for that matter. Under questioning, he refuses to divulge his motive for attacking the man in the bar. Perhaps he has said something to you?" Again the oblique, old, shrewd glance.

"Not to me," Rudolph said. "I have some notions, but . . ." He shrugged. "Of course they wouldn't mean anything in a court of law."

"So—there is no defense. No extenuating circumstances. Physical attacks are regarded seriously under French law." The lawyer breathed heavily. A touch of asthma, Rudolph thought, or a sign of approval, an unspoken pride in the civilized nature of France where hitting a man with a beer bottle was considered a matter of utmost gravity, as compared with the frontier attitude of America, where everybody struck everybody else with unpunishable lightness of heart. "Luckily," the lawyer went on, regaining his breath, "the Englishman is well out of danger. He will be discharged in a few days from the hospital. He, himself, has had several brushes with the local police regulations and is not disposed to bring charges. Also, the *juge d'instruction* has taken into consideration the age of the boy and the loss he has recently suffered and in a spirit of mercy has merely indicated that the boy will be taken to the nearest border or to the airport in the next eight days. Forgive me—that is one week in French." He smiled again, doting on his native language. "Don't ask me why." He smoothed the desk again, making a small, papery noise. "If the boy wishes to come back to France, to continue his education, perhaps—" With a little genteel snuffle into a handkerchief, the old man implied, with perfect politeness, that education was a rare commodity in America. "I am sure that after a year or so, when it has all been forgotten, I could arrange for him to be allowed back."

"I'm glad to hear that," Rudolph said. "From what

his father and Mr. Dwyer have told me, he likes it here and has done very well in school."

"He should continue on the *lycée,* at least until he gets his *baccalauréat.* If he ever wants to get anyplace in the world that, I would say, in our day and age, is the minimum requirement."

"I'll think about it. And, of course, talk it over with the boy."

"Good," the old man said. "I trust, my dear friend, that you consider that I have served you well and faithfully and, if I may say so, have used what small influence I have in this—this—" for once he hesitated over the English word "—in this *pays*—this section of the coast—to good effect."

"I thank you very much, *Maître,*" Rudolph said. At least he had learned how to address a lawyer in France. "How will it all be arranged?" he asked. "I mean— taken to the nearest border?" He frowned. "I mean, nobody I've ever known has been taken to the nearest border before."

"Oh, that," the old man said airly. It was an old, commonplace story for him. "If you will be at the Nice airport with a ticket for the boy one week from today, he will arrive accompanied by a detective who will make certain that he boards a plane for some other country. The United States, if you wish. Since the man will not be in uniform, it will arouse no curiosity: he will seem like an uncle, a friend of the family, wishing the boy *bon voyage.*"

"Has the boy been told?" Rudolph asked.

"I informed him myself this morning," the lawyer said.

"What did he say?"

"As usual, nothing."

"Did he seem happy, sad?" Rudolph persisted.

"He seemed neither happy nor sad."

"I see."

"I took the liberty of looking at the schedules of the American airlines that serve Nice. The most convenient would be the plane that will leave at eleven-thirty in the morning."

"I'll be there," Rudolph said. He reached out for Jean's passport and put it in his pocket.

"I must compliment you, *Monsieur* Jordache," the old man said, "on the calm, the gentlemanly equilibrium with which you have endured this painful episode."

"Thank you." The moment I leave this beautiful office, Rudolph thought, I will not be calm or demonstrate equilibrium of any kind, gentlemanly or otherwise. As he started to get up, he felt dizzy, almost as if he were going to faint, and had to steady himself by putting a hand against the desk. The old man looked at him quizzically. "A bit too much lunch?" he asked.

"No lunch at all." He had skipped lunch for seven days.

"It is important to guard one's health," the old man said, "especially when one is in a foreign country."

"Would you like my address in the United States," Rudolph asked, "so that you can mail me your bill?"

"That will not be necessary, *monsieur*," the old man said smoothly. "My clerk has it prepared for you in the outer office. You do not have to bother with francs. A check in dollars will do, if you will be kind enough to send it to the bank in Geneva whose address you will find on the bill."

Impressive, able, surrounded by gleaming eighteenth-century furniture, with a view of the blue sea and an untaxed account in Switzerland, the old man stood up, slowly, careful of his advanced years, and shook Rudolph's hand, then accompanied him to the door, saying, *"Enfin,* I must extend my sympathies to you and your family and I hope that what has happened will not prevent you from visiting this lovely part of the world in the future."

First things first, he thought as he walked away from the lawyer's house along the ramparts toward the port, past the Musée Grimaldi, with all the Picassos in it. The bad news to begin with. That meant Dwyer and Kate. He would have to tell them of his conversation with Heath yesterday. Together, preferably, so that there would be no misunderstanding, no suspicion of secret dealing. After that, the good news for Jean and Gretchen, that they were free now to go back home. He relished the thought of neither meeting. Then there would have to be the jail again, some decision made about where and how and with whom Wesley would stay in America. Maybe that would be the worst conversation of all. He hoped the boy had shaved by now. And taken a shower.

He stopped and looked out to sea, across the Baie des Anges toward Nice. The Bay of Angels. The French didn't care what they named things. Antibes, for example. Antipolis, the Greek settlers had called it— Opposite the City. What city? Athens, a thousand miles away by oared galley? Homesick Greeks? He himself was homesick for no place. Lucky Greeks. What were the laws then, what had those exemplary politicians judged a fair punishment for a boy who had hit someone in a tavern with a beer bottle? What civic spirit or lust for fame or profit had driven the lawmakers among the statutes and the measured rhetoric to leave their academies and festivals to seek election, take on the burden of ruling that intelligent and warlike race? He himself had made speeches on the hustings, had cajoled, promised, heard the cheers of crowds, won and accepted office. Why? He couldn't remember now.

There was a bustle of traffic around him, even on the

narrow stone road along the top of the ramparts. Antibes had once been a sleepy, forgotten town, but it was crowded now by the beneficiaries or the victims of the twentieth century, leaving winter behind them in the rush to the climate of the south, to work and live there, not only to play. Flowers and light industry. He himself was a northern man but he could use a few years of the south himself. If what had happened here had not happened, he might have settled cosily here, anonymous, unknown, retired gratefully, as some men did, in his thirties. He had the rudiments of French—think of Jeanne—he could have worked at it, learned to read Victor Hugo, Gide, Cocteau, whatever new men were worth reading, visited Paris for the theater. Dreams. Impossible now.

He breathed deeply of the salt balmy air off the sea. Almost every place was open for him, but not this particular, haunted, beautiful place.

He started walking again, down from the ramparts toward the port. He would get Dwyer to find Kate and they could have their discussion in a café, because Kate had said she never wanted to see the *Clothilde* again. She might have changed her mind by now, with the first shock over, she was not a sentimental woman, but he was not the one who was going to force her.

Just at the entrance to the port there was a small seamen's café. At a tiny table in front of it Dwyer was sitting with a woman, her back to Rudolph. When he called out to Dwyer the woman turned and he saw that it was Kate. She was thinner now, or was it the black dress she wore that made her look so? The nut brown of her complexion had faded and her hair was careless around her face. He felt a twinge of anger or something akin to anger. Knowing everything that he was trying to do for her, she had not even bothered to call to tell him where she was staying, and here she was sitting with

Dwyer, the two of them looking like an old married
couple, sharing secrets in the sunshine. She stood up to
say hello to him and he was embarrassed.

"May I join you for a moment?" he asked. There
were moments and moments.

Without a word, Dwyer drew up a chair from the
next table. He was dressed as usual, tanned, muscular,
his bantamweight arms ridged below the short sleeves of
the white jersey with the printing on it. What mourning
he carried was not on public display. "What will you
have to drink?" Dwyer asked.

"What are you two drinking?"

"Pastis."

"Not for me, thanks," Rudolph said. He didn't like
its sweet, licorice taste. It reminded him of the long,
black, pliant sticks of candy, like miniature snakes, that
his father had bought for him when he was a boy. He
was in no mood to be reminded of his father. "If I
could have a brandy?"

Dwyer went into the café to fetch the brandy. Rudolph looked across the table at Kate. She was sitting
there stolidly, no emotion showing on her face. She
could be a Mexican peasant woman, Rudolph thought,
all work done for the moment, sitting in front of an
adobe wall in the sunlight, waiting for her husband to
come home from the fields. She lowered her eyes, refus-
ing to look at him, a baked mud wall around her primi-
tive thoughts. He sensed hostility. Had the parting kiss
when she left the *Clothilde* been a sardonic salute? Or
had it been real, meant then and later regretted?

"How is Wesley?" she asked, her eyes still averted.
"Bunny told me all about it."

"He's all right. They're letting him leave France a
week from today. Most probably for the States."

She nodded. "I thought they might," she said. Her

voice was low and flat. "It's better that way. He shouldn't hang around this part of the world."

"That was a foolish thing he did," Rudolph said, "getting into a fight like that. I don't know what could've come over him."

"Maybe," Kate said, "he was saying good-bye to his father."

Rudolph was silent for a moment, ashamed of what he had said. He felt the way he had the day he had left the consulate for the first time, weeping in the streets. He wondered if his cheeks were wet with tears now. "You know him better than I do," he said. He had to change the subject. "And how are you, Kate?" he said, trying to sound tender.

She made a curious, deprecating, blowing sound. "As well as might be expected," she said. "Bunny's been company."

Maybe they ought to get married, Rudolph thought. Two of a breed. From the same graduating class, from the same hard school. Keep each other company, as she put it. "I had hoped you would call," he said, lying.

She raised her eyes, looking at him. "I knew where I could find you," she said levelly, "if I had piss-all to say to you."

Bunny came back with the brandy and two fresh glasses of pastis. Rudolph watched as they poured the water into the glasses and the pastis turned milky yellow. Rudolph raised his glass mechanically. "To . . ." He stopped, laughed uncertainly. "To nothing, I guess."

Dwyer raised his glass, but Kate just slowly twirled her glass on the table.

The brandy was raw and Rudolph gasped a little as it struck his throat. "There have been certain developments that I think you ought to know about . . ." I must stop sounding as though I'm addressing a board meeting, he thought. "I'm glad I found you both together . . ." Then, as clearly as he knew how, he explained the meaning of what Heath had told him about the estate. They listened politely, but without interest. Don't you care what happens to your lives? he wanted to shout at them.

"I don't want to be, what's the word . . . ?" Kate said slowly.

"Executrix." Heath had told him that was probably what the judge would do.

"Executrix. I don't know tuppence about executrix," Kate said. "Anyway, I plan to go back to England. Bath. My ma's there and I can go on the National Health for the baby and my ma can watch after it when I go out to work."

"What sort of work?" Rudolph asked.

"I was waitress in a restaurant," Kate said, "before I listened to the call of the sea." She laughed sardonically. "A waitress can always find work."

"There'll be some money left," Rudolph said, "when the estate's settled. You won't have to work."

"What'll I do all day, sit around and look at the telly?" Kate said. "I'm not an idler, you know." Her tone was challenging, the implication clear that he and his women were idlers all. "Whatever money there is, and I don't imagine there'll be much after the lawyers and them others, I'll put aside for the kid's education. Educated, if it's a girl, maybe she won't have to wait on table and iron ladies' dresses in a steaming ship's laundry, like her ma."

There was no arguing with her. "If you ever need anything—money, anything," he said, without hope, "please let me know."

"There won't be any need," she said, lowering her eyes again, still twirling her glass on the table.

"Just in case," Rudolph said. "Maybe, for example, one day you'd like to visit America."

"America's no attraction for me," she said. "They'd laugh at me in America."

"Wouldn't you want to see Wesley again?"

"Wouldn't mind," she said. "If he wants to see me, there're planes every day from America to London."

"In the meantime," Rudolph went on, trying to keep the note of pleading out of his voice, "while the estate's being held up, you'll need some money."

"Not me," she said. "I have my savings. And I made Tom pay me my wages, just like before, even when we were sleeping in the same bed and fixing to marry. Love is one thing, I told him," she said, a proud declaration of categories, "and work is another." She finally lifted her glass and sipped some of the pastis.

"I give up." Rudolph couldn't help sounding exasperated. "You sound as if I'm your enemy."

She stared at him, blank pueblo eyes. "I don't rightly remember saying anything that could be construed like enemy. Did I, Bunny?"

"I wasn't really paying much heed," Dwyer said uneasily, "I couldn't pass judgment."

"How about you?" Rudolph turned to Dwyer. "Don't *you* need money?"

"I've always been a saving type of man," Dwyer said. "Tom used to tease me, saying I was mean and miserly. I'm well set, thank you."

Defeated, Rudolph finished his brandy. "At least," he said, "leave me your addresses. Both of you. So I can keep in touch."

"Leave Wesley's address with the shipyard here," Kate said. "I'll drop them a line from time to time and they'll pass on a card. I'd like to let him know whether he's got a sister or brother when the time comes."

"I'm not sure where Wesley will be," Rudolph said. He was beginning to feel hoarse, his throat rasped by the brandy and the effort of talking to these two evasive, stubborn human beings. "If you write to him care of me, I'll make sure he gets the letter."

Kate stared at him for a long moment, then lifted the glass to her lips again. She drank. "I wouldn't want your wife to be reading any mail of mine," she said, putting down her glass.

"My wife doesn't open my mail," Rudolph said. He couldn't help sounding angry now.

"I'm glad to see she's a woman of some character," Kate said. There was just the hint of a malicious glint in her eye, or was he imagining it?

"I'm only trying to be of help," Rudolph said wearily. "I feel an obligation . . ." He stopped, but it was too late.

"I thank you for your intentions," Kate said, "but you're under no obligation to me."

"I say we just would do better not to talk about it, Mr. . . . Rudy," Dwyer said.

"All right, let's not talk about it. I'm going to be in Antibes for at least a week. When do you plan to leave for England, Kate?"

Kate smoothed the wrinkles in the lap of her dress with her two hands. "As soon as I get my things together."

Rudolph remembered the single, scuffed, imitation-leather suitcase Wesley had carried off the *Clothilde* for her. It probably couldn't take her more than fifteen minutes to get her things together. "How long do you think that will take?" Rudolph asked patiently.

"Hard to tell," Kate said. "A week. A fortnight. I have some good-byes to make."

"I'll have to have your address here, at least," Rudolph said. "Something may come up, may have to be signed in front of a notary . . ."

"Bunny knows where I am," she said.

"Kate," Rudolph said softly, "I want to be your friend."

She nodded slowly. "Give it a little time, mate," she said harshly. The kiss of parting in the saloon of the *Clothilde* had been one of numbness. A week's reflection had embittered her. Rudolph couldn't blame her. He turned to Dwyer. "How about you," he asked, "how long do you expect to stay?"

"You'll know that better than I do, Rudy," Dwyer said. "I mean to stay until they throw me off. They'll be arriving any day now with the new shaft and the new screw and that'll mean hauling her up on dock for at least three days, that is if the insurance comes in. . . . You *could* do me a favor—get after the insurance. They're slow as shit if you don't get after them. And you'd know how to talk to them better than me. So if . . ."

"Goddamn the insurance," Rudolph said, letting go. "You handle the insurance yourself."

"No need to yell at poor old Bunny," Kate said placidly. "He's just trying to keep the ship in shape so that when you sell it you won't have a rotten hulk on your hands."

"I'm sorry," Rudolph said. "I've been going through a lot . . ."

"To be sure, you have," Kate said. If it was ironic, there was no telling it from her tone.

Rudolph stood up. "I have to go back to the hotel now. What do I owe here?"

"The drinks're on me," Dwyer said. "My pleasure."

"I'll keep you posted about what's going on," Rudolph said.

"That's kind of you," said Dwyer. "I'd like to see Wesley before he leaves for America."

"You'll have to see him at the airport," Rudolph

said. "He's going right there from the jail. With a policeman."

"French cops," Dwyer said. "It don't pay to let them
get their hands on you, does it? Tell Wesley I'll be at
the airport."

"Take care of yourselves," Rudolph said. "Both of
you."

They didn't answer, but sat there in silence with their
glasses in front of them, in shadow now, because the
sun was going down and the building across the street
was blocking it out. Rudolph made a little gesture and
walked back toward the Agence de Voyages near the
square where he could buy the three plane tickets for
tomorrow's flight.

Husband and wife, he thought bitterly, as he passed
the antique shops and the cheese shops and the shops
that sold newspapers, they'd make a good pair. What's
wrong with me? What makes me so goddamn sure I can
take care of anybody? Everybody? I'm like those idiotic
dogs at the greyhound races. Show me a responsibility,
mine, not mine, anybody's, and I'm off after it, like the
dogs after the mechanical rabbit, even if they never
catch it, *know* they never can catch it. What disease in-
fected me when I was young? Vanity? Fear of not being
liked? A substitute for denied religion? It's a lucky thing
I never had to fight a war—I'd be dead the first day,
shot by my own men, stopping a retreat or volunteering
to go for the ammunition for a lost and surrounded gun.
My project for the next year, he told himself, is to learn
how to say, Fuck you, to one and all.

# CHAPTER 6

*From Billy Abbott's notebook—*

Monika disturbed me tonight. She was
working on the printed proofs of a
speech she had translated from the
French into English, when she looked
up and said, I've just noticed
something. In both languages--and in
most others, too--the verbs--to have,
to be, to go, and to die--are all
irregular. In English--I have, he has,
I had--not too much of a variation, but
there all the same. More striking in
French. J'ai, tu as, il a, nous avons.
<u>To be</u> wanders much more. I am, you are,
he is, we were, you are being, they had
been, I shall, he will. In French, je
suis, tu es, nous sommes, vous etes,
il sera. Then sois et soyons and je fus
and il fut in other tenses. Think of I
go, I went, I have been gone. And
aller--je vais, nous allons, ils vont.
Dying is a bit more in a straight line,

but it gives you pause. I die. I am
dead. In French, mourir in the
infinitive, but je meurs, nous mourions,
nous sommes morts. What does that all
mean--that actions--existing, owning,
moving from place to place, dying? That
we seek to disown or disguise or flee
from our most basic activities? The
verb to kill, however, is
straightforward as could be, I kill, you
kill, he kills. I killed, you killed.
He killed. Nothing to hide there or cope
with uneasily. The same with fuck. Is
there judgment there?

I am glad I am not a translator, I
told her. But it set me thinking and I
was up half the night worrying about
myself and my connection to language.

---

Gretchen was in the bar when Rudolph got back to
the hotel. She was drinking a champagne cocktail and
talking to a young man in tennis clothes. She had been
doing quite a bit of drinking the last few days, which
was not like her, and had been talking to any men who
happened to be around, which, he thought, maliciously,
was very much like her. Had he heard footsteps softly
passing his door last night, past the paired shoes, in the
direction of her room? Remembering Nice, he could
hardly complain. And whatever diversions she found to
amuse herself with in the limbo in which she found herself were at the very least excusable.

"May I introduce my brother, Rudolph Jordache,"
she said as Rudolph came over to the table at which
they were sitting. "Basil—I forget your second name,
dear."

She must have had at least three champagne cocktails, Rudolph thought, to say dear to a man whose name she'd forgotten.

The young man stood up. He was tall and slender, actorish, dyed hair, frivolously good-looking, Rudolph decided.

"Berling," the young man said, bowing a little. "Your sister's been telling me about you."

Berling, Basil Berling, Rudolph thought, as he nodded acknowledgment of the bow. Who has a name like Basil Berling? British, from his accent.

"Won't you sit down and join us?" Basil Berling said.

"Just for a moment," Rudolph said, without grace. "I have some things I have to discuss with my sister."

"My brother is a great discusser," Gretchen said. "Beware his discussions."

Four cocktails, not three, Rudolph thought.

"What will it be, sir?" Basil Berling asked, polite British member of Actors Equity, working hard on his speech, conscious that he came from a mediocre school, as the waiter came up.

"The same," Rudolph said.

"Three of the same," Basil Berling said to the waiter.

"He's been plying me with drinks," Gretchen said.

"So I see."

Gretchen made a face. "Rudolph is the sober one in the family," she explained to Basil Berling.

"Somebody has to be."

"Oh, dear, I fear the discussion to follow," Gretchen said. "Basil—what is the name again, dear . . . ?"

She's pretending to be further gone than she really is, Rudolph thought. To annoy me. Today I'm everybody's target.

"Berling," the man said, always pleasant.

"Mr. Berling is an actor," Gretchen said. "Isn't it a coincidence," she asked, her tone girlish and drunk at

the same time, "here we are at the very end of the
world and we meet by sheerest jolly happenstance in a
low bar and we're both in the flicks?" She was mocking
him now with a fake English accent, but the young man
seemed beyond offense.

"Are you?" The Englishman sounded surprised. "I
mean in films? I say—I should have guessed."

"Isn't that gallant?" Gretchen touched Rudolph's arm
flirtatiously, brother or no. "I have to admit the fearful
truth. I'm in the unglamorous part." She sipped at her
new drink, smiling over the rim at Basil Berling.

"Hard to believe," Berling said heavily.

Must get rid of him forthwith, Rudolph thought, before I ask the manager to throw him out.

"Oh, yes," Gretchen said. "Behind the scenes. I'm
one of those ladies with the black fingernails. Up to my
ass in acetate. Film editor. There, now, the secret's out.
Just a plain, humble cutter."

"You do honor to the profession," Basil Berling said.

God save me from the mating rites of others, Rudolph thought, as Gretchen said, "Sweet," and patted
the back of Berling's hand. For a moment Rudolph was
curious about how his sister *really* was in bed, how
many men were in her past, her present. She'd tell him
if he asked.

"Gretchen," Rudolph said, as Gretchen tilted her
head with too much charm at the actor, "I have to go
up and tell Jean she has to pack. I have her passport
and she'll want to be leaving tomorrow. I'd like a word
with you first, please."

Gretchen made a pretty grimace. Rudolph would
have liked to slap her. The day's events had worn his
nerves thin. "Drink up, dear," Gretchen said to Berling.
"My brother is a busy man, the conscientious bee going
from flower to flower."

"Of course." The actor stood up. "I'd better get out

of these clothes, anyway. I played three sets of singles and I'll come down with a monstrous cold if I sit around wet much longer."

"Thanks for the wine," Gretchen said.

"My pleasure."

Dwyer had said, "My pleasure," too, Rudolph remembered. Everybody was enjoying himself this afternoon, he thought sourly. Except him.

"Will I see you later, Gretchen? For dinner?" Berling said, tall, but with skinny, stringy legs, Rudolph noticed. I'd look better in tennis shorts, he thought meanly.

"I daresay," Gretchen said.

"A pleasure to have met you, sir," Berling said to Rudolph.

Rudolph grunted. If the man was going to call him sir, as though he were on the edge of the grave, he'd be crusty, as befitted his age.

Brother and sister watched the actor stride out, springy and virile, treading the boards.

"God, Gretchen," Rudolph said, when the actor had gone, "you certainly know how to pick them, don't you?"

"There's very little choice at this season," Gretchen said. "A girl has to take what comes along. Now, what unpleasant thing are you in such a hurry to tell me?" She wasn't drunk at all, he saw.

"It's about Enid," he said. "I'd like you to get on the plane with Jean and Enid tomorrow and keep an eye on her. On both of them."

"Oh, God," Gretchen said.

"I don't trust my daughter with Jean," Rudolph went on doggedly.

"What about you? Aren't you coming along?"

"I can't. There's too much still to attend to here. And when you get to New York I want you to stay with them in my apartment. Mrs. Johnson's off on a holiday in St. Louis for another week."

"Come on now, Rudy," Gretchen said. "I'm too old to take up baby-sitting."

"Damn it, Gretchen," Rudolph said, "after all I've done for you . . ."

Gretchen put her head back and closed her eyes as though by that physical act she was holding back an angry reply. Still in the same position, and with her eyes still closed, she said, "I don't have to be reminded every day of what you've done for me."

"Every day?" Rudolph bit off the words. "When was the last time?"

"Not in so many words, my dear brother." She opened her eyes and leaned forward again. "Let's not argue about it." She stood up. "You've got yourself a baby-sitter. Anyway, it will be nice to be back again in a place where murders happen in the newspapers, not in the bosom of your own family. What time does the plane leave?"

"Eleven-thirty. I have your ticket."

"Think of everything, don't you?"

"Yes. Everything."

"I wouldn't know what to do without you, Brother," Gretchen said. "I'd better start packing myself." She smiled at him, but he noticed the effort. "Truce?"

"Truce," he said.

On the way to the elevator he stopped at the desk to get his key. "While you were out, Mr. Jordache," the concierge said, "a lady came by and left a letter for you." He took an envelope out of the box and gave it to Rudolph with his key. The envelope had only his name on it, in a woman's handwriting that he felt he had seen someplace before. In the elevator he tore open the envelope and picked the single piece of paper out of it.

It was from Jeanne.

Dear American,
This is just to tell you to please not call me. You can guess the reason why. I'll call you when I can. It may not be for a week or two. It may be that they have called off the war in Paris permanently. I hope you are having a good time in Antibes and are prolonging your stay. The afternoons are dreary without you. If you wish to write me, do it through Poste Restante, Central Post Office, Nice. I hope I have spelled everything correctly.

Drive carefully,
*Jeanne*

He crumpled the letter and put it in his pocket, got out of the elevator, went over to the door of the suite, arranged his face, put the key in the lock and went in.

Jean was standing at the window, staring out to sea. She didn't turn around when he came in. Against the fading light which came through the open window, her silhouette was slender and young in a linen summer dress. She reminded him of the girls he had gone to college with, girls who wore their boyfriends' fraternity pins on their bosoms and went to the Saturday-afternoon football games in bulky fur coats and bright woolen stockings and to the proms at which he had played the trumpet in the band, to help pay his way through school. Standing at the door, looking at the illusion of vulnerable youthfulness which his wife created, he felt a pang of pity for her, unsought, unprofitable.

"Good evening, Jean," he said, advancing toward her. Jean, Jeanne, he thought. What's in a name?

She turned slowly. He saw that she had had her soft, shoulder-length hair done that day and that she had put on makeup. The old woman she would one day be had gone from her face.

"Good evening," she said gravely. Her voice, too, had returned to normal, if normal for her meant not rasping with drink or fury or self-laceration.

"Here's your passport," he said, giving it to her. "The lawyer got it back today."

"Thank you," she said.

"I have your ticket for the plane tomorrow. You can go back home now."

"Thank you," she said again. "And you?"

"I'll have to stay at least a week more."

She nodded, opened her passport, glanced at her photograph, shook her head sadly, threw the passport on the table.

My passport photo doesn't flatter me either, Rudolph would have liked to say.

"At least a week . . ." Jean said. "You must be exhausted."

"I'm all right." He sank into an easy chair. Until she had said he must be exhausted he hadn't realized how tired he really was. He had been sleeping badly, waking often in the middle of the night, with uneasy dreams. Last night he had had the most curious, disturbing dream. He had awakened with a start. The bed had seemed to be shaking and the first thought he had was that there was an earthquake. In his dream, he had remembered, he seemed to have been pinched all over his legs by invisible, mischievous fingers. Poltergeists, he remembered thinking in his dream. Awake, he had thought, Now where did that word come from? He had read it, of course, but he had never spoken it or written it.

"How is Enid?" he asked.

"Fine," Jean said. "I took her to Juan-les-Pins this afternoon and bought her a miniature striped sailor's jersey. She looks charming in it and she's been posing in

front of the mirror in it ever since. She's having her supper now with the nurse."

"I'll look in and say good night to her," he said. "In a
while." He loosened his collar and tie. Unyoked for the
day, he would put on an open-necked sports shirt for
dinner. "Gretchen will be on the plane with you and
Enid," he said.

"She needn't bother," Jean said, but with no hint of
resentment. "Perhaps she'd like to stay on. The weather's glorious now and I saw her walking up from the sea
with a handsome young man."

"She's anxious to get back to New York," he said.
"I've asked her to stay with you and Enid until Mrs.
Johnson gets back from St. Louis."

"That will be dull for her," Jean said. "I can take
care of Enid myself. I have nothing else to do." But
again calmly, without resentment or the tone of argument.

"I think it would be better if Gretchen was there to
help out," he said carefully.

"Whatever you say. Although I can stay sober for a
week, you know."

"I know," he said. "Just to be on the safe side."

"I've been thinking, Rudy," Jean said, standing with
her hands clasped in front of her, her fingers interlaced,
as though she were on a platform giving a prepared
speech. "About what we've been through."

"Why don't you forget what we've been through?"
Rudolph said. He was in no mood for prepared
speeches.

"I've been thinking about us," she said evenly, without hostility. "For your sake and for Enid's, I think
we ought to get a divorce."

Finally, he thought. At least I wasn't the one to say
the word. "Why don't we wait awhile to talk about
things like that?" he said gently.

"If you want. But I'm no good for you. Or for her. You don't want me anymore. . . ." Jean put up her hand, although he hadn't begun to say anything. "You haven't come near me in over a year. And you've found somebody down here, I'm sure. Please don't deny it."

"I won't deny it," he said.

"I don't blame you, dear," she said. "I've been poison for you for a long time. Another man would have left me long ago. And the crowd would have cheered." She smiled crookedly.

"I wish you'd wait until we were both home in America . . ." he started to say, although he felt that a great weight was being lifted from his shoulders.

"I feel like talking this evening," she said, without insistence. "I've been thinking about us all day and I haven't had a drink in more than a week and I'm as sane and sensible as I'm ever going to be for the rest of my life. Don't you want to hear what I've been thinking about?"

"I don't want you to say anything that you're going to regret later."

"Regret." She made a little awkward movement, as though she were jerking away from a wasp. "I regret everything I say. And just about everything I've done. Listen carefully, my dear. I am a drunk. I am disappointed with myself and I am a drunk. I will be disappointed with myself and remain a drunk all my life. And I won't get over it."

"We haven't tried hard enough up to now," he said. "The places you've gone to weren't thorough enough. There are other clinics that . . ."

"You can send me to every clinic in America," she said. "Every psychiatrist in American can poke among my dreams. They can give me antabuse and I can vomit my guts out. And I will still be a drunk. And I will scream at you like a shrew and disgrace you. . . .

Remember, I did it before and not only once . . . and I can ask forgiveness and I can do it again and I can risk my child's life driving her around drunkenly in a car and I can forget everything and go looking for a bottle over and over again until the day I die and I wish it was going to be soon only I don't have the courage to kill myself, which is another disappointment. . . ."

"Please don't talk like that, Jean," he said. He stood up and went toward her, but she pulled away, as though she feared his touch.

"I'm sober now," she said, "and I've dried out for more than a week and let's take advantage of this lovely, unexpected moment and look things in the face and make sober, world-shaking decisions. I will retire to myself somewhere, out of sight—is Mexico far enough away? Spain? I speak Spanish, did you know that? Switzerland? The clinics are excellent there, I am told, and for two or three months at a time you can expect great results."

"Okay," he said, "let's live two or three months at a time then. Divorce or no divorce."

"There's no use pretending I can hold down a job anymore." Nothing could stop the chanting, obsessed voice. "But thanks to my dear, dead father I can live more than comfortably—extravagantly. You must help me draw up a trust fund for Enid because when I'm drunk there's a chance I'll meet some scheming, dazzling young Italian who will conspire to rob me of my fortune and I wouldn't like that. I've even figured out a way of making you not feel guilty for neglecting me and letting me wander unprotected around this dark and dangerous world. I'll hire a nice, strong young woman, probably a lesbian, who will keep me company and make sure I come to no harm when I am steeped in drink . . . and if necessary will supply me with innocent and undangerous sex. . . ."

"You must stop," he cried. "Enough, enough."

"Don't sound so shocked, my dear Puritan Rudolph," she said. "I've done it before and haven't disliked it and I'm sure I can do it again, especially after a bottle or two, and not dislike it again. The truth is, darling, I can't struggle anymore. Even the Confederate Army finally surrendered. I've had enough dead. I'm out of room to maneuver. I have come to Appomattox. You see, my education has not been wasted on me. You can return my sword, General Grant. No, that sounds mocking. I don't mean to mock. I'm in despair. I can't fight anymore. I can't fight you or the drink or guilt or marriage, whatever *that* word means to you and me at this time. Occasionally, when I'm in a calm period, I'll appear, with my Lesbian companion, I'll make sure she's not too obvious, I'll have her dressed girlishly, as will I, and visit Enid. You need not be present. Don't say anything tonight, please, but remember what I've offered in the morning when you put me on the plane, and admire me for my renunciation. Take it before I change my mind and hang for the rest of my life around your neck like a corpse."

"Look," he said, "when you get away from here, away from this morbid atmosphere, you'll . . ."

"Between us, we've made shit out of your life, too," she intoned. "And you're not getting any younger, you can't just sit in a corner staring at the fire for another fifty years, you've got to do *something*. Be thankful for today. Grab the offer. Who knows how long the merchandise is going to be on the market? And now, I know you've had a long hard day, and want to shave and take a nice hot shower and put on fresh clothes and have a martini and go to dinner. While you're in the shower, I'll order you the drink. Never fear, I won't touch a drop between now and New York—I have spurts of superhuman willpower. And then, if you'll be

so kind, you'll take me to dinner, just you and I alone—
and we'll talk of other things—like the rest of your life
and what schools Enid should go to and what kind of
woman you might finally consider marrying and whom
you've been screwing on the Côte d'Azur and then
when it's late and we're both tired, we'll come back here
to our lovely, insanely expensive hotel suite and you'll
let me sleep in your bed with you because tomorrow I'm
taking a plane to America and you're staying on for the
rest of the summer weather to tie up all the loose ends
that I have loosened."

He stood up and went over and put his arms around
her. She was trembling violently. Her face was flushed
and she felt feverishly hot to his touch.

"I'm sorry," she whispered, trembling in his arms,
her head against his chest, her arms gripping him. "I
suppose I should have made this speech long ago—
before we were married, maybe, except I don't think I
was like this before I was married."

"Sssh, sssh," he said, helplessly. "When you get home
things will look different."

"When I get home," she said, "the only difference
will be that I'll be one day older." She pulled away,
smiled wanly at him. "It's hard to think of that as any
great improvement. Now go take your shower. I'll be
less eloquent when you come out and there'll be a martini here for you to remind you that all is not lost. I'll
join you for the cocktail hour. With another Coca-
Cola."

In the shower he allowed himself to weep. Somewhere along the years there must have been a moment
when she could have been saved. He had been too busy,
too preoccupied, to recognize the moment, make the
necessary gesture toward her, before all avenues of escape finally closed to her.

He couldn't seem to regulate the temperature of the

water. It seemed to come out too hot and burn his skin
like a thousand needles or when he turned the knob it
spurted out icy cold, freezing him, making him shiver,
as though he were standing naked in a sleet storm.

He got out, dried himself with a big rough towel,
looking at himself in the long mirror, ashamed of his
trim, adulterous body, the muscles all neat, strong, useless in the life he lived, his sex an impediment to charity. *Chair,* he thought. Flesh, in French. Close enough,
at least in spelling, to charity. Save that, he thought bitterly, for the afternoons in Nice.

He dressed slowly, the expensive, well-fitting clothing
agreeable against his skin. The body's small, restorative
pleasures. He put on a light wool shirt, soft cashmere
socks, pressed flannel trousers, snug polished moccasins
(the Communists in the corridors at night), a crisp
seersucker jacket. Gretchen would not say tonight that
he looked as though he had just been laid.

The martini was on the table near the couch when he
went back into the salon, and Jean was standing in front
of the window staring out at the fragrant darkness
pierced by bright points of color as the lights of the
coast that swept away west from the peninsula of Antibes went on. Jean had lit a single lamp and had a glass
of Coca-Cola in her hand. She turned when she heard
him come in. "Gretchen called while you were in the
shower," she said. "I told her we were having dinner
alone. Is that all right with you?"

"Of course."

"She's having dinner in Golfe Juan with a friend, anyway, she said."

"I met him," Rudolph said.

"I often wonder how she gets along with men. She
doesn't confide in me."

"She confides in me too much," Rudolph said.

"As does all the world," Jean said lightly. "Poor Rudolph."

She wandered aimlessly around the room, touching the back of a chair absently, opening a drawer in the desk. "Tell me, Rudy—I don't quite remember," she said. "Is this the room we had when we came here just after we were married?"

"I don't remember, either," he said, and picked up the martini.

"Well," she said, lifting her glass, "here's to . . . to what?" She smiled. She looked beautiful and young in the shadowed room. "To divorce, say?" She sipped at her Coca-Cola.

Rudolph put his glass down. "I'll have my drink later," he said. "I want to go in and say good night to Enid."

"Go ahead," Jean said. "I believe you ought to give the French girl a nice little bonus. She's been very good with Enid. Very gentle and patient. She's almost a child herself, but somehow she always seems to have been able to invent games to amuse Enid. It's a talent I don't have."

"Nor do I," Rudolph said. "Don't you want to come with me?"

"Not tonight," Jean said. "Anyway, I have to make some repairs on my face."

"I won't be long."

"No hurry," she said. "We have the whole night ahead of us."

Enid was just finishing her supper, dressed in the striped seaman's jersey. She was laughing when Rudolph came into the room. Somehow, although the nurse couldn't speak English, the two of them seemed to understand each other perfectly. Education, Rudolph thought, with a pang, will wipe out that particular shared gift. He kissed the top of Enid's head, said, *"Bon soir"* to the girl. The girl said in French, "I'm sorry about the shirt. She has had her bath all right, but she wouldn't put on pajamas; she insists she wants to sleep tonight in the shirt. I hope you don't mind? I didn't think it was worth a struggle. . . ."

"Of course not." Sensible, flexible Frenchwoman. "She'll sleep all the better for it." Then he told her to please have the child's things packed in the morning, as they were leaving for New York. By the time I'm through here, he thought, I'll be able to speak enough French even to talk to a Corsican policeman. One for the plus side.

The girl said, *"Bien, monsieur."*

Rudolph took a long look at his daughter. She looked healthy and happy, with a light bloom on her cheeks from the sun. Well, he thought, another plus; at least *someone's* getting some good out of this trip. Seeing her sitting there, contentedly playing with her food, and suddenly reaching out to hold the girl's hand, he thought, when I get back to New York I'm going to fire Mrs. Johnson. Mrs. Johnson was in her fifties, efficient and quiet, but she wasn't one for games.

He kissed the top of Enid's head again and bent down farther as she said, "Good night, Daddy," and planted a wet, oatmeally kiss inaccurately on his cheek. She smelled of soap and talcum powder and if the girl hadn't been there he would have picked her up from the chair on which she was sitting, propped up on pillows, and hugged her, hard.

But he merely said, "Good night, little sailor, sleep well," and went out of the room.

The dinner was excellent, the moon shone over the sea, the restaurant was uncrowded and the waiters buzzed devotedly around their table. Jean insisted that he order a bottle of wine for himself and he allowed himself to be persuaded. They found they had a great deal to say to each other, none of it important or troubling, and there were no uncomfortable lapses in the conversation. We are all made out of rubber, Rudolph thought, admiring Jean's soft hair as she bent slightly over her food; we stretch all out of shape and then, at least to all appearances, snap back again, back to the original form, or almost back to the original form.

They lingered a long time over coffee, looking, he was sure, content with themselves, with each other, in front of the big window that gave on the dark sea, with its silver path of moonlight shimmering away toward the distant islands.

They walked slowly up to the hotel and when they came into the suite, Jean said, "Get into bed, darling. I'll be in in a little while."

Naked, he lay in the bed in the dark room, waiting. The door opened softly; there was a rustling as Jean took off her robe and then she was in bed with him. He put his arm around her, her body not trembling, warm, but without the blaze of fever. They didn't move and in a little while they both were asleep. This night he didn't dream that the hotel was rocking in an earthquake or that he was visited by poltergeists.


Farther down the hall, Gretchen slept uneasily, alone. The dinner had been delicious, the wine had flowed freely, the young man had been almost the handsomest man in the room and had been attentive, then importunate: she had nearly said yes. But finally, she was sleeping alone. Before she dropped off, she thought, If only my goddamn brother hadn't said, "You certainly know how to pick them, don't you?" she wouldn't have been sleeping alone that night.

# CHAPTER 7

*From Billy Abbott's notebook—*

Happened to pick up a copy of the
international issue of the week's <u>Time</u>
magazine. Lo and behold, under CRIME
there was the saga of the Jordaches,
with nude photograph and whole
unpleasant history of the family.
Failure, murder and disgrace in several
hundred well-chosen words.
　I am clipping out the story and
putting it with my other notes. It will
give my descendants, if there are any,
a useful rundown on their family tree.

　　About the last place you'd expect to find the
three children of a Hudson River town, German-
immigrant suicide baker would be a yacht on the
Riviera. But after the recent Antibes waterfront
killing of Thomas Jordache, better known years
ago as middleweight **Tommy Jordan**, a number of
names from the past bubbled to the surface of a

French police murder dossier. Among them: **Rudolph Jordache,** 40, Tom's brother, millionaire, ex-mayor of Whitby, N.Y.; Jordan's teenage son, **Wesley; Jean Prescott Jordache,** Rudolph's wife and heiress to the Midwestern Prescott drug empire; and **Gretchen Burke,** sister to both Jordaches and widow of stage and screen director, **Colin Burke.**

Sources in Antibes say that Jordan was bludgeoned to death only days after his wedding and after he'd extricated his tipsy sister-in-law from the clutches of a harbor ruffian in a seedy Cannes nightspot.

Staying in the plush Hôtel du Cap while police continued their investigation, Jean Jordache says she was accosted while having a solitary, quayside nightcap. Jordan, appearing on the scene, savagely beat the man who had accosted her. Later, Jordan was found murdered on his yacht.

French police will only confirm that they have a list of suspects.

Luckily, it doesn't mention me. It would have to be an outside chance for anyone to connect me with Mrs. Burke, once married to eminent director, now dead, earlier to an obscure flack named Abbott. Monika would, of course, because I've talked to her a lot about my mother, but fortunately Monika doesn't read _Time._ Information for entertainment, she calls it, not information for the sake of truth.

I sometimes wonder if I shouldn't try to be a newspaperman. I am inquisitive and mischievous, two important qualities in the trade.

```
 Monika not home. Note on table. will
be gone a few days. She believes in the
double standard all right--but in
reverse.
 I miss her already.
```

———

The limousine that the concierge had ordered for them was packed. Gretchen, Jean and Enid were already on the back seat, Enid a little tearful because the French girl was being left behind. Rudolph had checked for the third time that he had all their plane tickets, and the chauffeur was holding the front door open for him to get in, when a car drove up to the courtyard in front of the hotel and stopped. A small, plump, plainly dressed woman with graying hair got out of the car and a small plump man in a business suit emerged from behind the wheel.

"Rudolph Jordache, if you please," the woman called, coming toward him.

"Yes?" The woman looked vaguely familiar.

"I suppose you don't remember me," the woman said. She turned to the small plump man. "I told you he wouldn't remember me."

"Yes, you told me," the man said.

"I remember you, though," the woman said to Rudolph. "Very well. I'm Tom's wife, Wesley's mother. I came to get my son." She dug into the big handbag she was carrying and pulled out a copy of *Time* Magazine and waved it at Rudolph.

"Oh, Lord," Rudolph said. He had forgotten about the newspaperman and the telex. But the newspaperman obviously hadn't forgotten about him. Poor Wesley, he thought, his name known for a week in millions of homes, the stares of the curious to be dealt with for years to come, the strangers approaching him wherever he went, saying, "Excuse me, aren't you the one . . . ?"

"May I see what the story's like?" Rudolph reached out for the magazine. The journalist had been down to the boat before Wesley had been jailed, but he might have followed up on the story. He winced, thinking of what *Time* might have done with the account of Wesley's fight in the nightclub and the Englishman in the hospital with a concussion.

Teresa drew back, put the magazine behind her. "You can go out and buy your own magazine," she said. "According to what it says, you can damn well afford it. You and your fancy naked wife."

Oh, God, Rudolph thought, they've dug up that old picture. What a blessing it would be for the entire world if the files in the office of every newspaper on the face of the globe suddenly went up in smoke in a single day.

"It's all in the magazine," Teresa said malevolently. "This time your money didn't bail my great ex-husband out, did it? He finally got what he was looking for, didn't he?"

"I'm sorry, Teresa," Rudolph said. Tom must have been dead drunk or drugged when he married her. The last time Rudolph had seen her, three years ago in Heath's office, when he had paid her off to go to Reno for a divorce, her hair had been dyed platinum blond and she must have been twenty pounds lighter. Looking no better and no worse than she looked now.

"Forgive me for not recognizing you. You've changed a bit."

"I didn't make much of an impression on you, did I?" Now the malevolence was more pronounced. "I'd like you to meet my husband, Mr. Kraler."

"How do you do, Mr. Kraler?"

The man grunted.

"Where's my son?" Teresa said harshly.

"Rudy," Gretchen called from the car, "we don't want to miss the plane." She hadn't heard any of the exchange.

Rudolph began to sweat, although it was a cool morning. "You'll have to excuse me, Mrs. Kraler," he said, "but we have to go to the airport . . ."

"You don't get off that easy, Mr. Jordache," Teresa said, waving the rolled-up magazine at him. "I didn't come all the way here from America to let you fly off just like that."

"I'm not flying off anywhere," Rudolph said, his voice rising, to match the woman's tone. "I have to put my family on the plane and I'm coming back here. I'll see you in two hours."

"I want to know where my son is," Teresa said, grabbing his sleeve and holding on as he started to get into the car.

"He's in jail, if you must know."

"In jail!" Teresa shrieked. She put her hand to her throat in a tragic gesture. Her reaction reassured Rudolph. At least that part of the story hadn't been in the magazine.

"Don't carry on so," Rudolph said sharply. Her shriek had been the loudest noise he had heard at the hotel since he had come there. "It's not that serious."

"Did you hear that, Eddie?" she screamed. "My son is behind bars and he says it's not serious."

"I heard him say it," Mr. Kraler said.

"That's the sort of family it is. Put a child in their hands," as loudly as before, "and before you know it he has a police record. It's a blessing his father got murdered or else I'd never have known where he was and God knows what these people would have made out of him. You know who belongs in jail—" She released Rudolph's sleeve and stepped back a pace to point a shaking, accusatory finger at him, her arm outstretched operatically. "You! With your tricks and your bribes and your crooked money."

"When you calm down," Rudolph said, moving to get into the front seat of the limousine, "I'll explain everything to you." Then to the chauffeur, *"Allons-y."*

She lunged at him and gripped his arm again. "No, you don't," she said. "You're not getting off that easy, mister."

"Let go of me, you silly woman," Rudolph said. "I haven't time to talk to you now. The plane won't wait, no matter how loudly you scream."

"Eddie," Teresa shrieked at her husband, "are you going to let him get away with this?"

"See here, Mr. Jordache . . ." the man began.

"I don't know you, sir," Rudolph said. "Keep out of this. If you want to talk to me, be here when I get back." Roughly, he shook the woman's hand off his sleeve, and the concierge, who had come out to say good-bye, moved, quietly threatening, toward her.

Rudolph got into the car quickly and slammed and locked the door behind him. The chauffeur hurried around to the wheel and started the engine. Teresa was standing, waving the magazine angrily at the car, as they drove out of the gate.

"What was that all about?" Gretchen asked. "I couldn't hear what she was saying."

"It's not important," Rudolph said shortly. "She's Wesley's mother."

"She certainly has changed," Gretchen said. "Not for the better."

"What does she want?"

"If she's running true to form," he said, "she wants money." He would have to get Gretchen aside and tell her to make sure Jean didn't get hold of a copy of *Time* Magazine.

From the terrace of the airport building Rudolph watched the plane take off. The good-byes had been quiet. He had promised to get back to New York as soon as possible. He had tried not to think of the comparison between today's subdued farewell and the holiday gaiety with which they had arrived at this same airport, with Tom waiting for them with his bride-to-be and the *Clothilde* in port ready to take them all out to the channel between the islands off Cannes for a swim and a reunion lunch.

When the plane was out of sight, Rudolph sighed, went through the building, fighting down the temptation to buy a copy of *Time* Magazine at the newsstand. Whatever the story was like, it certainly could not bring him joy. He wondered how people who were constantly being written about, politicians, cabinet ministers, actors, people like that, could ever bring themselves to open a morning newspaper.

He thought of the plump, graying woman and her round little husband waiting for him back at the hotel, and sighed again. How had that dreadful woman ever managed to find a husband? And a second husband, at that. Perhaps, he thought, if the man from *Time* were still in Antibes, he should ask him to dig up the newspaper photograph of Teresa, with her old fake name, being taken away by the police after the raid on the brothel. One photograph deserved another. Poor Wesley.

Delaying, he asked the chauffeur to drive into Nice, directed him to the street on which Jeanne lived. He didn't know what he would do if by chance he saw her coming out of the house with her children or her martial husband. Nothing, most likely. But she did not appear. The street was like any other street.

"Back to the hotel, please," he said. "Go the long way, along the sea."

When they got to Antibes, they skirted the port. He saw the *Clothilde,* in the distance, with Dwyer, a tiny figure, moving on the deck. He did not ask the chauffeur to stop.

"I know my rights," Teresa was saying. The three of them were sitting on the chairs in a little glade in the park of the hotel, where there was no one to hear their conversation. The couple had been sitting stiffly in two chairs facing each other in the hotel lobby when Rudolph had come in. Their expressions were grim and disapproving, their presence a silent rebuke to the idle, pleasure-seeking guests, dressed for sport, who passed them on their way to tennis or to the swimming pool. They had listened sullenly as Rudolph led them into the park, explaining quickly, keeping his voice calm and neutral, how Wesley had fallen into the hands of the police and about his departure for America.

"We've been to a lawyer in Indianapolis, where we live, Mr. Kraler and myself, and I know my rights as a mother." Teresa's voice grated on his ears like chalk on a blackboard. "Wesley is a minor and with his father dead, the lawyer said I am his legal guardian. Isn't that what the lawyer said, Eddie?"

"That's what the lawyer said," Mr. Kraler said. "Exactly."

"When I get him out of jail," Teresa went on, "I'm going to take him back to a proper home where he can get a decent Christian upbringing."

"Don't you think it would be wiser to leave religion out of this?" Rudolph said. "After all, the life you've lead . . ."

"You don't have to beat about the bush about the life I've led. Mr. Kraler knows all about it. Don't you, Eddie?"

"All about it." Eddie nodded, little pudgy sacks of flesh under his chin shaking rhythmically.

"I was a whore, and no bones about it," Teresa said, almost with pride. "But I've seen the light. The strayed lamb is dearer in the eyes of the Lord . . ." She hesitated. "You know the rest, I'm sure, even if you and your whole family are lost heathens."

"Actually," Rudolph said, with false innocence, "I don't know the rest."

"It makes no difference," she said quickly. "Mr. Kraler is a Mormon and by his efforts I have been converted and accepted into the fold. For your information, I don't dye my hair any longer, as you may have noticed, if you ever stoop to notice anything about me, and I don't drink alcohol or even coffee or tea."

"That may be most admirable, Teresa," Rudolph said. He had read somewhere that Mormonism was the fastest-growing Christian religion in the modern world, but with Teresa in the fold the believers must feel that they had cast their net too wide. He could imagine the shudder in the Tabernacle in Salt Lake City when the elders of the Church of Jesus Christ of Latter-day Saints had to accept Teresa Jordache into their blessed company. "But I don't really see what that's got to do with Wesley."

"One thing that it's got to do with him is that he'll stop being a jailbird. I know your family, I know the Jordaches, don't think I don't. Fornicators and mockers, all of you."

Teresa's vocabulary, Rudolph noted, had expanded considerably with her conversion. He was not sure it was an improvement. "I don't really think that Wesley's being in jail for a few days because he had a fight in a bar is because I happen to be an atheist," he said. "And for your information," he couldn't help adding, "fornication and mocking are not my principal occupations."

"I'm not accusing anyone," Teresa said, although there was accusation in every syllable she spoke and every gesture she made. "But it can't be denied that he was in your charge, you being his uncle and head of the family when he nearly killed a man. . . ."

"All right, all right," Rudolph said wearily. He wanted her to leave, disappear, with her pudgy, purse-lipped, righteous husband, but the thought of Wesley being at the mercy of the couple back in Indianapolis appalled him. He didn't know what he could do to prevent it, but he had to try to do what he could. "What do you want?" He had explained that Wesley was to be put on a plane to America in six days, but he hadn't told her of his own hardly formed notion of putting Wesley into a good boarding school in America for a year and then sending him back to France to continue his education there, or his own plan (selfish? generously avuncular?) to come back to France himself to keep an eye on the boy.

"What do I want?" Teresa repeated. "I want to make him a decent citizen, not a wild animal in the jungle, like his father."

"You realize, of course," Rudolph said, "that in a little more than two years, he'll be eligible for the draft if he stays in the United States, and may be sent to get killed in Vietnam."

"If that is God's will, that is God's will," Teresa said. "Do you agree with me, Eddie?"

"God's will," Mr. Kraler said. "My son is in the Army and I'm proud of it. The boy has to take his chances, just like everybody else."

"I don't want any favors for any son of mine," Teresa said.

"Don't you think you ought to ask Wesley what he wants to do?"

"He's my son," Teresa said. "I don't have to ask him

anything. And I'm here to make sure he's not going to
get gypped of his just share in his father's big fat estate."
Ah, Rudolph thought, now we come to the heart of the
matter. "When that fancy yacht they wrote about in the
magazine is sold," Teresa said shrilly, "you can bet your
boots that I'm going to be looking over everybody's
shoulder to make sure my son isn't left out in the cold.
And our lawyer is going to go over every slip of paper
with a fine-tooth comb, don't make any mistake about
that either, Mr. Jordache."

Rudolph stood up. "In that case," he said, "I don't
think there's any need to continue this conversation any
longer. Wesley's stepmother, who will probably be appointed as executrix for the estate, will hire a lawyer
and the two lawyers can work everything out between
them. I have other things to do. Good-bye."

"Wait a minute," Teresa said. "You can't keep running off like that."

"I have to take a nap," Rudolph said. "I've been up
since dawn."

"Don't you want to know where we're staying here?"
she cried, victory slipping from her grasp, the argument
won so easily that she was sure that it was a ruse on her
opponent's part. "Our address in America? Mr. Kraler
is a highly respected merchant in Indianapolis. He's a
bottler. He has three hundred people working for him.
Soft drinks. Give him your card, Eddie."

"Never mind, Mr. Kraler," Rudolph said. "I don't
want to have your address here or in Indianapolis. Bottle away," he added crazily.

"I want to see my boy in jail," Teresa cried. "I want
to see what they've done to my poor son."

"Naturally," Rudolph said. "By all means, do so."
Her maternal instincts had been less evident in Heath's
office when he had paid her off and she had signed

away custody of her son at the sight of a check made out in her name.

"I intend to adopt him legally," Mr. Kraler said. "Mrs. Kraler wants him to forget he was ever called Jordache."

"That will have to be settled between him and his mother," Rudolph said. "Although when I visit him in jail I'll mention the idea to him."

"When're you going to the jail?" Teresa asked. "I don't want you talking to him alone, filling his ear with poison. . . . I'm going with you."

"No, you're not going anyplace with me," Rudolph said. "I always make a point of visiting jails unaccompanied."

"But I don't speak French," she wailed. "I don't even know where the jail is. How will I convince the cops I'm his mother?"

"I'm afraid you'll have to figure all that out yourself, Mrs. Kraler," Rudolph said. "Now I don't want to see either of you two people ever again. Tell your lawyer that the law firm he will have to get into contact with is Heath, Burrows and Gordon. The address is in Wall Street. I believe you were there once before, Mrs. Kraler."

"You bastard," Teresa said, un-Mormon-like.

Rudolph smiled. "Have a pleasant afternoon," he said. He nodded and left the two plump, little angry people sitting silently on the bench in the shade of the pine trees. He was trembling with rage and frustration and despair for the poor boy in the jail in Grasse, but for the moment there was nothing he could do about it. It would take a rescue mission of enormous proportions to tear Wesley out of the grasp of his mother, and today he was not up to thinking even about the first step to be taken. Christian or not, when there was the scent of money in the air, Mrs. Teresa Kraler remembered the habits of her ancient profession. He dreaded having to tell Kate what was in store for her.

He packed quickly. The concierge had gotten him a reservation at the Colombe d'Or in Saint-Paul-de-Vence. A hotel in Grasse would have been closer to the jail he visited almost daily. Saint-Paul-de-Vence was closer to Jeanne. He had chosen Saint-Paul-de-Vence. There was no reason for his remaining any longer at the Hôtel du Cap and many reasons for leaving it. He had told the concierge to forward his mail, but under no circumstances to tell anyone where he was staying. He wrote to Jeanne, telling her where he was going to be, and sealed the note in an envelope addressed to her, care of Poste Restante, Nice.

When he went down to the desk, to pay his bill while his bags were being put in his car, he was relieved to see that the Kralers had gone. He was shocked at the size of his bill. You pay a lot for agony, he thought, on the Côte d'Azur. It was one of the best hotels in the world, but he knew he would never come back to it again. And not because of the cost.

He drove first to the port. Dwyer and Kate had to know where to find him. Dwyer was polishing one of the small brass bitts up forward when he came aboard. He stood up when he saw Rudolph and they shook hands.

"How're things?" Rudolph asked.

Dwyer shrugged. "It ain't no holiday," he said. "They ain't delivered the shaft and the propeller yet. They have to come from Italy and the Italians ain't going to send it across the border until they get paid. I been on the phone to the insurance every day, but they're in no hurry. They never are. They keep sending me new forms to fill out," he said aggrievedly. "And they keep asking for Tom's signature. Maybe the Italians don't think anybody dies in France. And I have to keep getting everything translated. There's a waitress in town who's a friend of mine, she got the language, only she don't know fuck-all about boats and she had to keep asking for the names of things like equipment, running lights, fathoms, flotsam, things like that. It's driving me up the wall."

"All right, Bunny," Rudolph said, suppressing a sigh. "Send all the papers to me. I'll have them attended to."

"That'll be a relief," Dwyer said. "Thanks."

"I'm moving to the Colombe d'Or in Saint-Paul-de-Vence," Rudolph said. "You can reach me there."

"I don't blame you, moving out of that hotel. It must have cost you a pile."

"It wasn't cheap."

"You look around you," Dwyer said, "all those big boats, all these expensive hotels, and you wonder where the money comes from. At least *I* do."

"Bunny," Rudolph said, absurdly feeling on the defensive, "when I was young I was poorer than practically anyone you ever knew."

"Yeah. Tom told me. You worked like a dog. I got no beef against people who came up the way you did. I admire it. I would say you're entitled to anything you can get."

"There're a lot of things I can get," Rudolph said, "that I'd gladly give away."

"I know what you mean," Dwyer said.

There was a short, uncomfortable silence between them.

"I had hoped Kate would be here with you," Rudolph said. "Something's come up that she has to know about. How is she?"

Dwyer looked at him consideringly, as though trying to decide whether or not he should tell him anything about Kate. "She's gone," he said. "She left for England this morning."

"You have her address?"

"I do. Yeah," Dwyer said carefully.

"I need it," Rudolph said. As quickly as possible, he told Dwyer about the Kralers' visit, about the legal problems that Kate would have to deal with, or at least would have to be handled in Kate's name.

Dwyer nodded slowly. "Tom told me about that wife of his. A real ball-breaker, isn't she?"

"That's the least of her virtues," Rudolph said. He saw that Dwyer was hesitant about giving him Kate's address. "Bunny," he said, "I want to ask you something. Don't you believe that I'm trying to do the best for Kate? And for Wesley? And for you, too, for that matter?"

"Nobody has to worry about me," Dwyer said. "About Kate——" He made his curious, almost feminine gesture with his hands, as if explaining the situation in words was beyond him. "I know she sounded . . . well . . . snappish the other day. It's not that she's sore at you or anything like that. I'd say, what it is——" Again the little gesture. "It's that she's——" He searched for the word. "She's *bruised*. She's a sensible woman; she'll get over it. Especially now that she's back home in England. You got a pencil and a piece of paper?"

Rudolph took a notebook and pen out of his pocket. Bunny gave him the address and Rudolph wrote it down. "She doesn't have a telephone," Bunny said. "I gather her folks ain't rolling in money."

"I'll write her," Rudolph said, "when anything develops." He looked around him at the scrubbed deck, the polished rails and brasswork. "The ship looks fine," he said.

"There's always something to be done," Dwyer said.

"I made a date to have it hauled up in the yard two weeks from today. The goddamn stuff ought to be here from Italy by then."

"Bunny," Rudolph asked, "how much do you think the *Clothilde* is worth? What it would sell for?"

"What it's worth and what it would sell for are two different things," Dwyer said. "If you figure what it cost originally and all the work and improvements Tom and me put into it and the new radar you gave him as a wedding present—that'll have to be installed, too—I'd say it would come to almost a hundred thousand dollars. That's what it's *worth*. But if you have to sell it fast, like you said when you were telling us about settling the estate—and in this month, with the season more than half gone—nobody likes to pay for the upkeep of a boat for a whole winter—if people're going to buy, they're most likely to buy in the late spring—if you have to sell it fast in the off months and people know you *have* to sell, why then, naturally, they'll try to cut your throat and maybe you'd be lucky if you got fifty thousand dollars for it. Anyway, I'm not the one to talk about this. You ought to go around, talk to some of the yacht brokers here and in Cannes, Saint-Tropez, you see what I mean, maybe they have somebody on their books'd be interested for a fair price. . . ."

"Has anybody approached you so far?" Rudolph asked.

Dwyer shook his head. "I really don't think anybody who knows Antibes'd make a bid. After the murder and all. I think you'd do better to change the name and sail her to another harbor. Maybe another country. Italy, Spain, somewhere like that. Maybe even in Piraeus, that's in Greece. . . . People're superstitious about ships."

"Bunny," Rudolph said, "I don't want you to get angry at what I'm going to say, but I have to talk to you about it. Somebody's got to stay with the boat until it's sold. . . ."

"I would think so."

"And he'd have to be paid, wouldn't he?"

"Yeah," Dwyer said uncomfortably.

"What would the usual salary be?"

"That depends," Dwyer said evasively, "how much work you expected him to do, if he was an engineer or not, things like that."

"You, for example. If you were on another ship?"

"Well, if I'd been hired on earlier—I mean people've got their crews fixed by now—I guess about five hundred dollars a month."

"Good," Rudolph said. "You're going to get five hundred dollars a month."

"I didn't ask for it," Dwyer said harshly.

"I know you didn't. But you're going to get it."

"Just remember I didn't ask for it." Dwyer put out his hand and Rudolph shook it. "I just wish," Dwyer said, "there was some way of Tom knowing all you're doing for me, for Kate and the kid, for the *Clothilde*."

Rudolph smiled. "I didn't ask for it," he said, "but I got it."

Dwyer chuckled. "I think there's still some whiskey left on board," he said.

"I wouldn't mind a drink," Rudolph said.

As they went aft, Dwyer said, "Your sister, Mrs. Burke—Gretchen—made me into a whiskey drinker. Did she tell you?"

"No. She kept your romance secret."

He saw that Dwyer didn't smile and said nothing more about Gretchen.

They had the whiskey in the wheelhouse, warm. Dwyer apologized for not having any ice. He didn't want to have the generator that supplied the electricity running, wasting fuel.

"It's a funny thing," Dwyer said, relaxed now, with the glass in his hand. "You and Gretchen and Tom all in the same family." He took a big gulp of his drink. "Fire and ice," he said obscurely.

Rudolph didn't ask him to explain what he meant by that.

As he left, Rudolph said, "If I don't see you before then, I'll see you at the airport when Wesley leaves. You remember the date?"

"I have it written down," Dwyer said. "I'll pack his things for him and bring them along with me." He hesitated, coughed a little. "He's got a whole folder full of photos up forward. You know—pictures of the ship, ports we put into, him and his father, me and Kate. . . . That sort of thing. Should I pack them in?" He lifted his glass and closed his eyes as he drank, as though the matter were of no great importance.

"Pack them in," Rudolph said. Memory hurt, but it was necessary baggage.

"I got a whole bunch of pictures from the wedding. All of us . . . you know—drinking toasts, dancing, stuff like that, all of us. . . ."

"I think it would be a good idea to leave them out," Rudolph said. Too much was too much.

Dwyer nodded. "Kate didn't want them either. And I don't think I have room to keep them. I'll be traveling finally, you know. . . ."

"Send them to me," Rudolph said. "I'll keep them in a safe place. Maybe after a while Wesley would like to see them." He remembered the pictures that Jean had taken that day. He would put the other ones with them.

Dwyer nodded again. "Another drink?"

"No, thanks," Rudolph said. "I haven't eaten lunch yet. Would you like to join me?"

Dwyer shook his head. "Kind of you, Rudy," he said, "but I already ate." Dwyer had a quota, Rudolph saw. One favor accepted a day. No more.

They put their glasses down, Dwyer carefully wiping away with a cloth the damp the glasses left.

He was going forward to finish polishing the bitts as Rudolph left the *Clothilde*.

After he had checked in at the new hotel Rudolph had lunch on the terrace overlooking the valley that looked as though it had been designed from a painting by Renoir. When he had finished lunch, he made a call to the old lawyer in Antibes. He explained that the *Clothilde* was for sale and that he would like the lawyer to act as agent for the estate in the transaction. "If the best offer you can get," he said, "is not at least one hundred thousand dollars, let me know. I'll buy it."

"That's most gentlemanly of you," the lawyer said, his voice thin over the faulty telephone wires.

"It's a simple business matter."

"I see," the lawyer said. They both knew he was lying. No matter.

After that Rudolph called Johnny Heath in New York and talked at length. "Oh, what a mess," Heath said. "I'll do my best. I await the letter from Mr. and Mrs. Kraler's lawyer with impatience."

Then Rudolph put on his swimming trunks and did forty laps in the pool, his mind empty in the swish of water, his body used and healthily tired by the time he had finished.

After the swim he sat drying off by the side of the pool, sipping at a cold beer.

He felt guilty for feeling so well. He wondered, displeased with himself for the thought, how he would act if the telephone rang and the call was for him and a voice announced that the plane with his family aboard had gone down into the sea.

Fire and ice, Dwyer had said.

———

# CHAPTER 8

*From Billy Abbott's notebook—*

Families. There's a subject.

Love and destroy. Not necessarily. But often enough to show up well in the averages. For Freud the stage for Greek tragedy--incest, patricide, other intimate delights. Dreadful to imagine what the good doctor's family life in Vienna had been like.

Was Jung more lenient? Must ask Monika, fountain of wisdom. Come to think of it, she never talks about <u>her</u> family. Skeletons in every closet.

Have never met Wesley Jordache. Poor little bastard. Lost in the shuffle. Will the murder of his father turn out to be an enlarging experience for his soul? My grandfather died when Rudolph and my mother were comparatively young and their souls do not seem noticeably enlarged.

I liked my grandmother because she doted on me. She did not dote on my mother and even on the day of her funeral my mother had no use for her. Will my mother have any use for me on the day of _my_ funeral? I have a premonition I will die young. My mother is made of steel, will last forever, outwearing man after man.

Does her sexuality offend me? Yes.

Does my sexuality, that of Monika, offend me? No. Injustice is the coin that is exchanged between the generations.

My mother is a promiscuous woman. My father, when younger and could manage it, was, by his own accounts, a promiscuous man. I am not. Like the drunkard's child, I stay away from the vice I see in the parent.

Sons revolt. Daughters run off. I did neither. I hid. The army has made it easier. It would be interesting to meet with Cousin Wesley, so far unknown to me, compare notes, the same blood running in our veins.

The flower children rearranged the idea of family. I could not live in a commune. Unhygienic entanglements. Desperate experiments, doomed to failure. We are too far past the tribe. I do not want someone else's child to disturb me while I am reading or shaving or taking my wife to bed.

Will I live in a suburb ten years from now and play bridge and watch football games on the television all

weekend long? Commute? Swap wives?
Vote for that year's Nixon?
  It is late. I miss Monika.

———————

Wesley was sitting, cleanly shaved, neatly dressed in a suit that Rudolph had brought him from the *Clothilde,* waiting for the *agent* who was to take him to the airport. The suit had been bought for him by his father more than a year ago and was now very much too short in the arms and too tight across the chest. As he had expected, his Uncle Rudolph had somehow fixed it for him. Although having to leave France wasn't such a great arrangement. He had never been happy in America—and he had been happy in France, at least until the day his father died.

It hadn't been so bad in the prison in Grasse. The cop he had hit in the bar was stationed in Cannes and hadn't been around to bug him, and among the guards and with the *juge d'instruction* who had examined him he had enjoyed a certain celebrity because of what had happened to his father and because he spoke French and had knocked out the Englishman, who had a moderate reputation as a barroom fighter with the local police. Also he had been polite and had caused nobody any trouble. The occasional bill his uncle had slipped to the guards and a call from the American consulate, which his uncle had prompted, hadn't hurt, either.

One good thing about Uncle Rudy, he never even hinted that Wesley ought to show some gratitude for what he'd done for him. Wesley would have liked to show gratitude but he didn't know how. Eventually, he thought, he'd have to work on that. As it was, there was nothing much he could think of saying to his uncle, who seemed embarrassed to see Wesley behind bars, as though it was somehow his fault.

One of the guards had even smuggled in a photograph from the police files of the man called Danovic his father had had the fight within the Porte Rose. Wesley would remember the face when it was necessary to recognize it.

He said nothing of this to anyone. He had never been an open boy—even with his father it had been difficult for him to talk about himself, although his father had told him almost everything he wanted to hear about his own life. Now, he kept what he was feeling to himself. He felt threatened, although he wasn't certain what was threatening him. Whatever it was, silence was the first line of defense. He had learned that a long time ago, when his mother had put him in that damned military school.

His mother was another ball game. She had screamed and cried and scolded and slobbered all over him and promised him he would lead a different life when she got him back with her new husband in Indianapolis. He didn't want to lead a different life. He had asked his uncle if he had to go to Indianapolis and Rudolph had looked sad and said, "At least while you're still a minor." It had something to do with money, he didn't understand just what. No matter. He could take a look at the scene and blow if he didn't like it.

He had learned about flight.

Meanwhile, he missed not being able to go to school when the year began. They were starting the basketball season in September. He had been the star of the team last year and he knew they had been depending upon him this year. He hoped they had a lousy season, so they would know how much they needed him. It seemed a piddling thing to be worrying about when your father had just been murdered, but school was a big part of his life and he couldn't just turn it off because it would be

unimportant to grown-ups at this time. He felt his father
would have understood, even if nobody else did.

Some of the boys had made fun of him in school because he was American and spoke funny. He had never
hit them, as he had wanted to, because his father would
have beat the shit out of him if he had found out Wesley was fighting. It would be different now, he thought
grimly. With the sorrow, there was a new sense of freedom. I make my own mistakes now, he told himself,
and people can just lump them or leave them. The mistake his father had made would take a lot of getting
over. He had prayed for his father, but he'd be damned
if he forgave him. One night, one crazy grandstand act,
and his father had left him in the shit. Shit, he thought,
sitting in his clean clothes, shit.

The *agent* who was going to take him to the airport
unlocked the door and came in. He was dressed in
slacks and a sports jacket but he could be dressed like a
ballet dancer and anybody would know he was a cop,
right off.

The air smelled wonderful outside. He had forgotten
how good air could smell.

They got into an unmarked car, Wesley sitting in
front beside the *agent*. The *agent* had a big belly and let
out a little poof through his broken nose as he squeezed
in under the wheel. Wesley would have liked to ask if
he had ever been hit with a beer bottle or shot a man,
but decided it would be better to keep the conversation
on other things.

The *agent* drove slowly down the winding mountain
road, with all the windows open. "The weather is beautiful," he said, "we might as well profit from it." It was
an easy morning's work for him and he was making the
most of it. He already smelled from wine. "So," he said,
"no more France for you. Pity. Next time you will learn
to hit people where there are no witnesses." He laughed

at his lawman's joke. "What are you going to do in America?"

"Keep away from the police," Wesley said.

The *agent* laughed again. "That's a smart young man. My wife keeps after me. We ought to visit America, she says." He wagged his head. "On a policeman's salary, you can imagine." He looked sidelong at Wesley. "Your uncle is a man of important wealth, isn't he?" he asked.

"One of the richest."

"It shows." The policeman sighed, looked down at his rumpled jacket. "I admire his clothes. He is a man of great authority. That is evident. No wonder you're on the way home."

Home was not the word to describe where he was going, Wesley thought.

"You will come back here eventually—as a tourist—and spend a great deal of money, I suppose," the *agent* said.

"If you don't turn Communist first," Wesley said. In the prison there had been two men who said they were Communists and the day was near.

"Don't say things like that," the *agent* said darkly. "Especially in America. They will turn their backs on us." On the subject now of the bad opinion Americans had of the French, he said, "You are not going back and tell the newspapers how you were tortured by the police to make you confess?"

"I had nothing to confess," Wesley said. "Everybody saw me hit the *salaud*. I might say something about how one of your friends beat me up in the car on the way to the *préfecture*, though," he added mischievously. He was enjoying the ride through the ripe, flowery country-side after the weeks indoors. And just talking idly away with the man, who was friendly enough, postponed having to think what was waiting for him at the airport and in Indianapolis.

"Ah, what would you expect?" the *agent* said aggrievedly. "To be knocked down with one blow by a child in full view of the entire world and not get a little bit of your own back in a dark car? We are all human, you know."

"All right," Wesley said magnanimously, "I won't say anything."

"You're a good boy," the *agent* said. "You made a good reputation for yourself in Grasse. I have seen the man your father had the *fracas* with. He looked as though he had been run over by a locomotive." He nodded, an expert in these matters. "Your father did an excellent job. Excellent." He looked sidelong again at Wesley, his face serious now. "The fellow is known to the police. Unfavorably," he said. "So far he has been able to escape the punishment he richly deserves. He associates with dangerous men. It is as much for your sake as for the sake of France that you are being sent on your way."

"It just seems queer," Wesley said, "that a man that everybody knows is responsible for a murder can get away with it."

"You just forget about what people know, my friend," the *agent* said censoriously. "You just forget everything and go home and be a nice young American."

"Yes, sir," Wesley said, remembering every detail in the photograph, the slit eyes, the high, sharp cheekbones, the thin mouth and dark curly hair. *You* forget the man who killed my father, he wanted to say, but didn't. You just try and forget. "I wonder if you could do me a favor."

"What is it?" The *agent*'s voice was professionally suspicious.

"Could you drive along the port? I'd like to take a look at the boat."

The *agent* glanced at his watch. "It's early yet," he said. "We have time. Why not?"

"That's very kind of you, sir," Wesley said. "*C'est très gentil de votre part, monsieur,*" in French. It was one of the first things his father had taught him when he had brought him to Antibes. Although his father knew almost no French, he had said, "There're two expressions the Frogs pay a lot of attention to. First—*S'il vous plaît,* that means please. And *C'est très gentil de votre part.* Got it? Repeat them."

Wesley had not forgotten the lesson.

"I have a son about your age," the *agent* said. "He's crazy about boats, too. He's always hanging around the ports, whenever he gets a chance. I told him I'd disown him if he ever became a sailor. If it wasn't for all the boats down here, the police would be put out of work. The people it attracts," he said gloomily, "Algerians, Yugoslavs, Greeks, Corsicans, Sicilians, nudists, English kids in trouble with the law back home, girls who've run away from home, rich playboys with giant dope habits . . ." He shook his head as he went over the list of seaborne malefactors. . . . "And now every stinking town with a view of the Mediterranean is building a new port. It will take the entire *gendarmerie* of France to control it. Witness your case." He shook his finger angrily at Wesley, reminded by his outburst that he was conducting a criminal to exile. "Do you think what happened to you would have happened if you inhabited Clermont-Ferrand, for example?"

"My case was an accident," Wesley said, sorry he had asked to see the port.

"That's what they all say. And who has to clean up the mess? The police."

"What would you like your son to be?" Wesley thought it was time to change the subject.

"A lawyer. That's where the money is, my boy. Take

my advice, go back to America and be a lawyer. How many lawyers do you know who have ever been in jail?"

"I was considering it," Wesley said, hoping to get the cop back into his earlier expansive mood.

"Consider it seriously."

"I intend to," Wesley said, sage and appreciative and wishing that the cop would shut up.

"And don't ever carry a weapon. Do you hear me?"

"Yes, sir."

"Listen to the advice of an older man who is interested in the next generation and who has seen the world."

Now Wesley knew why they had picked this particular cop for the errand this morning. Anything to get him out of the *préfecture* and avoid having to listen to his lectures.

The cop grumbled, wordlessly, and lit a cigarette, the car swaying dangerously as he took his hands momentarily off the wheel. The smoke came Wesley's way and he coughed. Neither his father nor Bunny had smoked.

"And don't ever smoke, either," the cop said. "I despise myself for the habit." He lapsed into silence.

When they came to the port, Wesley saw the *Clothilde,* its decks deserted. Unreasonably, he half expected to see his father come out of the wheelhouse and pull at a line. His father had always been nervous that a sudden storm might arise and the lines would give way. Stop it, Wesley thought, stop it, he's not going to come on deck ever again. For a moment he wondered what would happen if he suddenly opened the door of the car and jumped out and ran. He could lose the fat cop in a minute, hide out, slip onto the *Clothilde* at night and handle her out of the port into the open sea, make for Italy. That was the nearest border, actually. Would the cop use his gun? It bulged in a shoulder holster under his sports jacket. Too risky. Crazy. Today, at least, he had to be sane. He would come back to Antibes another day.

"Boats," the cop said contemptuously and stepped on the accelerator.

Wesley closed his eyes. He didn't want to look at the *Clothilde* anymore.

Rudolph and Dwyer were waiting for him at the check-in counter at the airport. Dwyer had Wesley's canvas and leatherette bag with him and was carrying a big manila envelope.

"Your mother and her husband," Rudolph said, "have gone through passport control already. They'll look for you inside. They're on the same plane with you."

Wesley nodded. He couldn't trust himself to speak.

"All is in order, *Monsieur* Jordache," the *agent* said respectfully. "I'll go through with him and put him on the plane."

*"Merci,"* Rudolph said.

"Here's your things," Dwyer said, indicating the bag. "You'll have to have it weighed." Dwyer had put on a suit for the occasion. Wesley didn't remember having seen Dwyer in a whole suit before, not even at the wedding. He seemed smaller than Wesley remembered, and a lot older, with tiny, fine wrinkles in his forehead and around his mouth. "And this," Dwyer said, giving him the envelope, "has some of the photos you kept up forward. I thought you might like to look at them sometime." His voice sounded wandery, vague.

"Thanks, Bunny," Wesley said, taking the envelope.

Rudolph gave him a slip of paper. "There are two addresses on that, Wesley," he said. "My home address and my friend Johnny Heath's office, in case I'm off someplace. If you ever need anything . . ." He, too, sounded unsure of himself.

He's not used to seeing members of his family being seen off from one country to another by a cop, Wesley thought as he took the slip of paper and put it in his pocket.

"Take care of yourself," Dwyer said, as Rudolph gave Wesley's ticket to the girl behind the counter and watched while the bag was being weighed.

"Don't you worry about me, old shipmate," Wesley said, trying to sound hearty.

"Never." Dwyer smiled, but it didn't look like much of a smile. "See you around, eh?"

"Sure." He didn't even try to smile.

"Well," the cop said in French, "time to go."

Wesley shook hands with his uncle, who looked as though he would be seeing Wesley in an hour or two and Dwyer, who looked as though he would never see him again.

Wesley didn't glance backward as he went through passport control with the *agent,* who showed his identification card as he came up to the desk and winked at the officer there.

His mother and her husband, whom he had never seen before, were standing in the departure lounge just as he passed through the control, as if to make sure he wasn't going to escape. "You look pale," his mother said. Her hair was all over her face. She looked as though she had been caught in a force ten gale.

"I feel fine," he said. "This is my friend." He touched the *agent*'s arm. "He's a policeman. He doesn't speak English."

The *agent* bowed a little. The affair had passed off without incident and he could afford to be gallant. "Explain to them that I have to see you safely aboard," he said in French.

Wesley explained. His mother drew back as though the policeman had an infectious disease. "Meet your new father," his mother said. "Mr. Kraler."

"Welcome," Mr. Kraler said, like a master of ceremonies on television greeting a famous guest. He extended his hand.

"Keep your hands off me," Wesley said calmly.

"Don't worry about him, Eddie," his mother said. "He's disturbed today. That's natural. He'll learn. Do you want a drink, baby? A Coca-Cola, an orange juice?"

"A whiskey," Wesley said.

"Now see here, young man . . ." Mr. Kraler began.

"He's joking," his mother said hastily. "Aren't you joking, Wesley?"

"No."

A woman's voice was announcing the departure of the plane over the loudspeaker system. The *agent* took his arm. "I'll accompany you aboard," he said in French. "Those're my orders."

Maybe, Wesley thought as he walked toward the gate, I should have taken my chances when we were down at the port. His mother and her husband followed them closely.


Rudolph drove Dwyer toward Antibes. Neither of them said a word on the entire trip. When they reached the entrance to the port, Dwyer said, "I'll get off here. I have to see someone." Both he and Rudolph knew that he was going to stop at the little café and get drunk and that he wanted to be alone. "You going to be around for a while?"

"A week or so," Rudolph said. "Until I get it all cleared up."

"See you," Dwyer said, and went into the café, un-

buttoning the collar of his shirt and tearing off his tie
and stuffing it carelessly into his pocket.

Rudolph started the car again. In his pocket he had a
letter from Jeanne. She would meet him for lunch at the
Colombe d'Or and could see him every afternoon that
week. The war in Paris was on again, she had written.

When the seat belt sign went off in the cabin of the
plane as it turned west in the sky above Monte Carlo,
Wesley was looking at the photographs that had been in
the envelope that Dwyer had given him. He didn't notice his mother cross the aisle to stand over him. She
looked down at the photographs in his hand. Suddenly,
she reached over and grabbed them all. "You won't
need these anymore," she said. "You poor baby, you
have a lot to forget."

He didn't want to make a scene, not this soon anyway, so he didn't say anything. He watched as she stood
there in the aisle, tearing the photographs one by one
and dropping the pieces in the aisle. She didn't have any
objections to making scenes, he thought. Boy, it was
going to be great in Indianapolis.

He looked out the window and saw the peninsula of
Antibes, green and beloved, sliding away into the blue
sea below him.

———

# VOLUME
---
## TWO

# CHAPTER 1

*From Billy Abbott's notebook—*

There is a lot of talk at NATO about
displaced populations, the Germans
kicked out of Poland, the East Germans,
refugees in West Germany, the
Palestinians, the Armenians, the Jews
kicked out of the Arab countries, the
Italians out of Tunisia and Libya, the
French <u>colons</u> from Algeria. More
undoubtedly to come. Natural
conversation among military men, on the
lookout for occasions for war.

It has occurred to me that I am a
displaced population all by myself, far
from home, with sentimental and no doubt
distorted memories of a happier life and
better time in another country, feeling
no allegiance to the society (the U.S.
Army) in which I spend my exile, even
though it feeds, clothes, and pays me
more generously than I, with my meager
talents and complete lack of ambition,

could ever hope to feed, clothe and pay
myself in my native land.

I have no allegiances, which is the
same as saying that I could become a
desperate man. My allegiance, such as it
is, to Monika, is temporary at best. A
casual transfer of posts, the colonel
appointed to an outfit in Greece or
Guam and not being sure he could find
a useful tennis partner there, a shift
in command ordered by someone in
Washington who does not know or care if
I am alive, an offer of a better job
for Monika in another country, and it
would be destroyed.

It might not even be anything as
accidental as that. Lately Monika has
become edgy. I find her watching me
more and more often with a speculative
look in her eye that bodes no good.
It would be the height of blind
egotism in me if I believed that the
speculation included sorrow at the
thought of losing me.

If Monika leaves me I will screw the
Colonel's wife.

––––––

Billy Abbott, in civilian clothes, feeling at peace with
the world, after an excellent meal at the restaurant that
overlooked La Grande Place of the city of Brussels,
came out into the cool night air, holding on to Monika's
arm. The meal had been expensive, as the restaurant
was overpraised in all the guidebooks, but it had been
worth it. Besides, he had won sixty dollars that afternoon playing tennis with the Colonel as his partner. The
Colonel was a tennis nut and tried to play at least an

hour a day, and as befitted a true graduate of West Point, liked to win.

The Colonel had seen Billy play when Billy was only a corporal and had liked Billy's style, which was cool and tricky, so that he could beat players who hit the ball twice as hard as he did. Billy was also very quick and could cover three-quarters of the court in doubles. Since the Colonel was forty-seven years old, he needed a partner who could cover three-quarters of the court. So now Billy was no longer a corporal, but a master sergeant in command of the motor pool, a job that meant considerable extra money beyond his sergeant's pay, what with an occasional grateful tip from officers who had motorized business to conduct that was not officially Army business, and the not so occasional opportunity to sell Army gasoline clandestinely at prices cannily just below the prices in the city. The Colonel also invited Billy to dinner. He liked to know what the enlisted men were thinking, as he often said, and the Colonel's wife thought Billy was a charming young man and behaved like an officer, especially in civilian clothes. The Colonel's wife liked to play tennis, too, and lived in hope of the day when the Colonel would be sent off on an assignment for a month or two, leaving Billy behind.

It was not the Old Army, the Colonel sometimes said, but you had to keep up with the times. While the Colonel was his commanding officer there was no danger that Billy would be sent to Vietnam.

Billy knew that it was through his Uncle Rudolph's good offices in Washington that he had been spared the unpleasant sound of hostile fire and one day he would show his gratitude. Right now, he had in his pocket a letter from his uncle which contained a check for one thousand dollars. Billy's mother had run dry as a source of funds, and Monika, to whom Billy had spoken about his rich uncle, had pushed him into writing for money.

She had been mysterious about why she needed it, but Billy had long ago resigned himself to the fact that she was a mysterious girl. She never told him anything about her family in Munich or why she had taken it into her head at the age of eighteen to take a degree at Trinity College in Dublin. She was always going off on secret appointments, but except for that, most of the time was extremely agreeable to live with. That had been the condition on which she had moved into his cosy little flat off the Place. He was to ask no questions when she said she had to be away for an evening or sometimes a week. There were some delicate meetings among the delegates to NATO that could not be talked about. He was not a curious young man when it came to matters that did not concern him.

Monika was not really pretty, with her black, tangled hair and low-heeled shoes and sensible stockings, but she had large blue eyes that lit up her face when she smiled and a lovely small figure. The small was important. Billy was only five feet six inches tall and slightly built, and he didn't like the feeling of inferiority taller women gave him.

If he had been asked on this evening what profession he intended to follow he would most probably have said that he was going to reenlist. Every once in a while, Monika would get angry with him and denounce him for his lack of ambition. With his engaging youthful athlete's smile, he would agree with her that he had no ambition. The melancholy darkness of his eyes, fringed by heavy black lashes, gave his smile an extra value, as though he had made a special sad effort at gaiety for its recipient. Billy knew enough about himself not to turn the smile on too often.

Tonight was one of the times Monika had a mysterious appointment. "Don't wait up for me," she said as they gazed at the spotlit gilt magnificence of the Place's walls and windows. "I may be late. Maybe all night."

"You're ruining my sex life," he said.

"I bet," she said. Trinity College, plus the troops of NATO, had given her an easy command of both the English and American languages.

He kissed her lightly and watched her get into a cab. She sprang into it as if she were doing the running broad jump at a track meet. He admired her energy. He couldn't hear the address that she gave the driver. It occurred to him that every time he put her in a cab, he never heard where she was going.

He shrugged and strolled toward a café. It was too early to go home and there was nobody else he especially wanted to see that night.

In the café he ordered a beer and took out the envelope with the check and his uncle's letter in it. There had been an exchange of letters, quite cordial, since Billy had seen the item in *Time* Magazine about Tom Jordache's death and the awful photograph of Rudolph's wife naked that they'd dug up somewhere. He hadn't mentioned the photograph in the letter to Rudolph and had been sincere, or as sincere as he could be, with his condolences. Uncle Rudolph had been chatty in his letters, with all the family news. He sounded like a lonely man who didn't know quite what to do with himself, and he had written sadly, if reticently, of his divorce and the claiming of Cousin Wesley by the lady from Indianapolis. He had not mentioned the police record of Wesley's mother as a common prostitute, but Billy's own mother had not been sparing in details. His mother's letters tended to be stern and admonitory. She had never forgiven him for his refusal to keep away from the army—she would have enjoyed playing the honored martyr, he felt resentfully, if he had gone to jail instead. Everyone to his or her principles. For himself, he preferred playing tennis with a forty-

seven-year-old colonel and living in comparative luxury
with a bright, shapely, multilingual, and—admit it—a
beloved *fräulein* in the civilized city of Brussels.

His letter to his uncle asking for a loan had been
graceful and rueful rather than importunate. There had
been some unlucky poker games, he had hinted, an expensive automobile breakdown, the necessity to buy a
new car . . . Rudolph's letter, which had arrived that
morning, had been understanding, although he had
made it clear that he expected to be repaid.

Monika wanted the cash the next morning and he
would have to go to the bank. He wondered what she
might need it for. What the hell, he thought, dismissing
the subject, it's only money and it's not even mine. He
ordered a second beer.

In the morning he discovered what she wanted the
money for. She woke him up when she came in at
dawn, made him a cup of coffee, sat him down and told
him the thousand dollars was to be used to bribe a sergeant at the Army arms depot, so that the people she
was working with, whom she wouldn't name or describe, could go in with a U.S. Army truck, which he,
Billy, was expected to supply from the motor pool, and
lift an unspecified number of guns, grenades and rounds
of ammunition. He himself was not to be involved in
the deal. Only to the extent of driving the truck out of
the pool one night, with authentic orders, and delivering
it half a mile down the road to a man who would be
dressed as a U.S. Army MP lieutenant. The truck
would be back before dawn. She said all this calmly,
while he sat in silence, sipping his coffee, wondering if
she had been on drugs all night. In the course of her
explanation, given in the same even tones she might
have used back in Trinity at a seminar on an obscure
Irish poet, she also explained that he had been picked

as her lover because of his job at the motor pool, although she admitted that she had become fond of him, very fond, since then.

He tried to control his voice when he finally spoke. "What the hell is all this stuff going to be used for?"

"I can't tell you, darling," she said, stroking his hand across the kitchen table. "And you'll be better off never knowing."

"You're a terrorist," he said.

"That's a word like any other," she said, shrugging. "I might prefer the word idealist, or a phrase like seeker after justice or an enemy of torture or just plain lover of the ordinary, traumatized, brainwashed common man. Take your pick."

"What if I just went to NATO and told them about you? About this crazy scheme?" He felt silly sitting there shivering in a small, cold, bourgeois kitchen, dressed only in an old bathrobe that was half open, with his balls hanging out, talking about blowing people up.

"I wouldn't try that, darling," she said. "First of all they would never believe you. I'd say that I had told you I'd leave you and this was your weird way of getting revenge. And some of the boys I know can be very nasty customers indeed. . . ."

"You're threatening me," he said.

"I guess you could call it that."

By the look in her eye he knew that she was deadly serious. Serious was exactly the word. And deadly. He felt cold and frightened. He had never posed as a hero. He had never even had a fistfight in his life. "If I do this, this once," he said, trying to keep his voice from quavering, "I never want to see you again."

"That's for you to decide," she said evenly.

"I'll tell you at noon," he said, his mind racing, searching for a way he could get out of the whole thing, fly to America, hide out in Paris, London, escape the whole insane, surrealist plot in six hours.

"That will be time enough," Monika said. "The banks are open in the afternoon. But I must tell you, for your own sake—you will be watched."

"What the hell kind of woman are you?" he shouted, his voice out of control.

"If you weren't so superficial and frivolous and self-satisfied," she said, without raising her voice, "you'd know by now, after living with me as long as you've done."

"I don't know what's so frivolous and self-satisfied about not wanting to kill people," he said, stung by her description of him. "Don't be so goddamned smug."

"Every day," she said, "you put on a uniform. In the same uniform, thousands of young men your age go out every day to kill hundreds of thousands of people who never did them any harm. I consider *that* frivolous." As she talked, her eyes finally were darkening with anger.

"And *you're* going to stop that?" he said loudly. "You and five or six other murderous thugs?"

"We can try. Among other things that we will try. At least we'll have the satisfaction of knowing that we tried. And what satisfaction will you have?" She sneered at him, her mouth an ugly grimace. "That you played tennis while it all was happening? That there isn't a single human being alive who has any respect for you? That you sat idly by while the men whose boots you lick morning, noon and night are plotting to blow up the world? When everything goes up in the final explosion, are you going to be proud of yourself as you die because you ate well and drank well and fucked well while it all was being prepared? Wake up! Wake up! There's no law that says you have to be a worm."

"Rhetoric," he said. "So what'll you do—hijack an Israeli plane, break some windows in an embassy, shoot a policeman while he's directing traffic? Is that your idea of saving the world?"

"First of all, this has nothing to do with the Israelis. We—my group and I—have varying opinions on that subject, so don't worry about your Jewish friends—my Jewish friends, for that matter."

"Thank you," he said sardonically, "for your German forbearance of the Jews."

"You bastard." She tried to slap him across the table, but he was too fast for her and caught her hand.

"None of that," he said. "You may be wonderful with a machine gun, but you're not a boxer, lady. Nobody's going to get away with hitting me. You've yelled at me and yelled at me and threatened me and asked me to do something that might get me killed or land me in prison for life and you haven't explained anything yet." Recklessly, he went on, raving now. "If I'm going to help you, it's not going to be because you're scaring me into it or bribing me or anything like that. I'll make a deal with you. You're right—there's no law that says I have to be a worm. You convince me and I'm with you. You sit down and keep your goddamn hands and your goddamn threats to yourself and calmly explain. Otherwise, no soap. You understand that?"

"Let go of my hand," she said sullenly.

He dropped her hand. She stared at him furiously. Then she began to chuckle. "Hey, Billy boy, there's something there after all. Who would have guessed that? I think we need some fresh coffee. And you're cold. Go in and get dressed and put on a sweater and we'll have a nice little talk over the breakfast table about the wonder of being alive in the twentieth century."

In the bedroom, while he was getting dressed, he started shivering again. But even while he was shiver-

ing, he felt crazily exhilarated. For once he hadn't
backed down or slid away or evaded. And it could be a
matter of life and death, he was sure of that. There was
no sense in underestimating Monika's toughness or passion. The papers were full of stories of hijackings,
bombings, political murders, theatrical massacres, and
they were plotted and carried out by people who sat at
the next desk from yours, who stood by your side in a
bus, who went to bed with you, ate dinner with you. It
was his tough luck that Monika was one of them. As
she had said, he should have guessed *something*. Her
insults had wounded him: it was one thing to know that
you were worthless, it was another to be told by a
woman whom you admired, more than that—much
more—loved, who acted as though she loved you, that
you had no value.

The chuckle in the cold, dawn-lit kitchen had been a
gift of respect and he accepted it gratefully. In Monika's
eyes now he was a worthy opponent and had to be
treated accordingly. Until now he had let the world go
its own way and had been satisfied to find a snug,
government-issue corner for himself. Well, the world
had caught up with him and he had to deal with it. He
was involved, whether he liked it or not. From one moment to another, almost instinctively, he had put a new
price on his existence.

The hell with her, he thought, as he put on a sweater.
Loss is the risk of breathing. The hell with all of them.

Monika was heating a fresh pot of coffee when he
went back into the kitchen. She had taken off her shoes
and was padding around in her stockinged feet, her hair
a dark mess, like any housewife newly risen from the
marital bed to make breakfast for her husband on the
way to the office. Terror in the kitchen, bloodshed over
a hot stove, victims designated among the clatter of pots

and pans. He sat down at the scarred wooden table, rescued from some Belgian farmhouse, and Monika poured the coffee into his cup. Efficient German *hausfrau*. She made good coffee. He tasted it with relish. She poured some coffee for herself, smiled at him gently. The woman who had told him that he had been selected as her lover because he happened to run a motor pool from which trucks could be obtained for deadly errands had disappeared. For the time being. For ten minutes on a cold morning, he thought, as he drank the scalding coffee.

"Well," he said, "where do we begin?" He looked at his watch. "It can't take too long. I have to be at work soon."

"We begin at the beginning," she said. "The state of the world. The world's in a mess. The Fascists are everywhere. . . ."

"In America . . .?" he said. "Come on, Monika."

"In America it's still disguised," she said impatiently. "They can still afford to disguise it. But who gives them the arms, the money, the smoke screens, finally, the real support? The fat cats in Washington, New York, Texas. If you're going to insist on being naive, I won't bother talking to you."

"You sound as though it all comes out of a book."

"Why not?" she said. "What's wrong with learning from a book? It wouldn't do you any harm to read a few books, either. If you're so worried about your beloved native land, you'll be relieved to hear that we're not operating in America now, not the people I'm with anyway, although I'm not saying there aren't some who do. There're bombs going off in America, too, and there'll be more, I promise you. America's at the base of the pyramid and in the end it will be the prime target. And you're going to be surprised how easily it will crumble in the end. Because the pyramid is shaky, it's based on lies, immoral privileges, stolen wealth, subjugated populations; it's based on sand that's hollow beneath the surface."

"You sound more like a book than ever," he said. "Why don't you just get it out of the library and I'll read it myself."

Monika ignored his gibe. "What we have to do," she went on, "is show that it's vulnerable as well as evil."

"How do you plan to do that with a few crazy gangsters?"

"Don't use that word," she said warningly.

"Whatever you want to call them. Gunmen. Assassins. Whatever."

"Castro did it in Cuba with eighteen men."

"America's not Cuba," he said. "And neither is Europe."

"They're near enough. Both of them. The attacks will multiply. The men in power will get uneasy, uncertain, finally frightened. They'll act out of fear, make one mistake after another, each one worse than the last. They'll apply pressure. They'll make disastrous concessions which will only make people realize that they were close to defeat and only inspire more incidents, more cracks in the walls."

"Oh," he said, "turn off the record, will you?"

"A bank president will be assassinated," she chanted, rapt in her vision, "an ambassador kidnapped, a strike paralyze a country, money lose its value. They won't know where the next blow is coming from, just that there will be a next blow. The pressure will build up, until the whole thing explodes. It won't take armies. . . . Just a few dedicated people . . ."

"Like you?" he said.

"Like me," she said defiantly.

"And if you succeed, then what?" he said. "Russia takes the whole pot. Is that what you want?"

"Russia's time will come," she said. "Don't think I'm fool enough to want *that*."

"What *do* you want, then?"

"I want the world to stop being poisoned, stop being headed to extinction, one way or another. I want to stop the warriors we have now, the spies, the nuclear bombers, the bribed politicians, the killing for profit. . . . people are suffering and I want them to know who's making them suffer and what they're getting out of it."

"All right," he said, "that's all very admirable. But let's speak practically. Supposing I get you the truck, supposing you put your hands on a few grenades, plastic, guns. Just what, specifically, are you going to do with them?"

"Specifically," she said, "we are planning to blow in the windows of a bank here in Brussels, get some explosive inside the Spanish embassy, wipe out a judge in Germany who's the biggest pig on the Continent. I can't tell you more than that. For your own sake."

"You're ready to do a lot of things for my sake, aren't you?" he said. He bowed sardonically. "I thank you, my mother thanks you, my colonel thanks you."

"Don't be flip," she said coldly. "Don't ever be flip with me again."

"You sound as though you're ready to shoot me right now, dear little gunlady," he said, mocking her, pushing himself to courage, although he was shivering again, sweater and all.

"I've never shot anybody," she said. "And don't propose to. That is not my job. And if your scruples are so delicate, perhaps you'd like to hear that we plan to operate in such a way here in Belgium that nobody will get killed. What we do is merely unsettle, warn, symbolize."

"That's Belgium," he said. "What about other places?"

"That doesn't concern you," she said. "You don't

have to know anything about it. Later on, if you are convinced and you want to take a more active part, you will be trained, you will be in on the discussions. Right now, all you are to do is go to the bank and cash your uncle's check and make a truck available for a few hours one night. Christ," she said fiercely, "it's nothing new to you, with your bribes—don't think I don't know how you live so high on a sergeant's pay—with your black market gasoline. . . ."

"My God, Monika," he said, "do you mean to say you can't tell the difference between a little petty larceny and what you're asking me to do?"

"Yes," she said. "One is cheap and distasteful and the other is noble. You've been leading your life in a trance. You don't *like* what you are, you despise everybody around you, I've heard you talk about your family, your mother, your father, your uncle, the animals you work with . . . Don't deny it." She put up her hand to stop him as he tried to speak. "You've kept everything narrow, inside yourself. Nobody's challenged you to face yourself, open up, to see what it all means. Well, I'm challenging you now."

"And hinting that something very nasty will happen to me if I don't do as you want," he said.

"That's the way it goes, laddy," she said. "Think over what I've just said as you work this morning."

"I'll do just that." He stood up. "I've got to get to the office."

"I'll be waiting for you at lunchtime," she said.

"I bet you will," he said, as he went out the door.

The morning in the office passed for him in a blur. As he checked out orders, requests, manifests, operation reports, he made dozens of decisions, each one over and over again, each one discarded, the next one reached and discarded in turn. Three times he picked

up the phone to call the Colonel, spill everything, ask
him for advice, help, then put the phone down. He
looked up the schedule of the planes flying out of Brussels to New York, decided to go to the bank, cash his
uncle's check and get on a plane that morning. He
could go to the CIA in Washington, explain his predica-
ment, get Monika put behind bars, be something of a
secret hero in those secret corridors. Or would he?
Would those men, deft in murder and complicated un-
derground maneuvers and the overthrow of govern-
ments, congratulate him and secretly, in their own style,
scorn him for his cowardice? Or even worse, turn him
into a double agent, order him back to join whatever
band Monika belonged to, tell him to report weekly on
their doings? Did he want Monika behind bars? Even
that morning, he could not honestly tell himself that he
didn't love her. Love? There was a word. Most women
bored him. Usually he made an excuse, after copulation, to jump out of bed and go home. With Monika the
night's entwining could never be called copulation. It
was absolute delight. To put it coarsely, he told himself,
I can come five times a night with her and look forward
eagerly to seeing her naked and rosy in bed at lunchtime.

He didn't want to be killed. He knew that, just as he
knew he didn't want to give up Monika. But there was
something titillating, deeply exciting, about the thought
that he was daring enough to make love to a woman,
make her gasp in pleasure and pain, at six in the morning and know that she was ready to order his execution
at noon.

What would it be like to say to her, "I'm with you"?
To slide in and out of shadows? To hear an explosion
somewhere nearby while he was playing tennis at the
immaculate club with the Colonel and know that he had
scheduled it? To pass a bank on whose board his Uncle

Rudolph sat and stealthily deposit a bomb that would explode before the bank opened its doors in the morning? To meet fanatics, who flitted from one country to another, who would be heroes in the history books, perhaps, a century from now, who killed with poison, with their bare hands, who could teach him their mysteries, who could make him forget he was only five feet six inches tall?

In the end, he did not call the Colonel, he did not cash the check, he made no arrangements at the motor pool, he did not go out to the airport.

What he did was drift, dazed, through the morning and when the Colonel called and said there was a game on at five-thirty that afternoon, he said, "Yes, sir, I'll be there," although he felt that there was a good chance he'd be dead by then.

She was waiting for him when he came out of the office. He was relieved that she had combed her hair, because the other men streaming past to go to lunch all looked at them speculatively, leers suppressed, mostly because of his rank, and he didn't like the idea of their thinking he consorted with a slob.

"Well?" she said.

"Let's have lunch," he said.

He took her to a good restaurant, where he knew the other men who wanted a change from the food in the Army mess were not likely to go. He wanted the reassurance of crisp tablecloths, flowers on the tables, attentive waiters, a place where there was no suggestion of the world tottering, desperate plotters, crumbling pyramids. He ordered for them both. She pretended not to be interested in what she ate and couldn't bother with the menu. Meanly, knowing at least that much about her, he understood why she tossed the menu aside. She

had to put on thick glasses to read and was vain enough
not to wish to be seen in public with them on. But when
the food came she ate heartily, more than he did. He
wondered how she kept her figure.

They ate quietly, talking politely about the weather, a
conference that was to start tomorrow at which she was
to act as translator, about his date for tennis with the
Colonel at five-thirty, about a play that was coming to
Brussels that she wanted to see. There was no reference
to what had passed between them that morning until the
coffee came. Then she said, "Well, what have you decided?"

"Nothing," he said. Even in the overheated, cosy restaurant he felt cold again. "I sent the check back to my
uncle this morning."

She smiled coldly. "That's a decision, isn't it?"

"Partially," he said. He was lying. The check was still
in his wallet. He hadn't known he was going to say it. It
had come out mechanically, as though something had
pushed a lever in his brain. But even as he said it, he
knew he *was* going to mail the check back, with thanks,
explaining to his uncle that his finances had taken a
turn for the better and there was no need at the moment
for help. It would prove useful later on when he really
needed something from Uncle Rudolph.

"All right," she said calmly, "if you were afraid that
the money could be traced, I understand." She
shrugged. "It's not too important. We'll find the money
someplace else. But how about the truck?"

"I haven't done anything about it."

"You have all afternoon."

"No, I haven't made up my mind yet."

"We can handle that, too, I suppose," she said. "All
you have to do is look the other way."

"I'm not going to do that, either," he said. "I have a
lot of thinking to do before I decide one way or an-

other. If your friends want to kill me," he said harshly, but keeping his voice low, because he saw their waiter approaching with more coffee, "tell them that I'll be armed." He had had one morning's practice with a .45, could take it apart and reassemble it, but had had a very low score when he had fired at a target for the record. Gunfight at the Brussels OK Corral, he thought. Who was it—John Wayne? What would John Wayne have done today? He giggled.

"What're you laughing about?" she asked sharply.

"I happened to think of a movie I once saw," he said.

"Yes, please," she said in French to the waiter who was standing over her with the silver coffeepot. The waiter filled both their cups.

After the waiter had left, she smiled at him strangely. "You don't have to a pack a gun. Nobody's going to shoot you. You're not worth a bullet."

"That's nice to hear," he said.

"Does *anything* ever make an impression on you, touch you?"

"I'll make out a list," he said, "and give it to you the next time we meet. If we meet."

"We'll meet," she said.

"When are you moving out of the apartment?" he asked.

She looked at him in surprise. He couldn't tell whether the surprise was real or feigned. "I hadn't intended to move out. Do you want me to move out?"

"I don't know," he said. "But after today . . ."

"For the time being," she said, "let's forget today. I like living with you. I've found that politics has nothing to do with sex. Maybe with other people, but not with me. I adore going to bed with you. I haven't had much luck in bed with other men. The orgasms are few and far between on the New Left—at least for me—and in this day and age ladies have been taught that orgasms are a lady's God-given right. You're the answer to a maiden's prayer for that, darling, if you don't mind my being a little vulgar. At least for this particular maiden. And I like good dinners, which you are obliging enough to supply. So—" She lit a cigarette. She smoked incessantly and the ashtrays in the apartment were always piled with butts. It irritated him, as he did not smoke and took seriously the warnings of the magazine articles about mortality rates for smokers. But, he supposed, you couldn't expect a terrorist who was constantly on the lookout for the police or execution squads to worry about dying from cancer of the lungs at the age of sixty. "So—" she said, exhaling smoke through her nostrils. "I'll divide my life, while it lasts, into compartments. You for sex and lobster and pâté de foie gras, and others for less serious occupations, like shooting German judges. Aren't you glad I'm such a sensible girl?"

She's cutting me to pieces, he thought, little jagged pieces. "I'm not glad about anything," he said.

"Don't look so mournful, laddy," she said. "Everything to his or her own talents. And now, I have most of the afternoon off. Can you sneak away for an hour or two?"

"Yes." He had long ago perfected a system of checking in and out of the office without being noticed.

"Good." She patted his hand. "Let's go home and get into bed and have a perfectly delicious afternoon fuck."

Furious with himself for not being able to stand up, throw a bill on the table for the check and stalk out of the restaurant, he said, "I have to go back to the office for ten minutes. I'll meet you home."

"I can't wait." She smiled at him, her large blue eyes lighting up her Bavarian-Trinity face.

# CHAPTER 2

*From Billy Abbott's notebook—*

```
This will be the last entry in this
notebook for some time.
   I had better not write anything about
Monika anymore.
   There are snoops, and authorized
burglars everywhere. Brussels abounds
in them.
   Monika edgier than ever.
   I love her. She refuses to believe me.
```

Sidney Altscheler was standing at the window of his office high up in the Time and Life Building, staring gloomily out at the lights of the buildings around the tower in which he worked. He was gloomy because he was thinking of all the editorial work ahead of him over the weekend.

There was a discreet knock on the door and his secretary came in. "There's somebody called Jordache here who wants to see you."

Altscheler frowned. "Jordache?" he said. "I don't know anybody named Jordache. Tell him I'm busy, let him write me a letter."

The secretary had turned to go when he remembered. "Wait a minute," he said. "We ran a story five, six months ago. About a murder. The man's name was Jordache. Tell him to come up. I've got fifteen minutes free before Thatcher comes in with his rewrite. Maybe there's a follow-up on the Jordache story we can use." He went back to the window and continued being gloomy about the weekend as he stared out at the lights in the surrounding offices, which would be dark tomorrow because it was Saturday and the vice-presidents, the clerks, the bookkeepers, the mailboys, everybody, would be enjoying their holiday.

He was still at the window when there was a rap at the door and the secretary came in with a boy in a suit that was too small for him. "Come in, come in," he said, and seated himself behind his desk. There was a chair next to the desk. He indicated it to the boy.

"Will you need me?" the secretary asked.

"If I do, I'll call you." He looked at the boy. Sixteen, seventeen, he guessed, big for his age. Thin, handsome face, with disturbing intense eyes. Trained down like an athlete.

"Now, Mr. Jordache," he said briskly, "what can I do for you?"

The boy took out a page torn from *Time*. "You did this story about my father." He had a deep, resounding voice.

"Yes, I remember." Altscheler hesitated. "Which one was your father? The mayor?"

"No," the boy said, "the one who was murdered."

"I see," Altscheler said. He made his tone more kindly. "What's your first name, young man?"

"Wesley."

"Have they found the murderer yet?"

"No." Wesley hesitated. Then he said, "That is—technically no."

"I didn't think so. I haven't seen any follow-up."

"I really wanted to see whoever wrote the article," Wesley said. "I told them that downstairs at the desk, but they telephoned around and found it was by a man named Hubbell and said he was still in France. So I bought a copy of *Time* and I saw your name up in front."

"I see," Altscheler said. "What did you want to see Mr. Hubbell for? Did you think the article was unfair or mistaken?"

"No. Nothing like that."

"Is there any new development you think we ought to know about?"

"No. I wanted to talk to Mr. Hubbell about my father and my father's family. There was a lot about all that in the article."

"Yes. But Mr. Hubbell couldn't help you. That was done here; the material came from one of our researchers."

"I didn't know my father well," Wesley said. "I didn't see him from the time I was little until just a couple of years ago. I'd like to know more about him."

"I can understand that, Wesley," Altscheler said kindly.

"In the article you seemed to know a lot more than I ever did. I have a list of people who my father had something to do with at different times in his life and I put *Time* on the list, that's all."

"I understand," Altscheler rang for his secretary. She came in immediately. "Miss Prentice," he said, "will you find out who did the research on the Jordache article? If I remember correctly it was Miss Larkin; take the young man to her office. Tell her to do anything she can for Mr. Jordache." He stood up. "I'm afraid I have to go back to work now," he said. "Thank you for coming to see me, Wesley. And good luck."

"Thank you, sir." Wesley stood, too, and followed the secretary out of the office.

Altscheler went back to the window and stared out. Polite, sad boy. He wondered what he would have done if his father had been murdered and he himself had been sure he knew who had done it. They did not consider these questions at Yale, where he had earned his B.A.

The researcher had a little office without windows, lit by neon tubes. She was a small young woman with glasses, carelessly dressed, but pretty. She kept nodding and looking timidly at Wesley as Miss Prentice explained what he was there for. "Just wait a minute right here, Mr. Jordache," she said, "and I'll go into the files. You can read everything I dug up." She flushed a little as she heard herself using the phrase. "Dug up" was not the sort of thing to say when you were talking to a boy whose father had been murdered. She wondered if she ought to censor the files before she let the boy see them. She remembered very well working on the story— mostly because it was so different from anything she herself had experienced in her own life. She had never been on the Riviera, in fact had never been out of America, but she had been a hungry reader in the literature courses she had taken in college and the south of France was firmly fixed in her imagination as a place of romance and tragedy—Scott Fitzgerald driving to a party or from a party on the Grand Corniche, Dick Diver, desperate and gay on the blazing beaches, with all the trouble ahead of them all when everything collapsed. She had kept her notes, which she didn't usually do, out of a vague feeling of being connected to a literary geography that she would one day explore. She looked at the boy—who had been there, had suffered there, now standing in her office in his clumsy suit— and would have liked to question him, discover if he knew anything of all that. "Would you like a cup of coffee while you wait?" she asked.

"No, thank you, ma'am," he said.

"Would you like a copy of this week's magazine to look through?"

"I bought a copy downstairs, thank you."

"I'll just be a minute," she said brightly. Poor little boy, she thought as she went out of the office. So handsome, too. Even in the ridiculous suit. She was a romantic girl who had read a great deal of poetry, too. She could imagine him, dressed in flowing black, twin to the young Yeats in the early photographs.

When she came back with the file the boy was sitting hunched over on the straight chair, his arms resting on his thighs, his hands hanging between his knees, like a football player on the bench.

"Here's everything," she said brightly. She had debated with herself about whether or not to take out the photograph of Jean Jordache naked, but had decided against it. The picture had been in the magazine, after all, and he must have seen it.

"Now, you just take your time," she said. "I have some work to do." She gestured toward the pile of clippings on her desk. "But you won't bother me." She was pleased to have him in the office. It broke the routine.

Wesley looked down for a long time at the file without opening it, as Miss Larkin busied herself at her desk, using scissors and making notes, occasionally looking at the boy, until he caught her at it, which flustered her. Still, she thought, excusing herself, he'd better get used to girls looking at him. They're going to be doing it in droves.

The first thing she saw him take out of the files was a photograph of his father in boxing trunks, with his fists cocked. He looked fierce and young. To Wesley, he hardly looked older than he himself was now. Every muscle stood out in his arms and torso. He must have scared the wits out of the guys he was going to fight.

Miss Larkin had looked at the picture, too, when she took it out of the files. She thought the fighter looked like a handsome ruffian, somebody it would be wise to stay away from. She preferred men who looked like intellectuals. She studied the boy frankly now, since he was paying attention only to the photograph in his hand. He looked surprisingly like his father, but there was nothing ruffianly about him. He must be at least nineteen, she thought; maybe it would be nice to invite him downstairs for a drink. These days, she thought, nineteen can be very mature for a boy. She was only twenty-four herself; you couldn't call it an impossible gap.

The photograph had been cut out from *Ring* Magazine and there was a little article about Tom Jordan pasted to the bottom of the picture. "Tom Jordan, promising middleweight, undefeated in fourteen bouts, 8 k.o.'s, on his way to London to fight Sammy Wales, contender for British middleweight championship, at Albert Hall. Arthur Schultz, Jordan's manager, predicts that with another four or five matches under his belt, Tommy will be ready for anybody in his division."

Clipped to the photograph, there was another sheet of paper with typing on it. Wesley started reading again. "Won fight in London by knockout. Fought René Badaud three weeks later in Paris. Knocked out in seventh round. From then on, record spotty, slipped down in class. Hired as sparring partner Freddy Quayles, Las

Vegas, Nevada (date). Quayles leading challenger middleweight title. Incident between Quayles and Jordan.
L.V. stringer reports rumor fight in hotel room over
Quayles' wife, later small-part actress Hollywood. Witness claims to have seen Quayles in hospital, badly battered. Quayles never regained form, quit ring, now
works as salesman sporting goods store, Denver, Col. T.
Jordan disappeared from Las Vegas, warrant out for his
arrest, auto theft. Has not surfaced since."

And that was it. A whole life in a few lines, all
summed up in four words—"Has not surfaced since."
He surfaced all right in Antibes, Wesley thought bitterly. He took out his pen and a piece of paper and
wrote, Arthur Schultz, Freddy Quayles.

Then he stared once more at the photograph of his
father, the left hand out, the right hand up under the
chin, the shoulders bunched, the fierce, confident young
face, ready, according to authority, after four or five
more matches, for anybody in his division. Not surfaced
since.

Wesley looked up at Miss Larkin. "I don't think I'd
recognize him if he came in through the door right now
looking like this." He laughed a little. "I'm glad he
didn't believe in hitting kids, with those shoulders."

Miss Larkin saw that Wesley was proud of the hard
body, the confident pugnacity of his father when he was
just a bit older than the boy was now.

"If you want the picture," she said, "I'll put it in a
big envelope for you so you won't crease it."

"You mean that?" Wesley said. "I can really have
it?"

"Of course."

"That's really great," Wesley said, "having the picture, I mean. I don't have any picture of him. I had
some, but they were all taken later. . . . He didn't
look like this. He looked okay," he said hastily, as

though he didn't want Miss Larkin to think that he was
running his father down or that he had turned into a fat,
bald, old man or anything like that. "He just looked
different. The expression on his face, I guess. I don't
suppose you can go through life always looking about
twenty years old."

"No, you can't," Miss Larkin said. She searched for
wrinkles around her eyes every morning.

Wesley dug in the file and brought out a biographical
note that Miss Larkin had prepared on the members of
the family.

Wesley went through the notes quickly. There was
very little in them that he didn't already know, his uncle's early success and the scandal at the college, his
aunt's two marriages, the outlines of his father's career.
One line he read twice. "Rudolph Jordache, when he
retired in his mid-thirties, was reputed to be a millionaire many times over." Many times over. How many
times would his father have had to fight, how many seasons on the Mediterranean would he have had to serve
even to be a millionaire just one time over?

He looked curiously at the pretty girl with glasses
working at her desk. Just by accident she had been chosen to learn so much about his family. He wondered
what she would say if he asked what she really thought
about the Jordaches. In her notes she had written that
Rudolph's was the standard American success story,
poor boy makes good in a big way. Would she say of his
father, poor boy makes bad in standard American way?

He made a funny little noise, almost a laugh. Miss
Larkin looked over at him. "That's about all there is,"
she said. "I'm afraid it isn't very much."

"It's okay," Wesley said. "It's fine." He didn't want
the nice young lady to think he wasn't grateful. He gave
her back the file and stood up. "Thank you very much.
I better be pushing along now."

Miss Larkin stood up, too. She looked at him strangely, as though she was making up her mind about something. "I'm just about finished here for the day," she said. "I was wondering if you'd like to go downstairs with me and have a drink?" She sounded as though she was appealing to him, but he couldn't tell for what. "I have a date later . . ." Even he could tell she was lying. "And I have an hour to kill . . ."

"They won't serve me a drink at a bar," Wesley said. "I'm not eighteen yet."

"Oh, I see." She flushed. "Well, thanks for the visit. If you ever come by again, now you know where my office is. If I can help in any way . . ."

"Yes, ma'am," he said.

She watched him go out of the office, the big shoulders bulging in the tight jacket. Not yet eighteen, she thought. Boy, am I dumb.

She sat staring at the papers on her desk for several minutes. She had a peculiar feeling that something strange was happening to her or was going to happen to her. She reread everything in the file. Murder, a rich brother, an intellectual sister, a brawling prizefighter done to death, the mystery unsolved. A beautiful son, still little more than a child, with strange, tragic eyes, looking for what—revenge?

The novel she was trying to write was about a girl very much like herself, growing up in a broken family, lonely, imaginative, her crushes on teachers, her first love, her first disillusionment with men, her coming to New York from a small town. She thought of it now with disdain. Written a thousand times.

Why wasn't the boy's story a novel? After all, Dreiser had started *An American Tragedy* after reading an article in a newspaper. Nobody in Dreiser's family had been murdered, he hadn't *known* anybody who'd been murdered, but he'd written a great novel, just the same.

Sitting in the same room with her just a few minutes ago was a handsome, complex boy, carrying the burden of remorse and sorrow on his shoulders almost visibly, nerving himself, she thought, shuddering deliciously, for the inevitable act. Hamlet as an American child. Why not? Revenge was among the oldest of literary traditions. Turn the other cheek, the Bible said, but also an eye for an eye. *Her* father, who was a rabid Irishman, cursed whenever he read what the English were still doing in Ireland, and there was a portrait of Parnell in the living room when she was a child.

Revenge was as much a part of all of us, she thought, as our bones and blood. We liked to pretend we were too civilized for it in the twentieth century, but the man in Vienna who spent his life tracking down Nazis who had killed Jews was honored all over the world. Her father said he was the last hero of World War Two.

She wished she had had the sense to ask the boy where he could be found. She would have to find him, study him, bring him to life on the page, with all his anger, his doubts, his youthfulness. It was cold-blooded, she told herself, but you either were a writer or you weren't. If he ever came into the office again, she would make sure that she'd find out all about him.

Feeling elated, as though she had come upon treasure, creative juices flowing, she carefully put all the papers back in the file and went out to where the master files were kept and put it back into place.

She could hardly wait to get back to her apartment and throw the sixty pages she had written on her novel into the fire.

# CHAPTER 3

Rudolph was sitting at the little upright piano, trying to pick out the melody of "On a Clear Day," when he heard the bell ring and Mrs. Burton came out of the kitchen to answer it. He saw her pass in the hall on the way to the front door. She had her hat and coat on. She only came in during the day as she had to go home each evening to feed her own family in Harlem. From the kitchen he heard the laughter of Enid, who was having her supper with her nurse there. Rudolph wasn't expecting anyone and he kept working on the melody. Getting the piano had turned out to be a good idea. He had originally bought it because the new nurse he had hired had a sweet voice and he had overheard her singing softly to Enid. She said she could play the piano a bit and he thought it would be useful for Enid to listen to someone actually making music in her own home. If it turned out that Enid had any talent it would be better for her than just hearing it from a box, as though Bach and Beethoven were as commonplace as an electric light, to be turned on or off by pushing a switch. But when the piano had been in the house for a few days he had found himself sitting down at it himself and fooling around with chords, then melodies. He had a good ear and he could pass hours amusing himself and not thinking of anything but the music at his fingertips. Whatever distracted him, even for a few minutes at a time, was so much profit. He had almost decided to take formal lessons.

He heard Mrs. Burton come into the living room. "There's a young man at the door, Mr. Jordache," Mrs. Burton said, "who says he's your nephew. Should I let him in?" Since Rudolph had moved to the two top floors of a brownstone, without a doorman, Mrs. Burton had been nervous about burglars and muggers and always kept the door chained. The neighbors, she complained, were careless about the front door and left it unlocked, so anyone could prowl the staircase.

Rudolph stood up. "I'll go see who it is," he said. In the letter from Brussels the week before from Billy, Billy hadn't said anything about coming to America. From the letters Billy had been writing him he seemed to have grown up into a nice, intelligent young man and on an impulse Rudolph had sent the thousand dollars Billy had asked for. Now he wondered if Billy had gotten into trouble with the army and deserted. That would explain the request for money. As for Wesley, there had been no word from him since Nice, and that was almost nine months ago.

Mrs. Burton followed him down the hallway. Outside the partially opened door, across the chain, Wesley was standing in the dim light of the ceiling bulb.

"It's all right, Mrs. Burton," Rudolph said. He slipped the chain free and opened the door. "Come in, Wesley." He put out his hand. After the slightest of pauses Wesley shook it.

"Will you be needing me any more tonight?" Mrs. Burton asked.

"No, thanks."

"Then I'll be moving along home. Have a nice week-end, Mr. Jordache."

"Thanks, Mrs. Burton." He closed the door behind her when she had left. Wesley merely stood there, his face thin, pale and expressionless, the ghost of his father as a boy, hostile and alert. He was in the same suit he had worn when he had left the jail in Grasse and it was smaller on him now than it had been then. He seemed to have grown and broadened considerably since their last meeting. His hair, Rudolph was happy to see, was not too long, but cropped at the neck.

"I'm glad to see you," Rudolph said as they went into the living room. "Can I get you something to drink?"

"A beer would be nice," Wesley said.

"Make yourself comfortable." Rudolph went into the kitchen where Enid was eating with the nurse. The nurse was a solid woman of about forty, with a marvelously gentle way of making Enid behave.

"Your Cousin Wesley is here, Enid," Rudolph said as he got a bottle of beer out of the refrigerator. He was about to tell her to come into the living room and say hello to Wesley after she had eaten, but thought better of it. He didn't know what Wesley had come for. If it was because of some emotional problem or dramatic adolescent disaster, it would only complicate matters to have Enid in the room. He kissed the top of her head and went into the living room with the beer and a glass. Wesley was standing awkwardly in the middle of the room just where Rudolph had left him. Rudolph poured the beer for him.

"Thank you," Wesley said. "Aren't you having anything to drink?"

"I'll have some wine with dinner. Sit down, sit down." Wesley waited for Rudolph and then sat in a chair facing him. He drank thirstily.

"Well," Rudolph said, "how're things? What brings you to New York?"

"I went to the wrong address," Wesley said. Rudolph noted that the boy didn't answer his question. "The doorman didn't want to tell me where you'd moved to. He wouldn't believe I was your nephew. I had to show him my library card." He sounded resentful, as though Rudolph had moved four blocks farther north just to avoid him.

"Didn't you get the letter I sent you?" Rudolph said. "I wrote you my new address the day I rented this apartment."

"I didn't get any letters." Wesley shook his head. "No, sir, no letters."

"Not even the one about how the estate would probably be finally settled and how much your share will be?"

"Nothing." Wesley drank again.

"What happens to your mail?" Rudolph tried to keep the irritation out of his voice.

"Maybe my mother doesn't approve of my getting mail. Anyway, that's my guess."

"Did you eat dinner yet?"

"No."

"I'll tell you over dinner what was in the letter I sent you."

"I didn't hitchhike all the way from Indianapolis to talk about money, Uncle Rudy," Wesley said softly. "It's a—well, I guess you might say it's a social visit."

"Does your mother know you're here?"

Wesley shook his head. "We're not on very good speaking terms, my mother and me."

"You didn't run away from home, did you?"

"No. It's the Easter vacation. I left a note saying I'd be back in time for school."

"That's a relief," Rudolph said dryly. "How're you doing in school?"

"Okay. I'm a hotshot in the French class." He grinned boyishly. "I teach my friends all the dirty words."

"They can come in handy," Rudolph said, smiling. "At times." Then more seriously, "Why did you have to hitchhike?"

"Money," Wesley said.

"Your mother gets quite a nice sum each month for your support for the time being," Rudolph said. "There's certainly enough for bus fare once a year to New York."

"Not a red cent," Wesley said. "I'm not complaining. I work after school. I get along."

"Do you?" Rudolph said skeptically. "Is that the only suit you have?"

"Like a whole suit—yeah. I got some sweaters and jeans and stuff like that for school and work. And there's an old mackinaw I wore in the winter that belongs to Mr. Kraler's son, he's a soldier, he's in Vietnam, so I don't freeze."

"I think I'll have to write your mother a letter," Rudolph said. "She's not allowed to use your money for herself."

"Don't make waves, please, Uncle Rudy," Wesley said carefully, putting his glass down on the floor beside him. "There's enough crap going on in that house without that. She says she'll give me every cent of the money she's supposed to if I go to church with her and Mr. Kraler, like a decent Christian."

"Oh," Rudolph said, "I'm beginning to get the picture."

"Some picture, eh?" Wesley grinned boyishly again. "The Spanish Inquisition in Indianapolis."

"I think I'll have a drink after all," Rudolph said.

He got up and went over to the sideboard and mixed himself a martini. "You want another beer, Wesley?"

"That'd be nice." Wesley picked up the glass from the floor, stood up and handed it to Rudolph.

"Enid's in the kitchen. Would you like to say hello to her?" He saw Wesley hesitate. "Her mother's not in there with her. I wrote you we were divorced." He shook his head annoyedly. "I don't suppose you got that letter, either."

"Nope."

"Damn it. From now on I'll write you care of General Delivery. Didn't you ever think it was queer that nobody wrote you?"

"I guess I never thought much about it."

"Didn't you write Bunny or Kate?"

"Once or twice," Wesley said. "They didn't answer, so I gave up. Do you hear from them?"

"Of course," Rudolph said. Dwyer sent him a monthly report, with the bills from the *Clothilde*. Dwyer had had to be told that Rudolph had bought the ship. The court-ordered official appraisal of the value of the boat had been a hundred thousand—Dwyer had been correct about that—but no other buyers had offered anything near that price and Dwyer had taken the ship for the winter to Saint-Tropez, where it was berthed now. "They're fine. Kate's had a baby. A boy. You've got a brother. A half brother, anyway."

"Poor little bastard," Wesley said, but the news seemed to cheer him. The blood survives, Rudolph thought. "When you write to Kate," Wesley said, "tell her I'll drop in on her in England someday. Kids. That makes my old man the only one in the family with more than one kid. He told me one night that he'd like to have five. He was great with kids. A couple would come on board with the worst little spoiled brat you ever saw and in a week my old man'd have him saying sir to everybody, standing up when grown-ups came on board, hosing down the decks in port, minding his language—everything." He fiddled with his beer, uncomfortably. "I don't like to boast, Uncle Rudy, but look what he did for me. I may not be much, even now, but you should have seen me when he grabbed me out of school—I was spastic."

"Well, you're not spastic now."

"Anyway," Wesley said, "I don't *feel* spastic. That's something."

"It certainly is."

"Talking about kids—you think it would be all right if I went in and said hello to Enid?"

"Of course," Rudolph said, pleased.

"She still talk a blue streak?"

"Yes," Rudolph said as he led the way into the kitchen, "more than ever."

For once, Enid was shy when they entered the kitchen and Wesley said, "Hello, Enid, I'm your cousin, Wesley. Remember?"

Enid looked up at him soberly, then turned her head away. "It's late," the nurse said defensively. "She gets a little temperamental this time of day."

"I'll come around in the morning sometime," Wesley said. In the small kitchen, his deep, mature voice sounded brassy and harsh and Enid put her hands over her ears.

"Manners, miss," the nurse said.

"I guess I talk too loud," Wesley said apologetically, as he followed Rudolph out of the kitchen. "You get in the habit on a boat, with the wind and the noise of the water and all."

In the living room, Rudolph poured the martini out of the shaker into a glass and twisted a piece of lemon peel over the top of the drink. He raised his glass to Wesley, suddenly glad that the boy had come to see him, had asked to see Enid. Maybe, he thought, in some dim, distant future we will be something like a family again. He had little left, he thought, self-pityingly; a family was something to cling to. Even the letter he had received from Billy, with its rather timid, offhand request for money, had been cordial in tone. With no sons of his own, he knew that if the boys permitted it, he would be their friend, more than friend. Lonely, no longer married, Jeanne an almost forgotten incident in the past, with his own child in the hands of a highly competent woman and still at an age at which he thought of her as no more than a kind of charming toy, he knew that once he began communicating with his nephews he would soon need them more than they would ever need him. He hoped that day would come—and soon.

"Whatever reason brought you to New York," he said, moved, as he raised his glass, "I'm very happy to see you."

Wesley raised his glass, too, self-consciously. "Thanks."

"No more fights in bars, I hope," Rudolph said.

"Don't worry," Wesley said soberly. "My fighting days're over. Though sometimes it's pretty tough to hold back. There're a lot of blacks in the school and the whites pick on them and they pick on the white boys. I guess I have the reputation of being chicken. But, what the hell, I can live with it. I learned my lesson. Anyway, I promised my father, the day he took me out of military school. I forgot only once. It wasn't what you would call a normal occasion." He stared down into his glass, grim, looking older than his years. "Just the once. Well, every dog is entitled to one bite, like they say. I guess I owe it to my father to keep my promise. It's the least I . . ." He stopped. His mouth tightened. Rudolph was afraid the boy was going to cry.

"I guess you do," he said quickly. "Where're you staying in New York?"

"The YMCA. Not too bad."

"Look," said Rudolph, "I'm taking Enid down to Montauk to her mother's tomorrow morning for the week, but I'll be coming back myself on Sunday. Why don't you ride down with me, get a breath of sea air . . .?" He stopped as he saw Wesley eyeing him warily.

"Thanks," Wesley said. "That would be nice. But some other time. I have to be getting back to Indianapolis."

"You won't have to hitchhike. I'll give you the air fare back." When will I ever stop offering people money, he thought despairingly, instead of what they really come for?

"I'd rather not," Wesley said. "Actually, I like to hitch rides. You get to talk to a lot of different kinds of people."

"Whatever you say," Rudolph said, rebuffed, but not blaming the boy for not wanting to run the risk of having to see Jean again, being reminded all over again. "Still," he said, "if you'd rather stay here for the night, I can fix you up on the sofa. . . . I don't have a guest room, but you'd be comfortable." Hospitality, family solidarity, not dollar bills.

"That's nice of you," Wesley said carefully, "but I'm fixed at the Y."

"The next time you come to New York let me know in advance. There're some nice hotels in the neighborhood and it would be convenient. We could take in a couple of shows, things like that. . . ." He stopped short. He didn't want the boy to think that he was attempting to bribe him.

"Sure," Wesley said unconvincingly. "Next time. This time, Uncle Rudy, I want to talk to you about my father." He stared soberly at Rudolph. "I didn't have the chance to know my father well enough. I was just a kid, maybe I'm still just a kid, but I want to know what he was like, what he was *worth*. . . . Do you understand what I mean?"

"I think so."

"I keep making up lists, names of people who knew my father at different times in his life—and you and Aunt Gretchen are first on that list. That's natural, isn't it?"

"I suppose so. Yes. That's natural." He was afraid of the questions he was going to be asked, the answers that he would be forced to give the tall, solemn, overgrown boy.

"When I got to know him—" Wesley went on, "just the short time we had together—I thought he was some kind of hero, a saint, almost, the way he treated me and Kate and Dwyer, how he got everybody to do what he wanted without ever even raising his voice, how, no matter what came up, he could handle it. But I know he wasn't always like that, I know my opinion of him was a kid's opinion. I've got to get a real fix on my father. For my own sake. Because that'll help me to get a fix on myself. On what kind of man I want to be, what I want to do with my life. . . . It sounds kind of mixed up, doesn't it . . . ?" He moved his bulky shoulders, as though he was irritated with himself.

"It's not so mixed up, Wesley," Rudolph said gently. "I'll tell you anything you want to know, anything I can remember. But first, I think, we ought to go out and have dinner." Postpone the past—the first rule of civilization.

"I could use a good meal," Wesley said, standing up. "I just ate junk food on the road. And the stuff I eat at home—" He made a face. "My mother is a health food nut. Fine for squirrels. Uncle Rudy," he smiled, "everybody keeps telling me how rich you are. Can you afford a steak?"

"I guess I'm rich enough for that," Rudolph said. "Anyway, a few times a year. Just wait here for me while I go up and say good night to the baby and get a jacket."

He was taking the jacket out of the closet when the phone rang. "Hello," he said, as he picked up the phone.

"Rudy . . ." It was Gretchen's voice. "What are you doing for dinner?" She was always most brusque and direct when she was slightly embarrassed. He hadn't spoken to her in weeks and it was a strange time for her to call, at a quarter past seven on a Friday evening.

"Well . . ." He hesitated. "I've had an unexpected visitor. Wesley. He hitchhiked in from Indianapolis. I'm taking him to dinner. Would you like to join us?"

"Is there anything special he wants to talk to you about?" She sounded disappointed.

"Not that I know of. Not anything he wouldn't want to say in front of you, as far as I know."

"I wouldn't like to interfere . . ."

"Don't be silly, Gretchen. Is there anything special *you* want to talk to me about?" The last time they had had a meal together she had seemed distracted and had let drop enough hints for him to guess that she was having trouble with the Hollywood director with whom she was working and having an on-again, off-again affair. What was his name? Kinsella. Evans Kinsella. Arrogant Hollywood sonofabitch. Gretchen had had luck once in her life with a man and that man had run a car into a tree. Rudolph supposed that Kinsella had something to do with her call, but she could bring that up if she wished after he had packed Wesley off to the YMCA.

"I just called," Gretchen said, "because I'm at something of a loose end for the evening. My boyfriend stood me up. For a change." She laughed mirthlessly. "So I thought about family. Weekends are a good time for loose ends and family." But she still didn't say whether she would come to dinner. Instead she said, "How's Wesley?"

"Getting along," Rudolph said. "Bigger than ever. As serious as ever. More so."

"In trouble?" she asked.

"No more than you and I," he said lightly.

"Do you think he'd object to seeing me?"

"Absolutely not. In fact he said we were at the top of the list of people he wanted to see."

"What did he mean by that?" She sounded worried.

"I'll fill you in after dinner. He wants a steak." He told her the name of the restaurant.

He hung up and put on his jacket and went downstairs. Wesley was standing in the middle of the living room staring about him. "You know something," Wesley said and grinned as he said it. "This is my idea of a real Christian home."


As they went down Third Avenue toward the restaurant, Rudolph noted how much like his brother Tom Wesley walked—the same almost-slouch, with a warning swinging of the shoulders. When he and Tom were young, Rudolph had thought it was a conscious pose, an advertisement that here was a predatory and dangerous male on the loose, to be avoided. Later as a grown man, Rudolph saw his brother's manner of walking as a way of avoiding pain, a signal that he wanted the world to leave him alone.

Rudolph's own gliding, slow walk, with shoulders stiff, was a manufactured gait, which he had developed as a youth because he thought it was gentlemanly, Ivy League. He no longer cared about seeming gentlemanly and he had met enough Ivy Leaguers in business not to be anxious to be taken as one of them. But his way of walking was now a part of him. To change it now would be an affectation.

When he had told Wesley that Gretchen was dining with them, Wesley's face had brightened and he'd said, "That's great. She's swell, a real lady. What a difference between her and some of the dames we had to put up with on the boat." He wagged his head humorously. "Money coming out of their ears, their tits showing day and night, and treating everybody like dirt." The two beers had loosened his vocabulary. "You know, I sometimes wonder how it happens some women who never lifted a finger in their lives can act like they own the whole goddamn world."

"They practice in front of a mirror," Rudolph said.

"Practice in front of a mirror." Wesley laughed. "I got to remember that. Aunt Gretchen works, doesn't she?"

"Very hard," Rudolph said.

"I guess that's what does it. If you don't work, you're just shit. You don't mind the way I talk, do you?" he asked anxiously.

"Not at all."

"My father was kind of free talking," Wesley said. "He said he didn't like people who talked as though they had an anchor up their ass. He said there was a difference between talking dirty and talking ugly."

"Your father had a point there." Rudolph, who had never gotten over his boyhood aversion to swearing and carefully censored his speech at all times, suddenly wondered if his brother had included him among the people who spoke as though they had an anchor up their ass.

"You know," Wesley went on, "Bunny thought your sister was something special, too. He told me *you* should have married somebody like her."

"That would have been a little awkward," Rudolph said, "seeing that we were sister and brother and I wasn't the pharaoh of Egypt."

"What's that?" Wesley said.

"I'm sorry," Rudolph said. His embarrassment—jealousy?—at Wesley's open admiration for his sister had made him pedantic in self-defense. "It was the custom in ancient Egypt in the families of the pharaohs."

"I get it," Wesley said. "I guess I'm not what you might call well educated."

"You're young yet."

"Yeah," Wesley said, brooding over his youth.

The boy had good stuff in him, Rudolph was sure, and it was criminal that by law the Kralers were given the right to warp or destroy it. He was going to see Johnny Heath in the morning when Johnny and his wife came to drive down to Montauk with him and Enid. He'd ask Johnny once more if there weren't some legal way to get the boy out of his mother's clutches.

"What about education?" Rudolph said. "Are you going on to college?"

The boy shrugged. "My mother says it'd be a waste of money on me. I read a lot, but not what they tell me to read in school. I've been studying up some on the Mormons. I guess I wanted to find out if Mr. Kraler and my mother were like they are because they're Mormons or because they're my mother and Mr. Kraler." He grinned. "The way I figure it now, they started out as awful people, and their religion brought out the worst in them. But," he said seriously, "it's a queer religion. They sure were brave, the Mormons, fighting off the whole United States and all, and going in wagons halfway across America and settling in the desert and making it bloom, the way they say. But all those wives! I look at my mother and I swear, it makes you wonder why anybody would ever want to get married. You lis-

ten for ten minutes to my mother and one wife is one
wife too many. Marriage in general . . ." He scowled.
"Our family, for instance. You got divorced, Aunt
Gretchen got divorced, my father got divorced . . .
What's it all about? I ask myself."

"You're not the first man to ask himself that question," Rudolph said. "Maybe it's the times we live in.
We're adjusting to new stances in each other, as the so-
ciologists would put it, and perhaps we're not ready for
it."

"There's a girl in school," Wesley said, scowling
again, "pretty as a ripe red apple and older than me.
I . . . well . . . I fooled around with her in the back
of a car, in her own house, when her parents were
out—a couple of times—and she started talking about
marriage. I couldn't get her off the subject. I just
stopped seeing her. You going to get married again?"
He peered fiercely at Rudolph, suspecting wedding
bells.

"It's hard to say," Rudolph said. "At the moment I
have no plans."

"Religion is a funny thing," Wesley said abruptly, as
though the exchange about marriage had embarrassed
him and he wanted to get away from it as quickly as
possible. "I want to believe in God," Wesley said earnestly. "After all, there *had* to be something that started
the whole shebang going, wasn't there? I mean how we
got here, what we're doing here, how everything works,
like how we have air to breathe, water to drink, food to
eat. I read the whole Bible through the last few months.
There're no answers there, I tell you—at least not for
me."

Oh, dear nephew, Rudolph wanted to say, when your
uncle was sixteen he was there before you. And found
no answers.

"What are you supposed to believe?" Wesley asked.

"Do you believe in those copper plates the Mormons say Joseph Smith found in upstate New York and never showed to anybody? How do they expect people to believe stuff like that?"

"Well, Moses came down off Mount Sinai with the Ten Commandments carved in stone by God," Rudolph said, relieved that Wesley had not asked him about his own beclouded lack of religion. "A lot of people have believed *that* story for thousands of years."

"Do you? I mean do *you* believe it?"

"No."

"In school, too, they tell you a lot of things that just want to make you laugh out loud. They spend hours trying to tell you that black and white are the same thing and all you have to do is go out the door and walk one block and you see it just ain't so. It was different in France. Or maybe *I* was different in France. I was doing fine in France, even with the language problem— but in Indianapolis . . ." He shrugged. "Most of the teachers seem full of shit to me. They spend most of the time trying to keep the kids from yelling in classroom and throwing spitballs, if they're not knifing each other. If college is anything like that, I'd say, Fuck it." He looked inquiringly at Rudolph. "What's your opinion about college? I mean, for me?"

"It's all according to what you want to do with your life," Rudolph said carefully. He was touched by the boy's naive garrulousness, his trust that his uncle would not betray him to the adult world.

"Who the hell knows?" Wesley said. "I have some notions. I'm not ready to tell anybody about them yet." His tone was suddenly cold.

"For example," Rudolph said, ignoring the change in Wesley's attitude, "you know something about the sea. You like it, don't you?"

"I did," Wesley said bitterly.

"You might want to go into the merchant marine."

"It's a dog's life, Bunny says."

"Not necessarily. It wasn't a dog's life for Bunny on the *Clothilde,* was it?"

"No."

"It isn't a dog's life if you're an officer on a decent ship, if you get to be a captain . . ."

"I guess not."

"There's a merchant marine academy right here in New York. When you get out of it you're an officer right off."

"Ah," Wesley said reflectively. "Maybe I ought to look into that."

"I'll ask around," Rudolph said, "and write you what I find out. Just remember to ask for your mail at General Delivery."

While they were waiting for Gretchen to arrive before ordering, Rudolph had a martini. It was as good a time as any to explain about the estate. "All told," Rudolph said, "after taxes and expenses for lawyers there should be a little over a hundred thousand dollars to be divided." He didn't intend to let either Wesley or Kate ever know that it was the amount he had paid for the *Clothilde* so that the estate could be liquidated. "One-third to Kate," he went on, "one-third in trust for her child, with Kate as the executrix—" He didn't tell the boy about the endless hours spent in legal wrangling to reach *that* compromise. The Kralers had fought tenaciously to have Teresa, as Wesley's mother, appointed as the administrator of the whole estate. They had some legal backing for their claim, as Kate was not an American citizen and was domiciled in England. Heath had had to threaten to bring up Teresa's two convictions as a prostitute and start proceedings to have her declared unfit on moral grounds to be Wesley's guardian, even though she was the boy's natural mother. Rudolph knew that for Wesley's sake he would never have allowed Johnny to go through with the action, but the threat had worked and the Kralers had finally given in and allowed Rudolph to be appointed administrator of the estate, which meant that he had to answer a long list of vengeful questions each month about the disposition of every penny that went through his hands. In addition, they were constantly threatening to sue him for faulty or criminal behavior in protecting Wesley's interest. What evil angel, Rudolph thought again and again, had touched his brother Tom's shoulder the day he asked the woman to marry him?

"That leaves approximately one-third to . . ." He stopped. "Wesley, are you listening?"

"Sure," the boy said. A waiter had gone by with a huge porterhouse steak crackling on a platter and Wesley had followed its passage across the room hungrily with his eyes. Whatever you could say about him, Rudolph thought, you could never fault him for being spoiled about money.

"As I was saying," Rudolph continued, "There's about thirty-three thousand dollars that will be put in a trust fund for you. That should bring in roughly about nineteen hundred dollars a year, which your mother is supposed to use for your support. At the age of eighteen you get the whole thing to use as you see fit. I advise you to leave it in the trust fund. The income won't be very much but it could help you pay for college if that's what you want. Are you following me, Wesley?"

Again he had lost the boy's attention. Wesley was gazing with open admiration at a flashy blond lady in a mink coat who had come in with two paunchy men with gray hair and white ties. The restaurant, Rudolph knew, was a favorite of the more successful members of the

Mafia and the girls who came in on their arms made for stern competition with the food.

"Wesley," Rudolph said plaintively. "I'm talking about money."

"I know," Wesley said apologetically. "But, holy man, that is something, isn't it?"

"It comes with money, Wesley," Rudolph said. As an uncle he felt he had to instill a true sense of value in the boy. "Nineteen hundred dollars a year may not mean much to you," he said, "but when I was your age . . ." Now he knew he would sound pompous if he finished the sentence. "The hell with it. I'll write it all down in my letter."

Just then he saw Gretchen come in and he waved to her. Both of the men stood up as she approached the table. She kissed Rudolph on the cheek, then threw her arms around Wesley and kissed him, hard. "Oh, I'm so glad to see you," she said. Her voice, to Rudolph's surprise, was trembling. He felt a twinge of pity for her as he watched the two of them, Gretchen staring hard into the boy's face, fighting with an emotion he could not identify. Perhaps she was thinking of her own son, lost to her, rejecting her, making excuses to her as to why she should not come to Brussels whenever she wrote him that she would like to visit him. "You look wonderful," Gretchen said, still holding onto the boy. "Although you could use a new suit."

They both laughed.

"If you'll stay over until Monday," Gretchen said, finally releasing Wesley and sitting down, "I'll take you to Saks and see if they have anything there to fit you."

"I'm sorry," Wesley said as he and Rudolph seated themselves. "I've got to be on my way tomorrow."

"You just came here for one day?" Gretchen said incredulously.

"He's a busy man," Rudolph said. He didn't want to

listen to Gretchen's predictable explosion of wrath if she heard about Mr. and Mrs. Kraler's Christian concept of money for the young. "Now, let's order. I'm starved."

Over the meal, Wesley began to ask the questions about his father. "I told Uncle Rudy, back in his house," Wesley said as he wolfed down his steak, "why I want to know—why I *have* to know, what my old man was like. Really like, I mean. He told me a lot before he died, and Bunny told me even more—but so far it hasn't added up. I mean, my father's just bits and pieces for me. There's all those stories about what a terror he was as a kid and as a young man, how much trouble he got into . . . how people hated him. How he hated people. You and Uncle Rudy, too. . . ." He looked gravely first at Gretchen and then at Rudolph. "But then when I saw him with you, he didn't hate you. He—well—I suppose I got to say it—he loved you. He was unhappy most of his life, he told me—and then—well, he said it himself—he learned to lose enemies—to be happy. Well, I want to learn to be happy, myself." Now the boy was frankly crying, while at the same time eating large chunks of the rare steak, as though he hadn't eaten in weeks.

"The crux of the matter," Gretchen said, putting down her knife and fork and speaking slowly, "is Rudy. Do you mind if I say that, Rudy?"

"Say whatever you want. If I think you're wrong, I'll correct you." Some other time he might tell the boy how and when his father had learned to be happy. The day he found out that Rudolph, unknown to him, had invested the five thousand dollars Tom had laid his hands on by blackmailing a kleptomaniac lawyer in Boston. The return of the blood money, Tom had called it, the same amount their father had to pay to get Tom out of the jail where he was facing a charge of rape. Tom had thrown the hundred-dollar bills on the hotel bed, saying, "I want to pay off our fucking family and this does it. Piss on it. Blow it on dames. Give it to your favorite charity. I'm not walking out of this room with it." Five thousand dollars which by careful babying along had grown to sixty thousand through the years when Rudolph hadn't known where Tom was, whether he was alive or dead, and which had finally enabled Tom to buy a ship and rename it the *Clothilde*. "Your father," he might say at that future date, "became happy through crime, luck and money, and was smart enough to use all three things for the one act that could save him." He didn't believe that saying it would help Wesley much. Wesley did not seem inclined to crime, his luck so far had been all bad and his devotion to money nonexistent.

"Rudy," Gretchen was saying, "was the white-haired boy of the family. If there was any love my parents had to spare, it was for him. I'm not saying he didn't deserve it—he was the one who helped out in the store, he was the one who got the highest marks in school, he was the one who was the star of the track team, he was the one who was expected to go to college. He was the one who got presents, birthday celebrations, he was the only one who had a freshly ironed shirt to go out in, an expensive trumpet, so he could play in a band. All the hope in the family was invested in him. As for me and Tom . . ." She shrugged. "We were outcasts. No college for me— when I finished high school I was sent out to work and had to pay almost all of my salary into the family kitty. When Rudolph went out with a girl, my mother would make sure he had pocket money to entertain her. When I had an affair, she called me a whore. As for Tom— I've heard our parents predict a hundred times that he'd wind up in jail. When they talked to him, which was as little as possible, they snarled at him. I think he said to himself, Well if that's the way you think I am, that's what I'm going to be. Frankly, I was terrified of him. He had a streak of violence in him that was frightening. I avoided him. When I was walking down the street with any of my friends I'd pretend I didn't see him, so I wouldn't have to introduce him. When he left town and dropped out of sight, I was glad. For years I didn't even think about him. Now I realize I was wrong. At least we two should have made some sort of combination, a common front against the rest of the family. I was too young then to realize it, but I was afraid he'd drag me down to his level. I was a snob, although never as much a snob as Rudy, and I thought of Tom as a dangerous peasant. When I went to New York and for a while became an actress, then started writing for magazines, I cringed in fear that he'd look me up and make me lose all my friends. When I finally did see him—Rudy took me to see him fight once—I was horrified, both by him and your mother. They seemed to come from another world. An awful world. I snubbed them and fled. I was ashamed that I was connected to them in any way. All this may be too painful for you, Wesley . . ."

Wesley nodded. "It's painful," he said, "but I asked you. I don't want any fairy tales."

Gretchen turned to Rudolph. "I hope I haven't been too rough on you, Rudy, with my little history of the happy childhood we spent together."

"No," Rudolph said. " 'Beauty is truth, truth beauty'—you know the rest. I was a prig, Wesley," he said, tearing at old scars, "and I imagine you guessed that. In fact, I wouldn't hold it against you if you thought so now. I don't suppose your father would have used that word. What he would have said, if he had thought it out, was that everything I did was fake—not for myself, but for its effects on other people, mostly older people, people in authority. The way I look back

on it now, I used the word prig. But back then the way
I acted was an escape hatch from the world my mother
and father were caught in." He laughed ruefully. "The
injustice of it is in that it worked. I *did* escape."

"You ride yourself too hard, Uncle Rudy," Wesley
said quietly. "Why don't you give yourself a break once
in a while? My father said that you saved his life."

"Did he?" Rudolph said, surprised. "He never told
me that."

"He didn't hold with praising people to their face,"
Wesley said. "He didn't praise me much, I can tell you
that. . . ." He grinned. He had even white teeth and a
sweet smile that changed the entire look of his sharp,
brooding face, made it seem boyish and open. Rudolph
wished he would smile more. "And he didn't go overboard praising Bunny or even Kate, except for her
cooking, and that was more of a joke than anything
else, because she was English. Even when I first got to
know him, when he was off by himself and didn't think
anybody was watching him, there was something sad
about him, as though there were a lot of bad things that
had happened to him that he couldn't forget. But he did
say you saved his life."

"I only gave him some money that was coming to
him," Rudolph said. "I guess you realize by now that
Gretchen was trying to show you how and why your
father became what he was as a young man. . . . That
the family made him that way."

"Yeah," Wesley said, "I see that."

"It's true," Rudolph said, "and again, it's not true.
There are some excuses, as there always are. It's not my
fault that I was the oldest son, that my father was an
ignorant and violent man with a hideous past that had
been no fault of his own. It wasn't my fault that my
mother was a frigid, hysterical woman with idiotically
genteel pretensions. It wasn't my fault that Gretchen

was a sentimental and selfish little fool. . . . Forgive me," he said to Gretchen. "I'm not going through all this for your sake or mine. It's for Wesley."

"I understand," Gretchen said, bent over her food, half hiding her face.

"After all," Rudolph said, "the three of us had the same genes, the same influences. Maybe that's why Gretchen said just now that your father was frightening. What she was afraid of was that what she saw in him she saw in herself, and recoiled from it. What I saw in him was a reflection of our father, a ferocious man chained to an impossible job, pathologically afraid of ending his life a pauper—so much so that he finally committed suicide rather than face up to the prospect. I recoiled in my own way. Toward money, respectability . . ."

Wesley nodded soberly. "Maybe it's lucky Kraler's kid is in Vietnam. Who knows what he'd do for me if I had to eat dinner every night with him?"

"There have been second sons before your father," Rudolph said, "in worse families, and they didn't go around trying to destroy everything they touched. I don't like to say this, Wesley, but until the day of our mother's funeral, I believed that your father was born with an *affinity* for destruction, an affinity that gave him great pleasure. Destruction of all kinds. Including self-destruction."

"It sure turned out that way," Wesley said bitterly, "didn't it?"

"What he did that night in Cannes," Rudolph said, "was admirable. By his lights. And to tell the truth, by my lights, too. You mustn't forget that."

"I'll try not to forget it," Wesley said. "But it's not easy. Waste, that's what I think it really was. Crazy *macho* waste."

Rudolph sighed. "I think we've told you everything

we could for now, as honestly as we could. We'll save the anecdotes for another time. You must be tired. I'll send you a list of names of people you might want to talk to who'll perhaps be more helpful than we've been. Finish your dinner and then I'll ride you over to the YMCA."

"No need," Wesley said shortly. "I can walk through the park."

"Nobody walks through the park in New York at night alone," Gretchen said.

Wesley stared at her coldly. "*I* do," he said.

Christ, Rudolph thought, as he watched the boy finish the last bit of his steak, he looks and sounds just like his father. God help him.

# CHAPTER 4

Rudolph stood on the sidewalk in the morning sunlight with Enid and her nurse, waiting for Johnny Heath and his wife to come by in their Lincoln Continental and pick Enid and himself up for the trip to Montauk. The nurse had a suitcase with her. She was off for her family in New Jersey for the week. Somehow, Rudolph thought idly, children's nurses never seemed to have families who lived in the same state in which they worked. Enid was carrying some schoolbooks and her homework to do over the holiday. The nurse had packed a bag for her. He had a small overnight bag with his shaving kit, pajamas and a clean shirt.

The night before, after they had said good-bye to Wesley, Rudolph had walked Gretchen to her apartment. He had invited her to come with him and the Heaths to Montauk. She had looked at him strangely and he remembered that she had once had an affair with Heath. "You want a lot of witnesses present when you see your ex-wife, don't you?" she had said.

He hadn't really thought about this, but as she said it, he recognized the truth of what she had said. Jean had

visited him once, with the burly masseuse she had hired
as her companion in Reno, and the meeting had been
an uncomfortable one, although Jean had been sober,
reasonable, subdued, even when she had played with
Enid. She was leading the quiet life, she said, in a small
house she had bought for herself at Montauk. Mexico
had not worked out. It was a drinking man's climate,
she had decided, too raw for her nerves. She was completely dried out, she had said, with a tiny smile, and
had even begun to take photographs again. She hadn't
tried to place them in any magazines. She was just
doing it for herself, proud of the fact that her hands
were steady again. Once more, except for the heavy
presence of the masseuse, she was so much the woman
he had married and loved for so long—shining of hair,
her delicate, pink-tinted complexion healthy and youthful—that he started wondering uncomfortably all over
again if he had done the right thing in consenting to the
divorce. Pity was mixed in his feeling, but pity for himself, too. When she had called a few days ago to ask if
she could have Enid for a week, he could not say no.

He had no fears for Enid, but feared for himself, if
he and Jean had to spend any time alone in what she
described as a cosy small house filled with the sound of
an uncosy large ocean. She had invited him to stay in
the guest room, but he had made a reservation at a
nearby motel. As an afterthought, he had invited the
Heaths. He didn't want to be tempted by an evening in
front of a blazing fire in a silent house, lulled by the
sound of the sea, to go back to domesticity. Let the past
belong to the past. Hence the Heaths. Hence Gretchen's
sharp question.

"I don't need any witnesses," he said. "Johnny and I
have a lot of things to talk about and I hate to have to
go to his office."

"I see," Gretchen had said, unconvincingly, and had

changed the subject. "What's your opinion about the boy. Wesley?"

"He's a thoughtful young man," Rudolph said. "Maybe too—well—interior. How he turns out all depends on if he can survive his mother and her husband until he's eighteen."

"He's a beautiful young man," Gretchen said. "Don't you think so?"

"I hadn't thought about it."

"It's a marvelous face for the movies," Gretchen said. "The tough bones, the sweet smile, the moral weight, to be fancy about it, the tenderness in the eyes."

"Maybe you're more perceptive than I am," was all that Rudolph had answered.

"Or more vulnerable." She smiled.

"You sounded on the phone as though there was something you wanted to talk to me about," he said. "Are you in trouble?"

"No more than usual." She smiled again. "I'll tell you about it when you get back to town."

He had kissed her good night in front of her apartment house and watched her go into the lighted lobby, guarded by a doorman. She looked trim, capable, desirable, able to take care of herself. Occasionally, he thought. Only occasionally.

The Lincoln Continental drove up, Johnny Heath at the wheel, his wife Elaine beside him. The nurse kissed Enid good-bye. "You're going to be a good little girl, aren't you, miss?" the nurse said.

"No," said Enid, "I'm going to be a horrid little girl." She chortled.

Rudolph laughed and the nurse looked at him reprovingly. "Sorry, Anna," he said, straightening his face.

Elaine Heath got out of the front of the car and

helped establish Enid in the rear with her. She was a
tall, exquisitely groomed woman, with hard, intelligent
eyes, fitting wife to a man who was a partner in one of
the most successful firms on Wall Street. The Heaths
had no children.

He got in beside Johnny. Enid waved at the nurse
standing with her bag on the sidewalk and they drove
off. "Hi, ho," Johnny said, at the wheel, "on to the orgies of Montauk, to the lobsters and the nude clam-
bakes on the white beaches." His face was soft and
round, his eyes deceptively mild, his hands on the wheel
pale, with only the smallest suggestion of fat, his paunch
just a tiny hint of things to come under his checked
sports jacket. He drove aggressively and well. Other
drivers were forced to respect Johnny Heath's right of
way, as other lawyers had to respect his tenacity and
purpose in a boardroom or before the bench. Rudolph
did not see Johnny often; after the Heaths' marriage
they had drifted apart somewhat, and each time Rudolph saw his old friend after a lapse of months, he
thought, with no regret, I might have looked like that,
too.

Behind him he heard the child prattling happily. He
heard Elaine whispering into her ear, making Enid
laugh. To look at her, one would think that Elaine
would dread embracing a child, fear that her handsome
tweed suit would be wrinkled or dirtied. When Rudolph
turned around he saw that Enid was mussing Elaine's
perfectly set hair and that Elaine was smiling happily.
You never could tell about anybody, Rudolph thought
as he turned back and watched the road. They were
crossing the Triborough Bridge and New York
stretched alongside the river, towers, glass, smoke, the
old, enormous, impossible engine glittering in the morning springtime sun. Only at certain moments, moments
like this one, when he saw the city as a great, challeng-

ing entity, its harsh, imperial beauty falling into a cohe-
sive pattern, did he feel any of the thrill, the satisfaction
of belonging, that had moved him daily when he was
younger.

Down below, on the swiftly moving river, a small
yacht chugged bravely against the current. Perhaps, he
thought, this summer I will board the *Clothilde* and set
sail for Italy. Might as well get some use out of the
boat. They had been on course once for Portofino but
had never reached it. Dispel ghosts. Get Jeanne somehow to escape her husband and children for two weeks
and make love at twelve knots and in a softer climate,
drink cold local wine out of a carafe at cafés along the
Ligurian shore. I must not allow myself just to become
a used-up old man. *Fantasia Italiana.*

He shook himself out of his reverie. "Johnny," he
said, "you told me over the phone that you wanted to
talk to me. What about?"

"I have a client," Johnny said; "actually it's a dead
client, whose estate has to be settled." Johnny, Rudolph
thought maliciously, makes more money out of the dead
than a cityful of undertakers. Lawyers. "The heirs are
squabbling," Johnny said, "as heirs will. You know all
about that."

"It has become my specialty," Rudolph said.

"To avoid litigation," Johnny went on, "there's a part
of the estate that's up for sale at a very decent, low
price. It's a big ranch out in Nevada. The usual income
tax benefits. I don't have to tell you about *that*."

"No," Rudolph said.

"You're not doing anything in New York," Johnny
said. "You don't look good, you certainly don't seem
happy, I don't know what the hell you do with yourself
day after day."

"I play the piano," Rudolph said.

"I haven't seen your name recently on the posters outside Carnegie Hall."

"Keep looking," Rudolph said.

"You're just sinking into decay here," Johnny said. "You're not in action anymore. Christ, nobody even sees you at any of the parties these days."

"How're the parties in Nevada?"

"Jamborees," Johnny said defensively. "It's one of the fastest-growing states in the union. People're becoming millionaires by the dozen. Just to show you I'm not kidding, if you say yes, I'll go in half with you—arrange the mortgages, help you find people to run it. I'm not just being altruistic, old buddy, I could use a place to hide from time to time myself. And I could also use a little tax shelter in the golden West. I haven't seen the place myself, but I've seen the books. It's viable. With some smart additional investment, a lot more than viable. There's a great big house there that with a little fixing up would be a dream. And there's no better place to bring up kids—no pollution, no drugs, a hundred miles away from the nearest city. And politics are nicely controlled there; it's a sweet, tight operation—you could move into it like a fish in water. And they never heard of Whitby, New York. Anyway, that's all forgotten by now, even in Whitby, even with that goddamn article in *Time*. In ten years you could wind up being senator. Are you listening to me, Rudy?"

"Of course." Actually, he hadn't been listening too closely for the last few seconds. What Johnny had said about its being a place to bring up kids had intrigued him. He had Enid to think of, of course, but there were also Wesley and Billy. Flesh and blood. He worried for them. Billy was a drifter—even as a boy in school he had been cynical, without ambition, a sardonic dropout from society. Wesley, as far as Rudolph could tell, had no particular talents, and whatever education he might receive was unlikely to improve his chances for an honorable life. On a modern ranch, with its eternal problems of drought, flood and fertility and the newer necessity for shrewd handling of machinery, employees, the marketplace, there would be plenty of work for the two of them to keep them out of trouble. And eventually they'd have families of their own. And there was always the possibility that he'd marry again—why not?—and have more children. "The dream of the patriarch," he said aloud.

"What was that?" Johnny asked, puzzled.

"Nothing, I was talking to myself. Seeing myself surrounded by my flocks and my progeny."

"It isn't as though you'd be stuck in the wilderness," Johnny said, mistaking the intention of what Rudolph had said, believing it to be ironic. "There's a landing strip on the property. You could have your own plane."

"The American dream," Rudolph said. "A landing strip on the property."

"Well, what's wrong with the American dream?" Johnny demanded. "Mobility isn't a venal sin. You could be in Reno or San Francisco in an hour whenever you wanted. What do you think? It's not like retiring, though it has a lot of its advantages. It's getting into action again—a new kind of action. . . ."

"I'll think about it," Rudolph said.

"Why don't you plan—why don't we *both* plan—to fly out there next week and take a look?" Johnny said. "That can't do any harm, can it? And it'd give me a good excuse to get away from the damned office. Hell, even if it turned out to be worthless, it'd be a vacation. You can bring your piano along."

Heavy irony, Rudolph thought. He knew that Johnny considered his having retired a kind of whimsical aberration, a vastly premature symptom of the male menopause. When Johnny retired it would be to the ceme-

tery. They had come up together, they had made a great
deal of money together, they had never cheated each
other, they understood each other, and Rudolph knew
that Johnny felt that as an act and seal of their friendship he had to get Rudolph moving again.

"Well," Rudolph said, "I've always dreamed of
riding across the desert on a horse."

"It's not desert," Johnny said testily. "It's ranchland.
And it's at the foot of the mountains. There's a trout
stream on the property."

"I can take a couple of days off this week," Rudolph
said, "while Enid's with Jean. Can you get away?"

"I'll buy the tickets," Johnny said.

While they drove swiftly past the endless graveyards
of Long Island, where the generations of New Yorkers
have hidden their dead, Rudolph closed his eyes and
dreamed of the mesas and mountains of the silver state
of Nevada.

Usually, Gretchen liked to work on Saturdays, just
she and her assistant, Ida Cohen, alone in the cutting
room in the deserted, silent building. But today Ida
could tell Gretchen wasn't enjoying herself at all as she
shuttled the moviola back and forth, running the film
irritably through her white-gloved hands, pushing the
slicing lever down with sharp little snaps and whistling
mournfully, when she wasn't sighing in despair. Ida
knew why Gretchen was in a bad mood this morning.
The director, Evans Kinsella, was up to his old tricks,
shooting lazily, incoherently, fighting a hangover, letting
the actors get away with murder, trusting that somehow
Gretchen would make sense out of the wasteful miles of
film he was throwing at her. And Ida had been in the
room the day before when Kinsella had phoned to say
that he couldn't take Gretchen to dinner as he had
promised.

By now, Ida, whose loyalty to the woman she worked with was absolute, loathed Kinsella with an intensity of feeling that she otherwise reserved for the cause of Women's Liberation, a movement whose meetings she attended religiously and at which she made passionate and somewhat demented speeches. Fat and short, she had even gone so far as to renounce wearing a brassiere, until Gretchen had scowled at her and said, "Christ, Ida, with udders like yours, you're putting the movement back a century."

Ida, forty-five years old and plain, with no man in her private life to bully her, believed that Gretchen, beautiful and talented, allowed herself to be taken advantage of by men. She had persuaded Gretchen to accompany her to two of the meetings, but Gretchen had been bored and annoyed by the shrillness of some of the orators and had left early, saying, "When you go to the barricades you can count on me. Not before."

"But we need women just like you," Ida had pleaded.

"Maybe," Gretchen had said, "but I don't need *them.*"

Ida had sighed hopelessly at what she told Gretchen was sinful political abdication.

Gretchen had more to bother her that morning than the quality of the film she was working on. During the week, Kinsella had tossed a screenplay at her and asked her to read it. It was by a young writer, unknown to either of them, but whose agent had been insistent that Kinsella look at it.

Gretchen had read it and thought it was brilliant, and when Kinsella had called the afternoon before to break their date for dinner had told him so. "Brilliant?" he had said over the phone. "I think it's a load of shit. Give it to my secretary and tell her to send it back." He had hung up before she could argue with him. Instead, she had stayed up until two in the morning re-reading it.

Although it was written by a young man, the central role was that of a strong-minded, young, working-class woman, sunk in the drabness and hopelessness of the people around her, a girl who, of all her generation in the small, dreary town in which she lived, had the wit and courage to break out, live up to her dream of herself.

It could be a bracing corrective, Gretchen believed, to the recent spate of films which, overcorrecting for the happy-ending fairy tales that Hollywood had been sending out for so long, now had all their characters aimlessly drifting, reacting with a poor little flicker of revolt against their fates, and then sinking hopelessly back into apathy, leaving the viewer with a taste of mud in his mouth. If the old Hollywood pictures, with their manufactured sugar-candy optimism were false, Gretchen thought, these new listless dirges were equally false. Heroes emerged daily. If it was true that they did not rise with their class, it wasn't true that they all *sank* with their class.

When she had finished reading, she was more convinced than ever that her first impression had been correct and that if Kinsella could be pulled up again to the level of his earlier work, he would finish with a dazzling movie. She had even called his hotel at two-thirty in the morning to tell him so, but his phone hadn't answered. All this was going through her mind, like a looped piece of film in which the action of a scene is repeated over and over again, as she worked on the shoddy results of Kinsella's last week of shooting.

Suddenly, she turned the machine off. "Ida," she said, "I have something I want you to do for me."

"Yes?" Ida looked up from her filing and registration of film clips.

Gretchen had the script with her in the big shoulder bag she always wore to work. She went over to where it was hanging and took it out. "I'm going to a museum for an hour or so," she said. "Meanwhile I want you to drop that trash you're fiddling with and read this for me." She handed the script to Ida. "When I get back, we'll go out to a girly lunch, just you and me, and I'd like to discuss it with you."

Ida looked at her doubtfully as she took the script. It wasn't like Gretchen to break off in the middle of work for anything more than a container of coffee. "Of course," she said. She adjusted her glasses and looked down at the script in her hands as though afraid it might contain an explosive device.

Gretchen put on her coat and went downstairs and into the bustle of Seventh Avenue, where the building was located. She walked swiftly crosstown and went into the Museum of Modern Art, to soothe her nerves, she told herself, wrongly, with honest works of art. When she came out, she was no more soothed than when she went in. She couldn't bear the thought of going back to the moviola after more than an hour of Picasso and Renoir and Henry Moore, so she telephoned the cutting room and asked Ida to meet her at a restaurant nearby. "And put some makeup on and straighten your stockings," she told Ida cruelly. "The restaurant is French and fancy, but fancy-fancy. I'm treating—because I'm in trouble."

Waiting for Ida in the restaurant, she had a Scotch at the bar. She never drank during the day, but, she told herself defiantly, there's no law against it. It's Saturday.

When Ida came in and saw Gretchen at the bar, she asked, suspiciously, "What're you drinking?"

"Scotch."

"You *are* in trouble." Philosophically in the vanguard of modern thought, as she believed she was, in her daily life Ida was grimly puritanical.

"Two Scotches, please," Gretchen said to the bartender.

"I can't work after I've had anything to drink," Ida said plaintively. "You know that."

"You're not going to work this afternoon," Gretchen said. "Nobody's going to work this afternoon. I thought you were against sweated female labor. Especially on Saturdays. Aren't you always telling me that what this country needs is the twenty-hour week?"

"That's just the theory," Ida said defensively, eyeing the glass that the bartender set down in front of her with repugnance. "Personally I *choose* to work."

"Not today," Gretchen said firmly. She waved to the maitre d'hôtel. "A table for two, please. And send over the drinks." She left two dollars, grandly, as a tip for the bartender.

"That's an awful big tip for just three drinks," Ida whispered as they followed the maitre d'hôtel toward the rear of the restaurant.

"One of the things that will make us women equal to men," Gretchen said, "is the size of our tips."

The maitre d'hôtel pulled out the two chairs at one of the tables just next to the kitchen.

"You see—Ida glared around her. "The restaurant's almost empty and he puts us next to the kitchen. Just because there isn't a man along."

"Drink your whiskey," Gretchen said. "We'll get our revenge in heaven."

Ida sipped at her drink and made a face. "While you were at it," she said, "you might have ordered something sweet."

"On to the barricades, where there are no sweet drinks," Gretchen said. "And now tell me what you think of the script."

Ida's face lit up. A well-done scene in a movie, a passage she admired in a book, could make her euphoric.

"It's wonderful," she said. "God, what a picture it's going to make."

"Except it looks as though no one is going to make it," Gretchen said. "I think it's been around and our beloved Evans Kinsella was the agent's last gasp."

"Has he read it yet—Evans?"

"Yes," Gretchen said. "He thinks it's a load of shit. His words. He told me to give the script to his secretary to send back."

"Vulgarian," Ida said hotly. "And to think what a big shot he is. How much is the picture we're on going to cost?"

"Three and a half million."

"There's something goddamn wrong with the business, with the world, for that matter," Ida said, "if they give a fool like that three and a half million dollars to play around with."

"He's had two big hits in the last three years," Gretchen said.

"Luck," Ida said, "that's all—luck."

"I'm not so sure it's only that," Gretchen said. "He has his moments."

"Not three and a half million dollars' worth," Ida said stubbornly. "And I don't know why you stick up for him. The way he treats you. And I'm not talking about only in the office, either."

"Oh," Gretchen said with a lightness that she didn't feel, "a little touch of masochism never hurt a girl."

"Sometimes, Gretchen," Ida said primly, "you drive me crazy, you really do."

The waiter was standing over them now, his pad and pencil ready.

"Time to order," Gretchen said. She looked at the menu. "They have roast duck with olives. That's for two. Do you want to share it with me?"

"All right," Ida said. "I don't like olives. You can have them all."

Gretchen ordered the duck and a bottle of Pouilly Fumé.

"Not a whole bottle," Ida said. "Please. I won't drink more than half a glass."

"A whole bottle," Gretchen said to the waiter, ignoring her.

"You'll be drunk," Ida warned her.

"Good," said Gretchen, "I have some big decisions to make and maybe I won't make them dead sober."

"You have a funny look in your eye today," Ida said.

"You bet your liberated brassiere I have," said Gretchen. She finished her second whiskey in one long gulp.

"What are you planning on doing?" Ida said. "Now don't be reckless. You're angry and you've got all that alcohol in you . . ."

"I'm angry," Gretchen said, "and I have a wee bit of whiskey in me and part of what I'm planning to do is drink most of the bottle of wine all by my little self, if you won't help me. And after that . . ." She stopped.

"After that, what?"

"After that," Gretchen said, "I'm not quite sure." She laughed. The laughter sounded so strange that Ida was convinced that Gretchen was in the first stages of descending alcoholism. "After that I'm going to have a little talk with Evans Kinsella. If I can find him, which I doubt."

"What are you going to say to him?" Ida asked anxiously.

"Some impolite home truths," Gretchen said. "For starters."

"Be sensible," Ida said, worriedly. "After all, no matter what else he is to you, he's still your boss."

"Ida," Gretchen said, "has anyone ever told you that you have a sick respect for authority?"

"I wouldn't say sick." Ida was hurt.

"What would you say then? Exorbitant, slavish, adoring?"

"I'd say normal, if you must know. Anyway, let's get off me for a while. Just what are you going to tell him?"

"I'm going to tell him that the picture we're working on stinks. That'll be the overture," Gretchen said.

"Oh, please, Gretchen . . ." Ida put her hands up as though to stop her physically.

"Somebody ought to buy you some rings," Gretchen said. "You have pretty hands and rings would set them off nicely. Maybe we'll spend the afternoon looking for rings for you if we can't find that bastard Kinsella."

Ida looked around worriedly. The restaurant had filled by now and there were two men sitting near them. "People can hear you."

"Let them hear," Gretchen said. "I want to spread the good word around."

The waiter was at the table and expertly carving their duck. The wine was in a cooler. "No olives for me, please," Ida said. "Give them all to the lady."

Gretchen watched admiringly as the waiter deftly sectioned the duck. "I bet *he* doesn't drink during working hours," she said. Kinsella had been known to do that, too, from time to time.

"Ssh," Ida said. She smiled at the waiter, apologizing for her eccentric friend.

"Do you?" Gretchen asked the waiter.

"No, ma'am," he said. He grinned. "But I would if it was offered."

"I'll send around a bottle the first thing in the morning," Gretchen said.

"Gretchen," said Ida, "I've never seen you like this before. What's come over you?"

"Fury," Gretchen said. "Just plain old healthy fury." She tasted the duck, "Mmm," she said and drank heartily of the wine.

"If I were you," Ida said, nibbling at her food, "I'd wait until after the weekend before you did anything."

"Never postpone fury. That's an old family motto in my family," Gretchen said. "Especially over the weekend. It's hard to be furious on Monday morning. It takes a whole week to get into the proper frame of mind for fury."

"Kinsella will never forgive you if you go on at him like this," Ida said.

"After the overture," Gretchen said, disregarding Ida's interruption, "we go into the full performance. About how I only consented to work on the piece of junk he's making because I wanted to continue to enjoy the favors of his pure white body."

"Gretchen," Ida said reproachfully, "you once told me you loved him." In her spinster heart romance held a prominent place.

"Once," Gretchen said.

"You'll infuritate him."

"That's exactly my intention," said Gretchen. "To continue—I will tell him that I've read the script he told me to send back to the agent and I find it original, witty and too good for the likes of him. However, since he's the only director I happen to be half living with at the moment, and certainly the only director I'm intimate with who can raise money for a picture on the strength of his name, I will tell him that if he has the brains he was born with he'll buy it tomorrow, even if he's doing it only because I'm asking him to."

"You know he'll say no," Ida said.

"Probably."

"Then what will you do? Burst into tears and ask for his forgiveness?"

Gretchen looked at her in surprise. Ida was not ordinarily given to sarcasm. Gretchen could see that the whole conversation was disturbing her. "Ida, darling," she said gently, "you mustn't let it worry you so. After all, I'm the one who's going to do the fighting."

"I hate to see you get into trouble," Ida said.

"There're times when it can't be avoided, and this is one of the times. You asked me what I will do if he says no."

*"When* he says no," Ida said.

"I'll tell him that I'm walking off the picture as of that moment. . . ."

"You have a contract. . . ." Ida cried.

"Let him sue me. He can also go to law to get me back into his bed."

"You know that if you quit, I'll quit, too," Ida said, her voice quivering at the immensity of what she was saying.

"In a war," Gretchen said harshly, "sometimes you have to sacrifice the troops."

"This isn't a war," Ida protested. "It's just a moving picture like a thousand other moving pictures."

"That's exactly the point," Gretchen said, "I don't want to spend my life working on pictures that are just like a thousand others." She saw that Ida was near tears, her soft dark eyes getting puddly. "You don't have to pay for my peculiar notions, Ida," she said. "There's no reason you have to quit if I do."

"I won't talk about it," Ida said.

"Okay," Gretchen said. "The matter's closed. Now finish your duck. You've barely eaten a bite. Don't you like it?"

"I . . . I . . . love it," Ida blubbered.

They ate in silence for more than a minute, Gretchen helping herself to more wine. She could see Ida making an effort to compose her soft, gentle face that could

have been that of a chubby child, and for a moment was
sorry that she had given Ida the script to read, burdened
her with her own problems. Still, with her experience of
Ida's stony integrity and purity of taste, she had had to
have confirmation of the value of the script. Without it,
she would never have been sure enough to confront
Kinsella. Evans Kinsella, she thought grimly to herself,
is in for a rough afternoon, if he's home, Ida Cohen or
no Ida Cohen. If he's home.

Finally, Ida spoke. "I've been thinking," she said, her
voice almost timid. "There's another way of going about
it. You don't have to do everything head-on, do you?"

"I suppose not. I'm not good at doing things slanty-
wise, though."

Ida chuckled. "No, you're not. However—maybe this
one time you'll listen to me. You know and I know he'll
never say yes. Especially if you argue with him."

"How do you know him so well?" Gretchen asked
with mock suspicion. "Have you been having a nasty
little affair with him behind my back?"

Ida laughed aloud, her spirits restored. "How could
I?" she asked. "He's not even Jewish."

They both laughed together. Then Ida's face became
grave. "My idea is this—finish cutting the picture—"

"Oh, God," Gretchen said.

"Hush. Listen to me for a minute. I listened to *you*,
didn't I?"

"You certainly did," Gretchen admitted.

"Don't even mention the script to him again. Pretend
you've forgotten all about it."

"But I haven't forgotten about it. It's haunting me
already. Even now I can see shot after shot . . ."

"I said *pretend*," Ida said crossly. "Get someone to
put up option money and buy it yourself."

"Even if I could get the money," Gretchen said,
thinking immediately of poor Rudy, "then what?"

"Then," Ida said triumphantly, "direct it yourself."

Gretchen leaned back in her chair. Whatever had been in Ida's head, she hadn't expected this.

"My heavens," she said, "what an idea."

"Why not?" Ida said eagerly, forgetting once more to eat. "In the old days most directors came out of the cutting rooms."

"The old days," Gretchen said. "And they were all men."

"You know I don't like talk like that," Ida said reprovingly.

"Forgive me. For the moment I forgot. But just for fun, Ida, give me the names of twenty-five woman directors."

"In the old days there weren't twenty-five women in the army, either." The meetings she attended gave a solid base to Ida's arguments and she was making the most of it. "You won't go to meetings, you won't even read the pamphlets we put out—but you could do us a lot more good by coming along with a beautiful movie than if you went to a million meetings. And if you have any doubts about whether you could pull it off or not, let me tell you, you know more about movies than Evans Kinsella ever did or ever will."

"It's an idea," Gretchen said thoughtfully, "now that the first shock is over, it's an idea."

"It's not an expensive picture to make," Ida went on quickly. "A small town, mostly location and easy indoor shots, a small cast, kids mostly; you couldn't find name actors for the parts even if you had the money to spend. I know some people who put money into pictures. I could go to them. You could go to your brother . . ."

Poor Rudy, Gretchen thought again.

"How much did Evans Kinsella's first picture cost?" Ida asked.

"One hundred and twenty-five thousand," Gretchen

said promptly. Kinsella was constantly boasting that his first picture, which had had a huge commercial success, had been brought in for peanuts and he always announced the exact sum.

"A hundred and twenty-five thousand," Ida said. "And now they give him three and a half million."

"That's show business," Gretchen said.

"Times have changed," Ida said, "and a hundred and twenty-five is impossible these days. But I bet we could do this one for no more than seven hundred and fifty thousand. Most of the actors'd work for scale, and with parts like these the leads would defer their salaries and take percentages. All the money would be on the screen, no place else."

"Dear Ida," Gretchen said, "you're already beginning to talk like a movie mogul."

"Just promise me one thing," Ida said.

"What's that?" Gretchen asked suspiciously.

"Don't call Kinsella today or tomorrow. Think everything over at least until Monday."

Gretchen hesitated. "Okay," she said, "but you're depriving me of a lovely fight."

"Just think of what Kinsella's face will look like when the movie comes out, and you won't mind giving up the satisfaction of telling him what a jerk he is."

"All right, I promise," Gretchen said. "Now let's order a gorgeous, gooey French dessert and then we'll indulge ourselves to the full the rest of the afternoon. Tell me—how many times have you seen Bergman's *Wild Strawberries?*"

"Five times."

"All right, I promise," Gretchen said. "Now let's play hooky this afternoon and make it an even half-dozen."

Driving home through the Sunday-afternoon traffic, in the rear of the Continental, with Johnny Heath at the wheel and Elaine in front beside him, Rudolph reflected upon the weekend. It had been a success, he thought. Jean's house had been cosy, as she had promised, and the view of the ocean glorious. The masseuse did not seem to be a lesbian and turned out to be a very good cook indeed. There had been no orgies, no nude clam-bakes on the beach, despite Johnny's prediction, but there had been long walks on the hard sand left by the ebbing tide, all of them together, with Enid holding her mother's hand. The two of them had been delighted with each other, and without saying anything about it, Rudolph had thought that it might be a good idea for Enid to stay with her mother and go to a small country school rather than face the perils of the streets of New York. He could always see the child on weekends and school holidays. Of course, if he was to take Johnny's wild idea about Nevada seriously there would be com-plications. Anyway, it wouldn't be tomorrow or next week, probably not even next year.

Jean had looked healthy and fit. She and the mas-seuse did Spartan exercises each morning and Jean wandered for miles each day along the shore looking for subjects to photograph. She seemed happy, in a dreamy, reticent way, like a child who had just wakened after a pleasant dream. She had been pleased to see the Heaths and content to spend the short weekend in a group. Nei-ther she nor the masseuse, whose name was Lorraine, had attempted to get him off for a private conversation. If Jean had any friends in the neighborhood, they did not appear either on Saturday or Sunday. When Ru-dolph had asked to see her photographs, she had said, "I'm not ready yet. In a month or so, maybe."

Sitting in the back of the comfortable car, speeding toward the city, he realized, not without a touch of sor-

row, that Jean had seemed happier that weekend than
at almost any time since their marriage.

There had been wine on the table, but no hard liquor. Jean had not reached for the bottle and Rudolph
had caught no warning looks to her from Lorraine.

She has come to terms with herself, Rudolph
thought. He could not say as much for himself.

Coming into New York over the bridge, he saw the
buildings rearing like battlements against the melo-
drama of the sun sinking in the west. Lights were being
turned on in windows, small, winking pinpoints like
candles in archers' loopholes in a stronghold at twilight.
It was a view and a time of day that he loved—the
empty Sunday streets through which they passed looked
clean and welcoming. If only it were always Sunday in
New York, he thought, nobody would ever leave it.

When the car stopped in front of his brownstone, he
asked the Heaths if they wanted to come in for a drink,
but Johnny said they had a cocktail party to go to and
were late. Rudy thanked Johnny for the ride, leaned
over and kissed Elaine on the cheek. The weekend had
made him fonder of her than before.

"Are you going to be all alone tonight?" Elaine
asked.

"Yes."

"Why don't you get back into the car and have the
evening with us?" she said. "We're going to Gino's for
dinner after the party."

He was tempted, but he had a lot of thinking to do
and he felt it would be better to be alone. He did not
tell her that he felt uncomfortable these days with a lot
of people around. It was just a passing phase, he was
sure, but it had to be reckoned with. "Thanks," he said,
"but I have a pile of letters to answer. Let's do it during
the week. Just the three of us."

"I'll call you tomorrow," Johnny said, "when I get the Nevada pilgrimage arranged."

"I'll be in all day," Rudolph said. As he watched the car drive away, he was sorry he had said it. He was afraid that in the car, one or the other of the Heaths was saying, "He'll be in all day because he doesn't know what to do with himself."

Carrying his bag, he went up the steps. He didn't have to use the key to open the front door. The people downstairs again. He would have to talk to them. As he went into the darkened hallway a man's voice said, "Don't move and don't make a sound. I've got a gun on you."

He heard the front door slam behind him.

"Which apartment is yours, mister?" the voice said.

He hesitated. If Enid had been upstairs, he wouldn't have answered. He thanked God she was safely with her mother, more than a hundred miles away. And the nurse was in New Jersey. There was nobody upstairs. He felt what might have been a gun jabbing him roughly in the ribs. "We asked you a question, mister," the voice said. He was conscious of a second man, standing next to him.

"Second floor," he said.

"Climb!" the voice commanded. He started up the steps. There was no light coming through the crack at the bottom of the door of the downstairs apartment. Nobody home. Sunday evening, he thought, as he went mechanically up the stairs, with the sound of two pairs of footsteps heavy behind him.

His hands trembled as he got out his keys again and unlocked the door and went in. "Turn on a light," the same voice said.

He fumbled for the switch, found it, pushed at it. The lamp in the hallway went on and he turned to see the two men who had been lying in wait in the vestibule downstairs. They were young, black, one tall, one medium-sized, both neatly dressed. Their faces were lean and tense and full of hatred. Hopheads, he thought. The tall man was holding a gun, pointing at him, blue-black, gleaming dully in the light of the lamp.

"Into the living room," he said.

They followed him into the living room and the second man found the light switch. All the lamps went on. The room looked comfortable and clean, the drapes drawn across the windows. The nurse had tidied up before they left the morning before. The clock on the mantelpiece ticked loudly. He saw that it was five-thirty. "Let's have your wallet," the tall man said, "and no funny business."

Rudolph dug into his jacket and took out his wallet. The man with the gun grabbed it roughly and tossed it to the other man. "See what's in it," he said.

The second man rifled the wallet. "Thirty dollars," he said, holding the bills in his hand.

"Shit," said the man with the gun. "What've you got in your pants?"

Rudolph took out his money clip and two quarters. The second man put his hand out and grabbed the clip and the change. "You can say shit again, brother," he said. "There's only eight bucks here." He let the two quarters drop to the rug.

"You got the nerve to drive up here in a Lincoln Continental and only have thirty-eight bucks on you?" the man with the gun said. "Smart, aren't you? Afraid of being mugged, aren't you, Mr. Rockefeller?"

"I'm sorry," Rudolph said. "That's all I have. And those credit cards." The credit cards were strewn on the floor now."

"This institution don't accept credit cards, does it, Elroy?" the man said.

"It sure don't," Elroy said. They both laughed hoarsely.

Rudolph felt remote, as though it weren't happening to him but to a tiny, numb figure far off in the distance.

"Where do you keep the money in the house?" the man with the gun demanded. "Where's the safe?"

"I don't keep any money in the house," Rudolph said. "And there's no safe."

"Smarter and smarter, ain't you?" the man said. With his free hand he slapped Rudolph, hard, across the eyes. Rudolph was blinded momentarily by tears and he stumbled back. "That's just to truthen you up a little, mister," the man with the gun said.

"Look for yourself," Rudolph said blindly.

"You got one last chance to show us where it is, mister," the man said.

"I'm sorry. There's nothing I can do about it."

The man with the gun was breathing heavily, irregularly, and his eyes were flicking about, reflecting the light from the various lamps fitfully. "What do you say, Elroy?" he asked.

"Teach the cocksucker a lesson," Elroy said.

The man with the gun palmed it in a sudden gesture and swung against Rudolph's temple. As he crumpled to the floor it seemed to Rudolph that he was falling slowly and not unpleasantly through space and the floor seemed like a beautiful soft bed when he reached it. After a while a voice somewhere far off said, "That's enough, Elroy, you don't want to kill the bastard, do you?"

He was dreaming. Even while he dreamed he knew it was a dream. He was searching for Enid on a beach. There was the roar of breakers. Somehow, there were buses parked on the beach, in an irregular pattern, and people kept running in and out of them, people he didn't know or recognize, who paid no attention to him, who sometimes blocked him, sometimes dissolved into shadows, as he pushed through them, shouting, "Enid! Enid!" He knew it was a dream but he was tortured just the same because he knew he would never find her. The sense of loss was intolerable.

Then he awoke. The lights were still on. Now they were a glare that stabbed his eyes. He was lying on the floor, and everything hurt, his head, his groin. It was torture to move. His face was wet. When he put up his hand it came away streaming with blood.

Around him the room was demolished. All the upholstered chairs and the sofa had been slashed with knives and the stuffing lay like heaps of snow on the floor. The clock was lying, shattered, on the brick apron of the fireplace. Every drawer in the desk and chests and sideboard had been pulled out, their contents thrown around the room. The mirror above the fireplace was splintered into jagged pieces. The wooden chairs and the coffee table and small sideboard had been fractured with the poker from the set of fireplace utensils and the poker itself was bent at a crazy angle. All the bottles from the sideboard had been hurled against the wall and there was broken glass everywhere and a pervading smell of whiskey. The front panel of the piano was leaning against the sofa and the exposed, torn strings hung, broken and loose, over the keyboard, like an animal's intestines. He tried to look at his watch to see how long he had been lying unconscious, but the watch had been cut away from his wrist and there was an ugly seeping wound there.

With a gigantic effort, groaning, he crawled to the telephone. He took the instrument off its cradle, listened. It was working. Thank God. It took him what seemed like many minutes to remember Gretchen's number. Painfully, he dialed. It rang and rang. He lay on the floor with the phone next to his cheek. Finally he heard the phone being picked up at the other end.

"Hello." It was Gretchen's voice.

"Gretchen," he said.

"Where've you been?" she said. She sounded cross. "I phoned you at five; you said you'd be back by . . ."

"Gretchen," he said hoarsely, "come over here. Right away. If the door is locked, get a policeman to break it open for you. I . . ." Then he felt he was falling again. He couldn't talk anymore. He lay there on the floor with Gretchen's voice in his ear, crying. "Rudy! Rudy! Rudy, do you hear me . . . ?" Then silence.

He let himself go all the way and fainted again.

He was in the hospital for two weeks and he never did get to Nevada with Johnny Heath.

# VOLUME

---

# THREE

# CHAPTER 1

He had delivered seventeen dollars' worth of groceries
to Mrs. Wertham from the supermarket and Mrs. Wertham had invited him to have a cup of coffee. Mr. Wertham worked in Mr. Kraler's bottling plant and that,
Wesley thought, bridged the social and sexual gap in
Mrs. Wertham's mind between a comfortably well-off
housewife and a sixteen-year-old delivery boy. He had
accepted the coffee. It was the last call of the day and
he never was served coffee at the Kralers'.

After the coffee, Mrs. Wertham, coyly, with a certain
amount of giggling, told him he was a very handsome
young man and invited him into her bed. Coffee was
not the only thing he wasn't being served at the Kralers'
and Mrs. Wertham was a generously built, dyed-blond
lady. He accepted that invitation, too.

The coffee had been good, but the sex better. He had
to perform quickly, because the store bike, with the delivery box between the two front wheels, was parked
outside, and it was a neighborhood with a lot of kids
who could be counted upon to steal anything they could
lay their hands on, even a bike with U.M. Supermarket
painted in big letters on the box.

That had been just a month ago. He had made ten deliveries to Mrs. Wertham since then. The order for groceries in the Wertham household depended upon the fluctuations in Mrs. Wertham's libido.

This time, as he was getting dressed, Mrs. Wertham put on a housecoat and sat smiling at him as though she had just had a big, creamy dessert. "You sure are a strong-built young man," she said admiringly. "You could lift up my husband with one hand."

"Thanks, ma'am," Wesley said, getting into his sweater. He had no desire to lift Mr. Wertham with one hand.

"I don't usually do things like this," Mrs. Wertham said, perhaps forgetting that Wesley knew how to count, "but . . ." She sighed. "It makes a nice break in the day, doesn't it?"

"Yes, ma'am," Wesley said.

"It would be a sweet gesture on your part," Mrs. Wertham said, "if the next time you have to make a delivery here, you just kind of slipped a little present into the package. Half a ham, something like that. I'm always home between three and five."

"Yes, ma'am," Wesley said ambiguously. That was the last time Mrs. Wertham was going to get him into her bed. "I have to go now. My bike's outside. . . ."

"I understand," Mrs. Wertham said. "You'll remember about the ham, won't you?"

"Yes, ma'am," Wesley said.

The bike was still downstairs. He swung on it and pedaled, disgusted with himself, toward the post office. Half a ham. She thought he came at bargain prices. It was degrading. He felt he had reached a turning point in his life. From now on he wasn't going to accept anything just because it was offered. America was full of wonderful girls. The nice, shy one in the *Time* office in New York, for example, old as she was. He wasn't going to settle for trash anymore. Outside of Indianapolis there must be a girl somewhere whom he could talk to, admire, laugh with, explain about his father and himself, a girl he could love and feel proud of, a girl who wouldn't make him feel like a pig after he left her bed. Meanwhile, he decided, he could just wait.

At the post office there were two letters for him at General Delivery, one from Bunny, the other from Uncle Rudolph. Since he had used Uncle Rudolph's idea and picked up his mail at General Delivery, he had received letters from Bunny and Kate regularly. They made life in Indianapolis almost bearable. He stuffed the letters in his pocket, unread, because Mr. Citron, the manager of the U.M., always looked at him sharply if Wesley took even five minutes more than Mr. Citron thought was absolutely necessary, and Mrs. Wertham had already put him slightly behind schedule. Mr. Citron, Wesley thought, smiling innocently at the manager when he got back to the store, must have a time clock in his head. Try always to be your own boss, his father had said, it's the only way of beating the bastards.

In the stockroom behind the market he took the letters out of his pocket. He opened Bunny's letter first. His strong, clear handwriting looked as though it were written by a man who weighed over two hundred pounds.

Dear Wesley,
The news is that the *Clothilde*'s been sold for a hundred and ten thousand dollars. More dough for you and Kate and Kate's kid. Congratulations. Now I can finally tell you that the real owner wasn't Johnny Heath, as it says in the ship's papers, but your Uncle Rudolph. He had his reasons for hiding it, I suppose. I was beginning to think that we'd never sell it. I tried to talk your uncle

into letting me change the name, but he wouldn't hear of it. He's got principles. Maybe too many principles. The new owners are German, very nice people; they knew about what happened, but it didn't seem to bother them. I guess Germans aren't superstitious. They fell in love with the *Clothilde* at first sight, the lady told me. They wanted me to stay on as captain, but I decided against it. There're a lot of reasons and I don't think I have to tell you what they are.

I got to know an American couple with two boys aged around 11 and 9 hanging around St. Tropez who have a 43-foot Chris-Craft and they asked me to work it. I'm the only one in crew, but the kids can help clean up and the wife says she don't mind doing the cooking. The father says he can read a chart and handle the wheel. We'll see. So I'm still on the good old Mediterranean. It should be ok. It's nice having two kids on board.

Heard from Kate. She's got a job as barmaid in a pub not far from where she lives, so she gets to see a lot of her kid. I guess you know she named him Thomas Jordache.

Sorry you fell into a pile of shit in Indianapolis. According to your uncle when you're eighteen you can split. It's not so far off and time goes fast, so sweat it out and don't do anything crazy.

The name of my new ship is the *Dolores*—that's the lady's first name and her home port is St. Tropez, so you can keep writing me here care of the Captain of the Port.

Well, that's the news, friend. If you find yourself along the coast, drop in and see me.

Au revoir,
*Bunny*

Wesley folded the letter carefully and put it back in the envelope. He'd written Bunny twice asking him if he'd heard anything about Danovic, but Bunny never mentioned him. Times goes fast, Bunny had written. Maybe on the Mediterranean. Not in Indianapolis. There were few things he liked in Indianapolis. One was the big old market building, with its high ceiling and stalls heaped with fruit and vegetables and the smell of baked bread over everything. He went there as often as he could, because it reminded him of the market near the port in Antibes.

When he opened his uncle's letter two twenty-dollar bills fell out. He picked them up and put them in his pocket. He hadn't asked for money—ever—but he was grateful when it came. His uncle had a habit of coming through at odd times for everybody. It was nice, if you could afford it. And Uncle Rudolph obviously could. Don't rap it. The letter began,

> Dear Wesley,
> Note the address on top of the page. I finally moved out of New York. Since the robbery, the city has lost much of its charm for me and I began to worry, exaggeratedly, I'm sure, for Enid's safety. I've rented this house here in Bridgehampton out on Long Island for a year for a trial run. It's a quiet, charming community, except in the summer months, when it's enlivened by artistic and literary folk, and my house is near the beach and just about fifteen minutes' drive from my ex-wife's house. Enid stays with her during the school week and visits me on the weekends and with that arrangement no longer needs a nurse to look after her. She is happy in the country and even if it were only for her sake the move would be a good one.
> I've fully recovered from the two operations on

my face, and although I snort like an old war-
horse when I jog along the beach, due to certain
rearrangements made on my nasal passages after
my accident, I feel fine. The doctors wanted to operate on my nose once more for cosmetic reasons,
but I said enough is enough. Gretchen says I look
more like your father now, with my flattened nose.

Gretchen, incidentally, is off on a new career.
She finishes with the movie she is cutting with Mr.
Kinsella this next week and is launching out as a
director, having bought a screenplay that she likes
and that I've read and liked very much myself. In
fact, not knowing just what to do with my money,
I am investing in it and counseling Gretchen as
tactfully as possible on the business end of the ven-
ture. Be careful the next time you see her. She
thinks you would have a great success in one of the
roles in the movie. We have had almost everything
in the family by now, but never a movie star and
I'm not sure how that would reflect on the family
name.

I'm afraid that in the to-do after I got beaten up
I forgot to keep my promise about sending you the
names of some of the people you wanted to know
about who might give you information about your
father. There's Johnny Heath, of course, who
chartered the *Clothilde* with his wife. I don't remember if you were already on board at that time
or not. Then there're Mr. and Mrs. Goodhart, who
also chartered the ship in different seasons. I'm
writing the addresses on the enclosed sheet of paper. If you want to go as far back as when your
father was the age that you are now, there was a
boy—now a man, of course—called Claude
Tinker, in Port Philip, who was a partner of your
father in some of his escapades. The Tinker fam-

ily, I have heard, is still in Port Philip. Then there's a man named Theodore Boylan, who must be quite old by now, but who had intimate ties with our family.

I only saw your father fight professionally once—against a colored boy named Virgil Walters, and perhaps he would have something to remember. Your father had a manager called Schultz and I found him once through *Ring* Magazine when I wanted to get in touch with your father.

If other names occur to me I'll send them along to you. I'm sorry you couldn't come to visit me this summer and hope you can manage it another time.

I'm enclosing a little gift to start the new school year with. If by any chance you need more, don't hesitate to let me know.

Fondly,
*Rudolph*

Wesley folded the letter and put it back into the envelope, as he had with Bunny's letter. He *writes* with an anchor up his ass, Wesley thought. He *isn't* like that, there's just a wall between what he is and what he sounds like. Wesley wished he could like Uncle Rudolph more than he did.

He gave two letters to Jimmy when Jimmy came in to help sweep up. Jimmy was the other delivery boy. He was a black, the same age as Wesley. Jimmy kept the photograph of his father in boxing trunks that the lady from *Time* had given him and whatever letters Wesley got, because Wesley's mother went through everything in his room at least twice a week looking for signs of sin and whatever else she could find. Letters from his uncle and Kate and Bunny would be incriminating evidence of a giant conspiracy by everybody to rob her of her

son's love, an emotion she spoke about often. Her occasional outbursts of affection were hard to bear. She insisted upon kissing him and hugging him and calling
him her sweet baby boy and telling him that if he only
got a haircut he would be a beautiful young man and if
he would accept the joys of religion he would make his
mother blissfully happy and there wasn't anything she
and Mr. Kraler wouldn't do for him. It wasn't an act
and Wesley knew his mother *did* love him and want him
to be happy—but in her way, not his. Her demonstra-
tiveness left him uneasy and embarrassed. He thought
of Kate with longing.

He never spoke about his mother or Mr. Kraler to
Jimmy, although Jimmy was the only friend Wesley had
in town. He had avoided all other overtures, except that
of Mrs. Wertham, and that didn't really count. He
didn't want to feel sorry at leaving anything behind
when he departed from Indianapolis.

He didn't feel like going home for dinner, first of all
because he knew the meal would be lousy and second
because the house, which had been bad enough before,
had been as gloomy as the grave since Mr. Kraler had
gotten the telegram saying his son Max had been killed
in Vietnam. They were expecting the body home for
burial any day now and the time of waiting for it had
been like one long funeral.

He invited Jimmy to have dinner with him. "I can
splurge tonight," he told Jimmy. "My rich uncle came
through again."

They ate in a little restaurant near the supermarket
where you could get a steak dinner for one fifty and
where the owner didn't ask for proof you were of age
when you ordered a beer.

Jimmy wanted to be a rock musician and sometimes
he took Wesley over to his house and played his clarinet
for him with one of his sisters who played the piano,

while his other sister brought in the beers. Jimmy's sisters treated Jimmy as though he were a precious object, and anybody Jimmy liked they couldn't do enough for. There was no question of anybody's robbing them of Jimmy's love or theirs for him. Jimmy's crowded warm house, filled with the presence of the two pretty, laughing girls, was another place in Indianapolis that Wesley liked. Indianapolis, with its factories and pale tides of workmen morning and night and its flat expanses of identical houses and its littered streets, made Antibes seem like a suburb of a city in heaven.

Wesley didn't tell his mother about Jimmy. She was polite with blacks, but she believed in their keeping their distance, she said. It had something to do with being a Mormon.

After dinner, he remembered to tell Jimmy that from now on he'd appreciate it if Jimmy would make the deliveries to Mrs. Wertham's house. He didn't say why and Jimmy didn't ask him. That was another good thing about Jimmy—he didn't ask foolish questions.

He walked home slowly. There was an unspoken rule that if he got home by nine o'clock there wouldn't be any hysterical scenes about his tomcatting around town, disgracing his family, like his father. The usual routine was bad enough, but the scenes, especially late at night, tore at his nerves and made it almost impossible for him to get to sleep after them. He had thought again and again of just taking off, but he wanted to give his mother every chance possible. There had to be *something* there. Once, his father had loved her.

When he got home, Mr. Kraler was sobbing in the living room and holding his son's framed photograph. The picture had been taken with Max Kraler in a private's uniform. He was a thin-faced, sad-eyed boy, who looked as though he knew he was going to be killed before he was twenty-one. Wesley's mother took him into the hallway and whispered that Mr. Kraler had received notice that Max's body was going to arrive in two days and had spent the afternoon making funeral arrangements. "Be nice to him, please," she said. "He loved his boy. He wants you to get a haircut tomorrow and go with me to buy a new dark suit for the funeral."

"My hair's okay, Ma," Wesley said. "I'm not going to cut it."

"At a time like this," his mother said, still whispering. "You might just this once—to show respect for the dead."

"I can show as much respect for the dead with my hair the way it is."

"You won't even do a little thing like this to please your mother?" She began to cry, too.

"I like the way my hair is," Wesley said. "Nobody but you and him . . ." he gestured toward the living room, "ever bothers me about it."

"You're a stubborn, hard boy," she said, letting the tears course down her cheeks. "You never give an inch, do you?"

"I do when it makes sense," he said.

"Mr. Kraler won't let me buy you a new suit with that hair."

"So I'll go to the funeral in my old suit," Wesley said. "Max won't care."

"That's a sick joke," she wept.

"I didn't mean it as a joke."

"That old suit and that wild-Indian hair will make us all ashamed in church."

"Okay. I won't go to church. And I won't go to the cemetery. I never even *met* Max. What difference does it make?"

"Mother," Mr. Kraler called from the living room, "can you come in here for a minute?"

"Coming, dear," Teresa called. She glared harshly at Wesley, then slapped him, hard.

Wesley didn't react, but merely stood there in the hallway. His mother went into the living room and he went upstairs to his room.

They left it at that. When Max Kraler was buried, Wesley was delivering groceries.

Corporal Healey, who had also served in Vietnam but had not known Mr. Kraler's son, accompanied the body of the boy to Indianapolis. Mr. Kraler, who was a veteran of the Korean War, invited the corporal as a comrade in arms to stay in the house instead of going to a hotel. The night after the funeral Wesley had to share his bed with Healey, because of Mr. Kraler's married daughter, Doris, who lived in Chicago, was using the guest room across the hall. Doris was a small, mousy young woman who looked, Wesley thought, like Mr. Kraler.

Healey was a short, likable man, about twenty-three, who had a Purple Heart with two clusters on his blouse. Mr. Kraler, who had been a clerk in the quartermaster's in Tokyo during the Korean War, had talked Healey's ear off all day about *his* experiences as a soldier, and Healey had been polite, but had signaled to Wesley that he would like to break away. In a pause in Mr. Kraler's conversation Healey had stood up and said he'd like to take a little walk and asked if they'd mind letting Wesley go with him so he wouldn't get lost. Mr. Kraler, one soldier to another, said, "Of course, Corporal," and Teresa had nodded. She hadn't said a word to Wesley since the scene in the hallway and Wesley was grateful to Healey for getting him out of the house.

"Phew!" Healey said as they walked down the street, "that's heavy duty in there. What's the sister like, that Doris?"

"I don't know," Wesley said. "I met her for the first time yesterday."

"She keeps giving me the eye," Healey said. "Do you think she means it?"

"I wouldn't know."

"Sometimes those plain-looking little dolls are power-houses when it comes to putting out," Healey said. "You wouldn't object if I gave it a try, would you?"

"Why should I?" Wesley asked. "Just be careful. My mother patrols the house like a watchdog."

"We'll see how the situation develops," Healey said. He was from Virginia and his speech was soft and drawled. "That Mr. Kraler is something. The way he talks it was hand-to-hand combat every day in Tokyo. And he kept eating up all the gory details about how I was wounded. One thing for sure, I'm not joining the American Legion. I had my war and I don't want to hear word one about that war or anybody else's war. Where can we get a couple of beers?"

"It's not far from here," Wesley said. "I guessed you could use a drink."

"You'd think that if a fella came along with the body," Healey complained, "there'd be a little nip of something to cheer everybody up a bit. Not even a cup of coffee, for Christ's sake."

"They're Mormons."

"That must be some sorrowful religion," Healey said. "I go to Mass every Sunday I can, but I don't spit in the face of Creation. After all, God made whiskey, beer, wine—Christ, he even made coffee and tea. What do they think He made them for?"

"Ask Mr. Kraler."

"Yeah," Healey said mournfully.

They sat in a booth at the restaurant where Wesley had eaten dinner with Jimmy and drank beer. Wesley had explained to Healey that was the one place he was sure he wouldn't be called on being under eighteen.

"You're a big kid," Healey said. "It must be a nice feeling, being big, nobody picks on you much. I tell you something, a guy my size sure gets his share of shit."

"There're a lot of ways of getting picked on," Wesley said, "that got nothing to do with size."

"Yeah," Healey said. "I noticed Mr. Kraler and your mother aren't all warm loving-kindness with you."

Wesley shrugged. "I grin and bear it."

"How old are you, anyway?"

"Sixteen."

"You could pass for twenty-one."

"If necessary," Wesley said.

"What're you going to do about the draft when you're eighteen?"

"I haven't decided yet," Wesley said.

"You want some advice from someone who's been there and almost didn't make it back?" Healey said. "No matter what you do, don't give 'em your name and let them give you a number. It ain't fun, Wesley, it ain't fun at all."

"What can you do?"

"Anything. You just don't want to let them get you in the army. You never saw such a lot of hopeless, disgusted men in your life, getting shot at, getting blown up on mines, coming down with every kind of disease and jungle rot you can think of, and nobody knowing what he's doing there. . . . Believe it or not, Wesley, I enlisted. *Enlisted,* for God's sake!"

"My father told me once," Wesley said, "don't ever volunteer for any wars."

"Your father knew what he was talking about," Healey said. "The army sure knows how to take the

patriotism out of a man and it wasn't enemy action that
did it for me, either, boy. The final cherry on the
whipped cream was when a pal of mine and myself got
off the plane in San Francisco, all gussied up in parade
dress, with our ribbons and all. There were two pretty
chicks walking in front of us at the airport and we hurried a little and caught up with them and I said,
'What're you girls doing tonight?' They stopped and
looked at me as though I was a snake. They didn't say
nary a word, but the girl nearest me spit at me, right in
the face, just as calm as could be. Imagine that. Spit!
Then they turned around and walked away from us."
Healey shook his head. "We were home from the wars
just ten minutes, with our Purple Hearts, and that was
the welcome we got. Hail the conquering hero!" He
laughed sourly. "You don't want to put your ass on the
line for people like that, Wesley. Just keep on the move,
float around, so they can't put their hands on you. The
best place to get lost, the guys say, is Europe. Paris is
the number one spot. Even if you have to register at the
embassy, they don't take the trouble to smoke you out."

Talk around the campfire, Wesley thought. Old bat-
tles and loving thoughts of home. "I've been in Europe," he said. "I can speak French pretty good."

"I wouldn't wait too long if I was you, Wesley. You
just make sure you're in gay Paree on your eighteenth
birthday, pal," Healey said and waved for two more
beers. The coffin he had accompanied to Indianapolis
had been draped with the flag at the church and at the
graveside. Mr. Kraler had the flag and had said at dinner that he was going to hang it in Max's room, which
was Wesley's now.

The house was dark when they reached it, so there
was something to be thankful for. If his mother had
been up and smelled the beer on them, there would
have been tears and a scene.

They went upstairs quietly and were just starting to get undressed when there was a little knock on the door and the door opened and Doris came in. She was bare-footed and was wearing a nightgown that you could see through. She smiled at them and put her finger to her lips as she carefully closed the door behind her. "I heard you boys come in and I thought it might be nice to have a little gabfest. To get better acquainted, so to speak," she said. "Do either of you have a cigarette by any chance?" She talked in a mincing, self-conscious way, as though she had used baby talk until she was through with high school. She had droopy breasts, Wesley saw, though he tried not to keep looking, and a fat, low-slung ass. If I looked like that, he thought, I wouldn't go around dressed like that, except in total darkness. But Healey was smiling widely and there was a new gleam in his eye. He had already taken his shirt off and was naked from the waist up. He didn't have much of a build, either, Wesley noted.

"Here you are, dear lady," Healey said, courtly Virginia gentleman, "I have a pack right here in the pocket." He crossed the room to where his shirt was hanging over the back of a chair. He took out the cigarettes and matches, then started to take the shirt off the chair.

"You don't need to get dressed for Doris," Doris said. She wiggled her thin shoulders and smiled girlishly at Healey. "I'm a married woman. I know what men look like."

She *did* mean it, Wesley thought, when she gave Healey the signal during the day.

Healey gallantly lit Doris's cigarette. He offered one to Wesley. Wesley didn't like cigarettes but he took one because he was in Mr. Kraler's house.

"God," Doris said as she puffed at her cigarette and blew smoke rings, "I'm back in the land of the living.

Poor Max. He wasn't much when he was alive, and he turned up dead for his one moment of glory. Boy, the bishop had a hard time making poor Max sound like something in his speech." She shook her head commiseratingly, then looked hard at Wesley. "Are you as bad as *they* say you are?"

"Evil," Wesley said.

"I bet," Doris said. "With your looks. *They* say you're a terror with married women."

"What?" Wesley asked, surprised.

"Just for your information," Doris said, "and because I think you're a nice boy, you better tell a certain Mrs. W. that she'd better get to the mailbox every morning before her husband."

"What the hell are you talking about?" Wesley asked, although he could guess. Some neighborhood gossip must have noticed the U.M. bike parked in front of Mrs. Wertham's house more than once and blabbed to his mother.

"While you were out you were the subject of discussion," Doris said. "First of all that you were so different from Max and not different better, I can tell you that."

"I can guess," Wesley said.

"Your mother did not have many kind words for your father, either," Doris said. "He must have been something, if half of what she said was true. And you're following in his footsteps, she said, arrested and all in France for nearly killing a man in a drunken brawl."

"Hey," Healey said, "good for you, pal."

"And," Doris went on, "a virtual sex maniac like the old man. What with that disgusting Mrs. W., who's old enough to be your mother, and God knows how many other houses you go to and deliver more than the groceries." She giggled, her droopy breasts quivering under the transparent nightgown.

"Hey, I have a good idea," Wesley said. He felt he

was being choked in the small room, with the loops of cigarette smoke and the coquetting, almost-naked malicious girl and the leering soldier. "You two obviously have a lot to talk to each other about . . ."

"You can say that again, Wesley," said Healey.

"I'm not sleepy," Wesley said, "and I could use another breath of air. I'll probably be an hour or so," he said warningly. He didn't want to come back to the room and find the two of them in his bed.

"I may just stay for another cigarette," Doris said. "I'm not sleepy yet either."

"That makes three of us," said Healey.

Wesley started to stub out his cigarette, when the door was flung open. His mother was standing there, her eyes stony. Nobody said anything for a moment as Teresa stared first at him, then at Healey, then, for what seemed minutes, at Doris. Doris giggled.

"Wesley," his mother said, "I'm not responsible for the conduct of Mr. Healey or Mr. Kraler's daughter, who is a married woman. But I am responsible for *your* conduct." She spoke in a harsh whisper. "I don't want to wake up Mr. Kraler, so I'd appreciate it if whatever you do or say you do it quietly. And, Wesley, would you be good enough to come downstairs with me?"

When she was formal, as she was now, she was worse than when she was hysterical. He followed her downstairs through the darkened house to the living room. The flag from the coffin was folded on a table.

She turned on him, her face working. "Let me tell you something, Wesley," she said in that harsh whisper, "I've just seen the worst thing in my whole life. That little whore. Who got her in there—you? Who was going to lay her first, you or the soldier?" In her passion her vocabulary lost its pious euphemisms. "To do that on the very night that a son of the family was laid to rest after giving his life for his country. . . . If I told Mr. Kraler what's been going on in his house, he'd take a baseball bat to you."

"I'm not going to explain anything, Ma," Wesley said. "But you can tell Mr. Kraler that if he as much as tries to lift a finger to me, I'll kill him."

She fell back as though he had hit her. "I heard what you said. You said kill, didn't you?"

"I sure did," Wesley said.

"You've got the soul of a murderer. I should have let you rot in that French jail. That's where you belong."

"Get your facts straight," Wesley said roughly. "You had nothing to do with getting me out of jail. My uncle did it."

"Let your uncle take the consequences." She leaned forward, her face contorted. "I've done my best and I've failed." Suddenly she bent over and grabbed his penis through his trousers and pulled savagely at it. "I'd like to cut it off," she said.

He seized her wrist and roughly pulled her arm away. "You're crazy, Ma," he said. "You know that?"

"From this moment on," she said, "I want you to get out of this house. For good."

"That's a good idea," he said. "It's about time."

"And I warn you," she said, "my lawyer will do everything possible to make sure you don't get a penny of your father's dirty money. With your record it won't be too hard to convince a judge that it doesn't make any sense to put a fortune into the hands of a desperate murderer. Go, get out of here, go to your whores and hoodlums. Your father will be proud of you."

"Stuff the money," Wesley said.

"If that your final word to your mother?" she said melodramatically.

"Yeah. My final word." He left her in the middle of the living room, breathing raucously, as though she were on the verge of a heart attack. He went into his room without knocking. Doris was gone, but Healey was lying propped up on the bed, smoking, still bare from the waist up, but with his pants on.

"Holy shit," Healey said, "that lady sure barged in at the wrong moment, didn't she?"

"Yeah." Wesley began throwing things into a small bag.

Healey watched him curiously. "Where you going, pal?"

"Out of here. Somewhere," Wesley said. He looked into his wallet to make sure he had the list of names he had been adding to ever since he got out of jail. He never left his wallet anywhere that his mother could find it.

"In the middle of the night?" Healey said.

"This minute."

"I guess I don't blame you," Healey said. "Breakfast is going to be a happy meal here." He laughed. "The next time the army sends me out with a coffin I'm going to tell them they got to give me a complete rundown on the family. If you ever get to Alexandria, look me up."

"Yeah," Wesley said. He looked around him to see if he had forgotten anything important in the room. Nothing. "So long, Healey," he said.

"So long, pal." Healey flicked ashes on the floor. "Remember what I said about Paris."

"I'll remember." Silently, his old windbreaker zipped up against the night's cold, he went out of the room, down the dark stairs and out of the house.

He remembered, too, as he walked along the windy dark street, carrying the small bag, that his father had told him that it had been one of the best days of his life when he realized he didn't hate his mother anymore. It had taken time, his father had said.

It would take time for the son, too, Wesley thought.

A day later he was in Chicago. He had gone into an all-night diner on the outskirts of Indianapolis when a truck driver came in who told the girl behind the counter that he was on the way to Chicago. Chicago, Wesley thought, was just as good a place to start whatever he was going to do as anyplace else and he asked the driver if he could come along. The driver said he'd be glad for the company and the trip had been comfortable and friendly and aside from having to listen to the driver talk about the troubles he was having with his seventeen-year-old daughter back in New Jersey, he had enjoyed it.

The driver had dropped him off near Wrigley Field and he'd looked at his list of addresses and seen William Abbott's address. Might as well start somewhere, he'd thought, and had gone to the address. It was about noon, but Abbott was still in pajamas and a rumpled bathrobe, in a beat-up, one-room studio littered with bottles, newspapers and coffee containers and crumpled pieces of paper near the typewriter.

He had not been favorably impressed with William Abbott, who pretended to know a lot more about Thomas Jordache than he really knew, and Wesley left as soon as he could.

The next two days he tried to get a job at two or three supermarkets, but they weren't hiring people at supermarkets that week in Chicago and people kept asking him for his union card. He was low in funds and he decided Chicago was not for him. He called his Uncle Rudolph in Bridgehampton, collect, to warn him he was coming there, because he didn't know where else to go.

Rudolph sounded funny on the phone, uneasy, as though he were afraid somebody who shouldn't be listening in was listening in.

"What's the matter?" Wesley said. "If you don't want me out there, I don't have to come."

"It's not that," Rudolph said, his voice troubled over the wire. "It's just that your mother called two days ago to find out if you were with me. She has a warrant out for your arrest."

*"What?"*

"For your arrest," Rudolph repeated. "She thinks I'm hiding you someplace."

"Arrest? What for?"

"She says you stole a hundred and fifty dollars from her household money, the money she kept in a pitcher over the stove in the kitchen, the night you left. She says she's going to teach you a lesson. *Did* you take the money?"

"I wish I had," Wesley said bitterly. That goddamn Healey, he thought. The army had taught him how to live off the land. Or even more likely, that cheese-faced Doris.

"I'll straighten it out," Rudolph said soothingly, "somehow. But for the time being I don't think it would be wise to come here. Do you need money? Let me know where you are and I'll send you a money order."

"I'm okay," Wesley said. "If I get to New York I'll call you." He hung up before Rudolph could say anything else.

That's all I need, he thought, the jug in Indianapolis.

Then he decided he'd go to New York. Rudolph wasn't the only person he knew in New York. He remembered the nice girl at *Time* saying that if he needed help to come to her. Nobody would think of looking for him at *Time* Magazine.

He was on the road the next morning.

# CHAPTER 2

He did not talk to his uncle for almost two months after the telephone call from Chicago.

When he got to New York he went directly to Alice Larkin's office. He must have looked pretty awful after his days on the road, because she gasped as though someone had thrown a bucket of cold water over her when he came into her cubicle. He had had almost nothing to eat in days and had done his sleeping in truck cabs; he needed a shave, his collar was frayed, his pants were stained with grease from helping a driver change a tire on the big semitrailer outside Pittsburgh; and he had forty-five cents in his pocket.

But after the first shock, Miss Larkin seemed happy to see him and insisted on buying him lunch downstairs even before he could tell her what he was there for.

After he had eaten and was feeling like a human being again he had told her just about everything. He tried to make it sound unimportant, and joke about it, because he didn't want that nice girl to think he was an overgrown crybaby. She was easy to talk to, looking across the table at him intently through her glasses, her small, pink-cheeked face alert, as he explained why he had left Indianapolis and about the warrant for his arrest and the division of the estate, everything.

She didn't interrupt him as he poured it all out, just sighed or shook her head every once in a while in sympathy and indignation.

"Now," she said, when he had finished, "what're you going to do?"

"Well, I told you, the other time I was here," he said, "I sort of have the feeling that I'd like to look up the people who knew my father and get an idea of what he seemed like to them—you know—different people, different times of his life. I knew him less than three years." He was speaking earnestly now, not trying to sound ironic or grown up. "I feel as though there's a great big hole in my head—where my father ought to be—and I want to fill it as much as I can. I guess it sounds kind of foolish to you . . ."

"No, it doesn't," she said, "not at all."

"I told you I had a list of people . . ." He took his wallet out of his pocket and put the worn, creased sheet of paper with the names written on it onto the table. "The magazine seems to be able to find just about anybody they want to," he said, "and I thought, if it wasn't too much trouble for you, maybe in your spare time . . ."

"Of course," Miss Larkin said, "we're not as omniscient as you might . . ." She stopped when she saw the puzzled look on his face. "I mean as all-knowing as you might think, but we're pretty good at hunting down people." She looked at the list. "This is bound to take some time and there's no guaranteeing I can turn them *all* up, but . . ." She looked at him curiously. "Will you be staying in New York?"

"I suppose so."

"Where?"

He moved uncomfortably in his chair. "I haven't decided on any place yet. I came right here."

"Wesley," Miss Larkin said, "tell me the truth—how much money have you?"

"What's the difference?" he said defensively.

"You look like a scarecrow," she said. "You ate as though it was your first meal in a week. How much money have you got on you?"

He grinned weakly. "Forty-five cents," he said. "The heir to the Jordache fortune. Of course," he said hastily, "I could always call my uncle and he'd stake me, but for the time being I'd rather not."

"Do you mind if I take this list with me?" Miss Larkin said. "You'll have to tell me just who they are and where you think they might be found, of course. . . ."

"Of course."

"It might take weeks."

"I'm in no hurry."

"And you expect to live for weeks on forty-five cents?" She sounded accusing, as though she were angry with him.

"Something'll turn up," he said vaguely. "Something always does."

"Would you be offended if I told you that something *has* turned up?" Unaccountably, she blushed.

"What?"

"Me," she said, louder than she realized. *"I've* turned up. Now listen carefully. I've got two rooms and a kitchenette. There's a perfectly comfortable sofa on which you can sleep. I'm not much of a cook, but you won't starve. . . ."

"I can't do that," Wesley protested.

"Why not?"

He grinned weakly again. "I don't know why not."

"Do you have any other clothes?"

"I have a clean shirt and a pair of socks and some

underwear. I left them downstairs at the desk in your building."

She nodded primly. "A clean shirt," she said. "As far as I can tell, these people on the list are scattered all over the country. . . ."

"I guess so. My father moved around some."

"And you expect to travel all over the United States and go into people's homes and ask them the most intimate questions with one clean shirt to your name?"

"I hadn't thought about it much," he said defensively.

"You'd be lucky to get past the dogs, looking like that," she said. "It's a wonder they let you come up to my office."

"I guess I haven't looked in a mirror the last few days," he said.

"I'm going to tell you what I'm going to do with you," she said, sounding more certain of herself than she actually felt. "I'm going to have you stay with me and I'm going to lend you some money to buy some clothes and . . ."

"I can't let you do that."

"Of course you can," she said crisply. "You heard me say 'lend,' didn't you?"

"God knows when I'll ever get my money."

"I can wait," she said.

He sighed deeply. She could see how relieved he was. "I don't know why you want to be so nice to me," he said. "You hardly know me. . . ."

"I know enough about you to want to be nice to you," she said. Then she sighed, in her turn. "I have to be honest with you and tell you something. I'm not doing this out of random charity. I have an ulterior purpose. You know what ulterior means?"

"I've read a book, Miss Larkin," he said, a little hurt.

"Alice."

"I'm not as stupid as I look is what I meant to say."

"I don't believe you're stupid at all. Whatever," she said, taking a deep breath. "I have my own private, selfish reasons for doing what I'm doing and you might as well know them now as later. I just hope you won't be hurt."

"How can I be hurt if somebody wants to give me a place to live and dress me up like a decent human being?"

"I'll tell you how," she said. "When you left my office last time—No. Let me go back further than that. Like just about everybody else on the magazine I want to be a writer. I think of myself as a novelist. I had sixty pages of a novel done when I met you. When you left I went home and burned them."

"Why'd you do that?" he asked. "What's that got to do with me?"

"It's got everything to do with you. After doing the research and then hearing your story I decided what I was writing was junk—flat, worn-out, repetitive junk. I decided I wanted to write a story about a young boy whose father had been murdered. . . ."

"Oh," Wesley said softly. Now he eyed her cautiously.

"The young boy," she went on, avoiding his glance, looking down at the table, "wants to find out several things—who did it, why it was done, what his father's life was like— He didn't know his father, his parents had been divorced when he was a small boy, and his father had wandered off. If it worries you, let me tell you that the murder doesn't take place in Europe—I don't know anything about Europe, I've never been there. But the plan, in general, isn't so different from what you're doing. . . ."

"I see."

"So you can see what my ulterior purpose is."

"Yes."

"I'll have you right under my nose, I'll be able to study you, I'll be helping you to find all kinds of people. In a way, it could be considered a fair exchange. Would that bother you?"

Wesley shrugged. "Not necessarily," he said. "I don't quite see myself as a character in a book, though."

"It doesn't work like that," Miss Larkin said. "You'll be a character in my head and I'll take what I need and what I can use and hope for the best."

"What if you find out I'm not worth the trouble?"

"That's the chance I take."

"How does the book turn out?" Wesley asked curiously. "Does he find the murderer?"

"Eventually, yes."

"Then what does he do?"

"He takes his revenge."

Wesley chuckled sourly. "Pretty easy in a book, isn't it?"

"I don't intend to make it easy," she said.

"And what happens to the kid?"

She took another deep breath. "He gets killed," she said.

Wesley drummed absently on the tabletop, without looking at her. "That sounds logical," he said.

"It will be fiction, of course," she said.

"Some fiction," he said.

"If you get mixed up with writers," she said seriously, "or even somebody like me who *thinks* she's a writer, that's the chance you take. They'll try to steal a part of your soul."

"I didn't know I had one," Wesley said.

"Let me be the judge of that," Alice said. "Look—if the whole thing seems awful to you—or absurd—you don't have to go along with it."

"Will you write the book anyway?"

"Yes, I'll try."

"What the hell." He grinned. "If I do have a soul I guess I have enough to spare for a few pages in a book."

"Good," she said briskly, although her hands were trembling. She dug in her pocketbook. "I have to go back to work. But here's my charge account card at Bloomingdale's. It's on Fifty-ninth Street and Lexington Avenue." As she spoke she scribbled on a sheet of *Time* stationery. "You take this note along with my card so they'll know I authorized you to use it. You go into there this afternoon and buy yourself a couple of shirts and some flannel pants. Have them sent here, so they know it's my order. You can't go around looking like this. Then come back here about six o'clock and I'll take you home. Oh, and you'll need some money for bus fares and stuff like that." She dug in her bag again and gave him five dollars in singles and change.

"Thanks," he said. "Remember—whatever you give me is only a loan. I'm due to get about thirty thousand bucks when I'm eighteen."

"I'll remember," she said impatiently.

"Write it down," he insisted. "Five dollars and the date."

She made a face. "If you want." She took out a pen and her notebook and wrote in it. She pushed it across the table at him. "Satisfied?"

He looked at the page of the notebook gravely. "Okay," he said.

She put the notebook back in her bag.

"Now that I'm a character in a book," he said, "do I have to behave in any particular way? Do I have to watch my language or save maidens in distress or anything fancy like that?"

"You just behave any way you want," she said. Then she saw that he was grinning and that he had been making fun of her. She laughed. "Just don't be wise beyond your years, boy," she said.

He was on his way to Port Philip. Might as well start at the place where it all began, he had said, when Alice had found out that Theodore Boylan was still alive and still living there. Wesley's father had told him something about Boylan's connection with the family and it was just a couple of hours by train from the city.

He was neatly dressed now in flannel slacks and a sports jacket and good brown shoes from Bloomingdale's and Alice had insisted on trimming his hair, not too short, but neat. She seemed glad to have him around the small apartment on the West Side, near the park. She said she was beginning to feel melancholy living alone and that she looked forward to seeing him there when she got back after work. When young men called to take her out she introduced him as her cousin from the Midwest who was staying with her for a few weeks.

While waiting for Alice to come up with the information he had asked her for, he enjoyed wandering around the city. He went to a lot of movies and investigated things like the Radio City Music Hall and the United Nations building and the garish carnival of Broadway. At night, sometimes, Alice took him to the theater, which opened up a whole new world for him, since he had never seen a live show before.

When they were alone together in the apartment he tried to keep out of her way while she tapped away at the typewriter in her room. She never offered to let him read anything that she was writing and he didn't ask her any questions about it. Sometimes, he felt strange, sitting reading a magazine in the living room and listening to the typewriter and knowing that someone was in there writing about him or inventing somebody who might conceivably be him. Occasionally, she would come out and stare at him silently, a long time, as though she were studying him, trying to get inside his head, then go back into her room and start at the machine again.

Whenever she took him to the theater or bought him a meal he made her put the amount of the tickets or the dinner in her notebook.


The train rattled north along the Hudson River. It was a clear sunny day and the river looked bright and clean and he thought how nice it would be to have a small boat and sail up its broad reaches, past the green cliffs, the small drowsy towns, and tie up at night and see what the life was like in them.

He saw the big, forbidding pile of Sing Sing at Ossining and felt a pang of kinship with the men pent up there, with the great free river just below their barred windows, counting off the years. Never, he thought, never for me. Whatever else happens.

When he got to Port Philip, he got into a taxi at the station and said, "The Boylan mansion." The driver looked at him curiously through the rearview mirror as he started the motor. "I don't reckon I've had a fare there for more than ten years," the driver said. "You going to work there?"

"No," Wesley said. "It's a social visit."

The driver made a sound. It was hard to figure out whether it was a cough or a laugh.

Wesley stared out the window as they drove through the town. It was shabby, the streets unkempt, as though the people who lived there, long ago, in the certainty of defeat, had given up the last attempt at civic beautification. In a funny way it reminded Wesley of bums lying on park benches, who, when aroused, spoke in good, college-educated accents.

The gates at the entrance to the Boylan grounds were broken and off their hinges, the gravel road leading up the hill toward the house was full of potholes and the lawns were overgrown, the wild hedges untrimmed. The house itself looked like a smaller version of Sing Sing.

"Wait a minute," he told the driver as he got out of the cab and paid him. "I want to see if they let me in." He pushed at the bell at the front door. He didn't hear any sound inside and he waited, then pushed again. He looked around as he waited. The weeds were almost waist high on the lawns and there were wild vines crawling over the garden walls.

A couple of minutes went by and he was about to turn back to the taxi and return to town when the door opened. A bent old man in a striped butler's vest stood there, peering at him. "Yes?" The man said.

"I'd like to talk to Mr. Boylan, please," Wesley said.

"Who should I say is calling?"

"Mr. Jordache," Wesley said.

The old man peered at him sharply, leaning forward to get a better look. "I will see if Mr. Boylan is in," he said and closed the door again.

The taxi driver honked his horn impatiently.

"Wait just a minute, will you?" Wesley called.

Thirty seconds later, the door opened again. "Mr. Boylan will see you now," the old man said.

Wesley waved to the driver to go and the taxi spurted around the potholed circle in front of the house and sped down the hill.

The old man led Wesley down a long dark hall and opened a door. "If you please, sir," the old man said, holding the door open for him.

Wesley went into a big room, which was dark, too, because of the heavy drapes, although it was sunny outside. A man was sitting in a big winged leather chair, reading a book. At a table near one of the tall windows

that let out onto the terrace, where there was some sunlight, two young women were sitting across from each
other playing cards. They looked at him curiously as he
came into the room. Although it was the middle of the
afternoon, they were dressed in nightgowns, with frilly
robes over them.

The man in the leather chair slowly stood up, carefully putting the book he had been reading facedown on
the wing of the chair. "Ah," he said. "Mr. Jordache?"
His voice was thin and dry.

"Yes, sir," Wesley said.

"Jordache," the man said. "I know the name." He
chuckled thinly. "I'm Theodore Boylan. Sit down." He
indicated an identical winged chair facing the one he
had been sitting in. He didn't offer to shake hands. He
had bright blond hair that had to be dyed, over that
lined, quivering old face, the nose sharp, the eyes milky.

Wesley sat, feeling stiff and uncomfortable, wishing
the two women weren't there, conscious of their staring
at him.

"Whose pup are you?" Boylan asked, seating himself
again. "The merchant prince's or the thug's?"

"Thomas," Wesley said. "Thomas Jordache was my
father."

"Dead now." Boylan nodded, as if with approval.
"Not long for this world. In the cards. Murdered." He
addressed the women at the window. "In a pretty part
of the world." He squinted maliciously at Wesley.
"What do you want?"

"Well," Wesley said, "I know you knew my family . . ."

"Intimately," Boylan said. "All too intimately."
Again he spoke to the women at the window. "The
young man's aunt was a virgin when I met her. She was
not a virgin when she left me. Believe it or not, at one

moment I asked her to marry me. She refused." He turned on Wesley. "Has she told you that?"

"No," Wesley said.

"There are many things, I'm sure, they haven't told you. Your aunt and uncle used to take great pleasure in coming to this house. It was in better condition then. As was I." He chuckled again, a raucous little noise. "I taught them many things when they were young and hungry. They learned valuable lessons in this house. They have not been back to visit the old man for lo, these many years. Still, as you see, young man, I am not without company. . . ." He waved carelessly at the two women, who had gone back to playing cards. "Youthful beauties," he said ironically. "The advantages of wealth. You can buy youth. They come and go. Two, three months at a time, selected for me by a discreet madam who is an old and valued acquaintance of mine in the great city of New York and who is constantly surprised at what she hears from their ruby lips about the indomitable appetite of the old man."

"Oh, come off it, Teddy," one of the women said, shuffling the cards.

"My dears," Boylan said, "I would appreciate it if you would leave the men to their conversation for a while."

The woman who had spoken sighed and stood up. "Come on, Elly," she said, "he's in one of his goddamn moods."

The other woman stood up and they both went out, swinging their hips, their high-heeled mules making a clacking noise on the polished floor.

"There is one great advantage to paying for labor," Boylan said when the women had left the room, closing the big door behind them. "The employees are obedient. When one gets old one values obedience above all other virtues. So—young man—you are curious about the noble roots of your family. . . ."

"Actually," Wesley said, "it's my father mostly that I . . ."

"I was only acquainted with him by his deeds," Boylan said, "but Gretchen and Rudolph I knew all too well. Your Uncle Rudolph, I'm afraid, suffered, from an early age, from a prevalent American disease—he was interested only in money. I attempted to guide him, I showed him the way to eminence, an appreciation of the finer things of life, but the almighty dollar was raging in his veins. I warned him he was laying waste to himself, but he suffered from the Jew's deformation . . ." Boylan rubbed his middle finger against his thumb. "The clink of coin was heavenly music in his ears. Not content with the fortune he could amass himself, he married great money and in the end it did him in. He was foredoomed and I warned him, but he was deafened by the harps of gold." He laughed gleefully. Then he spoke more soberly. "He was a man who lacked the essential virtue of gratitude. Well, he's paid his price and I, for one, do not mourn for him."

"Really, Mr. Boylan," Wesley said stiffly, "what I came for was . . ."

"As for Gretchen," Boyland went on as though Wesley had not spoken, "prettiest girl in town. Ripe as a peony, blooming on a slag heap. Demure, she was, eyes downcast and modest. In the beginning. Not later. She could have had a life of ease and respect, travel; I was ready to offer her anything. I once bought her a bright red dress. When she came into a room shimmering in red, every man in the place felt anguish clutching at his throat." He shrugged. "What I offered she spurned. She wanted cheap young men, quick with false words, into bed, out of bed. She destroyed herself with her unbri-

dled sensuality. If you see her, please remember my
words and repeat them carefully to her."

Gaga, Wesley thought, absolutely gaga, with a crazy
gift of gab. He tried not to think of his Aunt Gretchen
walking into a room in a red dress bought for her by
this loony old man. "What I'm trying to get at," he said
doggedly, "is what my father . . ."

"Your father," Boylan said contemptuously, "was a
criminal and an arsonist and belonged behind bars. He
came here to spy on his sister and he burned a cross on
the hill outside because on one of his marauding raids
he discovered that his sister was upstairs in my bed and
he saw me naked in this very room fixing her a drink.
A burning cross. Symbol of bigotry and ignorance."
Boyland spat out the words, still outraged after all the
years by the flaming insult on his doorstep. "All this
came out many years later, of course—the boy who was
his accomplice—Claude Tinker by name, now a respectable citizen in this very town—confessed everything to me over a splendid dinner in my own dining
room. Your father." Boylan wrinkled his long, thin, old
man's reddened nose. "Good riddance, I'd say. I followed his career. As was to be expected, he failed at
everything, even at keeping alive."

Wesley stood up. "Thank you very much, Mr. Boylan," he said, hating the man. "I believe I've heard
enough. I'll be going now."

"As you wish," Boylan said carelessly. "You know
the way to the door. I thought you might be interested
in the truth—at your age the truth is often a useful
guide for your own conduct. I'm too old to lie or cosset
random young scum because once I was kind to a relative or two." He picked up his book from the wing of
the chair and started reading.

As he went out of the room and walked quickly toward the front door, Wesley thought, My old man

shouldn't have just burned a cross, he should have set
fire to the whole goddamn place. With that sonofabitch
in it.

He walked the few miles down the hill and to the
station and was lucky because a train was just pulling
into the station as he reached it.

When he got to the apartment Alice had dinner waiting for him. She saw that his lips were tight, his jaw
tense, and they ate in silence. She didn't ask him how it
had gone in Port Philip.

———————

Dominic Joseph Agostino, who in his fighting days in
the twenties and thirties had been known as Joe Agos,
the Boston Beauty, and who had been in charge of the
gym at the Revere Club when Thomas Jordache had
worked there, was still alive, Alice told Wesley, and still
working at the Revere Club. Tom Jordache had told
Wesley that Agostino had been good to him, had saved
his job once when he was suspected of rifling the members' lockers and had even persuaded him that he was
good enough to start in the amateurs. All things considered, Thomas had told Wesley, he was glad he had had
his fling at the fight game, even if in the end he had
wound up as a bum. "What the hell," Thomas had said,
"I enjoyed fighting. Getting paid for it was so much
gravy. For a while, anyway." There was one wonderful
thing about Agostino, Thomas had said, he had been as
polite as a lady's maid with the members of the club
with whom he sparred and full of compliments about
how good they were and how they were improving in
what he called The Art, but had managed never to let
on for a minute that what he really would have liked to

do was blow up every one of them, along with the building itself, with its fancy rooms and oil portraits of the old aristocracy of Boston on the walls.

"He was a model of deportment," Thomas had said admiringly, "and he taught me a lot."

Wesley took the shuttle to Boston from LaGuardia— thirty-six dollars round trip, as he wrote in the notebook he now kept for himself, to make sure that Alice wasn't slyly cheating herself about the money she advanced him. The trip would have been enjoyable, except for the ex-paratrooper who sat next to him, who started sweating as soon as the plane began taxiing and digging his nails into the palms of his hands and kept saying, once they were in the air, "Listen to the sound of that port engine. I don't like the sound of that port engine, we're going to crash, for Christ's sake and those guys up front don't give a damn."

The more you knew about anything, Wesley thought, the less you liked it.

The plane didn't crash and once they were on the ground the ex-paratrooper stopped sweating and looked like any other passenger as they got off the plane.

At the Revere Club, the old man at the front desk looked at him queerly when he asked if he could speak to Mr. Agostino.

"I'm Mr. Agostino," the man said. He had a husky, whispery, hoarse voice and he was small and skinny, with his uniform hanging loosely around his bones and his big Adam's apple moving up and down in his stringy neck.

"I mean the one who used to work in the gym," Wesley said.

"That's me." The man eyed him suspiciously. "I ain't worked in the gym for fifteen years. Too fucking old.

Besides the arthritis. They made me the doorman. Out of the goodness of their hearts. What'd you want to see Agostino about?"

Wesley introduced himself. "Tommy Jordan's son," Agostino said flatly. "What do you know? I remember him. He got killed, didn't he? I read it somewhere." There was no emotion in the whispering, hoarse voice, with the flat South Boston accent. If the name stirred any pleasant memories in the balding head, decorated by a few wispy gray hairs, he kept them to himself. "You looking for a job?" His tone was accusing. He eyed Wesley professionally. "You got a good built on you. You planning to go into the ring or anything like that?"

"I'm not a fighter," Wesley said.

"Just as well," Agostino said. "They don't box anymore in this club. They decided it wasn't a sport for gentlemen. All those niggers and all. Now, when they have to settle a difference of opinion, they sue each other." He laughed, his breath whistling through the gaps in his teeth.

"I just wanted to talk to you about my father for a few minutes," Wesley said, "if you have the time."

"Your father. Umm. He could punch, your father, with his right. You might just as well have tied his left hand behind him, all the good it did. I saw him fight pro once. I saw him knock the bum out. But after the fight I told him, 'You'll never go to the top,' I told him, 'until you get yourself a left hand.' I guess he never did. Though the way things are now, he might of got himself a couple good paydays, being white and all. He wasn't a bad kid, your old man. Had a streak of larceny in him, I suspected; not that I blamed him, with the wall in this joint practically papered with dollar bills. There were all sorts of stories after he left. Somehow the word got around that he blackmailed one of the members, a lawyer, for God's sake, for five thousand bucks. The guy's father got wind of it and let it be known that his poor little son was sick, he was a kleptomaniac. Money kept disappearing all over the place, and I guess your old man caught the guy at it once and made him pay to keep quiet. Your father ever tell you any of this?"

"Yes," Wesley said. "He said it was his lucky day."

"That's a nice chunk of dough," Agostino said, "five big ones. What did he do with it?"

"He invested it," Wesley said. "Or rather his brother did it for him. He finished with a yacht."

"I read that, too, in the magazine," Agostino said. "A yacht. Shit. I wish I had a brother like that. A young punk like that winding up with a yacht!" He shook his head. "I got along with him okay, bought him a couple of beers from time to time. I wasn't too surprised he got killed. Yeah, I'll talk to you, if that's *all* you want. . . ." Now he sounded suspicious. "I'm not going to contribute to any Tom Jordan Memorial Fund or anything like that, if that's what you're after."

"All I want to do is talk awhile," Wesley said.

Agostino nodded. "Okay. I get a fifteen-minute break in a few minutes. The headwaiter from the dining room takes the desk for me. There's a saloon about five doors down. I'll meet you there. This time you can pay for the beers."

A portly gentleman in a black coat with a velvet collar came up to the desk and said, "Good afternoon, Joe. Any mail for me?"

"Good afternoon, Mr. Saunders," Agostino said, bowing a little. "It's nice to see you in the old place again. You out of the hospital for good now?"

"Until the next time," the portly gentleman said and laughed. Agostino laughed with him, wheezing.

"Age, you know, Joe," the man said.

"Isn't it the sad truth?" Agostino said. He turned and

was reaching into the pigeon hole with S printed over it
as Wesley went out of the club.

"The thing I remember best about him," Agostino
was saying over the beers at the end of the dark bar,
"was the day I was sparring with one of the members,
big guy he was, young, twenty-five, twenty-six, old
fucking Boston family—" the hatred was plain in his
voice, in the still-fierce, coal-black, Sicilian eyes, "—won
some sort of crappy intercollegiate championship,
pretty boy by the name of Greening, I remember the
name to this day, Greening, thought he was hot shit
with the gloves, light heavyweight, me I was still one
thirty-six, one thirty-eight at the time, he never changed
that cold, superior look on his face, the sonofabitch
caught me one on the chin, an uppercut, all his weight
behind it, I thought he'd broke my goddamn jaw. I had
a bad cold that day, I couldn't breathe, sparring in the
gym, for Christ's sake, you didn't dare tap one of the
members any harder than you'd stroke a pussy, you'd
be out on your ass before you could say boo if you drew
two drops of blood from their beautiful Beacon Hill
noses and this sonofabitch knocked me down, my teeth
loose and my mouth all bloody, not being able to
breathe, something to laugh about at the bar later with
the other fancy pisspots, sucking the blood of the poor,
the bastards." Agostino shook his head, the wisps of
hair floating on the bald pate, his hand up to the bony
jaw, as though he were still feeling to see if it was broken, the grating, furious old voice quiet for a moment.
Looking at him, Wesley found it almost impossible to
imagine him young, moving lightly around a ring, giving
and receiving blows. One thing I'm sure of, he thought,
watching Agostino noisily slurping his beer, I don't ever
want to get that old.

"After that," Agostino went on, "it was pure pleasure. Greening was miffed, he hadn't gotten his day's exercise, he said it didn't hardly pay him to have undressed and he asked your father if he wanted to go a round or two. I gave your old man the sign and he put on the gloves. Well, boy, it was a treat to the eyes. That good, old, intercollegiate, straight-up stance didnt mean balls to your father, though he took a couple of real hard ones to the head before he caught on the shit meant business with *him*, too. Then he just massacred the guy, they didn't stop for rounds or anything polite like that, they just tore into each other. For a minute there I felt that boy there was making up to me, personally, for my whole lousy life. Finally your father caught him a beauty and the old Boston family went glassyeyed and started moving in circles like a drunk comedian and Tom was ready to put the crusher on him, but I stepped in and stopped it. I wasn't worried about Tom, he knew what he was doing, but I had my job to consider. Mr. Greening, sir, came back to the land of the living, blood smeared all over his fucking Harvard Quadrangle face and just walked off with never a thank you. Your old man didn't have any doubts. 'There goes my job,' he said. 'Probably,' I said. 'It was worth it. For me.' " Agostino cackled merrily at the memory of the far-off golden moment. "Four days later I was told I had to fire him. I remember the last thing I told him— 'Never trust the rich,' I told him." He looked at the clock above the bar. "I better be gettin' back. Nice of you to come and visit, son. Thanks for the beers." He picked up the visored uniform cap he had placed on the bar and put it on his head, very straight. It was too large for him and under it his pale, bony face looked like a starved child's. He started to leave, then turned and came back. "Tell you something, son, there're a lot of people I'd have liked to see killed before your old man."

Then he shuffled, bent and arthritic, out the door to take up his post at the front desk of the club, where he would hand out the mail and laugh obsequiously, full of Sicilian dreams of vengeance and destruction, at the jokes of the members until the end of his days.

———

When he got back to New York that evening Alice could see that he was in a different mood from when he had returned from the visit to Boylan in Port Philip. "That fellow Agostino," he told her as he helped her prepare dinner in the kitchen, which consisted mostly of putting out plates and cutlery, "is a marvelous, weird old man. He sure was worth the trip." Then he told her as well as he could remember everything that the old boxer had said. She asked him to repeat sentences . . . "in the man's own words, if possible, Wesley," over and over again, as though she was trying to memorize them and get the exact tone of the man's voice, the rhythms of his speech and a picture of what he actually looked like.

"Back home in Sicily," she said, "he probably would have been burning crops and kidnapping *principessas*. Poor man, stuck in Boston, handing out mail. Oh," she said, "I got some news for you today in the office. I wrote a letter to an old newspaperman in Elysium, Ohio, who occasionally strings for us when there's anything of interest happening in that part of the world, and I think he's found your father's Clothilde for you."

"How the hell did he do that?" Wesley asked, although after Alice had discovered the whereabouts of Dominic Joseph Agostino he had begun to believe that nobody could avoid being pinpointed by *Time* Magazine if it were looking for him.

"It seems that there was a juicy divorce in Elysium

quite a few years ago," Alice said, "a respected burgher named Harold Jordache—the name's familiar to you, I imagine . . . ?" She smiled at him over the platter of cold cuts.

"Oh, come on," he said.

"His wife sued him for divorce because she found him in bed with the maid. It was big news in Elysium, Ohio, and our stringer, his name is Farrell, you might look him up if you have time, covered it for the local sheet. Farrell said the wife walked away with a bundle, the house, half the business, alimony, a woman publicly scorned and all that in a small, God-fearing town. Anyway, can you guess the name of the lady taken *in flagrante delicto?*"

"You tell me," Wesley said, although he could guess the name and even guess what *flagrante delicto* meant.

"Clothilde," Alice said triumphantly. "Clothilde Devereaux. She runs a Laundromat just down the street from Farrell's paper. I have the address in my pocketbook. How does that grab you?"

"I'll leave for Ohio tomorrow," Wesley said.

He stood in front of the Laundromat on the sleepy street. From the bus station he had called the Jordache Garage and Ford Dealer, with the idea of seeing his Great-Uncle Harold for a few minutes before looking up Clothilde Devereaux. Might as well get the ugly part over first. When Harold Jordache finally came to the phone and Wesley told him who he was, the man started to yell at him over the phone. "I don't want to have anything to do with you. Or anybody in your family." He spoke curiously, the traces of the German accent in his speech accentuated because of the high pitch of his voice. "I've had enough trouble from the goddamn Jordaches to last me a lifetime, if I live to be ninety. Don't you come snooping around here or my

house or I'll have the police on you. I don't want anything to do with the son of the man who defiled my
home. The only good thing I have to say about your
father is that he's dead. Do you hear me?"

"I hear you," Wesley said and hung up the phone.
He left the booth, shaking his head. He had been impressed by the neatness and beauty of the town as he
came in on the bus, the trimmed lawns, the white-
painted, New England—style houses, the wooden
churches with their narrow steeples, and he wondered
how anybody could remain angry as long as his Great-
Uncle Harold obviously had managed to in a pleasant
town like this. Divorce had plainly not improved his
great uncle's temper. Idly, as he walked toward the address Alice had given him for the Laundromat, he speculated on how Great-Uncle Harold and his own mother
would get along.

The Laundromat belonged to a chain and was like
any other establishment of the kind—a big plate-glass
window through which he could see rows of machines
with chairs opposite them on which some women were
sitting talking, waiting for their wash to be done.

He hesitated before going in. The way his father had
spoken about Clothilde, with such a melancholy note of
longing and regret for her beauty and goodness of character, made it seem almost silly for him to go past the
swishing machines and the gossiping women to a
counter behind which stood a thickset, short woman
handling other people's laundry and making change, to
say, "I am my father's son. He told me he loved you
very much when he was about my age."

Still, he hadn't come all the way from New York to
Ohio just to stare at a Laundromat window. He squared
his shoulders and went in and ignored the curious stares
of the women who had fallen silent to examine him as
he passed them.

The woman had her back turned to him; she was putting paper-wrapped bundles of clean laundry into the racks as he came up to the counter. Her arms were bare and he noticed that they were strong and full, the skin dark. Her hair was pitch black and she had it tied carelessly on top of her head so that he could see the powerful muscles in her neck work as she tossed the bundles into place. She was wearing a loose print dress that made her back and shoulders seem even broader than they were. He waited at the counter until she had finished with the bundles and turned around. "Yes?" she said pleasantly. Her face was broad, with high cheekbones, and almost coppery complexion, and the whole effect, he thought, with the coal-black hair and the deep black eyes, was that of an Indian squaw. He remembered his father telling him that he thought that she had Indian blood in her, some tribe in the wilderness of Canada. To him, she looked very old.

"I'm looking for Mrs. Devereaux, Mrs. Clothilde Devereaux," he said.

She stared at him, unsmiling, studying him, frowning a little, as though she was trying to remember something. "I know you," she said. "You're Tom Jordache's son, aren't you?"

"Yes," he said.

"Good God Almighty," she said. "I thought I was seeing ghosts." She smiled. "The haunted Laundromat." She chuckled. She had a deep, throaty chuckle. He liked her after the chuckle, but, being honest with himself, he couldn't see any of the beauty his father had found in this aging, wide lady. "Lean over the counter, please," she said.

He leaned over and she took his face in her hands, the palms soft and firm, and stared at him, hard, for a moment, close up, then kissed him on the forehead. Behind him he heard one of the women opposite the washing machines giggle.

She released him and he stood erect again, still feeling the touch of soft lips on his forehead. Clothilde smiled, a little, almost dreamy, sad smile. "My Lord," Clothilde said softly, "Tom's son in this town." She began to undo the strings of the apron she wore over the print dress. "We'll get out of this place," she said. "We can't talk here. Sarah!" she called to the back of the store, behind the laundry racks, "will you come here, please?"

A blond young woman with straggly hair shuffled out and Clothilde said, "Sarah, I'm taking off the rest of the afternoon. It's only an hour before closing, anyway, and I have an important date. Take over here for me and lock up like a good girl, will you?"

"Yes, ma'am," the woman said.

Clothilde hung up her apron and did something with her hair, so that it fell straight to her shoulders. It made her look more Indian than ever. She pushed up a hinged portion of the counter and came out. She had wide hips, a generous bosom and thick, strong, unstockinged legs, and suddenly she reminded him almost unbearably of Kate.

She took his arm as they passed the sitting women, who were now staring frankly at the couple, nasty little smiles curling the corners of their mouths. When they were outside, Clothilde said, "Ever since the court case, the ladies of the town keep looking at me as though I'm the Whore of Babylon." She was still holding his arm and they started walking down the street. She breathed deeply. "My," she said, "it's good to get out in the air after smelling dirty laundry all day long." She looked obliquely at him. "You've heard about the case?"

"Yes," he said. "That's how I found out where you were."

"It's an ill wind," she said. "I know your father is dead." She said it flatly, as though whatever emotion she had suffered when she heard the news had been long ago put under control. "I saw in the article that he married twice. Was he happy?"

"The second time."

She nodded her head. "I was afraid he'd never be happy again. They all kept hounding him so. . . ."

"He owned a boat. A yacht," Wesley said. "On the Mediterranean. He loved the sea."

"Imagine that," she said wonderingly. "Tom on the Mediterranean. I always meant to travel, but . . ." She left the sentence unfinished.

"He named the boat the *Clothilde.*"

"Oh, God," she said, still walking briskly, holding his arm. "The *Clothilde.*" Then he saw that she was crying, the tears falling unheeded from the dark eyes, glistening on the thick black lashes.

"When people asked him how he happened to pick the name *Clothilde* for his ship, he used to say it was the name of an old queen of France. But he told me the real reason."

"After all those years," she said, wonderingly, her voice choked. "After what happened." Now her voice turned harsh. "Did he tell you about that, too?"

"Enough," Wesley said. "That his uncle found you and him—well—together, and threatened to have you deported back to Canada for corrupting the morals of a minor. . . ."

"Did he tell you the rest of it?" Her voice was even harsher than before.

"Enough. About you and his uncle. The stuff that came out in the trial and the papers," Wesley said uncomfortably.

"That ugly, slobbering man," Clothilde said fiercely.

"I was a servant in his house. I couldn't run the risk of
going back to Canada, my husband would have killed
me. I tried to make Tom understand. He refused to understand. He wanted me to run away with him. A
sixteen-year-old boy . . ." She laughed, the sound sad
on the sunny, tree-lined street.

"He understood in the end," Wesley said. "He told
me so. The name of the boat proves that, doesn't it?"

"I suppose so." She walked in silence, drying her
tears roughly with the back of her hand. "Did he tell
you I put in a note with his sandwiches one day when
he went to work?"

"I don't think so."

"I wrote, 'I love you,'" she said. "That's how it all
started." She laughed abruptly. "My God, he had an
appetite. I never knew anybody, man or boy, who could
eat like that. The meals I cooked for him! The roasts,
the garden vegetables, the best of everything, when his
uncle and the terrible family were away in Saratoga and
we had the house to ourselves. I used to sing over the
stove in the afternoons, waiting for him to come home.
Those two weeks I'll remember all the days of my life."
She stopped walking, as though pulled up by an invisible leash, and turned him around and held him by both
arms as she stared into Wesley's eyes. "Why've you
come here? Do you need anything from me?"

"No," he said. "I came just for what you're doing—
talking about him."

After a moment of silence, in which the dark eyes
searched his face, she kissed his forehead again.

"It's uncanny," she said, "how much you look like
him. He was a beautiful young man—I told him he
looked like Saint Sebastian—he looked it up in the encyclopedia in the library—that's where he found out
where my name came from, too. It was hard to imagine

him, the sort of wild boy he was, looking up anything in the encyclopedia." Her face softened as she spoke, and Wesley imagined that she must have had very much the same expression on her face when his father had come back from the library and told her what he had learned there.

"Are you disappointed?" she asked.

"In what?"

"After what your father must have told you about me, naming a boat after me and all, queen of France . . ." She laughed briefly. "And then you see a fat old lady behind the counter of a Laundromat."

"No," Wesley said, "I'm not disappointed." He wasn't quite sure he was telling the truth. She must have been a lot different when she was younger, he thought.

"You're a decent boy," she said, as they started walking again. "I hope you're having a better time than your father did."

"I'm okay," Wesley said.

"After we—well—after we broke up, in a manner of speaking, although we still lived in the same house and I saw him every day and served him his meals with the family in the dining room, but we never said another word to each other, except for good-bye, he turned ferocious, as though he was tormented. He'd come home bloody from fights night after night, people began to treat him as though he was a stray, dangerous dog, he screwed every little tart in town. I heard about it, of course, I guess it was a kind of revenge, I didn't begrudge him it, although I knew it would one day catch up with him, in this nasty, hypocritical town. They put him in jail for rape—rape, mind you, when every girl and woman in town with hot pants was after him like kids after a fire engine. Did he tell you about that?"

"Yes."

"And the twins he was supposed to have knocked up and the father made the complaint?"

"Yes, he told me."

"He must have loved you very much," Clothilde said, "to tell you things like that."

"I guess he did. He liked to talk to me." Nights on deck, under the stars, or in the dark pilothouse.

"Naturally they would pick on him, his reputation here and all, everybody was glad to believe the worst about him," Clothilde said bitterly. "Those twins had a choice of fifty fathers! Including the cop who arrested Tom. I see them—the twins—they're still in town, grown women. I advise you not to look *them* up. One of the kids looks as though he was your brother." Clothilde chuckled merrily. "Finally, there's some decent blood running through a few veins in this town. Ah . . ." she said softly, "sometimes late at night, I take to wondering what it would have been like, how it all would have turned out if I'd listened to his crazy begging and run off with him, a twenty-five-year-old servant and a sixteen-year-old boy, without a penny between us. . . . I couldn't do it to him, could I?" she asked, pleading.

"No, I guess not," Wesley said.

"Ah, I keep on talking. About myself. About ancient history." Clothilde shook her head impatiently. "What about you? Are you all right?"

"Not too bad," Wesley said.

"You having a good time?"

"I wouldn't go as far as to say that."

"Still," she said, "you look as though you're being taken care of—nice clothes and all, like a young gentleman."

"I've been lucky," Wesley said. "In a way. Somebody is taking care of me. Sort of."

"You can tell me all about yourself over dinner. You're in no hurry to leave town, are you?"

"Not really," Wesley said. "I figured tomorrow."

"I'll make you a roast loin of pork, with mashed potatoes and applesauce and red cabbage. It was one of your father's favorite meals." She hesitated. "I have to tell you something, Wesley," she said. "I'm not alone. I'm living with a nice man, he's the foreman at the furniture factory. We're not married. He's got a wife and two kids and they're Catholics. . . . He'll be at dinner. You don't mind?" she asked anxiously.

"It's got nothing to do with me," Wesley said, "or my father."

"People're funny," Clothilde said. "You never know how they're going to react." She sighed. "A woman can't live alone. At least not me. Ah, you live two days—every day, with the man coming home and sitting down at night to read his paper and drink his beer and not say anything much to you, and in your memory, the wonderful days you had when you were younger, with a wild boy. Wesley, I have to tell you, your father was the gentlest and tenderest man a woman could ever hope to find in her travels on this earth. And he had the softest skin, like silk, over all those young muscles, that I've ever felt. You don't mind my talking like this, do you?"

"I want to hear it," Wesley said, feeling the tears come to his eyes now, not for himself or even for his dead father, but for this wide-shouldered, Indian-dark, aging woman, marked by a lifetime of work and disappointment, walking by his side.

"Do you like wine with your dinner?" Clothilde asked.

"I wouldn't mind a glass," Wesley said. "I was in France for quite a long time."

"We'll stop in at the liquor store," Clothilde said gaily, "and buy a delicious bottle of red wine to celebrate the visit of my love's beautiful son to an old lady. Frank—that's my man, the foreman at the furniture factory, can give up his beer for the occasion."

————

Schultz, his father's old manager, was, Alice told him, in the Hebrew Home for the Aged in the Bronx.

"He's that fat old man sitting in the hall with his hat and coat on as though he's going out," the attendant told Wesley. "Only he never goes out. He sits like that all day, every day, never saying anything. I don't know if he'll talk to you. He don't talk to anyone else."

Wesley walked down the bare hall to where an enormously fat man, bloating out of his suit and overcoat, a derby hat squarely on his head, his features little squiggles in the immense expanse of his face, sat on a straight wooden chair, staring at the opposite wall, the eyes half closed, the breath coming in snorts.

"Mr. Schultz," Wesley said, "can I talk to you for a minute?"

The fat man's wrinkled eyelids lifted heavily and the eyes slowly turned in Wesley's direction, although the head, with its derby, remained rigid.

"What's it to you if I'm Schultz or I'm not Schultz?" the fat man said. His voice was guttural and there was a clacking of dentures as he spoke.

"My name is Wesley Jordache," Wesley said. "A long time ago you managed my father. Tom Jordan."

The eyes slowly went back to their original position, staring at the peeling paint of the wall of the corridor. "Tom Jordan," the fat man said. "I don't allow that name to be used in my presence. I hear tell he got himself killed. Son or no son, don't think you're going to hear old Schultzy say he's sorry. He had it in him to go someplace and he screwed it away. Two weeks with an

English whore, eating and drinking like a pig, after all I did to bring him along. And then, when he was down on his ass I got him a salary in Las Vegas. He got fifty bucks a day sparring with Freddy Quayles—there was a boy, my one chance in my whole miserable life to handle a champion—and what does he do, he shacks up with Quayles' wife, and then when Quayles goes to his room to object to his conduct, he near murders him. And Quayles couldn't beat my mother after that. If I hadn't taken pity on your stupid old man and loaned him my car to get out of Vegas, the mob would've cut him to little pieces with steak knives. Your old man wasn't anything to be proud of, boy, and that's for certain, but he sure was dynamite in a hotel room. Only, for money, you have to fight in a ring twenty-four by twenty-four feet, with a referee on the premises. If they let your old man fight in a closet and charged admission he'd still be the champion of the world, the sonofabitch. My once chance, Freddy Quayles, moved like a dancer, wrecked for cunt. You want to hear about your old man—I'll tell you about your old man—he let his cock destroy him."

"But you were with him before that," Wesley said, "there were other things . . ."

"Destroyed by his cock," the fat man said, with the clacking of dentures, as he stared straight ahead of him. "I said my say. Get the fuck out of here, I'm a busy man."

Wesley started to say something else, then realized it was hopeless. He shrugged and went out, leaving the fat man in his overcoat and derby hat staring at the wall across from him.

Dutifully, now knowing whether to laugh or cry as he spoke, Wesley made his report of the visit with Schultz to Alice. When he finished, he said, "I don't know whether I want to talk to anyone else who knew him, at least on this side of the Atlantic. Maybe there are some things a son shouldn't hear about his father. A lot of things, maybe. What's the sense in my listening to people smear him all over the country? He must have been a different man while he was in America. There's no connection between the man I knew and the man these people're talking about. If I hear one more person tell me how rotten my father was and how glad they are he's dead, maybe I'll go back to Indianapolis and let my mother cut my hair and take me to church and forget about my father once and for all. . . ." He stopped when he saw the disapproval on Alice's face.

"That's quitting," she said.

"Maybe that's the name of the game," Wesley said. "At least my game."

"Clothilde didn't talk like that about your father," Alice said, her eyes angry behind her glasses.

"A fat lady in a Laundromat," Wesley said cruelly.

"Say you're sorry you said that," Alice said, sounding schoolteacherly.

"All right," he said listlessly, "I'm sorry. But, I have a feeling I'm just wasting time and money. My time," he said, with a wry smile, "and your money."

"Don't you worry about my money," she said.

"I suppose," Wesley said, "the character in your book is a fine, upstanding young man who never gets down in the dumps and he finds out that his father was one of nature's noblemen, who went around while he was alive doing good deeds and helping the poor and being nice to old ladies and never screwing a friend's wife. . . ."

"Shut up, Wesley," Alice said. "That's enough of that. Don't you tell me what I'm writing. When the book comes out, if it ever comes out, you can buy it and then tell me what the characters are like. Not before."

They were in the living room, Alice seated in an easy chair and Wesley standing at the window looking out at the dark street. Alice was dressed to go out because she had a date to go to a party and was waiting for the man who was going to escort her.

"I hate this goddamn city," Wesley said, staring down at the empty street, "I wish I was a thousand miles out to sea. Oh, hell!" He moved away from the window and threw himself full length on the sofa. "Christ, if I could only be back in France, just one night, with people I love and who I know love me . . ."

"Take your shoes off the sofa," Alice said sharply. "You're not in a stable."

"Sorry," he said, moving his legs so that his feet were on the floor. "I was brought up uncouth, or so people keep telling me."

Then he heard her sobbing. He lay still for a moment, closing his eyes, wishing the dry, uneven sound would go away. But it didn't go away and he jumped up and went over to the chair in which she was sitting with her head in her hands, her shoulders moving convulsively. He knelt in front of her and put his arms around her. She felt small and fragile and soft in her pretty black party dress.

"I'm sorry," he said gently. "Honest, I didn't mean what I said, honest. I'm just sore at myself and that's how it came out. Don't think I don't appreciate everything you've done for me. I don't want to let you down, only sometimes, like tonight . . ."

She raised her head, her face tearstained. "Forgive me for crying," she said. "I hate women who cry. I had an awful day, too, people were yelling at me all day. You can put your shoes on the sofa anytime you want." She laughed, through her tears.

"Never again," he said, still holding her, glad that she had laughed, wanting to protect her against disappointment and people yelling at her all day and the city and his own black character.

They looked at each other in silence, her clear wet eyes magnified by her glasses. She smiled tremulously at him. He pulled her gently toward him and kissed her. She put her arm around him and held him. Her lips were as soft as anything he had ever imagined, the very essence of softness. Finally, she pulled away from him. All tears were gone. "So, that's what a girl has to do to get a kiss around here," she said, laughing.

The doorbell rang from downstairs. She jumped out of the chair and he stood up. "There's my date," she said. "Entertain him while I fix my face. His field is archaeology."

She fled into the bathroom.

There was a knock on the door and Wesley opened it. A tall, skinny young man with a domed forehead and steel-rimmed glasses was standing there. "Hello," the man said. "Is Alice in?"

"She'll be out in a minute," Wesley said, closing the door as the man came in. "I'm to entertain you until she's ready. My name is Jordache. I'm her cousin."

"Robinson," the man said. They shook hands.

Wesley wondered how he was expected to entertain him. "You want to listen to the radio?" he asked.

"Not especially," the man said. "May I sit down?"

"Of course."

Robinson sat down in the easy chair and crossed his long legs and took out a package of cigarettes. "Smoke?" he said, offering the package to Wesley.

"No, thanks." He watched Robinson light his cigarette. How did you talk to a man whose field is archaeology? "I saw some ruins in France when I was there," he offered hopefully. "The arena in Nîmes, Arles, stuff like that," he said lamely.

"Is that so?" Robinson said, blowing smoke. "Interesting."

Wesley wondered if Robinson would be so offhand if he was told that just before he rang the bell, Wesley had kissed Alice Larkin, Robinson's date for the night, in the very chair he was sitting in and that before that he had made her cry. He felt condescendingly superior to the lanky man in his baggy slacks and five-colored, nubbly tweed jacket with leather patches on the elbows, although maybe that was the way all archaeologists dressed, maybe it was a uniform that commanded respect in those circles. "Where did you dig?" he said abruptly.

"What's that?" Robinson stopped his cigarette in midair, on the way to his mouth.

"I said, where did you dig?" Wesley said. "Alice told me you were in the field. Isn't that what archaeologists do—dig?"

"Oh, I see what you mean. Syria mostly. A little bit in Turkey."

"What did you find?" Alice had asked him to entertain the man and he was doing his best.

"Shards, mostly."

"I see," Wesley said, resolving to look up the word. "Shards."

"You interested in archaeology?"

"Moderately," Wesley said.

There was a silence and Wesley had the impression Robinson wasn't being entertained. "What's Syria like?" he asked.

"Grim," Robinson said. "Grim and beautiful. You ought to go there some day."

"I plan to," Wesley said.

"What college you go to?" Robinson asked.

"I haven't made up my mind yet," Wesley said.

"I would go to Stanford," said Robinson. "If you could get in. Marvelous people out there."

"I'll remember that."

Robinson peered at him nearsightedly through the steel-rimmed glasses. "You said you were Alice's cousin?"

"Yes."

"I didn't know she had a cousin," Robinson said. "Where you from?"

"Indianapolis," Wesley said promptly.

"Dreadful place. What're you doing in New York?"

"Visiting Alice."

"Oh, I see. Where do you stay in New York?"

"Here," Wesley said, feeling as though the man were excavating him.

"Oh." Robinson looked around at the small room gloomily. "A little cramped, I'd say."

"We make do."

"It's a convenient location. Near Lincoln Center and all . . ." Robinson seemed depressed. "Where do you sleep?"

"On the sofa."

Robinson stubbed out his cigarette and lit another. "Well," he said, sounding more depressed than ever, "I suppose . . . cousins . . ."

Alice came in, bright as a rosebud, with her party contacts in place, so she wouldn't look like a secretarial mouse, as she had explained to Wesley other times she had gone out on dates.

"Well," she said gaily, "have you two gentlemen had a nice chat?"

"Fascinating," Robinson said gloomily as he heaved

himself to his feet. "We'd better be going. It's late." Alice must be pretty hard up, Wesley thought, if Robinson was the best she could do, a man who spent his life digging up shards. He wished, despairingly, that he was twenty-seven years old. He was glad he wasn't going to be around when Alice had to explain to the archaeologist just what sort of cousins they were.

"Wesley," Alice said, "there're two roast beef sandwiches and some beer in the icebox if you get hungry. Oh—I nearly forgot—I found the address and telephone number of the man you were looking for—Mr. Renway, who was a shipmate of your father's. I called him today and he said he's looking forward to seeing you. I got his address through the National Maritime Union. It's right near here, in the West Nineties. He lives with his brother when he's not at sea. He sounded awfully nice on the telephone. You going to see him? He said he'd be in all day tomorrow."

"I'll see how I feel tomorrow," Wesley said ungraciously and Alice gave him a reproachful look.

Robinson helped Alice on with her coat, and said as they went out the door, "Remember Stanford."

"I will," Wesley said, thinking, the reason he's so keen on Stanford is it's three thousand miles away from Alice Larkin.

He had no idea what time it was when he was awakened, as he slept under the blanket on the sofa, by the sound of murmured conversation on the other side of the front door. Then there was the click of the key in the lock and he heard Alice come in, softly, alone. She came over silently to the sofa and he felt her staring down at him, but he kept his eyes closed, pretending to be asleep. He heard her sigh, then move away. A moment later he heard her door shut and then the sound of her typewriter.

I wonder what she expected me to do? he thought, just before he fell back to sleep.

———————

Calvin Renway reminded Wesley of Bunny Dwyer. His skin was coffee-colored, almost the same as Bunny's when Bunny had been out in the sun all summer, and he was small and delicate-boned and the muscles of his arms showed sharply in his short-sleeved flowered shirt and his voice was gentle, with an underlying permanent tone of politeness, as he welcomed Wesley at the door of his brother's home, saying, "Well, this is a nice day, the son of Tom Jordache come to visit. Come in, boy, come in. The nice lady on the phone said you'd be coming up, come in."

He led Wesley into the living room and pushed the biggest chair a couple of inches toward him and said, "Make yourself comfortable, boy. Can I get you a beer? It's past noon, time for a beer."

"No, thank you, Mr. Renway," Wesley said.

"The name's Calvin, Wesley," Renway said. "I sure was surprised when that nice lady called and said you'd be looking for me—I haven't seen your father for all these years—you ship out with a man and he means something special to you that you carry with you all your days, and then he goes his way and you go yours—ships that pass in the night, as you might say—and then a big young man rings your doorbell—by God the time does pass, doesn't it?—I never got married, never had any son, to my sorrow, a seaman's life, one port after another, no time to court a woman and the ones who want to enter into wedlock"—he laughed heartily, gleaming white teeth in the wide, kindly mouth "—not the sort you'd want as the mother of your kids, if you ever could be sure, if you know what I mean. But there's no mistaking about you, boy, the moment you appeared at the door, there was no mistake, there was Tom Jordache's kid, yes, sir, I bet he's proud of you, a big strong boy, with Tom Jordache printed all over your face. . . ."

"Mr. Renway—Calvin, I mean—" Wesley said uneasily, "didn't the lady tell you over the phone?"

Renway looked puzzled. "Tell me what?" he said. "All the lady said to me was, Are you the Mr. Renway was once on the same cargo vessel with Tom Jordache? and when I said, Yes, ma'am, the same, she said, Tom Jordache's boy is in town and he'd like to talk to you for a few minutes, that's all she said and asked if my address was the same she got from the Maritime Union."

"Calvin," Wesley said, "my father's dead. He got murdered in Antibes."

"Oh, Lord," Renway whispered. He said nothing more, but turned his face away to the wall, silently, for a long minute, hiding pain, as though somehow it was a breach of manners to show unbearable sorrow publicly. His long dark hands clenched and unclenched in an unconscious spasm, as though his hands were the only part of him that hadn't learned the lesson that it was useless to let the world know when he was hurting.

Finally, he turned back to Wesley. "Murdered," he said flatly. "They sure do away with the good ones, don't they? Don't tell me the story, boy. Some other time. It can wait, I'm in no hurry for any details. It's kind of you to come and tell me what happened—I could've gone on for years without knowing and I might be in a bar in Marseilles or New Orleans or someplace, drinking a couple of beers and talking about the old days when we crewed together on the *Elga Anderson,* maybe the nastiest vessel on the Atlantic or any other ocean, when he saved my life, in a manner of speaking, and somebody would say, 'Tom Jordache, why he died ages ago.' It's better this way and I thank you. I suppose you want to talk about him, boy—that's why you're here, I take it . . . ?"

"If you don't mind," Wesley said.

"Times were different then," Renway said. "On ships, anyway. They didn't call us blacks those days or mister, we were niggers and never forget it. I'm not saying your father was a special friend or a preacher or anything like that, but when he passed me in the morning, it was always, Hi, bud, how're they treating you, nothing special, just a normal human greeting, which was like a band playing those days on that nasty ship, the way just about everybody else was treating me. Your pa ever mention the name Falconetti to you?"

"I know something about him."

"The nastiest man I ever had the misfortune to come across, black or white," Renway said. "Big bull of a man, terrorized the crew, he beat up on men just for the animal pleasure of it and out of meanness of spirit and he said he wouldn't let no niggers sit down in the same messroom with him and I was the only black on board and that meant whenever he came into the room, even if I was in the middle of supper, I'd have to get up and go out. Then your pa took him on, the only one out of a crew of twenty-eight who had the guts to do it—he didn't do it for me, Falconetti'd been bugging Bunny Dwyer too—and your pa gave him the licking of his life, maybe he went too far, like the other men said, he shamed him every day, whenever they happened to pass each other, your pa'd say, come over here, slob, and punch him hard in the stomach, so that that big bull of a man would be left standing there, with people watching, bent over, with tears in his eyes.

"One night, it was dark and stormy, waves thirty feet

high, in the messroom Falconetti quiet as a lamb, your pa came and got me and took me back to the messroom, the radio was on, and he said, 'We're just going to sit down like gentlemen next to this gentleman here and enjoy the music.' I sat myself down next to Falconetti—my heart was beating, I can assure you, I was still scared—but nobody said as much as boo and finally, after a while, your pa said to the man, 'You can go now, slob,' and Falconetti got up and looked around at the men in the room, none of them looking at him, and he went out and up to the deck and jumped over the side.

"It didn't make your pa popular with the other men; they said it's one thing to beat up on a man, but it's another to send him to his death like that. I'm not a vengeful man, Wesley, but I didn't go along with that talk—I kept remembering how I felt sitting down next to that nasty man, with the music playing, and him not saying a single word. I tell you it was one of the greatest, most satisfactory moments of my life and I remember it to this day with pleasure and I owe it to your pa and I'll never forget it."

Renway had been talking in a kind of singsong chant, with his eyes almost closed, as though seeing the whole thing over again, as though he was not in the neat little living room in the West Nineties in New York City, but back in the hushed messroom among the silent, uncomfortable men, tasting once more the moment of exquisite pleasure, safe, protected by the courage of the father of the boy sitting across from him.

He opened his eyes and looked thoughtfully at Wesley. "I tell you, boy," he said, "if you turn out to be half the man your father was, you should bless God every day for your luck. Wait here a minute." He stood up and went into a bedroom that gave off the living room.

Wesley could hear a drawer opening, then closing a few seconds later. Renway came back into the living room carrying something wrapped in tissue paper. He took off the tissue paper and Wesley saw that he was holding a small leather box, inlaid with gold. "I bought this box in Italy," Renway said, "in the town of Florence, they make them there, it's a specialty of the town. Here." He thrust it toward Wesley. "Take it."

Wesley held back. "It's your box, Calvin," he said. "It must have cost an awful lot of dough. What do you want to give it to me for, you didn't even know I was alive until yesterday afternoon?"

"Take it," Renway said harshly. "I want the son of the man who did what he did for me to have something I cherish." Gently, he placed the box in Wesley's hand.

"It's a beautiful box," Wesley said. "Thanks."

"Save your thanks for a time they're needed," Renway said. "Now I'm going to put on my coat and I'm going to take you up to One Hundred and Twenty-Fifth Street and I'm going to feed you the best lunch money can buy in Harlem in the city of New York."

The lunch was enormous, fried chicken and sweet potatoes, and they drank a lot of beer with it and Renway put sorrow aside for a time and told Wesley stories about Glasgow and Rio de Janeiro and Piraeus and the Trieste and said his brother kept after him to quit the sea but whenever he thought of living on land and never seeing a new town rising up from the sea as they made port, he knew that he could never bring himself to stop wandering on good ships and bad ships across the length and breadth of the oceans.

When they said good-bye, he made Wesley swear that whenever he heard he was in town he would come and have a meal with him again.

Going downtown in the subway, with the gold-inlaid, hard leather box in his pocket, Wesley decided he was going to throw away his list. I'm going to quit while I'm ahead, he told himself, feeling a weight lifting from his heart.

# CHAPTER 3

Rudolph was sitting on the deck in front of the house he had rented, looking out over the high dune at the stretch of white beach and the rollers of the open Atlantic. It was a mild, mid-September morning and the sun was pleasantly warm, reflecting off the script of Gretchen's screenplay that he was rereading. Next to him, stretched out on an air mattress in a bathing suit, lay Helen Morison, who had a house farther down the beach, but who spent several nights a week with him. She was a divorcée, who had come over to him at a neighbor's cocktail party and introduced herself because she recognized him. She was a friend of Gretchen's. They had become acquainted at one of Ida Cohen's Women's Liberation meetings, where, according to Gretchen, Helen Morison's ironic, efficient manner of presenting facts and programs was in marked contrast to Ida's wild lunges at the perfidy of the male sex. Helen had no enmity toward the male sex. Rudolph had noted. "Quite the contrary," he had told her and she had laughed and agreed. The fact that she was living on Mr. Morison's alimony and sending her thirteen-year-

old son to an exclusive, all-boys' Episcopal school, also
at Mr. Morison's expense, did not seem to trouble her.
Rudolph, who knew how often his own actions hardly
reflected his principles, never pressed the point with
her.

She was a tall, slender woman, with a profile that
could be stern in repose. She did not need a brassiere
and she wore her dark, reddish-brown hair long and often put it up in the evenings when he came to take her
to dinner. In a rigorously Republican community, she
was at the forefront of the Democratic Party affairs and
had lost friends in the process. She was one of those
women who could be depended upon more than most
men to act courageously in a disaster.

She had been for her daily swim that morning, even
though the sea was growing colder every night and the
air was cool. She did not neglect her body. She made no
secret of the fact that they were lovers.

He was very fond of her. Perhaps more than that.
But he was not the man to rush to expose his emotions
or make declarations that would haunt him later, when
all the facts were in, the emotions added up.

For the moment he was engrossed in Gretchen's
movie project. In rereading the screenplay he liked it
more than ever. It was called *Restoration Comedy*, a
play on words, since the plot involved the young heroine in bullying, cajoling, begging and arguing an entire
dying mill town in Pennsylvania, a fictitious community
called Laundston, into restoring five streets of fine old
town houses that had fallen into neglect when the mill
had shut down. The script was full of the energy of the
girl who, with guile, good looks, coquetry and a wild
sense of humor, combined with a pragmatic, womanly
attitude toward occasional dishonesty, captured cynical
bankers, crooked politicians, starving young architects,
lonely secretaries, stultified bureaucrats, failing contrac-

tors, dragooned college students into doing day-
laborers' work, in the process of creating an esthetically
satisfactory, financially sound, middle-income suburb,
which now, because of the new highways, was easily ac-
cessible to commuters from Philadelphia and Camden.
The interesting part of it, to Rudolph, was that even
though it was a complete work of fiction and no such
place existed, it seemed to him, as a hardheaded businessman, like an eminently practical idea.

He was not sure of two things, though: the title,
which he thought smacked a little of a course in English
literature, and Gretchen's ability to bring it off. Still, it
wasn't only brotherly indulgence that had made him
back Gretchen to the tune of a third of the film's budget
and spend countless hours with Johnny Heath wrangling over contracts in Gretchen's behalf. Ida Cohen
and Gretchen herself had found backers for the rest of
the cost of the picture and given enough time could
have got all the financing without him.

It amused him, and he didn't mind driving into New
York twice a week for it, and now he didn't have to say
to friends that they could call at any time, he'd be at
home all day.

It had taken months and months to get this far and
Rudolph had learned a great deal about the movie business, not all of it agreeable, but Gretchen had called to
ask him to come to New York the next day, not in his
capacity as an angel, but as an "idea man," as she put
it, because, when they were talking together about
where to find a suitable location, he had suggested, half
jokingly, their old hometown, Port Philip, where a
whole quarter of great old houses had lain derelict for
more than twenty years. Gretchen had gone up there
with architects and the scene designer and they had all
told Rudolph that the place was perfect and Gretchen
was well on her way toward making a deal with the

mayor and the town board to get all the help necessary
for shooting the picture there. Rudolph was not sure he
was ever going to visit the company on location. In the
end, Port Philip and the neighboring town of Whitby
did not have the most pleasant associations for him.

He finished reading the script with a last little
chuckle.

"You still like it?" Helen asked.

"More than ever." He knew that Helen thought the
script wasn't openly partisan enough in its politics. She
also said the same thing about *his* politics. "You have
been numbed by the Cold War," she said, "and the cor-
ruption in Washington and Vietnam and general hardening of the arteries. When was the last time you
voted?"

"I don't remember," he said, although he did—for
Johnson in 1964. After that, the process had seemed
footless.

"Shame," Helen said. She voted ferociously, whenever she got the opportunity. There was no hardening of
the arteries for Helen Morison. "Don't you think
Gretchen needs a political adviser? I'd do it for free."

"I would think that's the last thing she needs," Rudolph said. "For free or no."

"I will finally convert you," Helen said.

"To what?"

"Jeffersonian democracy," she said. "Whatever *that*
means."

"Please," Rudolph said, "spare me Jeffersonian democracy. Whatever it means."

Helen chuckled. She had a nice, open chuckle.
"Now," she said, "this is the sort of place to talk about
politics. On the beach in the sunshine after a nice brisk
swim. There'd never be a war."

He leaned over and kissed her. Her skin was salty
from the ocean. He wondered why he had gone so long

without a woman since Jeanne. With Helen just a little
way down the dunes from him there was no need to
cross the sea. In recent years doctors had been publicly
advocating regular sexual activity as a deterrent to heart
disease. Think of Helen as a health measure, he thought
with an inward smile, because he knew how furious she
would be if he said it aloud. "In your own way," he said
lightly, "you are glorious."

"Have you ever paid a woman a compliment," she
asked, "without adding a modifying clause?"

"I don't remember," he said. "Actually, I don't remember any other women."

She laughed, mockingly. "Should I wear my scarlet
letter into New York tomorrow?"

"Don't forget your wimple, either," he said.

"If we made love right out here, with me all salty and
sandy and you thinking about money and contracts,"
she said, "would the neighbors be shocked?"

"No," he said. "but I would."

"You've got a long way to go, brother," she said.

"You bet. And I won't go there."

"After lunch? I'm cooking."

"What're you cooking?"

"Something light, nourishing and aphrodisiacal," she
said. "Like clam chowder. See how you feel at two P.M.
The phone's ringing inside." She had a remarkably
acute sense of hearing and he was always amused when
she repeated, word for word, whispered conversations,
usually malicious ones about herself, that she had somehow overheard across a noisy room while she was holding forth to two or three captive listeners on some pet
subject of hers. "Should I answer it? I'll say I'm the
butler and that you're upstairs doing your yoga and
can't be disturbed."

"I'll take it," he said. It still made him a little uneasy
whenever she answered the phone and made it plain

that she was very much at home in his house. "Just be
here when I get back."

"Never fear," she said. "This sun is sleepy-making."

He stood up and went into the house. The maid only
came three times a week and this was not one of her
days. As always, he was pleased with the way the house
looked as he went through the big glass doors facing the
sea and saw the pale wood and comfortable corduroy
couches and the wide old polished planks of the floor of
the living room.

"Rudolph," Gretchen said, "I've got a problem. Are
you busy?"

He repressed a sigh. Gretchen had at least one problem a week that she called him about. If she had a husband, he thought, her telephone bill would be decreased
by half. Last week the problem had been Ida Cohen's
uncle, who had been a movie producer in Hollywood
and had retired after a stroke. He was a shrewd old
man who knew the business and when Ida had shown
him the script he had volunteered to work for them, sitting in the little office in New York and wrangling with
actors' agents and coming up with ideas on casting and
distribution and doing the daily dirty work of signing
actors' and technicians' contracts and politely letting
down candidates for jobs. But he had been sick for
three days and Gretchen was afraid he'd had another
stroke and she wanted to know what Rudolph thought
she ought to do about Ida Cohen's uncle. Rudolph had
said talk to his doctor and Gretchen had found out that
it was merely a head cold.

Then there was the problem of Billy Abbott, which
Gretchen had called Rudolph about in the middle of the
night, her voice full of emotion. Billy's father had telephoned from Chicago. "This time sober," Gretchen had
said, to underline the gravity of the situation. "Billy's
written his father," Gretchen had said, "telling him he's

going to reenlist. Willie's just as against it as I am. A
professional noncom! That's just what he and I wanted
our son to be! Willie wants us both to go over to Brussels together to talk him out of it, but I can't leave New
York for a minute at this time, you know that. Then
Willie suggested that I offer Billy a job on the picture—
third assistant director, anything. But Billy doesn't
know the first thing about movies—I don't think he's
seen three in his life—he's not normal for this day and
age—and he's lazy and disloyal—and if he took the job
it would be the same kind of nepotism that sent the old
Hollywood studios into oblivion. Even if it didn't mean
much money, it would just be stealing from our backers,
including you. I told Willie I couldn't give him a job
and I couldn't go to Brussels and why didn't *he* go himself and see what he could do and he said he didn't have
the money and would I advance the fare? Advance!
Hah! Anyway, every cent I have I've got tied up in
*Restoration Comedy,* and he said why didn't I get it
from you and I said I absolutely forbade him to ap-
proach you." As the date for the actual shooting neared,
Gretchen's sentences had become more and more
rushed and her voice had risen in tense crescendo. It
was a bad sign, Rudolph felt, and would give rise to
nervous explosions later.

"How about you?" Gretchen had said, hesitant now.
"You don't have to be going over to Europe for anything, do you?"

"No," Rudolph had said. "I've finished with Europe
for the time being. Anyway, what's so terrible about
having a son in the army?"

"You know as well as I do," Gretchen said, "that
sooner or later there's going to be another war."

"There's nothing much either you or I can do about
it," Rudolph said. "Is there?"

*"You* can say that," she'd said. "You have a daughter." And had hung up.

Then there was the call about the problem of casting the role of the heroine's young brother, the part Gretchen had thought she wanted to test Wesley for. He was supposed to be beautiful and sad and cynical, constantly throwing cold water on his sister's enthusiasm, given to repeating the line, "You can't beat the numbers, man!" In the script, although he was supposed to be intellectually advanced far beyond his years and full of a variety of talents, he deliberately wasted himself, scornfully taking a job as a serviceman at the local airport and playing semiprofessional football on Sundays and consorting with the lowest and idlest and least salvageable of the ruffians of the town. Gretchen was sure, she said, that Wesley would be wonderful for it, just by the way he looked, with a minimum of acting, and none of the other boys she had tested had satisfied her and she had written to Wesley time and time again, but the letters had all been returned unclaimed, with no forwarding address, from General Delivery in Indianapolis. She wanted to know if Rudolph knew where to find Wesley, but Rudolph told her that he hadn't heard from Wesley since the telephone call from Chicago. He had never told Gretchen about the warrant for Wesley's arrest in Indianapolis. He was sure that Wesley would turn up eventually, but that wouldn't help Gretchen with her casting now. He also doubted that Wesley could be useful as an actor. If Wesley had a single outstanding characteristic it was that he kept his emotions to himself, not the highest recommendation for a film career. Added to that there was Rudolph's own unstated but ingrained snobbishness toward the profession of acting. Overpaid, narcissistic grown men at play, he would have said if pressed.

From where he was standing at the phone in the living room he saw Helen rise from the air mattress and begin to do slow and difficult exercises, stretching, bending, like a ballet dancer, outlined in salt against the glittering sea. Gretchen's voice in the receiver grated on his ears.

"What's the problem now?"

"This one's serious," Gretchen said. She said the same thing about each of her problems, but he didn't remind her of that. "Evans Kinsella called me this morning," Gretchen said. "He just got in from California last night. He's changed his mind. He wants to do *Restoration Comedy* himself now. He says he's got two million to do it and major distribution and two stars. He's ready to pay everybody off, with a profit of ten percent for all the backers."

"He's a sonofabitch," Rudolph said. "What did you tell him?"

"I told him I had to think it over," Gretchen said. "We have a date to meet at his hotel in a half hour."

"Talk to him," Rudolph said, "and call me back. Say no, if you want to, but don't say yes until you've talked to me." He hung up the phone. Ten percent on his investment in only two months, he thought. Not a bad return. Still, the idea of it gave him no pleasure. Outside, on the deck, Helen was still doing her exercises. After Gretchen's call he could use the aphrodisiacal lunch this afternoon.

Gretchen carefully put on her makeup, fluffed up her hair, chose her smartest suit and dabbed herself with Femme, a perfume that Evans had once said he liked on her. Ida Cohen would not have approved, she thought, heightening her femininity, making herself the alluring female animal for what, being realistic, was merely a business appointment, and one with unsavory overtones at that. At my age , it gets harder and harder,

Gretchen thought, looking in the full-length mirror, to make myself into an alluring female animal. Getting to sleep these nights was difficult, and she had been taking pills and it showed. Damn Evans Kinsella. She put on an extra dab of perfume.

Evans was freshly shaved and was wearing a jacket and tie when she went up to his apartment in the Regency Hotel on Park Avenue. He usually met her in his shirt-sleeves or in a robe when he summoned her to his place. He had decided on charm for this meeting. She felt a tingling all over her body as he kissed her first on one cheek then on the other, a salutation he had brought back with him when he had made a picture in Paris. She resented her body for the tingle.

In the ornate salon with him was Richard Sanford, the young author of *Restoration Comedy,* dressed, as usual, in an open-necked wool shirt, a windbreaker, jeans and high, unpolished boots. Careless, unconventional poverty was the public expression of his background and his beliefs. Gretchen wondered what he would dress like in Hollywood after his third picture. He was a pleasant young man, with a wide, slow smile and respectful manner, and had always been most friendly with Gretchen in all their dealings. Although she had been seeing him almost every day, he had never mentioned that he even knew Kinsella. Conspiracy was the word that crossed her mind.

Today, she saw, Richard Stanford was not going to be friendly, not friendly at all. He would go a long way in California, would Richard Sanford.

Beware young men, Gretchen thought, looking at the two young men. Although at the age of thirty-three, Evans Kinsella, with what he had learned, copied and stolen, could hardly be considered a young man. She should have brought Ida Cohen with her to balance the company, but it would have been like bringing along a small volcano just waiting to erupt. She had not yet told Ida about Kinsella's call. Time enough for that.

"Would you like a wee drop?" Kinsella gestured toward the table on which the bottles were neatly placed, with glasses and ice. There must be a single waiter in hotels like this one, Gretchen thought, expert in his field, who rushes from room to room, distributing bottles in strict formal arrangement as soon as the telex comes announcing the impending arrival of the nabobs of the new aristocracy—the abundance and quality of the arrangement depending upon the current importance of the particular nabob in the manager's files. Gretchen saw, with some malice, that the display on Kinsella's bar was merely medium. His last picture had been a flop and the hotel manager's private *Almanach de Gotha* reflected it. "Our young genius and I have been regaling oursleves," Kinsella said. "In a modest fashion. To get into the proper festive mood for your arrival. What's the lady's pleasure?"

"I'll skip it, thank you," Gretchen said. "It's a little early for a working girl." She was going to keep the tone light and calm, even if it meant bursting a blood vessel. "Young genius," she said, smiling blandly at the boy. "Evans must have changed his mind about you, Richard."

"I happened to reread the script," Kinsella said hastily. "I must have read it the first time on a bad morning."

"As I remember," Gretchen said, her voice honeyed, "you told me it was a load of shit." One assassination deserved another. She saw with pleasure that Sanford flushed as he put his glass down and stared at Kinsella.

"Artists make mistakes all the time, Dick," Kinsella said. Gretchen noted the familiar diminutive. "There're always a thousand people pulling you every which way. Atonement is possible." He turned his attention, smiling with difficulty at Gretchen. "Among other reasons for this little conference," he said, "is that Dick and I have talked the script over and we've agreed on some changes that would be helpful. Rather drastic changes. Haven't we, Dick?"

"Yes," Sanford said. He was still flushed.

"Two days ago," Gretchen said to the young man, "you told me it was ready to go, you didn't want a word changed."

"Evans pointed out a few things to me that I'd missed," Sanford said. He sounded like a little boy who was being stubborn and knew he was going to be punished for it. The conspiracy went back weeks, perhaps months.

"Let's be honest, Gretchen," Kinsella said. "With two million in the pot, Sanford is going to get a guarantee about three times what you've offered him. He's not a rich man, as you know. He has a wife and a young child to support . . ."

"Maestro," Gretchen said, "will you play the violin, tremolo, with that line?"

Kinsella scowled. "You've forgotten what it's like to be poor and struggling for each month's rent, my dear. With your rich brother you've always had a big fat cushion to fall back on. Well, Dick hasn't any cushion."

"What I'd like you to forget, Evans," Gretchen said, "is that I have a brother. Fat or skinny or any shape whatever. And what I'd like you *not* to forget, Richard . . ." She emphasized his name. ". . . is that you have a contract with me."

"I was coming to that," Kinsella said. He was speaking smoothly again now. "I in no way want to shut you or your little friend Ida Cohen, the Jewish Joan of Arc, out of the project. It was always my intention to ask you to come on as associate producer with full perks, of

course. And promote Ida to head cutter. There—" He
beamed. "What could be fairer than that?"

"I suppose, Richard," Gretchen said, "you agree with
Evans in all this? I'd like to hear it in your own words.
You also are pleased, no doubt, to hear Ida Cohen, who
has slaved to get your script on the screen, described as
a Jewish Joan of Arc?"

Sanford flushed again. "I don't go along with that
part of it, no. But I do go along with the idea that you
can make a better picture with two million dollars than
with seven hundred and fifty thousand dollars. And before you called me up, I'll be honest with you, it never
occurred to me that a woman could do this picture. . . ."

"And now . . . ?"

"Well . . ." The boy was flustered. "I know you're
smart and I know you've had a lot of experience—but
never as a director. It's my first picture, Gretchen, and
I'd just feel better if a man like Evans Kinsella, with all
his hits and his reputation . . ."

"His reputation stinks," Gretchen said flatly. "Where
it counts. Like with me. If he does one more picture like
the last, he won't be able to rent a Brownie in California."

"See, Dick," Kinsella said, "I told you she'd turn
female and vindictive. She was married to a director
who she thought was Stanislavski come again, although
I've seen his pictures and I could have lived without
them, to say the least. Since he died, she wants to get
even on something, anything, everybody, every director,
and she's become the great deballer of the twentieth
century. And old Polish Ida, the flower of the ghetto,
who couldn't get a man to touch her with a ten-foot
pole, has puffed her up to think that she's been elected to
lead womankind into an Academy Award."

"You awful, conspiring, despicable man," Gretchen

said. "It would serve you both right if I gave you the picture and let you turn it into the load of shit you said it was in the first place."

"When I hired her," Kinsella went on, all constraint lost, "a friend told me, never hire the rich. Especially a rich woman. And don't screw her. She'll never forgive you the first time you look at another girl. Get out of here, you bitch." He was screaming shrilly. "I'll come to your opening and have a good laugh."

"Gretchen . . ." Sanford said piteously. He looked appalled and sorry he had ever touched a typewriter. "Please . . ."

"Richard," Gretchen said calmly, feeling wonderfully cleansed and dizzily free, "when we start shooting you're most welcome to come or not come, as you please. Good day, gentlemen," she said and swept grandly out of the beflowered, bebottled, becursed salon.

In the elevator she smiled and she wept, without worrying about the other passengers. Wait till I tell Ida about this morning, she thought.

But on the street she made a resolution: no more younger men. No matter how bright their eye, how white their teeth, how brimming their vitality, how promising their promise, how clear their skin, how sweet their smell. From now on, if she chose any man he would be older than she and grateful for her and not expect her to be grateful for him. She didn't know how that fit in with Ida Cohen's philosophy and she didn't care.

———

They were in the middle of lunch, the clam chowder and hot biscuits that Helen had prepared, and Helen had just said, "I love cooking for a man who doesn't have to watch his weight," when the doorbell rang.

Helen said, "Damn."

The lunch had been interrupted once before by a telephone call from Gretchen. Gretchen had taken fifteen minutes to tell Rudolph what had happened between Kinsella and herself that morning and had said that she was sure Rudolph would have approved. He was not as sure as she thought he would be.

Now it was the doorbell. Rudolph got up from the table and went to the door and opened it. Wesley was standing there, in the oceanic September sunshine, neatly dressed in slacks, and a sports jacket, looking a bit gaunt, his cheekbones prominent, his hair cut and neatly combed, neither long nor short, his eyes, as always, old and veiled.

"Hello, Wesley," Rudolph said. "I knew you'd turn up sooner or later. You're just in time for lunch. Come in."

# CHAPTER 4

Billy watched with interest as George, which Billy knew was not the man's real name, carefully worked at the table on the timing device. Monika, whom George addressed as Heidi, stood on the other side of the table, her face in shadow, above the sharp vee of light the work lamp cut over the table. "Are you following this closely, John?" George said in his Spanish-accented English, looking up at Billy. John was the name assigned to Billy in the group. Monika called him John, too, when members of the group were around. It reminded him of the hocus-pocus of secret societies he had started in the yard of the progressive school in Greenwich Village when he was a small boy. Only George wasn't a small boy and neither was Monika. One laugh, he thought, and they'd kill me.

There were only two other associates of George and Monika-Heidi whom Billy had met, but they were not present this afternoon in the small room in the slum section of Brussels where George was working on the bomb. Billy had never seen George in the same room twice. He knew from various references in George's

conversation that there were cells like the one he had
joined in other cities of Europe, but so far he had no
notion of where they were or what exactly they did. Although for his own safety he was not particularly anxious to know any more than he was told, he could not
help resenting the fact that he was still treated as an
untested and scarcely trusted outsider by the others,
even though he had twice supplied them with a half-ton
from the motor pool and had driven the car in Amsterdam the night George had bombed the Spanish tourist
office there. He didn't know what other bombings
George and Monika had been in on, but he had read
about explosions in a branch of an American bank in
Brussels and outside the office of Olympic Airways. If
Monika and the man he knew as George had been responsible for one or all of them, Monika was keeping
her promise—no one had been hurt either in Amsterdam or Brussels.

"Do you think you could put this together yourself, if
necessary?" George was saying.

"I think so."

"Good," George said. He always spoke quietly and
moved deliberately. He was dark and small, with gentle
sad eyes and looked totally undangerous. Regarding
himself in the mirror, Billy couldn't believe that anyone
could imagine that *he* was dangerous, either.

Monika was a different story, with her tangled hair
and her eyes that blazed when she was angry. But he
lived with Monika, was frightened of her, and loved her
more than ever. It was Monika who had said he must
reenlist. When he said that he couldn't face any more
time in the army, she had turned furiously on him and
had told him it was an order, not a suggestion, and that
she would move out if he didn't do as she said.

"Next time we meet," George said. "I'll let you put
together a dummy, just for practice."

George turned back to his work, his fine, small hands moving delicately over the wires. Neither he nor Monika had told Billy where the bomb was going to be used or when or for what purpose, and by now he knew that it would be useless to ask any questions.

"There we are," George said, straightening up. "All done." The small plastic charge with the clockwork attachment and detonator lay innocently on the table under the harsh light. "Lesson over for the day. You leave now, John. Heidi will remain with me for a while. Walk to the bus. Take it in the direction *away* from your apartment for eight blocks. Then get off, walk for three more blocks and get a taxi. Give the driver the address of the Hotel Amigo. Go into the hotel. Have a drink at the bar. Then leave the hotel and walk home."

"Yes, George," Billy said. That was about all he ever said to the man. "Will I be seeing you for dinner tonight?" he asked Monika.

"That depends on George," she said.

"George?" Billy said.

"Don't forget," George said. "At least ten minutes in the Hotel Amigo."

"Yes, George," Billy said.

Sitting in the bus going in the opposite direction from the house where he lived, surrounded by women going home after a day's shopping to prepare the family dinner, by children on the way home from school, by old men reading the evening newspaper, he chuckled inwardly. If only they could guess what the small, mild-looking young American in the neat business suit had just been doing on one of the back streets of their city. . . . Although he hadn't shown it in front of George and Monika, while he was watching the bomb being assembled he had felt his pulse race with excitement. Coldly, now, in the everyday light of the rumbling bus, he could call it by another name—pleasure. He had felt the same weird emotion racing away from the tourist office in Amsterdam, hearing the faint explosion six blocks behind him in the dark city.

He didn't believe, as Monika did, that the system was tottering and that a random bomb here and there was going to topple it, but at least he himself was no longer just an insignificant, replaceable cog in the whole lousy inhuman machine. His acts were being studied, important men were trying to figure out who he was and what he meant and where he might strike next. The disdain of his comrades in arms for him as Colonel's pet was now an ironic joke, made juicier by the fact that they had no notion of what he was really like. And Monika had had to admit that she had been wrong when she had said he was worthless. Finally, he thought, they would put a weapon in his hand and order him to kill. And he would do it. He would read the papers the next day and would report meekly to work, filled with secret joy. He didn't believe that Monika and George and their shadowy accomplices would ever achieve their shadowy purposes. No matter. He himself was no longer adrift, at the mercy of the small daily accidents of the enlisted man who had to say, "Yes, sir," "Of course, sir," to earn his daily bread. Now *he* was the accident, waiting to happen, the burning fuse that could not finally be ignored.

He counted the blocks as the bus trundled on. At the eighth block he got off. He walked briskly through a light drizzle the three blocks that George had told him to cover, smiling gently at the passersby. There was a taxi at the corner of the third block, standing there as though it had been ordered expressly for him. He settled back in it comfortably and enjoyed the ride to the Hotel Amigo.

He was just finishing his beer at the dark bar at the Amigo, the small room empty except for two blond men at a corner table who were talking to each other in what he took to be Hebrew when Monika walked in.

She swung up on a stool next to him. "I'll have a vodka on ice," she said to the barman.

"Did George order you to come?" he asked.

"I am having a social period," she said.

"Is it Monika or Heidi?" he whispered.

"Shut up."

"You said social," he said. "But it isn't. You were sent here to see if I followed instructions."

"Everybody understands English," she whispered. "Talk about the weather."

"The weather," he said. "It was rather warm this afternoon, wasn't it?"

"Rather," she said. She smiled at the barman as he put her drink in front of her.

He nursed the last bit of his beer at the bottom of the glass. "What would you do," he asked, "if I were sent back to America?"

Monika looked at him sharply. "Are you being shifted? Have you been keeping something from me?"

"No," he said. "But the Colonel's been getting restless. He's been here a long time. Anyway, in the army, you never can tell . . ."

"Pull wires," she said. "Arrange for someplace in Germany."

"It's not as easy as all that," he said.

"It can be done," she said crisply. "You know that as well as I do."

"Still," he said, "you haven't answered my question. What would you do?"

She shrugged. "That would depend," she said.

"On what?"

"On a lot of things. Where you were sent. What kind of job you got. Where I was needed."

"On love, perhaps?"

"Never."

He laughed. "Ask a silly question," he said, "and you get a silly answer."

"Priorities, John," she said, accenting "John" ironically. "We must never forget priorities, must we?"

"Never," he said. He ordered another beer. "There's a chance I'll be going to Paris next week."

Again she looked at him sharply. "A chance?" she asked. "Or definitely?"

"Almost definitely. The Colonel thinks he has to go and he'll put me on orders to accompany him if he does go."

"You must learn not to spring things like this suddenly on me," she said.

"I just heard about it this morning," he said defensively.

"As soon as you know for sure, you let me know. Is that clear?"

"Oh, Christ," he said, "stop sounding like a company commander."

She ignored this. "I'm not talking idly," she said. "There's a package that has to be delivered to Paris next week. How would you go? Civilian plane?"

"No. Army transport. There's an honor guard going for some sort of ceremony at Versailles."

"Oh, good," she said.

"What will be in the package?"

"You'll know when you have to know," she said.

He sighed and drank half the fresh beer. "I've always been partial to nice, uncomplicated, innocent girls."

"I'll see if I can find one for you," she said, "in five or six years."

He nodded dourly. In the corner the two blond men

were talking more loudly, as though they were arguing.

"Are those two men speaking Hebrew?" he asked.

She listened for a moment. "Finnish," she said.

"Are they close? Hebrew and Finnish, I mean?"

"No." She laughed and kissed his cheek. She had decided to be Monika now, he saw, not Heidi.

"So," he said, "business hours are over."

"For the day."

"For the day," he said and finished his beer. "You know what I would like to do?"

"What?"

"I'd like to go home with you and fuck."

"Oh, dear," she said with mock gentility, "soldier talk."

"The afternoon's activities have made me horny," he said.

She laughed. "Me, too," she whispered. "Pay the nice man and let's get out of here."

It was dark by the time they got to the street where they lived. They stopped on the corner to see if they were being followed. As far as they could tell they were not. They walked slowly on the opposite side of the street from his house. There was a man standing, smoking a cigarette, in front of the building. It was still drizzling and the man had his hat jammed down low over his forehead. There wasn't enough light for them to see whether they had ever seen the man before.

"Keep walking," Monika said in a low voice.

They went past the house and turned a corner and went into a café. He would have liked another beer but Monika ordered two coffees.

When they came back fifteen minutes later, they saw, from the opposite side of the street, that the man was still there, still smoking.

"You keep walking," Monika said. "I'll go past him

and upstairs. Come back in five minutes. If it looks all right, I'll turn on the light in the front room and you can come up."

Billy nodded, kissed her cheek as though they were saying good-bye and went on toward the corner. At the corner he looked back. Hazard of the trade, he thought. Eternal suspicion. The man was still there but Monika had disappeared. Billy turned the corner, went into the café and had the beer that Monika had vetoed. When he left the café he walked quickly around the corner. He saw that the front room light was on. He kept on walking, his head down, over to the side of the street where the man was waiting in front of the house and started up the steps, taking his keys out.

"Hello, Billy," the man said.

"Holy God! Dad!" Billy said. In his surprise he dropped his keys and he and William Abbott almost bumped heads as they both bent over to pick them up. They laughed. His father handed Billy the keys and they embraced. Billy noticed that the smell of gin, which he had associated with his father since early childhood, was absent.

"Come on in," Billy said. "How long have you been waiting?"

"A couple of hours."

"You must be soaked."

"No matter," Abbott said. "Time for reflection."

"Come on upstairs," Billy said, opening the door. "Uh—Dad—we won't be alone. There'll be a lady there," he said as he led the way upstairs.

"I'll watch my language," Abbott said.

Billy unlocked the door and they both went into the little foyer and Billy helped his father off with his wet raincoat. When Abbott took off his hat, Billy saw that his father's hair was iron gray and his face puffy and yellowish. He remembered a photograph of his father in his captain's uniform. He had been a handsome young man, dark, smiling at a private joke, with black hair and humorous eyes. He was no longer a handsome man. The body, which had been erect and slender, was now saggy under the worn suit, a little round paunch at the belt line. I will refuse to look like that when I am his age, Billy thought as he led his father into the living room.

Monika was in the small, cluttered living room. Monika did not waste her time on housework. She was sitting in the one easy chair, reading, and stood up when they came into the room.

"Monika," Billy said, "this is my father."

Monika smiled, her eyes giving a welcoming glow to her face. She has sixty moods to the hour, Billy thought as Monika shook hands with Abbott and said, "Welcome, sir."

"I saw you come in," Abbott said. "You gave me a most peculiar look."

"Monika always looks at men peculiarly," Billy said. "Sit down, sit down. Can I give you a drink?"

Abbott rubbed his hands together and shivered. "That would repair a great deal of damage," he said.

"I'll get the glasses and ice," Monika said. She went into the kitchen.

Abbott looked around him approvingly. "Cosy. You've found a home in the army, haven't you, Billy?"

"You might say that."

"Transient or permanent?" Abbott gestured with his head toward the kitchen.

"Transiently permanent," Billy said.

Abbott laughed. His laugh was younger than his iron-gray hair and puffy face. "The history of the Abbotts," he said.

"What brings you to Brussels, Dad?"

Abbott looked at Billy reflectively. "An exploratory

operation," he said. "We can talk about it later, I suppose."

"Of course."

"What does the young lady do?"

"She's a translator at NATO," Billy said. He did not
feel called upon to tell his father that Monika also was
plotting the destruction of the capitalist system and had
almost certainly contributed to the recent assassination
of a judge in Hamburg.

Monika came back with three glasses, ice and a bottle of Scotch. Billy saw his father eyeing the bottle hungrily. "Just a small one for me, please," Abbott said.
"What with the plane trip and all and walking around
Brussels the whole, livelong day, I feel as though I've
been awake for weeks."

Billy saw that his father's hand shook minutely as he
took the glass from Monika. He felt a twinge of pity for
the small man, reduced in size and assurance from the
father he remembered.

Abbott raised his glass. "To fathers and sons," he
said. He grinned crookedly. He made the ice twirl in his
glass, but didn't put it to his lips. "How many years is it
since we've seen each other?"

"Six, seven . . ." Billy said.

"So long, eh?" Abbott said. "I'll spare you both the
cliché." He sipped at his drink, took a deep, grateful
breath. "You've weathered well, Billy. You look in
good shape."

"I play a lot of tennis."

"Excellent. Sad to relate. I have neglected my tennis
recently." He drank again. "A mistake. One makes mistakes in six or seven years. Of varying degrees of horror." He peered at Billy, squinting like a man who has
lost his glasses. "You've changed. Naturally. Matured, I
suppose is the word. Lines of strength in the face and
all that. Most attractive, wouldn't you say, Monika?"

"Moderately attractive," Monika said, laughing.

"He was a nice-looking child," Abbott said. "But unnaturally solemn. I should have brought along baby pictures. When we get to know each other better, I'll take you to one side and ask you what he says about his father. Out of curiosity. A man always worries that his son misjudges him. The sting of siredom, you might call it."

"Billy always speaks of you lovingly," Monika said.

"Loyal girl," said Abbott. "As I said, the opportunities for misjudgment are infinite." He sipped at his drink again. "I take it, Monika, that you are fond of my son."

"I would say so," Monika said, her voice cautious. Billy could see that she was unfavorably impressed by his father.

"He's told you, no doubt, that he intends to reenlist." Abbott twirled his glass again.

"He has."

Ah, Billy thought, that's what brought him to Brussels.

"The American Army is a noble and necessary institution," Abbott said. "I served in it once, myself, if my memory is correct. Do you approve of his joining up again in that necessary and noble institution?"

"That's his business," Monika said smoothly. "I'm sure he has his reasons."

"If I may be inquisitive, Monika," Abbott said, "I mean—using the prerogative of a father who is interested in his son's choice of companions—I hope you aren't offended . . ."

"Of course not, Mr. Abbott," Monika said. "Billy knows all about me, don't you, Billy?"

"Too much," Billy said, laughing, uneasy at the tenor of the conversation.

"As I was saying," Abbott said, "if I may be inquisitive—I seem to detect the faintest of accents in your speech—could you tell me where you come from? I mean originally."

"Germany," she said. "Originally, Munich."

"Ah—Munich." Abbott nodded. "I was in a plane once that bombed Munich. I am happy to see that you are too young to have been in that fair city for the occasion. It was early in nineteen forty-five."

"I was born in nineteen forty-four," Monika said.

"My apologies," Abbott said.

"I remember nothing," Monika said shortly.

"What a marvelous thing to be able to say," Abbott said. "I remember nothing."

"Dad," Billy said, "the war's over."

"That's what everybody says," Abbott took another sip, slowly. "It must be true."

"Billy," Monika said, putting down her half-finished glass, "I hope you and your charming father will excuse me. I have to go out. There are some people I have to see. . . ."

Abbott rose gallantly, just a little stiffly, like a rheumatic old man getting out of bed in the morning. "I hope we will have the pleasure of your company at dinner, my dear."

"I'm afraid not, Mr. Abbott. I have a date for dinner."

"Another evening . . ."

"Of course," Monika said.

Billy went into the foyer with her and helped her into her raincoat. He watched as she wrapped a scarf around her tangled hair. "Will I see you later?" he whispered.

"Probably not," she said. "And don't let your father talk you out of anything. You know why he's here, I'm sure."

"I suppose so. Don't worry," he whispered. "And come back tonight. No matter what time. I promise still to be horny."

She chuckled, kissed his cheek and went out the door. He sighed, inaudibly, fixed a smile on his face and went back into the living room. His father was pouring himself another drink, not a small one this time.

"Interesting girl," Abbott said. His hand was no longer shaking as he poured the soda into his glass. "Does she ever comb her hair?"

"She's not concerned with things like that," Billy said.

"So I gathered," Abbott said as he sat down again in the easy chair. "I don't trust her."

"Oh come on now, Dad," Billy said. "After ten minutes. Why? Because she's German?"

"Not at all. I know many good Germans," Abbott said. "I say that, although it isn't true, because it is the expected thing to say. The truth is I don't know *any* Germans and have no special feeling about them one way or another. Although I do have special feelings about ladies, a race I know better than I know Germans. As I said, she gave me a most peculair look when she passed me coming into the house. It disturbed me."

"Well," Billy says, "she doesn't give *me* any peculiar looks."

"I suppose not." Abbott looked judgingly at Billy. "You're small—too bad you took after me and not your mother in that respect—but with your pretty eyes and manner, I imagine you arouse a considerable amount of female affection."

"Most of the ladies manage to contain themselves in my presence," Billy said.

"I admire your modesty." Abbott laughed. "I was less modest when I was your age. Have you heard from your mother?"

"Yes," Billy said. "She wrote me after you told her I

was going to reenlist. I didn't know you kept in such close touch with her."

"You're her son," Abbott said, his face grave, "and you're my son. Neither of us forgets that, although we manage to forget many other things." He took a long gulp of his whiskey.

"Don't get drunk tonight, please, Dad."

Abbott looked thoughtfully at the glass in his hand, then, with a sudden movement, threw it against the small brick fireplace. The glass shattered and the whiskey made a dark stain on the hearth. The two men sat in silence for a moment. Billy heard his father's loud, uneven breathing.

"I'm sorry, Billy," Abbott said. "I'm not angry at what you said. On the contrary. Quite the contrary. You have spoken like a dutiful and proper son. I'm touched by your interest in my health. What I'm angry about is myself." His voice was bitter. "My son is on the verge of making what I consider a huge and perhaps irrecoverable mistake. I borrowed the money for the voyage from Chicago to Brussels from the last man in the world who can occasionally be prevailed upon to lend me a dollar. I came here to try to persuade you to . . . well . . . to reconsider. I walked around this town all day in the rain marshaling arguments to get you to change your mind. I managed not to order even one drink on the plane across the ocean, because I wanted to be at my best—" he smiled wryly "—which is not a very handsome best at best—for my meeting with you. I have antagonized you about your girl, whom I don't know, as you pointed out, because of a peculiar look on a doorstep, and I have begun the proceedings by pouring a double Scotch, which is bound to remind you of painful weekends with your father when your mother lent you to me for paternal Sabbath guidance. Willie Abbott rides again." He stood up abruptly. "Let us go to dinner. I promise not to touch another drop tonight until you deposit me at my hotel. After that I promise to drink myself into oblivion. I will not be in glorious shape tomorrow, but I promise to be sober. Where's the john? I've been standing in the rain for hours and my bladder is bursting. For the sake of you and the United States Army I didn't want to be caught pissing on the good burghers of Brussels."

"Through the bedroom," Billy said. "I'm afraid there's a lot of stuff lying around. Monika and I have to get to work early in the morning and most of the time we don't get back until dinner." He didn't want his father to think that Monika was a slob, although he occasionally complained to her about the mess they lived in. "There's nothing in Marx or Mao or Ché Guevara," he had said recently to her, "about good revolutionaries having to leave their underwear on the floor." "We clean up on the weekends," he said to his father.

"I will make no remarks, Billy," Abbott said, "about the life-style of you and your lady. I am not the neatest man in the world, but paradoxically consider neatness in a woman a useful virtue. No matter. We make do with what comes along." He looked searchingly at Billy. "You're not in uniform, soldier. How is it if you're in the noble and necessary army of the United States Army you're not in uniform?"

"Off duty," Billy said, "we can wear civilian clothes."

"It was different in my day," Abbott said. "I didn't wear civilian clothes for four years. Ah, well, wars change." He walked steadily out into the hall on his way to the bathroom. As he went out, Billy thought, That suit must be at least ten years old. I wonder if he'd let me buy him a new one.

His father said a lot of things over dinner, on a variety of subjects. He insisted upon Billy ordering wine for himself but turned his own glass over when the waiter poured. He said the food was first-rate, but just picked at it. By turns, he was expansive, apologetic, regretful, cynical, optimistic, aggressive, self-denigrating and boastful.

"I'm not through yet," was one of the things he said, "no matter what it looks like. I have a million ideas: I could eat up the field of public relations like a dish of whipped cream if I stayed off the booze. Ten of the top men in the field in Chicago have told me as much—I've been offered jobs in six figures if I joined Alcoholics Anonymous—but I can't see myself making public confessions to a group of professional breast-beaters. If you'd forget this crazy idea of sticking with the army— I can't get over that, I really can't, a smart young man like you, with your education, not even an officer—what the hell do you do all day, just check out cars like a girl in a radio taxi office? Why, if you came out to Chicago with me, we could set up an agency—William Abbott and Son. I've read your letters—I keep them with me at all times—the first thing I pack when I move from one place to another is the box I keep them in—I've read them and I tell you you can write, you really can turn a phrase with the best of them. If I had had your talent, I tell you I just wouldn't have a pile of unfinished plays in my desk drawer, no sir, not by a long shot. We could dazzle the folks, just dazzle them—I know the business from A to Z, you could leave that end of it to me, we'd have the advertisers knocking the door down to beg us to take their accounts. And don't think that Chicago is small time. Advertising *started* there, for God's sake.

"All right, I have a pretty good idea of what you think of the advertising business—the whore of the consumer society, all that crap. But like it or not, it's the

only society we have and the rule of the jungle is con-
sume or be consumed. Trade a couple of years of your
life and you can do whatever you damn well please
after it. Write a book—write a play. When I get back to
Chicago I'll have your letters Xeroxed and send them
to you, you'll be amazed at yourself reading them all at
once like that. Listen, your mother made a living, a
damn good living, writing for the magazines, and just
the things you dash off to me in a few minutes have
more—what's the word I'm looking for?—more *tone,*
more spirit, more sense of what writing is about than
she had in her best days. And she was highly thought
of, let me tell you, by a lot of intelligent people—the
editors were always after her for more—I don't know
why she quit. Her writing was good enough for the editors, for the public, but not for her. She has some insane
idea of perfectionism—be careful of that—it can finally
lead to molecular immobility—there's a phrase, my
boy—and she quit. Christ, *somebody* in the family
ought to finally make it. She complains to me you almost
never write her. I'm pleased, of course, you write me as
often as you do, but after all, she's your mother, it
wouldn't kill you to drop her a line from time to time. I
know I was shitty to her, I disappointed her, I was a
lousy husband. The truth is, she was too much for me—
in every department—physically, intellectually, morally.
She swamped me, but that doesn't prevent me so many
years later from appreciating her quality. There's no
telling how far she could have gone, with another man,
with better luck. . . . Colin Burke being killed.

"That family—the Jordaches—the old man a suicide,
the brother murdered, and sainted Rudolph just about
beaten to death in his own apartment. That would have
been something for your mother, if he'd have knocked it
off. Three for three. Two brothers and a husband. What
a percentage! And the kid—Wesley—did I write you

he came to Chicago and looked me up? He wanted me
to tell him what I knew about his father—he's haunted
by his father—the ramparts of Elsinore, for Christ's
sake—I guess you can't blame him for that—but he
looks like a zombie, his eyes are scary—God knows
how *he's* going to end up. I never even met his father,
but I tried to pretend that I'd heard he was a fine fellow
and I laid it on thick and the kid just stood up in the
middle of a sentence and said, 'Thank you, sir. I'm
afraid we're wasting each other's time.'

"You're half Jordache—maybe more than half—if
every a lady had dominant genes it was Gretchen Jordache—so you be careful, don't you ever trust to inherited luck, because you don't have it, on either side of
the family tree. . . .

"I'll tell you what—you get through with the goddamn army and you come out to Chicago to work with
me and I'll swear never to touch a drop of liquor again in
my whole life. I know you love me—we're grown men,
we can use the proper words—and you're being offered a
chance that very few sons get—you can save your father's life. You don't have to say anything now, but
when I get back to Chicago I want to see a letter from
you waiting for me telling me when you're arriving in
town. I'll be there in a week or so. I have to leave for
Strasbourg tomorrow. There's a man there I have to
see. Delicate negotiations for an old account of mine. A
chemical company. I have to sound out this Frenchman
to see if he'll take a fee, an honorarium—not to mince
words, a bribe, for swinging my client's business to his
company. I won't tell you how much money is involved,
but you'd gasp if I did tell you. And I get my cut if I
deliver. It's not the jolliest way to earn a living, but it
was the only way I could borrow enough money to
come over here to see you. Remember what I said
about the consumer society.

"And now it's late and your girl is undoubtedly waiting for you and I'm deadbeat tired. If you give one little goddamn for the rest of your father's life, that letter will be waiting for me in Chicago when I get there. And that's blackmail and don't think I don't know it. One last thing. The dinner's on me."

When he got back home after putting his father in a taxi and walking slowly through the wet streets of Brussels, with little aureoles of foggy light around the lampposts, he sat down at his desk and stared at his typewriter.

Hopeless, hopeless, he thought. Poor, hopeless, seedy, fantasizing, beloved man. And I never did get the chance to tell him I'd like to buy him a new suit.

When he finally went to bed, it was alone.

Monika didn't come in that night.

She came home before he went to work in the morning, with the package he was to deliver to an address on the rue du Gros-Caillou in the 7th arrondissement in Paris when he went to the capital of France with his colonel. The package was comparatively harmless—just ten thousand French francs in old bills and an American Army, .45-caliber automatic pistol, equipped with a silencer.

———

The .45 and the extra clips of ammunition were in his tennis bag as he got out of the taxi at the corner of the Avenue Bosquet and the rue St. Dominique at twenty minutes past three in the afternoon. He had looked at the map of Paris and seen that the rue du Gros-Caillou was a short street that ran between rue St. Dominique and rue de Grenelle, not far from the Ecole

Militaire. The ten thousand francs were folded in an envelope in the inner pocket of his jacket.

He was early. Monika had told him he would be expected at three-thirty. Under his breath he repeated the address she had made him memorize. He strolled, peering in at the shop windows, looking, he hoped, like an idle American tourist with a few minutes to spare before meeting his partners for their tennis game. He was still about thirty yards from the arched gate that led into the street, when a police car, its siren wailing, passed him, going in the wrong direction, up the rue St. Dominique and stopped, blocking the rue du Gros-Caillou. Five policemen jumped out, pistols in their hands, and ran into the rue du Gros-Caillou. Billy quickened his pace, passed the opening of the street. He looked through the arch and saw the policemen running toward a building in front of which there were three other policemen who had come from the other end of the street. He heard shouting and saw the first three policemen plunge through the doorway. A moment later there was the sound of shots.

He turned and went back, making himself walk slowly, toward the Avenue Bosquet. It was not a cold day, but he was shivering and sweating at the same time.

There was a bank on the corner and he went into it. Anything to get off the street. There was a girl sitting at a desk at the entrance and he went up to her and said he wanted to rent a safe-deposit box. He had difficulty getting out the French words, *"Coffre-fort."* The girl stood up and led him to a counter, where a clerk asked him for his identification. He showed his passport and the clerk filled out some forms. When the clerk asked him for his address he thought for a moment, then gave the name of the hotel he and Monika had stayed at when they were in Paris together. He was staying at another hotel this time. He signed two cards. His signature looked strange to him. He paid a year's fee in advance. Then the clerk led him down into the vault, where he gave the key to the box to the guardian at the desk. The guardian led him to a row of boxes in the rear of the vault, opened one of the locks with Billy's key and the second lock with his own master key, then went back to his desk, leaving Billy alone. Billy opened the tennis bag and put the automatic, the extra clips and the envelope with the ten thousand francs in it into the box. He closed the door of the box and called for the guardian. The guardian came back and turned the two keys and gave Billy his.

Billy went out of the vault and upstairs. Nobody seemed to be paying any attention to him and he went out onto the avenue. He heard no more shots, saw no more police. His father, it had turned out, had been needlessly pessimistic when he had warned him not to trust in inherited luck. He had just had ten minutes of the greatest luck of his or anybody's life.

He hailed a cruising taxi and gave the driver the address of his hotel off the Champs Elysées.

When he got to the hotel, he asked if there were any messages for him. There were none. He went up to his room and picked up the phone and gave the girl at the switchboard the number of his apartment in Brussels. After a few minutes his telephone rang and the girl at the switchboard said there was no answer.

The Colonel had given him the afternoon and evening off and he stayed in his room, calling the number in Brussels every half hour until midnight, when the switchboard closed down. But the number never answered.

He tried to sleep, but every time he dozed off, he woke with a start, sweating.

At six in the morning, he tried the number in Brussels again, but there still was no answer.

He went out and got the morning papers, *Le Figaro* and the *Herald Tribune*. Over coffee and a croissant at a café on the Champs Elysées, he read the stories. They were not prominently featured in either of the papers. A suspected trafficker in drugs had been shot and killed while resisting arrest in the 7th arrondissement. The police were still trying to establish his identity.

They are playing it cosy, Billy thought, as he read the stories—they're not giving away what they know.

When he went back to the hotel, he tried the apartment in Brussels again. There was no answer.

He got back to Brussels two days later. The apartment was empty and everything that had belonged to Monika was gone. There was no note anywhere.

When the Colonel asked him some weeks later if he was going to reenlist, he said, "No, sir, I've decided against it."

# CHAPTER 5

Coming in out of the bright seashore sunlight Wesley squinted in the shadow of the hallway as he followed his uncle into the house. A woman was sitting at a table laid for two in front of a big plate-glass window that overlooked the dunes and the Atlantic Ocean. Her face was still a blur against the brilliance of the window, and for a moment he was sure it was his uncle's ex-wife and he was sorry he had come. He hadn't seen her since the day of his father's death and he had spent a good deal of his time since then in trying to forget her. But then his eyes became accustomed to the light and he saw it was not Jean Jordache, but a tall woman with long, reddish-brown hair. Rudolph introduced her.

The woman smiled at him pleasantly and got up and went into the kitchen and came in with a tray with a glass and some plates and some silver on it and set a place for him. The smell from the big crockery pot on the table, mixed with the warm aroma of newly baked biscuits, was tantalizing. He had been on the road, hitchhiking, since seven o'clock in the morning and had walked the mile or two from the main road to the beach

and had not had lunch. He had to swallow to hide the
fact that his mouth was watering.

The woman was in a bathing suit and was deeply
tanned and did not remind him of Mrs. Wertham. The
clam chowder was delicious and he tried not to eat too
fast. Alice fed him adequately, but she was so busy at
the *Time* office that her meals were made up of odds
and ends she picked up as she rushed home from work.
The satisfactory memory of the feasts Kate used to prepare on the *Clothilde* was being engulfed in floods of
tuna salad and cold roast beef sandwiches. He was
grateful to Alice for her hospitality and he knew she
worked hard both at the office and at her apartment,
where she tapped away at her typewriter till all hours of
the night, but her interests were not in the kitchen, and
he couldn't help thinking that she had better succeed
with her writing as she would never earn any honors as
a cook.

When he finished the chowder, accompanied by four
biscuits, dripping with butter, Mrs. Morison insisted
upon filling his bowl again and getting some hot biscuits out of the oven.

"I guess I came at the right time," Wesley said, grinning, as he finished the second bowl.

His uncle didn't ask him any important questions
over lunch, just how he had come out to Bridgehampton
and how he had found the house. Wesley did not volunteer any information. He would answer questions when
they were alone.

"We hadn't planned on any dessert," Mrs. Morison
said, "but I think we can rustle up something from the
icebox for a young member of the family. I have a son
myself and I know about youthful appetites. I believe
there's some blueberry pie left over from last night and
I know there's some ice cream in the freezer."

Wesley decided that he liked the woman and wondered if his uncle would have been a different man if he had met her and married her long ago, before the other one.

After lunch the woman said she had to be going and put on a beach robe. Rudolph walked out with her to her car, leaving Wesley alone in the house.

"God, he's a handsome boy," Helen said as she got into her car.

"Gretchen says he looks like a young prince in a Florentine painting," Rudolph said. "She wants to try him out for a part in her movie."

"What does he say?"

"I haven't asked him yet," Rudolph said. "That's all we need in our family—a movie actor."

"He did come at the wrong time, though," Helen said.

"You're right. The lunch was aphrodisiacal, as promised."

Helen laughed. "There's always tomorrow," she said.

"What's wrong with tonight?"

"Busy," she said. "Undermining the Republican Party. Anyway, I imagine the boy wants to have a long talk with his uncle. He didn't come all the way out here just for lunch." She leaned over and kissed him and then started her car. He watched thoughtfully as she drove off, a woman with a purpose. He wondered if he ever again would have a purpose, sighed and went back into the house.

Wesley was standing in front of the big window, staring out to sea. "If ever I settle down," Wesley said, "I would like it to be in a place like this—with a whole ocean in front of me."

"I was lucky to find this place," Rudolph said.

"Yeah," Wesley said. "Lucky. Boy, that was some meal. She's a nice lady, isn't she?"

"Very nice," Rudolph said. The description of his re-

lations with Helen Morison and an appraisal of her
qualities could wait until later. "Would you like to go
for a swim? People keep leaving bathing trunks around
and I guess I could find a pair that would fit you." He
knew he was looking for ways to postpone whatever
problem Wesley had brought along to present to him.
"The water's pretty cold, but you'll have the whole
ocean to yourself."

"That'd be great," Wesley said. "A swim."

They went out onto the deck and down the steps under it to the cubicle where four or five pairs of trunks
were hanging. Rudolph left Wesley to undress and went
out onto the beach.

When Wesley came out in the swimming trunks, with
a towel slung around his neck, Rudolph walked with
him to the edge of the water. Wesley dropped the towel
to the sand and hesitated a moment before going in. He
had sloping powerful shoulders, an athlete's flat belly
and long muscled legs. His face, Rudolph thought, was
a refined version of his father's face, but the body, although a little taller, was his father's body. Maybe, Rudolph thought, as the boy suddenly started running toward the breakers, the water foaming around him,
maybe Gretchen is right about him. He watched the boy
plunge into a wave, then begin swimming easily through
the waves and into the swell. Enid was still afraid
of the ocean and only paddled cautiously near the
shore. He had not tried to force her to be more en-
terprising. He was not going to be one of those fathers
who, disappointed in not having a son, tried to make a
daughter into one. He had known one or two of those
overmuscled ladies and he knew that whatever they said
about their fathers, they cursed them in their hearts.

Wesley kept going farther and farther out, until his
head was just a small dot in the glittering blue distance.

Rudolph began to worry. Was it possible that the boy had come out to see him for the sole purpose of drowning himself in his presence? His old uneasiness with his nephew, the feeling that at any moment the boy was likely to do or say something unpredictable, dangerous or at least embarrassing came back to him. If he only could have more than a few hours at a time with the boy, perhaps he could get over the feeling that the boy was constantly judging him, measuring him against some private, impossible scale of values. He had to restrain himself from waving and calling to the boy to come in. Abruptly, he turned and went back into the house.

Five hundred yards out, Wesley floated on his back, enjoying the sensual feeling of going gently up and down with the swells. He daydreamed, looking up at the unclouded blue sky, that Alice was there with him, that they sank under the surface, kissing, their bodies weightless and laced in the rolling water, to rise again to stare at each other's faces, wet with the ocean's tingle, their love announced on land and sea. The truth was that since the one kiss when he made her cry, they had not touched each other, and a new tension, a shy drawing back on both their parts, had changed their relationship, and not for the better.

But now, rising and falling in the gentle sea, he thought of Alice with a longing he wouldn't dare confess to her—or to anybody else.

His father had told him that once when he was a young man he had made love to a girl while they were taking a bath together and that it had been an amazing experience. If it was amazing in a bathtub, what would it be like in the Atlantic Ocean?

If it had been his father on the beach he wouldn't have dared go out so far because his father would have bawled the bejesus out of him for showing off and taking a chance like that, all alone, no matter how good a swimmer he was. "Take chances," his father had said to him, "only when they mean something. Don't do anything just for show or to prove to yourself how all around marvelous you are."

He began to feel cold and turned and began swimming to shore. The tide was running out and he had to swim as hard as he could to get to where the waves were breaking. He rode in on a wave, tumbling in the curl of foam. He pulled himself to his feet on the smooth sand and got up to the beach. He stood there, drying his face and torso with the towel, looking out at the ocean going off to the horizon, with not a ship in sight. Whatever I finally do, he thought, I am going to end up with the sea.

Dry and dressed, after a shower in the cubicle, he went up to the deck and into the house, carrying his jacket over his shoulder. His uncle was talking on the phone in the living room. ". . . if he hasn't swum all the way to Portugal by now," he heard his uncle saying. His uncle smiled at him. "Wait a minute," Rudolph said into the phone. "He's just walked in. Looking a little waterlogged." He extended the phone toward Wesley. "It's your Aunt Gretchen," he said. "She'd like to say hello."

Wesley took the phone. "How are you?" he said.

"Busy," said Gretchen. "I'm glad you finally turned up. I've been trying to reach you for months. Where've you been?"

"Here and there," Wesley said.

"Listen, Wesley," Gretchen said, "Rudolph's driving into town early tomorrow and meeting me. Can you come with him? I'm dying to see you. He'll explain why."

"Well . . ." Wesley said. "He hasn't asked me to stay all night."

"Consider yourself asked," Rudolph said.

"Okay," Wesley said. "I'll try to make it."

"Don't just try," Gretchen said. "Make it. You won't be sorry."

"Do you want to talk to Rudolph again?"

"No time," Gretchen said. "Good-bye, honey."

Wesley put down the phone. "You sure I'm not fouling up your evening?" he asked Rudolph.

"On the contrary," Rudolph said. "I'm looking forward to it."

"She said you'd explain something to me," Wesley said. "Is there anything wrong?"

"No. Sit down. Let's make ourselves comfortable."

They sat across from each other at the table in front of the window. In the strong light the changes in Rudolph's face were most noticeable. The broken nose and the scar above one eye made him less frosty and distant. His uncle's face, Wesley thought, looked *used* now, more human. For the first time, he thought, his uncle looked unmistakably like his father. Until now he had never seen the resemblance between the brothers. "They must have given you quite a going over," he said, "those two guys."

"It's not too bad, is it?" Rudolph said.

"No," Wesley said. "I kind of like it. I guess I'm used to busted noses. It's more homelike." The reference to his father was easy and natural and they both laughed.

"Gretchen was after me to have it operated on," Rudolph said, "but I told her I thought it gave me character. I'm glad to hear that you agree."

"What's that about explaining . . . ? On the phone . . . ?"

"Oh, I wrote you she was trying to put together a movie, didn't I?"

"Yeah."

"Well, she finally got everything squared away. She starts shooting in about a month. For some reason," Rudolph said lightly, "she thinks you're a beautiful young man. . . ."

"Oh, come on," Wesley said uneasily.

"Whatever. There's no accounting for tastes," Rudolph said. "Anyway, she thinks you might be just what she needs for a certain part and she'd like to try you out."

"Me?" Wesley said incredulously. "In the movies?"

"I'm no judge," Rudolph said, "but Gretchen knows a great deal about pictures. If she thinks so . . ."

Wesley shook his head. "I'd like to see Gretchen again," he said, "but I won't do anything like that. I have a lot of things I have to do and I don't want to waste my time. I also don't want people walking up to me in the street and saying I recognize your face, Mr. Jordache."

"Those would be my sentiments, too," Rudolph said, "but I think it would be more polite to listen to Gretchen first before you say no. Anyway, they wouldn't say Mr. Jordache. In the movies they change everybody's name, especially if it's one like Jordache. They'd tell you nobody would know how to pronounce it."

"That mightn't be such a bad idea," Wesley said. "Changing my name, I mean. And not just for the movies."

Rudolph stared soberly at his nephew. It was a strange thing for the boy to say. He half understood it, but it troubled him, he wasn't sure quite why. Time to change the subject, he thought. "Tell me," he said, "what have you been doing?"

"I left home," Wesley said.

"You told me on the phone."

"By invitation," Wesley said. "I didn't tell you that."

"No."

"My mother." Wesley said. "I guess you could say we just didn't get along. I don't blame her. We don't belong in the same house together. In the same world, maybe . . . Has she been bugging you about me—about the warrant and all that?"

"That's all been arranged," Rudolph said.

"I suppose by you." Wesley sounded almost accusing.

"The less said about it the better," Rudolph said lightly. "Incidentally, where *have* you been all this time?"

"A lot of places," Wesley said, evasively. "In and out of New York a few times . . ."

"You didn't let me know." Rudolph tried not to sound aggrieved.

"You have troubles enough of your own."

"I might have helped."

Wesley grinned. "Maybe I was saving you for when I really needed help." Then he became grave. "I was lucky. I found a friend. A good friend."

"You look well," Rudolph said. "Almost prosperous. That's a nice suit you're wearing. . . ." It suddenly occurred to him that perhaps Wesley had been taken in by somebody who was using him for some shady undertaking, picking up poor girls at the bus terminal and turning them over to pimps or acting as a courier for a drug dealer. Since his beating, New York had taken on a new and sinister aura for him, a hunting ground where all were victims and no one safe. And a young, inexperienced boy wandering penniless around New York . . . "I hope you're not into something illegal."

Wesley laughed. "No," he said. "At least not yet. It's somebody up at *Time* Magazine. A lady. She helped me when I came to New York looking up the dope on my father. I thought maybe she could help me with finding

some other people who knew him. Addresses, things like
that. They seem to know everything about everybody up
there. I guess she was sorry for me. Anyway, my hunch
was right. She put me on a lot of trails."

"Did she buy you that suit?"

"She loaned me the money," Wesley said defensively.
"And she picked out the suit—a couple of other
things."

"How old is she?" Rudolph had a vision of an ancient spinster, preying on country youth, and was disturbed by the thought.

"A couple of years more than me."

Rudolph smiled. "I guess anything under thirty is
okay," he said.

"She's got a long way to go to thirty."

"Are you having an affair with her?" Rudolph asked.
"Excuse me for being blunt."

Wesley didn't seem hurt by the question. "No," he
said. "I sleep on her couch. She calls me Cousin."

"I'd like to meet the young lady."

"You'll like her. She's awfully nice," Wesley said.
"She really did some digging around for me."

"Whom did you talk to?" Rudolph asked curiously.

"Four or five people, here and there," Wesley said.
"Some good, some bad. I'd rather keep it all to myself,
if you don't mind. I still have some thinking to do about
it—see if I can figure out what it all means."

"Do you think you know your father any better
now?"

"Not really," Wesley said soberly. "I knew in general
he got into an awful lot of trouble when he was young. I
just picked up a few facts about the *kinds* of trouble.
Maybe I admire him more for turning out the way he
did after a start like that—I don't know. What I do
know is that I *remember* him better. I was afraid I
would start to forget him and I didn't want that. This

way," he said earnestly, "he's with me all the time. Inside my head, sort of, almost as if he's there talking to me, if you know what I mean."

"I think I do," Rudolph said. "Now—what did you really come for—?" With a little laugh, "Aside from lunch."

Wesley hesitated. "I came to ask you for a favor," he said, staring down at the table. "Two favors, actually."

"What are they?"

"I want to go back to Europe. I want to see Kate and her kid. And Bunny. And Billy Abbott. I'd like to see how the other son in the family survived. And a couple of other people around Antibes. I'm not at home in America, somehow. I haven't had a good day since I came here." His voice was too passionate to make it sound like a complaint. "Maybe that'll pass, but it hasn't yet. You once told me that the lawyer in Antibes said he thought in a year or so he could arrange for me to be let back into France. I was wondering if you could write him and . . . well, see what he can do."

Rudolph stood up and paced slowly toward the fireplace. "I'm going to be blunt again, Wesley," he said. "Have you told me your real reasons for wanting to go to Europe or—" He stopped.

"Or what?" Wesley asked.

"Or are you thinking of looking up the man your father had the fight with?"

Wesley didn't answer immediately. Then he said, "The thought may have crossed my mind."

"That would be foolish, Wesley," Rudolph said. "Very foolish. And very dangerous."

"I promise to be careful," Wesley said.

"I hope I don't have the occasion to remind you of your promise," Rudolph said. "Now, what's the other favor?"

"This is harder," Wesley said. Now he stared out to

sea. "It's about money. I won't be eighteen for another year, when I get my share of the inheritance. I thought if it didn't press you too hard, you'd lend me say a thousand dollars and I'd pay you back on my eighteenth birthday. . . ."

"It's not the money," Rudolph said, although he couldn't help thinking that somehow money was involved in almost every decision he had ever made—in paying Wesley's mother off to get a divorce, in helping Gretchen start in her new profession, in achieving his own reconciliation with Wesley's father, in his move to where he was living now, on the shores of the Atlantic, because of the few dollars and change in his pocket when he was ambushed by the two men in the hallway of his house in New York. Even in getting Wesley out of jail because the wily old lawyer in Antibes could be paid his handsome fee in the numbered account in Switzerland. "No, it's not the money," he repeated. "It's your future I'm thinking about."

"I'm thinking about my future, too," Wesley said bitterly. "I want to be in France on my eighteenth birthday, when I have to register for the draft. I don't want my future to be a grave in Vietnam."

"That could be arranged, too, without leaving America," Rudolph said, going over to the boy and standing at his side and looking out with him at the sea. "I wrote you about the Merchant Marine Academy . . ."

"I remember," Wesley said. "It sounded like a good deal."

"How are you in mathematics? That's important for getting accepted."

"Pretty good," Wesley said. "It comes easy to me."

"That's fine," Rudolph said. "But you have to be a high-school graduate. And be recommended by a congressman. I'm sure I could manage *that*. And . . ." He was struck by a sudden idea. "You could come here and live with me—it's not a bad place to live, is it?"

"No. It's great."

"Frankly, I'd like it very much. I think you'd be able to say that you finally had some good days in America. You could finish high school here. That is, if your aunt doesn't make a movie star out of you. . . ."

"Don't worry about that."

"By the time you got out of the academy, the war is bound to be over. It has to end sometime."

"Who says?" Wesley said.

"History," said Rudolph.

"I haven't read that particular book," Wesley said sardonically.

"I'll find it for you. You don't have to make up your mind right away. Meanwhile I'll write the lawyer. Is that fair enough?"

"Fair enough," Wesley said.

# CHAPTER 6

As Billy was packing his bags to leave Brussels, he looked at the piece of paper. Honorable Discharge, he read. He smiled wryly as he slipped the document into a stiff envelope. Don't believe everything you see in print.

The next piece of paper he put into the envelope was a letter from his father. His father was happy that he had decided wisely about the army and unhappy that he had decided not to come to Chicago, although he understood the attractions of Europe for a young man. Chicago could wait for a year or two. There was news about his mother, too. She was directing a picture. His father believed Billy should write and congratulate her. Of all things, his father added, one of the leading actors in the movie was Billy's cousin, Wesley. A sullen boy, Wesley, at least in William Abbott's opinion. The Jordaches took care of the Jordaches, his father wrote. A pity he, Billy, was not on better terms with his mother.

The next thing Billy put in his bag was a Spanish-English dictionary. A Belgian businessman with whom he had played tennis and who was involved in building a complex of bungalows and condominiums at a place called El Faro near Marbella, in Spain, with six tennis courts, had offered him a contract for a year as a tennis pro. The idea of Spain was attractive after Brussels and it was no contest against Chicago, and after all, the only thing he did well was play tennis and it was a clean and well-paying job, in the open air, so he had said yes. He could stand some sunshine. Beware the *señoritas,* his father had warned him.

The last piece of paper was undated and signed Heidi. It had been in an unstamped envelope that he had found in his mailbox the night before. "Had to depart suddenly because of the death of a friend. Understand you are not re-enlisting. Leave forwarding address, although I am sure I can find you. We have unfinished business to attend to."

He did not smile as he read the letter and tore it into small pieces and flushed it down the toilet. He did not leave a forwarding address.

He took the train to Paris. He had sold his car. Monika knew it too well, make, year, license number. Who knew how many people had its description and might be looking for it on the roads of Europe?

He could buy a new car in France. He could afford it. There was a modest but sufficient legacy waiting for him in the vault in the bank on the corner of the Avenue Bosquet in the 7th arrondissement in Paris.

———

"Cut," Gretchen said, and the day's shooting was over and the hum of conversation suddenly started from the actors and crew members on the set. The scene had been shot in front of a dilapidated mansion that now had a false facade and a fake lawn leading to the street. In the scene Wesley and the girl who played his sister had a violent argument about the way Wesley was lead-

ing his life. It had taken all day to shoot. His Uncle
Rudolph, who had come up for the day, was on the set,
and although he had merely waved at Wesley, his presence had made Wesley a little more self-conscious than
usual. But since he played the part of a boy who was
supposed to be taciturn and unresponsive and the girl
had to do most of the work, it had not mattered too
much.

After the first few days, during which Wesley had
been stiff and trying to hide his shyness about play-
acting in front of so many people, he had caught on to
what was wanted from him—his Aunt Gretchen had
taken him aside and told him not to try to act—and had
begun to enjoy the whole affair. Gretchen had told him
he was doing very well, although she had said it in private, with nobody else around to hear her. But he had
learned she was not a lady who lied.

He liked the atmosphere of the company. Most of the
people were young and friendly, constantly joking, and
anxious to be helpful. He had never had many friends
who were near his own age, and it was relaxing not to be
always on your best behavior just because you were
with people who were a lot older than you.

Gretchen allowed him to use the name Wesley Jordan. After all, his father had used the name Jordan professionally before him, so he had half a claim to the
title. Originally, he had allowed himself to be cajoled
into taking the job mostly because he was getting three
thousand dollars for a month's work, which would mean
he could pay Alice back what he owed her and wouldn't
have to depend on his uncle to get to Europe, but now
he found himself eager to get on the set each morning,
even when he wasn't due for any scenes himself. The
entire business fascinated him, the expertness of the
camera, lighting and soundmen, the devotion of the actors, the calm but firm way in which his aunt ran every-

thing. In her manner of handling people she reminded
him of his father. According to Frances Miller, the girl
who played his sister and who was only about twenty-
two but had been in show business since the age of
fourteen, not all movie sets were like that by a long
shot. Hysteria and temper were more often than not the
order of the day, and she'd told Wesley that she'd take
Gretchen as a director any time over most of the men
she had worked with.

Frances was a beautiful girl in a funny, wild way,
freckled, her eyes wide and deep in her sharply angled,
moody, youthful face, her body petite and deliciously
rounded, her skin an invitation to the most extreme
dreams. She was outspoken and occasionally foul-
mouthed. Occasionally, too, she liked to drink. More
often she also liked to make love to him, which she had
started early on in Port Philip, when she had come to
his room in their hotel to run over the lines for the next
day's shooting and stayed the night. Wesley was dazzled
by her beauty and by the idea that she had chosen him.
He would never have dared make the first move himself. It had not yet occurred to him that he was an ex-
traordinarily handsome young man. When strange
young women stared at him he had the uneasy feeling
that somehow he was doing something wrong or that
they were disapproving of the way he was dressed. For
a while, he had felt guilty, because he had thought that
he was in love with Alice Larkin. But Alice Larkin still
called him Cousin and he still slept on her couch in the
living room when he was in New York. Besides,
Frances made love with such happy abandon it was
hard to feel guilty about anything in her presence.

Frances was married to a young actor who was in
California where she ordinarily lived. Wesley tried to
forget about the husband. As far as Wesley knew, nobody in the company had any inkling of what was going

on between him and the leading lady. When they were in public she treated him as though he were in fact what he was in the movie—a younger brother.

His Aunt Gretchen had caught on, of course. He had discovered that she caught on to everything. She had had dinner alone with him one night and warned him that when the shooting was over Frances would go back to California and then on to a new picture and would almost certainly sleep with another young man in the new company who caught her fancy, because she was known to do things like that, and that he was not to take it too seriously. "I want this whole thing to be a wonderful experience for you," Gretchen said. "I don't want you to hate me for getting you into something you can't handle."

"I can handle it," he said, although he wasn't sure he could.

"Remember what I said about that girl," Gretchen said. "She's messed up the lives of older men than you before this." What she didn't say was that she knew Frances Miller had had an affair for six months with Evans Kinsella and that he had asked her to get a divorce and marry him. And that the day after the picture Frances was doing with him was finished, she stopped answering his calls. She also didn't say that she, Gretchen, was still jealous of Frances and regretted that she was the girl she had thought would be wonderful in the part. You couldn't cast or not cast a picture out of bedrooms, although many people had done so, to their sorrow. "Just remember," Gretchen said.

"I'll remember," said Wesley.

"You're dear and vulnerable, Old Toughie," Gretchen said. She leaned over and kissed his cheek. "Defend yourself. You're in a much rougher racket than you know."

That night he had made love to Frances almost the

whole night long, brutally, until he had had to smother her face in a pillow so that the entire hotel wouldn't be awakened by her screams. She was a girl who made no secret about whether she was enjoying herself.

As they both lay side by side, exhausted, he had thought, triumphantly, She's not going back to anyone after tonight.

At dinner he and the other actors ate together as usual in the hotel dining room. Gretchen and Ida Cohen and Ida Cohen's uncle, along with the scene designer and Uncle Rudolph, ate upstairs in the living room of Gretchen's suite. After dinner, Wesley and Frances decided to go for a walk. It was a cool autumn night with a moon that was almost full and they walked arm in arm, like any young couple out on a date.

The main street was almost empty, neon-lit from forlorn store windows. Port Philip watched television and went to bed early. Frances looked idly at the displays in the windows as they passed. "There's nothing here I'd ever buy," she said. "Imagine living in a place like this. Ugh."

"My family comes from here," Wesley said.

"Oh, my God," Frances said. "You poor boy."

"I never lived here. My father, my grandfather . . ." He stopped himself before he said, my Aunt Gretchen. He hadn't told Frances or any of the company that Gretchen was his aunt, and Gretchen was careful to treat him like any other novice actor in the company.

"Do you see any of them—" Frances asked. "I mean, your family, while you're here?"

"There're none left. They all moved away."

"I can understand why," Frances said. "This town must have gone downhill from the first day they put up the post office."

"My grandmother told my father that when she first

came here as a young girl, it was a beautiful place,"
Wesley said. He was walking the streets of the town in
which his father was born and which had formed him
and he didn't like the idea of its being thought of as a
dreary backwater by a girl from California. Somewhere
in the town, he thought, his father must have left a
mark, a sign that he had been and gone. He had burned
a cross here. Theodore Boylan, at least, remembered.
He wondered what his father would have thought of his
son walking the old same streets arm in arm with a
beautiful, almost famous movie actress. And, more than
that, making three thousand dollars for four weeks'
work, which was more play than any work his father
had ever known. "There were trees everywhere, my
grandmother told my father," Wesley said, "and all
those big houses were painted and clean and had big
gardens. My father used to swim in the Hudson
River—it was clean then—and the riverboats used to
stop by and there was great fishing . . ." He stopped
before telling the girl that aside from the boats and the
fishing, his grandfather had used the river in which to
drown himself.

"Things get worse, don't they?" Frances said. "I'll
bet there was a lot of screwing in those big gardens
then. Nothing else to do in the evening and no motels."

"I suppose everybody got his share."

"And her share," Frances said, laughing. "Like now.
It's too bad you're on this picture."

"Why?" Wesley asked, hurt.

"If you weren't," she said. "I'd have gone through
*War and Peace* by now, these long nights."

"Sorry?"

*"War and Peace* can wait," she said. She hugged his
arm. "By the way, I've been meaning to ask you—what
drama school did you go to?"

"Me?" He hesitated. "None."

"You act as though you've had years," she said. "Incidentally, how old are you?"

"Twenty-one," he said, without hesitation. He had made the mistake of telling Alice how old he was and she treated him as a child. He wasn't about to make that mistake again.

"How is it you're not in the army?"

"Football knee," he said promptly. Since he had come back to America he had learned how to lie at a moment's notice.

"I see." She sounded suspicious. "Where've you acted before?"

"Me?" he said again, foolishly. "Well . . . noplace." Frances was too knowing about things like that to take a chance on lying.

"Not even summer stock?"

"Not even summer stock."

"How'd you get this job then?"

"Mrs. Burke . . ." It sounded funny in his ears to talk about his aunt as Mrs. Burke. "She saw me at a friend's house and asked me if I wanted to test. What're you asking all these questions for?"

"It's natural for a girl to want to know a few facts about the man she's having an affair with, isn't it?"

"I suppose so." He was pleased with the word "affair." It gave him a new sense of maturity. Teenagers had dates or girlfriends, not affairs.

"There's one thing about me," Frances said, very definitely. "I can't go to bed with a man whom I don't respect." It embarrassed Wesley when Frances spoke in that offhand, plural way about other men she had known. But, he told himself, she had been an actress since she was fourteen, what could he expect? Still, some day soon, he promised himself, he would tell her to keep her reflections on that particular subject to herself.

"You came as a surprise, I must admit," she said cheerfully. "I took one look at the list of the cast and said this is going to be chastity-belt time for me."

"What changed your mind?"

"You." She laughed. "I knew just about all the others, but Wesley Jordan was a new name for me. I didn't know you'd be the prize of the litter. By the way, is that your real name?"

"No," Wesley said, after a pause.

"What is it?"

"It's long and complicated," he said evasively. "It would never look good over the title."

She laughed again. "This is your first picture, but you're learning fast."

He grinned. "I'm a quick study." He was enjoying being in the movies more and more and his vocabulary reflected it.

"What're you going to do after this picture?"

"Don't know." He shrugged. "Go to Europe if I can."

"You're awfully good," she said. "That isn't only my opinion. Freddie Kahn, the cameraman, has seen all the rushes and he's raving about you. You going to try Hollywood?"

"Maybe," he said cautiously.

"Come on out," she said. "I promise you a warm welcome."

Wesley took in a big gulp of air. "I understand you're married," he said.

"Who told you that?" she asked sharply.

"I don't remember. Someone. It just came up in the conversation."

"I wish people would keep their goddamn mouths shut. That's my business. Does that make any difference to you?"

"What would you say if I said it did?"

"I'd say you're a fool."

"Then I won't say it."

"That's better," she said. "Are you in love with me?"

"Why do you ask that question?"

"Because I like it more when people are in love with me," she said. "That's why I'm an actress."

"All right," he said, "I'm in love with you."

"Let's drink to that," she said. "There's a bar on the next block."

"I'm on the wagon," he said. He didn't want to be asked in front of Frances for proof of his age by the bartender.

"I like to drink," she said, "and I like men who don't drink. Come on, I'll buy you a Coke."

When they went into the bar they saw Rudolph and the set designer, a red-bearded young man by the name of Donnelly, sitting at a booth, absorbed in conversation.

"What ho," Frances whispered, "the brass."

Everybody in the cast knew that Rudolph was on the financial end of the undertaking and had been instrumental with the authorities in Port Philip when difficulties had arisen about permits, shooting at night and the use of the town police to block off streets. The cast didn't know, however, that he was Wesley's uncle; on the few occasions that Wesley had spoken to Rudolph in public he had addressed him as Mr. Jordache, and Rudolph had replied, gravely and courteously, by addressing his nephew as Mr. Jordan.

Frances and Wesley had to pass the booth in which the two men sat. Rudolph looked up and smiled at them and stood up and said, "Good evening, ladies and gentlemen."

Wesley mumbled a greeting, but Frances smiled her most winsome smile and said. "What new plot are you two gentlemen concocting against us poor actors in this noisome den now?"

Wesley winced at the false, girlish smile, the fancy language. Suddenly he realized that Frances had too many different ways of addressing different people.

"We were sitting here praising the performance of you two young people," Rudolph said.

Frances giggled. "Aren't you the polite man," she said. "What a delightful lie."

Donnelly grunted.

"Do sit down," Frances said. "In Hollywood nobody ever stands up for the help."

Again Wesley winced. At certain moments, aside from using her abundant charm, Frances managed to remind people whom she considered important of the bright career she had already put behind her.

The two men sat down, Donnelly staring morosely at the glass in front of him. No one had as yet seen him smile during the course of the shooting.

"Mr. Donnelly," Frances said, her voice still girlish, "I haven't dared to tell you this before, but now that the picture's almost over, I'd like to say that it's just wonderful what you've been doing with the sets. I haven't seen any of the film yet—" she made a small grimace— "us poor actors aren't let in on the decisions on who lives and who dies in the projection room, so I don't know how they look on film, but I do have to tell you that as far as I'm concerned I've never been as comfortable moving around in front of the camera as I have in the acting space you've designed for us to work in." She laughed, as though she were a little embarrassed at speaking so boldly.

Donnelly grunted again.

Wesley could see Frances's jaw set then. "I won't disturb you any longer while you two gentlemen arrange our fates," she said. "Young Wesley and I—" Now she

made it sound as though Wesley were ten years old. —
"have some problems in our scene tomorrow that we
thought we'd do a little homework on."

Wesley tugged at her arm, and with a last dazzling
smile, she moved off with him. She made a move to sit
in the next booth, but Wesley guided her firmly to the
last booth in the rear of the bar, well out of earshot of
Donnelly and his uncle.

"What a goddamn performance," he said as they sat
down.

"Honey catches more flies than vinegar, darling,"
Frances said sweetly. "Who knows when those two nice
men will do another picture and have the final say
about who's going to be in it and who's going to be out
on his or her ass?"

"You put on so many acts," Wesley said, "I bet
sometimes you have to call up your mother to find out
who you really are."

"That's the art, dear," Frances said coolly. "You'd
better learn it if you want to get anyplace."

"I don't want to get anyplace at that price," Wesley
said.

"That's what I used to say," she said. "When I was
fourteen years old. By the time I was fifteen, I changed
my mind. You're just a little retarded, dear."

"Thank God for that," Wesley said.

The waiter was standing over them now and Frances
ordered for both of them, a gin and tonic for her and a
Coke for him.

When the waiter had gone over to the bar Wesley
said, "I wish you wouldn't drink gin."

"Why not?"

"Because I don't like the way your breath smells
when you drink gin."

"There's no need to worry tonight, dear," Frances
said coldly. "I'm due for an early call with the hair-

dresser tomorrow and I'm not up to any gymnastics tonight."

Wesley sat in glum silence until the waiter brought the drinks.

"Anyway, even if you're so horrendously critical of a few little harmless, girlish tricks," Frances said, sipping at her gin and tonic, "there are others who find them entrancing. That cute Mr. Jordache, with all that money, for example. His eyes light up like a billboard sign whenever he sees me."

"I hadn't noticed," Wesley said, honestly shocked that anyone could call his uncle that cute Mr. Jordache.

"I have," Frances said firmly. "I bet he'd be something. That icy Yankee exterior with a volcano underneath. I know the type."

"He's old enough to be your father, for God's sake."

"Not unless he started awfully young," Frances said. "And I bet he did."

Wesley stood up. "I'm not going to sit here and listen to crap like that. I'm going home. See how you get on with that cute Mr. Jordache with all that money."

"Dear, dear," Frances said, without moving, "aren't we the touchy young man this evening."

"Good night," Wesley said.

"Good night," Frances said calmly. "Don't bother with the check."

Wesley strode past the booth where his uncle was sitting. Neither of the two men looked up as he passed. He went out into the street, feeling childish, hurt and foolishly emotional.

Five minutes later Frances got up and walked toward the door. She stopped and spoke for a moment to the two men, but they didn't ask her to join them. When she went back to the hotel she didn't go down the corridor and open Wesley's door as she did on all other nights, but continued on to her own room and stared at

herself in the mirror over the dressing table for a long
time.

Back at the bar, the two men were not talking about
making movies. Donnelly was an architect who had
drifted into scene designing when he discovered that he
was offered only unprofitable commissions for mediocre
small buildings which he considered beneath his talent.
In the course of the preparations for *Restoration Comedy* he and Rudolph had become friendly, and at first
timidly, then more enthusiastically, he had spoken
about an ambitious project that he was involved in but
so far had not been able to get financing for. Now he
was giving Rudolph the details. "We live in the age of
what the British call redundancy," he was saying, "not
only because of new machines or shifts in population,
but redundancy because of age. Men retire from business because they're bored and can afford it, or because
they can't stand the strain or because younger men are
called in to fill their jobs. Their children have grown up
and moved away. Their houses are suddenly too big for
them, the city in which they live frightens them or has
exhausted its attraction for them. Their pensions or savings don't permit them to keep the servants they once
had, the neighborhoods where they can afford to find
small apartments are crowded with young couples with
small children who treat them as invaders from another
century, they are separated from friends of their own
age who have similar problems but have looked for
other solutions in other places— They want to keep
their independence but they're frightened of loneliness.
What they need is a new habitat, a new atmosphere that
fits their condition—where they're surrounded by people approximately their own age, with approximately
the same problems and needs, people who can be depended upon in an emergency, just as it gives them a

sense of their own humanity to know that they're ready
to come to a neighbor's aid when *he* needs help." Donnelly spoke with great urgency, as though he were a
general, outlining plans for the relief of a besieged gar-
rison. "It has to be a real community," he continued,
gesturing eloquently with his large hands, as if already
he was molding brick, mortar and cement into livable,
populated shapes, "shops, movies, a small hotel where
they can entertain visitors, a golf course, swimming
pools, tennis courts, lecture rooms. . . . I'm not talking
about the poor. I don't know how they can be taken
care of except by the state and I'm not vain enough to
think I can rearrange American society. I'm talking
about the middle-income group, the ones whose way of
life is most drastically affected when the breadwinner
stops working." His voice dropped to bitterness. "I
know all about this in the case of my own mother and
father. They have a little money and I help some, myself, but from being a hearty, outgoing couple, they're
now a depressed, fretful pair of people, fiddling the last
years of their lives away in useless boredom. My idea
isn't so new. It's been tried and found successful all over
the country, but so far I haven't been able to get any
money men interested in it, because there isn't much
profit to be made, if any. What it needs to begin with is
to buy a huge piece of land in some pleasant country
spot—not too isolated—so that when people want a little city life it's easily available to them—and build a
small, but complete village of modest, well-designed,
but cheaply built attached homes, say in groups of four
or five, scattered in a parklike landscape, houses that
can be handled easily by two aging people. With bus
service, doctors and nurses on hand, a congenial but unobtrusive management. It wouldn't be an old folks'
home, with all the despair that entails—there'd be a
constant flow of young people—sons and daughters and

grandchildren, hopeful and lively, a view on the future. Your sister has told me that you're a public-spirited man and that you have access to money and you're looking for something to occupy your time. From what I've seen so far, I don't think getting mixed up in movies is exactly your idea of public service. . . ."

Rudolph laughed. "No," he said, "not exactly."

"She also said that you're a born builder," Donnelly went on, "that when you were young you bulled through the idea of a shopping center in what was then practically a wilderness and made almost a whole small town of it. I went out to look at it the other day, the Calderwood complex near here, and I was deeply impressed—it was way ahead of its time and it showed real imagination—"

"When I was young," Rudolph said reflectively. He hadn't shown anything of what he thought as he listened to Donnelly's speech, but he felt an excitement that was both new and old to him as Donnelly spoke. He had been waiting for something, he hadn't known what. Perhaps this was what he was waiting for.

"I've got whole sets of drawings," Donnelly said, "models of the sort of houses I want to put up, schedules of approximate costs . . . everything. . . ."

"I'd like to take a look at them," Rudolph said.

"Can you be in New York tomorrow?"

"No reason why not."

"Good. I'll show them to you."

"Of course," Rudolph said, "the whole thing would depend on just what piece of land you could get, what its suitability was, what the cost would be—all that."

Donnelly looked around him at the empty bar, as though searching out spies. "I've even picked out the spot," he said, lowering his voice. "It's a beauty. It's abandoned, overgrown farmland now and cheap. It's in Connecticut, rolling hill country, and it's no more than an hour from New Haven, maybe two from New York. It's made for something like this."

"Could you show it to me?"

Donnelly glared at him, as though suddenly suspecting him of some dark purpose. "Are you *really* interested?"

"I'm really interested."

"Good," Donnelly said. "You know something—" His voice was solemn now. "I think it was fate that made me say yes to your sister when she asked me to work on this movie. I'll drive you out there and you can see for yourself."

Rudolph left a bill on the table to pay for the drinks. "It's getting late," he said as he stood up. "Shall we go back to the hotel?"

"If you don't mind," Donnelly said, "I'd rather stay here and get drunk."

"Take two aspirin before going to bed," Rudolph said. Donnelly was ordering another whiskey as he went out of the bar, offering a libation to fate, which had brought him and Rudolph Jordache together.

Rudolph walked slowly, alone, down the familiar streets. They had aged since he had pedaled along them, delivering rolls for the family bakery at dawn every morning, but he had the incongruous feeling this night that he was a young man again, with grandiose plans in his head, achievement in his future. Once again, as he had felt on the gravelly strand in Nice, he was tempted to sprint in the darkness, renewing the elation of his youth when he was the best 220 high hurdler in the high school. He even took a few tentative, loping steps, but saw a car's headlights approaching and relapsed into his usual dignified walk.

He passed the big building which housed the Calderwood Department Store and looked into the windows and remembered the nights he had put in arranging the displays. If his fortune had started at any one place, it had started there. The windows were shabby now, he thought, an old lady putting makeup carelessly on her face, the lipstick awry, the eye shadow sloppy, the simulation of youth weary and unconvincing. Old man Calderwood would have bellowed. A dead man's life's work. Useful? Useless?

He remembered, too, marching, playing the trumpet at the head of a column of students on the evening of the day the war had ended, the future a triumphant panorama ahead of him. Yesterday, he had read in the town newspaper, there had been another parade of students, this time to protest the war in Vietnam, the youths chanting obscene slogans, defacing the flag, taunting the police. Eleven students had wound up in jail. Truman then, Nixon now. Decay. He sighed. Better not to remember anything.

When he had suggested to Gretchen that Port Philip would be a good place to shoot her movie—a neglected town, withdrawn from its prosperous and honorable past on the banks of the great river—he had resolved not to have anything to do with the actual machinery of the production or even visit the town. But problems had arisen and Gretchen had called for help and he had reluctantly made the trip, talked to the officials, fearing that they would recall his downfall when the students had turned against *him* and driven him away.

How beautiful Jean had been in those days.

But the officials had been respectful, eager to accommodate him. Scandals passed. New men arrived. Memories faded.

Donnelly reminded him of himself when he was young—passionate, hopeful, driving, self-centered, sure of his purposes. He wondered what Donnelly would feel ten years from now, many accomplishments behind

him, the streets of his native town, wherever it was,
changed, everything changed. He liked Donnelly. He
knew Gretchen liked him, too. He wondered if there
was anything between them. He wondered, too, if Donnelly's idea was practical, workable. Was Donnelly too
young, too ambitious? He cautioned himself to move
slowly, check everything, as he thought he himself had
checked everything when he was that age.

He would talk it over with Helen Morison. She was a
hard-headed woman. She could be depended on. But
she was in Washington now. She had been offered a job
there on the staff of a congressman whom she admired
and she had moved on. He would have to catch up with
her somehow.

He thought of Jeanne. There had been a few letters,
with less and less to say in each succeeding one, the
emotion of the week on the Côte fading. Perhaps when
Wesley finally went to France, he would take it as an
excuse to visit her. The lawyer in Antibes had finally
written that it had been arranged that Wesley could
come back, but he hadn't told Wesley that. He was
waiting until the movie was finished. He didn't want
Wesley suddenly to take it into his head to quit the picture and fly across the ocean. Wesley was not a flighty
boy, but he was driven, driven by his own ghosts, unpredictable.

He himself had been driven by the ghost of his own
father, despairing, a failure, a suicide, drunk on poverty
and destroyed hopes, so he could half understand his
nephew. Weird, that that subterranean, hidden boy
could turn out to be such a touching actor.

There had never been anybody with that kind of talent in the family before, although Gretchen had been
briefly on the stage, without success. You never could
tell where it comes from, Gretchen had told him after a
session in the projection room in which they had

watched and marveled at what the boy could do. And it wasn't only that particular talent. It was every kind of talent. In America especially, no maps to tell where anybody had set out from or what ports they would sail to. No dependable genealogical trees anywhere.

He went into the sleeping hotel and up to his room and undressed and got into the cold bed. He found it difficult to sleep, thought of the pretty, coquettish girl in the bar, her jeans tight across her hips, her professionally inviting smile. What would it be like, he wondered, that perfect young body, open to invitation? Ask my nephew, he thought enviously, he's probably in bed with her now. A different generation. He had been a virgin, himself, at Wesley's age. He was ashamed of his envy, although he was sure the boy would suffer later. Was suffering now—he'd left the bar alone. Not used to the tricks. Well, neither was he. You suffered according to your capacity to suffer and there was something about the boy that made you feel his capacity was dangerously great.

He hovered between sleeping and waking, missing the body in the bed beside him. Whose body? Jean's, Helen's, Jeanne's, someone he had never met but who would finally lie beside him? He had not found any answer by the time he fell into a deep slumber.

He was awakened by the sound of drunken singing in the street. He recognized Donnelly's voice, harsh and tuneless, singing "Boola, Boola." Donnelly had gone to Yale. Not a typical graduate, Rudolph thought dreamily. The singing stopped. He turned over and went back to sleep.

---

In her room, Gretchen was alone, going over the setups she wanted for the next day's shooting. When she was on the set she made herself seem calm and certain of herself, even at times she wanted to scream in anger or anguish. But when she was alone like this, working by herself, she could sometimes feel her hands shaking in fear and indecision. So many people depended on her and every decision was so final. She had seen the same division of conduct in Colin Burke when he was directing a movie or a play and had wondered how he could manage it. Now she wondered how any human being could survive a whole month at a time, or longer, being cut in half like that. Private faces in public places, in Auden's phrase, had no part in the business of making movies.

Then she heard Donnelly singing "Boola, Boola" outside the hotel. Sadly, she shook her head at the relation between talent and liquor in the arts in America. There again she thought of Colin Burke, whom she had never seen drunk and who rarely even took a drink. An exception. An exception in many ways. She thought of him often these days, while she worked, trying to imagine how he would set up the camera, what he would say to a balky actor, how direct a complicated scene. If you couldn't plagiarize a dead husband, she thought defensively, whom could you plagiarize?

The singing outside stopped and she hoped that Donnelly wouldn't feel too shaken in the morning. For his sake, not for hers—she didn't need him for the next day's shooting—but he always looked so shamefaced when he came onto the set after the night before.

She smiled, thinking of the artful, dour, complicated man, who, she thought, looked like a young Confederate cavalry colonel, with his jutting beard and fierce, unsatisfied eyes. She liked him and she could tell he was attracted to her and, despite her vow never to let a younger man touch her again, if she wasn't so obsessed with the picture, she might . . .

There was a knock on her door.

"Come in," she said. She never locked her door.

The door opened and Donnelly came in, walking almost straight.

"Good evening," she said.

"I have just spent a momentous hour," he said solemnly, "with your brother. I love your brother. I thought you had to be told."

She smiled. "I love my brother, too."

"We are going to engage in grand—grandiloquent undertakings together," Donnelly said. "We are of the same tribe."

"Possibly," Gretchen said good-naturedly; "our mother possibly was Irish, or at least that was what she claimed. Our father was German, though."

"I respect both the Irish and the Germans," Donnelly said, leaning against the doorpost for support, "but that is not what I meant. I am talking of the tribe of the spirit. Do I interrupt you?"

"I'd just about finished," Gretchen said. "If you want to talk don't you think it would be a good idea to shut the door?"

Slowly, with dignity, Donnelly closed the door behind him and leaned against it.

"Would you like some coffee?" Gretchen indicated the thermos pitcher on her desk. She drank twenty cups a day to keep going.

"People are always offering me coffee," Donnelly said pettishly. "I find it degrading. I despise coffee."

"I'm afraid I have nothing harder to drink," Gretchen said, although there was a bottle of Scotch, she knew, in the cupboard.

"I have no need of the drink, madam," Donnelly said. "I come merely as a messenger."

"From whom?"

"From David P. Donnelly," Donnelly said, "himself."

Gretchen laughed.

"Deliver the message," she said, "and then I advise bed."

"I have delivered half the message," Donnelly said. "I love your brother. The other half is more difficult. I love his sister."

"You're drunk."

"Correct," he said. "Drunk I love his sister and sober I love his sister."

"Thank you for the message," Gretchen said, still seated, although she wanted to stand up and kiss the man.

"You will remember what I have said?" He glowered at her over his beard.

"I'll remember."

"In that case," he said oratorically, "I shall retire for the night. Good night, madam."

"Good night," she said. "Sleep well."

"I promise to toss and turn. Ah, me."

Gretchen chuckled. "Ah, you."

If he had stayed another ten seconds she would have sprung from her chair and embraced him. But he waved his arm grandly in salute and went out, almost straight.

She heard him singing "Boola, Boola" as he went down the hallway.

She sat staring at the door, thinking, Why not, why the hell not? She shook her head. Later, later, when the work is over. Perhaps.

She went back to marking her script in the quiet room, which now smelled from whiskey.

On the floor below, Wesley tried to sleep. He had kept listening for the soft turning of the door handle and the rustle of cloth as Frances came into the darkened room. But the door handle didn't turn, there was no sound except the complaint of the bedsprings as he turned restlessly under the covers.

He had said he loved her. True, she had more or less forced it out of him, but when he had said it he had meant it. When you loved someone, though, did you notice when she was faking, putting on an act, did you let her know that she was behaving foolishly? People talked about love as though it was all one piece, as though once you said you were in love nothing else mattered. In the movie he was doing the young politician who fell in love with Frances never criticized her for her behavior, which he adored, but only for some of the wilder schemes she concocted to sway the other characters in the script to see things her way. Love is blind, the saying went. Well, he certainly hadn't been blind that evening. He had felt that the performance Frances had put on in the bar was phony and disgusting and he had told her so. Maybe he had better learn to keep his opinions to himself. If he had, he wouldn't be in bed alone at two o'clock in the morning.

He ached for the touch of her hand, the softness of her breast as he kissed it. If that wasn't love, what was it? When she was in bed with him he couldn't believe she would go back to her husband, be attracted to another man, despite what his aunt had told him. He had enjoyed the women on the *Clothilde*, while their husbands had slept below or been off at the casino, he had liked what he did with Mrs. Wertham, but he had known, with certainty, that what he was feeling then wasn't love. You didn't have to be an experienced man of the world to know the difference between what he had felt then and what he felt with Frances.

He remembered the times when Frances was in his arms in the narrow bed, their bodies entwined in the dark, and Frances had whispered, "I love you." What had she meant those times? He groaned softly.

He had told Frances to call her mother to find out who she really was. Whom could he call to find out who *he* really was? His own mother? She would probably say that like his father he was a defiler of decent Christian homes. His uncle? To his uncle he most likely seemed like an inherited nuisance, with no sense of gratitude, who only showed up when he needed something. His Aunt Gretchen? A freak, who by some mysterious trick of nature was gifted with a talent he was too stupid or unambitious to want to use. Alice? A clumsy, unsophisticated boy who needed pity and mothering. Bunny? A good deckhand who would never be anywhere near the man his father was. Kate? Half brother to her son, a painful, living memory of her dead husband. How put all this together and make one whole person out of the parts?

Was it only because he was so young that he felt so split up, so uncertain of himself? Retarded, Frances had said that evening. But other people around his age didn't seem to suffer, they put themselves together all right. Jimmy, the other delivery boy at the supermarket, with his music and the firm knowledge that his sisters and his mother had a single, uncomplicated opinion of him, and that opinion based on love. His own mother said she loved him but that kind of love was a whole lot worse than hate.

He thought of Healey, the wounded soldier who had come back with Kraler's son's body. Healey lived on one certainty, that he was a man who always got a raw deal from the world and that nothing would ever change for him and that the world could go fuck itself.

There was only one thing he was certain of, Wesley

thought, *he* was going to change. Only he had no inkling, as he lay there alone in the dark room, in what direction. He wondered, if by some miracle he could get a glimpse of himself at the age of twenty-one, twenty-five, thirty, what he would think of himself.

Maybe, after he was finished with Frances, he would finally do what his aunt wanted him to do and become an actor. Learn to live with all the different parts of himself and make full use of them, act not only in front of a camera, but like Frances, every minute of the day. Maybe she had it figured out—that's what the world wanted and that's what she gave it.

In the morning, he knew, on the set, he would be expected to seem like a savage, irresponsible ruffian. It was an easy role for him to play. Maybe he would try it for a year or two. It was as good a starting point as anyplace else.

When he finally slept he dreamed that he was in Alice's living room eating a roast beef sandwich and drinking a beer, only it wasn't Alice across the table from him, but Frances Miller.

# CHAPTER 7

*From Billy Abbott's notebook—*

Back at the typewriter again. Bad habits
die hard. Besides, everyone takes a
siesta here after lunch and I've never
gotten into the habit of sleeping
during the day and since there's nobody
else to talk to, I might as well talk
to myself. Anyway, there's no reason to
believe that Franco's police would be
interested in the ramblings of an
American tennis pro in this enclave of
the rich on the edge of the blue sea.
It was different in Belgium. Is it
possible that privacy is easier to
achieve under Fascism than under
democracy? Must study the question.
    After Brussels, the climate of
southern Spain is the weather of heaven
and it makes you wonder, how, if people
had any choice in the matter, they would
continue to live north of the Loire.

Drove down in the neat little
secondhand open Peugeot with French
transit TTX plates that I got at a good
price in Paris. As soon as I crossed
the Pyrenees, between the green
mountains and the ocean, I felt a
peculiar pleasure, as though I
recognized the villages and the fields
and rivers from another life, as though
I were returning home from a long
journey, and this was the country for
me.

Until I open my mouth I can pass as a
Spaniard. Is it possible that the
coloring of the Abbott family is the
result of a slipup at the time of the
Spanish Armada? Shipwrecked, potent
Andalusians on the coast of England
and Scotland?

The hotel I live in is brand new and
good at least a dozen years before it
succumbs to wind and tide. But it's
solid enough now and I have a
comfortable, airy room with a view of a
golf course and the sea. Aside from the
lessons I have to give to beginners and
dubs, there are enough good players
around for two hours of fast tennis
almost everyday. A simple man, myself,
with simple tastes.

The Spaniards here are handsome and
agreeable and schooled in courtesy, a
change after the American Army. The
others are on holiday and on their best
behavior. Up to now I have not been
insulted or challenged to a duel,
forced to see a bullfight or requested
to help bring down the system.

Careful to be most correct with the

ladies, accent or no. They're likely to
have husbands or escorts in the
background who have a tendency to be
suspicious of a young American
professional athlete who spends at least
an hour a day, scantily dressed, with
their partners. They suddenly appear
on the sidelines during lessons,
brooding darkly. I have no desire to be
ridden out of town in disgrace, charged
with dishonoring some Spanish
gentleman's wife or mistress. For a
year at least it is my intention to stay
out of trouble.

After Monika the joys of celibacy are
to be recommended. Turmoil, in and out
of bed, is not my specialty.

I'm brown from the sun and in better
shape than ever before and have taken
to admiring myself naked in a mirror.

The pay is good, the tips generous.
I find myself actually saving quite a
bit of money, something new and strange
in my life.

The parties are numerous here and I'm
invited to most of them. New boy in
town, I suppose. I make sure not to
drink too much or speak to any one lady
for more than fifteen minutes at a time.
By now I know enough Spanish to
understand most of the fierce political
arguments that erupt here late at night.
The participants are likely to bring up
such subjects as the menace of
bloodshed, expropriation, Communism, and
what will happen to the country when the
old man dies. I keep silent at such
times, thanking my stars that I have
settled, even if only for a short

period, in a beautiful country which suits my temperament so well, without having to express any opinion more inflammatory than how to grip the handle of a racket when serving.

Once more I have to doubt my father's warning that I come from an unlucky family.

My mother has written me several letters. As usual, she got my address from my father, whom I write on the vain presumption that my letters are the only thing that keeps him from jumping into Lake Michigan. My mother's letters have mellowed in tone. She takes it that my decision not to re-enlist has something to do with her protests and represents a new and welcome maturity in me. She now finishes her letters with "Love, Mother." For years it was just "Mother," a trick of signing off that I understood, I think correctly, as a sign of her complete disgust with me. I have returned the compliment and signed my one letter to her, "Love, Billy."

She tells me that she is enjoying her new career as a director, which comes as no surprise to me, considering her penchant for bossing people around. She writes with great enthusiasm of the ability of my Cousin Wesley as an actor. It's a trade I should have considered, since I can be as false or sincere as any man, but it's too late now. Wesley wants to visit me, my mother writes. How should I greet him? Welcome, Brother Sufferer.

Holy God! Two days after I wrote the above, Monika appeared, accompanied by a middle-aged German tycoon who sells frozen foods. She is in a prosperous period, all decked out in sleek, expensive-looking clothes, with her hair combed. So far she has pretended not to know me, but it may be the lull before the storm. Thoughts of flight haunt me.

I lost in  straight sets to a man I have beaten on six consecutive days.

---

Freddie Kahn, the cameraman, led the singing of "For she's a jolly good fellow," holding Gretchen's hand aloft like a winning prizefighter's, at the traditional party on the set in the studio in New York at the finish of the last day's shooting. The singing of the cast, the technical men, and the grips and the friends invited was loud and hearty. Gretchen was somewhere between tears and laughter as the singing rang out on the set strewn with cables, the cameras hooded, the liquor and sandwiches on improvised, flower-decorated tables set on trestles. Ida Cohen was frankly crying and had her hair done for the occasion. Kahn presented a wristwatch to Gretchen as a gift from the cast, to which Wesley had contributed fifty dollars, and called on Gretchen to make a speech.

"Thank you, thank you everybody," Gretchen said, her voice trembling a little. "You've all been wonderful and I want to congratulate one and all for making my first stab at being a director such a happy one. Although, as the saying goes in Hollywood, Show me a happy company and I'll show you a stinker of a movie."

There was a wave of laughter and a few shouts of, "No, not this time."

Gretchen raised her hand for silence. "For all of you, the job is over and I hope you go on to bigger and better things and that your flops will be forgotten and your hits remembered forever—or at least until the next Academy Award night. But for some of us, the cutters, the people who do the dubbing, the composer and musicians, and for Mr. Cohen, who will have the unenviable job of selling the picture for distribution without all of us being stolen blind, the job is just really beginning. Wish us well, because there're months of work ahead of us, and what we do from now on can mean the difference between success and failure."

She spoke modestly, but Wesley, who was standing near her, could see the light of triumph in her eyes. "Ida," she said, "do stop crying. This isn't a funeral—yet."

Ida sobbed.

Somebody put a glass of whiskey into Gretchen's hand and she raised it in a toast. "To us all—from the oldest here—" She turned to Wesley. "And to the youngest."

Wesley, who had a glass of whiskey in his hand, which he had not yet touched, raised his glass with the others. He was not smiling or looking exuberant, like most of the company, because he had just seen Frances Miller, who was standing to one side with her husband, clink glasses with him and exchange a kiss. Wesley and Frances had made up after the night in the bar in Port Philip and she had again come to his room in the hotel and had let him stay with her for the night several times in her apartment in New York when they resumed shooting interiors there. That was until three days ago, when her husband had arrived from California. Wesley had not yet met her husband, a handsome blond man built like a football player, who, Wesley had to admit to himself, looked nice enough, in a standard

Hollywood way. But the familiar manner in which
Frances and her husband looked at each other as they
raised their glasses, and the tenderness of their kiss,
made him wish there had been some way of avoiding
the party.

Alice was there, too, although for the moment he
could not see her in the shadows of the set. As always,
she made herself as unobtrusive as possible. She had
behaved peculiarly after the nights he had not come to
the apartment to sleep on the sofa, aloof and efficiently
nurselike. When he had told her about the party, she
had said she'd love to come, she had never been to a
party on a movie set before. He had tried to seem gra-
cious about inviting her, but it had been an effort.
When you get older, he thought, trying not to look in
the direction of Frances and her husband, maybe you
can learn how to handle things like this.

He took a big gulp of his whiskey and soda, remembering that the last time he had drunk hard liquor was
the night in the Porte Rose in Cannes. The whiskey
tasted fine and he took another gulp.

Gretchen walked around the set, shaking hands or
kissing people on the cheek and some of the other
women were teary-eyed, too. Everybody seemed reluctant to leave, as though they wished to prolong as much
as possible the ties they had formed with each other in
their common labor over the months. Wesley overheard
a middle-aged character woman say to Gretchen, "Bless
you, dear; from here on, it's got to get worse."

Wesley wondered how the simple act of just making a
movie, which must have become a routine experience to
all these professional people, could arouse so much
emotion. He himself had enjoyed making the movie, but
aside from Frances and Gretchen, he wouldn't care if
he never saw any one of them again. Maybe, no matter

what Gretchen told him, deep down he was not really cut out to be an actor.

When Gretchen came up to him and kissed him on the cheek and said, "Wesley Jordan, I'm going to miss you," he could see that she meant it.

"That was a nice little speech," he said. "You sure know how to decorate an occasion."

"Thank you, honey," she said. But she kept looking over her shoulder as though she was searching for someone. "Wesley," she said, "did Rudolph say anything to you about not coming here or being late?"

"No." All his Uncle Rudolph had said to him in the last few days of shooting was that the lawyer in Antibes had written that it was okay to come back to France. He had not yet bought his ticket. Without admitting it to himself, he had the feeling that he was not ready to leave America just yet, that there were too many things left unsettled.

"He had to go up to Connecticut again today with Mr. Donnelly," Gretchen said, still searching over the heads of the people who surrounded them, "but he promised to be back by five o'clock. It's past seven now. It's not like Rudolph to be late. I can't leave the party just yet, so will you be a dear and telephone his hotel to see if he left a message?"

"Of course," Wesley said and searched for coins as he went off the stage to the telephone outside to call the Hotel Algonquin, where his uncle kept a room for the nights he had to stay over in the city.

He had to wait to make the call because Frances was there, talking and giggling. He moved away because he didn't want to overhear what she was saying. She took a long time over her conversation and kept feeding dimes into the machine. He had carried his glass with him and by the time she had finished, he had drained it. He could feel his muscles tense as he waited, listening to

the tone of the voice without hearing the words, and he
was uncomfortably conscious of a spasmodic tingle in
the nerves around his groin and in his balls. Never
again, never again, he told himself, although he knew
he was lying.

With a last soft giggle, Frances hung up and came
toward the door to the stage, outside which he was
standing. Her hair was hanging long over her shoulders
and she swung it back with a womanly gesture of her
hand. "Ah," she said, and she giggled again, "the boy
wonder, lying in wait."

"I have a call to make," he said, "but first I want to
do something." Suddenly, he grabbed her and kissed
her on the mouth.

"Well, now," she said, giggling, "you've finally taken
acting lessons. How to be passionate in the presence of
husbands." Her voice was a little thick from drink.

"When am I going to see you again?" Wesley gripped
her arms, as though by the strength in his hands he
could keep her from slipping away.

"Who knows?" Frances said. She giggled. "Maybe
never. Maybe when you grow up."

"You don't mean that," he said, his voice tortured.

"Who knows what I mean," she said. "Least of all
me. I have some good advice for you. We had our fun
and it's over. Now forget it."

The door from the stage swung open and Frances'
husband bulked against the light from the set.

"Let go of her," the man said.

Wesley dropped his hands and stepped back a little.

"I know what you two have been up to all this time,"
the man said, "don't think I don't. Slut."

"Oh, cool it, Jack, please," Frances said carefully.

The man slapped her face. The sound was flat and
ugly. "As for you, you little bastard," he said to Wesley,

"if I ever catch you hanging around my wife again I'll break you in half."

"Oh, the great big he-man," Frances said mockingly. She hadn't put her hand to her face, it was as though her husband hadn't touched her. "Everywhere but in bed."

The man took a deep breath that was more of a gasp, like a rush of air from a suddenly opened door. Then he slapped Frances again, much harder this time.

Still, Frances didn't put her hand to her face. "Pig," she said to her husband. "You and your spies."

The man grabbed her arm. "Now you're marching back in there," he said, "and you're smiling because your husband, who was detained on business on the Coast, has managed to come to New York to spend the weekend with you."

"Whatever you say, pig," Frances said. She took his arm and without looking at Wesley went through the door with her husband onto the set, where there was the sound of music now, a piano and a trumpet and a set of drums, and couples dancing.

Wesley stood immobile in the dimly lit hall, only the muscles in his face working. Then he crushed the empty plastic cup in his hand and threw it against the wall. He took two minutes, until he was sure he wouldn't rush through the door, past the dancing couples, and throw himself at the man's throat.

When he felt he could trust his voice, he called the hotel, where the operator told him that Mr. Jordache had left no messages. He stood beside the phone on the wall for another moment, then went onto the set and found his aunt and repeated what the operator had said. After that he went to the bar and ordered a whiskey, which he drank straight off, then ordered another.

While he was finishing the drink, he felt a tap on his arm. He turned to see Alice standing there, that aloof, nurselike look on her face that he had begun to fear. "I think maybe it would be a good idea," Alice said calmly, "if you repaired your face. You've got lipstick all over it."

"Thank you," he said woodenly, taking out his handkerchief and dabbing at his lips and cheeks. "That better?"

"Much better," she said. "Now I think I'll be going. I've found out movie parties aren't as dazzling as people would lead a girl to believe."

"Good night," Wesley said. He wanted to ask her forgiveness, change that distant, cold expression in her eyes, but he didn't know how to say it or just what she could forgive him for. "I'll see you later."

"Perhaps," she said.

Christ, he thought, as he watched the small girl with the straight, honest walk disappear among the dancers, Christ, am I a mess, I've got to get out of this town. Then he turned back to the bar and asked for another drink. He was taking it from the bartender when Rudolph came up to him. "Having a good time, Mr. Jordan?" Rudolph said.

"Marvelous," Wesley said. "Gretchen is looking for you. She's worried. I called your hotel for her."

"I was delayed," Rudolph said. "I'll go find her. I'd like to talk to you later. Where'll you be?"

"Right here," Wesley said.

Rudolph frowned. "Take it easy, lad," he said. "I'm sure you'll be able to find another bottle of whiskey somewhere in New York tomorrow if you look hard enough." He gave Wesley's arm a friendly small pat, then went looking for Gretchen.

Gretchen was talking to Richard Sanford, the author of *Restoration Comedy,* when Rudolph saw her on the other side of the space where people were dancing. Sanford had made no concessions in his dress, Rudolph saw, for the celebration of the finishing day of shooting for his first opus. He was wearing his usual uniform of open-necked wool shirt and windbreaker.

"What I'm worried about," Sanford was saying earnestly, "is that there aren't enough close-ups of the girl in what I've seen so far. Somehow, I don't get enough emotion in the medium shots and in the . . ."

"Dear Richard," Gretchen said, "I'm afraid that like so many other authors, you are smitten with an actress's charms to the detriment of her talent . . ."

"Oh, come on now," Sanford said, flushing, "I've barely spoken to the girl."

"She's spoken to you," Gretchen said. "That's more than enough with a young lady like that. I regret for your sake that she was otherwise occupied."

"You underestimate me," Sanford said angrily.

"That's been the problem of artists for five thousand years," Gretchen said. "You'll learn to live with it, sonny."

"We're not friends, you and I," Sanford said. "You resent my—my maleness. I've known that from the beginning."

"That's beside the point," Gretchen said. "Aside from being pure bullshit. And if you haven't known it before, let me tell it to you now, young man—art is not created out of friendship."

"You're a bitter, aging woman." Months of resentment grated in his voice. "What you need is a good fuck. Which nobody is polite enough to give you."

Gretchen rubbed her eyes before replying. "You're a talented, unpleasant young man. You will be less unpleasant, and I'm afraid, less talented as you grow older."

"You don't have to insult me, Gretchen," he said.

"In our profession," Gretchen said, "insults are beside the point. You weary me. And I suppose I weary

you, too. Also beside the point. But, my dear Richard—" she touched his cheek lightly, half a caress,
half a threat of manicured long nails—"I promise to
serve you well. Don't ask for more. I promise you all
the close-ups you can use and all the emotion anybody
can stand. The problem with that girl is not too little,
it's too much."

"You've always got an answer to everything," Sanford said. "I never win an argument with you. Kinsella
warned me . . ."

"How is dear Evans?" Gretchen asked.

"He's okay." Sanford shifted his feet uneasily. "He's
asked me to do his next picture."

"And you're on your way to Hollywood."

"Actually . . . yes."

"Goody for you," Gretchen said. "And goody for
him. I know you'll be happy together. And now, if
you'll excuse me, I see my brother waiting to talk to
me."

As Gretchen walked toward Rudolph, he saw Sanford shake his head despairingly. Rudolph was chuck-
ling as Gretchen came up to him.

"What're you laughing about?" she asked.

"The expression on that young man's face when you
left him," he said.

Gretchen grimaced. "We were engaging in that most
creative of occupations—wounding each other. One
picture and he thinks he's the editor of *Cahiers du
Cinéma*. A lost soul. No great tragedy. America is full
of one-shot talents. I was worried about you. Where've
you been all this time?"

Rudolph shook his head. "We've run into a holy
mess in Connecticut. Donnelly's ready to slit his throat.
The whole project looks as though it's going to come
apart."

"Why?" Gretchen asked. "What's happened?"

"Some damned society for the preservation of the environment or something like that is suing us for an injunction to stop us from building," Rudolph said. "We spent the whole day with lawyers."

"I thought it was all set," Gretchen said.

"So did I," said Rudolph. "Until yesterday. We thought we had bought a tract of abandoned farmland. Now it turns out we have bought a precious piece of Connecticut wilderness, full of rare birds, herds of darling deer, lovely snakes. Three lynx have also been sighted there in recent years. Instead of being semiphilanthropic benefactors of aging humanity, it seems we are grasping city slickers out to pollute the pure air of the sovereign state of Connecticut, besides being the enemy of the lynx." He shook his head again, half-humorously.

"What do the lawyers say?"

"It will take years, even if we finally win. Donnelly almost wept with remorse when he realized how long our money was going to be tied up."

"Where is he?" Gretchen asked. "Donnelly?"

"I put him to bed. Dead drunk. He'll feel even worse tomorrow."

"I'm so sorry," Gretchen said.

"The roll of the dice," said Rudolph. "Don't let it spoil your big night. Another thing. I got a call from California yesterday. From a man I know, an agent called Bowen."

"I know him, too," Gretchen said. "He's got a good office."

Rudolph nodded. "He says the word has gotten around about Wesley. He says he can get him a fat contract. If Wesley's going to continue as an actor he'll need an agent and Bowen's as honest as any of them. I have to talk to the young man."

"He was holding up the bar the last I saw of him," Gretchen said, "smeared with lipstick."

"I saw him. I'll give him some sage, avuncular advice." Rudolph leaned over and kissed Gretchen on the cheek. "Congratulations for everything. You've done a wonderful job. And it isn't only your brother who thinks so."

"Things went smoothly. I was afraid it was going to be amateur night from beginning to end."

"Don't be so modest, Sister," Rudolph said and squeezed her hand. "You're in the major leagues now."

"We'll see. Let's keep our fingers crossed," Gretchen said, but she couldn't keep back a pleased smile.

"Now for the young man," Rudolph said. "Save me a dance for when I've finished with him."

"I haven't danced in years."

"Neither have I," Rudolph said. "I'll ask the boys to play a waltz."

Then he went back to the bar, but Wesley was no longer there. The bartender said that he had left five minutes ago.

---

Alice was sitting reading in the living room when Wesley got to the apartment. He had stopped at two bars on the way home. The bars had been too dark for anyone to ask him for proof of his age. Walking on the city streets had proved something of a problem, as the sidewalks seemed to be sliding away from him at different angles and he had stumbled twice at the curbs at corners.

"Good evening," he said gravely to Alice.

"Good evening," she said. She did not look up from her book. He noticed that the sofa was not made up as usual with sheets and blankets. He had the curious feeling that it was not Alice he was seeing, but a reflection of her in rippling water.

He misjudged the distance when he tried to sit down and just barely made the edge of the chair. He stared intently at Alice, who was still rippling.

"I'm no good," he said. "You're wasting your time worrying about me."

"You're drunk," she said. "And I'm not worrying about you."

"Tomorrow," he said, his voice sounding strange and faraway in his ears, "I will pay you every cent I owe you and I will de—de—depart."

"None too soon," Alice said, still looking down at her book. "I'm sure you'll be able to find another place to sleep. And don't talk about money to me. You don't owe me a cent. What I've done for you I didn't do for money."

He looked at her, focusing with difficulty. "Do you mind if I say thanks?" he said.

"I mind everything you say," she said fiercely. "Hollywood bum."

"I've never been to Hollywood. Not even to California," he said foolishly.

"You and your tarts." She threw the book to the floor. "What am I reading this damned book for? It's a terrible book."

"I thought you were my . . . well . . ." He spoke confusedly. "Well—my sister."

"I'm not your sister."

He groped for what he wanted to say, feeling his brain and tongue misted over. "You say I die," he said. "In your book. You want me to be noble and die. You're asking for too much . . ."

"Oh, my God," she said. She rose from her chair and came over to him and took his head into her hands and pressed him to her body. "I'm so sorry. I don't want you to die, Wesley. You've got to believe that."

"Everybody wants something from me I can't give," Wesley said, his mouth muffled against the stuff of her dress. "I don't know where I am. Tomorrow ask for me in the Lost and Found Department."

"Please, Wesley," she whispered, "don't say things like that."

"You said once you were stealing a piece of my soul . . ." He moaned as he spoke. "I hear you typing at night and I say to myself, There goes another bit of my soul."

"Please, please, Sweet . . ." She held his head tighter to her as though to keep him from saying another word. "You're killing me."

"Everybody shames me." He pulled his head sidewise, so he could speak. "What I went through tonight . . . Now you . . . I haven't lived up to you, I know that, but . . ."

"Sssh, sssh, baby," she crooned.

"I love you," he said.

She pulled him, hard, against herself. Then, amazingly, she laughed. "Why the hell did it take you so long to say that?" She dropped to her knees and kissed him, briefly. Then she moved her head back so that she could look at him. "Say it again," she said.

"I love you," he said.

"You look awful," she said.

"I *feel* awful. This is the second time in my life I've been drunk. Excuse me, please, I have to puke." He stood up, unsteadily, and reeled into the bathroom and there all the whiskey of the night came up. He felt no healthier, still weak and wobbly. He undressed carefully, brushed his teeth for two whole minutes, then took a cold shower. He felt a little better as he dried himself, although when he turned his head he had to do it with great care and his stomach felt as though he had swallowed nails. He put on a robe that Alice had picked out for him and went back, his hair wet, steadying himself with his hand against the wall, into the living room.

The living room was empty and the sofa was still not made up for sleeping.

From the bedroom, he heard Alice's voice. "I'm in here. You don't have to find any other place to sleep tonight."

Still weak and with his head feeling as though a carousel were going around in it, with the calliope playing, he stumbled into the bedroom. There was only one small lamp on and the bedroom was dim, but he saw Alice, still rippling, under the covers of the big bed.

"Come here," she said. "Get in."

He started to climb into the bed with his robe still on.

"Take that damned thing off," she said.

"Turn out the light." The idea of Alice Larkin, that shy and most ladylike girl, seeing him naked was shocking to him.

She chuckled as she turned the lamp off. He stumbled as he dropped the robe on the floor and he barked his shins against a dressing table as he felt his way to the bed. She was small and her skin soft and fragrant as he put his arms around her, but he still felt terrible.

"I can't do anything," he whispered. "I love you and I can't do anything. You should have told me earlier tonight, before I drank all that booze."

"I didn't know earlier," she said. "No matter." She kissed his ear as she pulled closer to him. "You'll be all right in the morning."

And he was.

# CHAPTER 8

*From Billy Abbott's notebook—*

She is still here.

She hasn't made a sign that she knows
me. She and her frozen-food manufacturer
from Dusseldorf speak, as far as I can
tell, to no one. I never see them with
anyone else. He plays golf every day.
They are not at any of the parties to
which I am invited. I have found out
that she is registered at the hotel as
<u>Senorita</u> Monika Hitzman, which was not
her name when I knew her before. When
we pass each other by accident, whether
she is alone or with her friend, we pass
as strangers, although I feel a glacial
current of air, very much like the chill
you might feel sailing past an iceberg.

Occasionally, sometimes alone,
sometimes with her friend, she passes
by the tennis courts. More often than
not she stops for a moment or two to

watch the sport, as do many other of the
guests.

My game is deteriorating daily.

There is another complication. I am
being wooed, if that is the word, by a
young Spanish girl, by name Carmen (is
there no escaping that melodic echo?)
from Barcelona, who plays a fierce,
tireless game of tennis, and whose
father, I have learned, was in a high
position in the Franco government in
Barcelona. He is sometimes with her and
sometimes not, an erect, gray-haired
gentleman, with an unforgiving face.

His daughter is twenty years old, with
dangerous dark eyes, blond hair and a
tigerish manner of moving, off the court
and on, as though she feels it incumbent
upon her to live up to the libretto of
the opera. She extends me in singles.
She also finds opportunities to offer me
a drink when we have finished playing
or at other moments, and entrusts me
with confidences that I do not wish to
hear. She has been to school in England
and speaks the language well, although
with a strong accent. With her I retreat
into my stupid athlete role, although
she says she sees through me, which I'm
afraid she does. Among the things she
has told me is that her father, although
Catalan, fought in Franco's armies, and
has the outlook on life of the captains
of Ferdinand and Isabella who drove the
Moors and the Jews from Spain. She
infuriates her father by speaking
Catalan to him and she loves him
profoundly. She will not be happy, she
says, until the Catalonian flag flies

over Barcelona and the poets of what she
calls her country write in that
language. She and Monika, who also sets
store on the linguistic division of
Europe, would have a great deal to say
to each other, although I doubt that
Carmen has as yet thrown her first bomb.
She distributes pamphlets that may or
may not be against the law. She has a
marvelous, lithe body and I do not know
how long I can continue to resist her,
although I fear her father, who when
he looks at me, which is seldom, does so
with the coldest suspicion. Carmen tells
me he looks at all foreigners,
especially Americans, with the same
suspicion, but I cannot help but feel
that there is a repugnance there that is
not purely chauvinistic.

She looks like the kind of young
woman you see standing at the barrera
in Spanish newpaper photographs as
matadors dedicate bulls to them. She
does not look like the sort of girl one
meets in America who distributes
pamphlets.

She is like Monika in at least one
respect. She will never make any man a
good wife.

———

The next day was a bad one for Billy Abbott. Monika came down to the courts with her friend and signed
up for a week of instruction, every day at 11:00 A.M.

Billy gave her her first lesson. She was hopeless. He
couldn't say anything to her, as her friend sat watching
during the entire forty-five minutes. She addressed Billy

as Mr. Abbott and he addressed her as *Señorita* Hitzman. As he tossed balls at her, which more often than not she missed, he thought, I must get her aside somehow and ask her just what she is up to; it can't be coincidence that brought her to El Faro.

In the afternoon he was very nearly beaten by Carmen. She was in a cranky mood and played ferociously.

Later, in the bar of the hotel, where they were alone, he asked her what was the matter.

"Did you read the paper this morning?"

"No."

"On the front page there was a picture of one of your admirals being decorated by Franco."

He shrugged. "That's what admirals are for," he said. "Actually, I don't mind his getting a medal. What I mind is his being here, him and his ships and our air force with its planes. I was in the army a long time and I'm skeptical about how useful we would be if it came to the crunch."

Carmen glared at him. "What would you like to see happen—the Russians overrun Europe?"

"If they had wanted to overrun Europe," he said, "they'd have done it by now. We're in Europe in just enough numbers to annoy the Russians and not in enough to do much about them. If it came to a war, the missiles would do the fighting, not the men on the ground. They'd just be sacrificed on the first day. I was a man on the ground and I wasn't too happy about it."

"I certainly am glad," Carmen said sarcastically, "that I have my own private American military expert to explain the facts of life to me."

"It's all for show," Billy said. He didn't know why he was arguing with her. Probably because the last set had gone to eight-six. Maybe because he was tired of being lectured on politics by attractive young women. "A base here and there just gives the military boys a chance to flex their muscles and squeeze more money out of Congress so that they can ride around in big cars and live five times better here than they ever could at home." Then, more to tease her than because he meant what he was saying, he said, "If we took every American soldier out of uniform and sent him home to do some useful work it would be better for everyone concerned—including the Spaniards."

"The weak and lazy always find excuses for their weakness and laziness," Carmen said. "Thank God, all Americans aren't like you." Her politics were complicated. She hated Franco and hated the Communists and now, it seemed, she hated him, as well as the American admiral. "Being here is moral," she said. "Letting a man like Franco pin a medal on your chest if you're an American is immoral. It's one thing to be ready to defend a country in your own interest, after all; it's another to help prop up the reputation of a disgusting regime. If I were an American I'd write to Congress, to the State Department, to the president, to the newspapers, protesting. There—you want to do something useful—at least write a letter to the *Herald Tribune*."

"How long do you think I'd last here if that letter was ever published?"

"Twenty-four hours," Carmen said. "It would be worth it."

"A boy has to eat, too."

"Money," Carmen said disdainfully. "Everything is a question of money for people like you."

"May I remind you," Billy said, "that I don't have a rich father, like some folks I know."

"That's a disgraceful thing to say. At least that's one thing you can say about Spaniards—they don't measure out their lives in dollars and cents."

"I see some pretty rich Spaniards around here," Billy said, "who spend their time making more and more money. Buying up olive groves down here, for example, and turning them into tourist traps. All those big yachts in the harbor aren't owned by people who've taken the vow of poverty."

"Scum," Carmen said. "A fraction of the population. Without soul. Doing whatever Franco and his criminals tell them to do just so they can hold on to their *fincas*, their yachts, their mistresses, while the rest of the country starves. I hate Communism but when I see what the ordinary man or woman has to do to feed a family here, I can understand why they're attracted to it. Out of despair."

"What do you want to see—another civil war?" Billy said. "Another million dead? Blood running in the streets?"

"If it comes to that," Carmen said, "it will be your friends, the yacht owners, who will bring it about. Of course I don't want to see it. What I want to see is decent, orderly change. If you can do it in America, why can't it be done here?"

"I'm not a student of the Spanish character," Billy said, "but somewhere I've heard that your fellow citizens, when aroused, are likely to be bloodthirsty and cruel and violent."

"Oh, I'm so tired of talk like that," Carmen cried. "As though Spain was all bullfights and flagellants and people taking revenge for the honor of their families. How is it that nobody says how cruel and violent the Germans are as a race—after what they did to Europe? Or the French, after Napoleon? And I won't say anything about what the Americans have done in their time, you poor, useless tennis player." They were sitting at the hotel bar during this conversation and Carmen contemptuously signed the chit for their drinks. "There. You've saved the price of four gin and tonics. Aren't you glad you came to cruel and violent Spain and became the lackey of the rich here?"

"Maybe," Billy said, stung, "we ought not to see each other anymore. Find somebody else to play tennis with."

"You will play tennis with me," Carmen said, "because you are paid to play tennis with me. Same time tomorrow." She strode out of the bar, leaving him sitting alone in the big, empty room. God, he thought, and I believed she was wooing me! First Monika with her bombs and now this.

The next morning Monika came to the courts alone. Billy had to admit that she *looked* like a tennis player, small and trim, with good legs, and dressed in a becoming short tennis dress, with a band around her head to keep her neatly set hair in place.

As they walked out onto the court together, Billy said in a low voice, "Monika, what sort of game are you up to?"

"My name is *Señorita* Hitzman," she said coldly, "Mr. Abbott."

"If you want the money I took to Paris—and the other—the other part of the package," Billy said, "I can get it for you. It would take some time, but I could do it . . ."

"I don't know what you're talking about, Mr. Abbott."

"Oh, come on, now," he said, irritated. "Mr. Abbott. You didn't call me Mr. Abbott when we were fucking all afternoon in Brussels."

"If you go on like this, Mr. Abbott," she said, "I'll have to report you to the management for wasting valuable time in conversation instead of doing what you're supposed to do—which is to teach me how to play tennis."

"You'll never learn to play tennis."

"In that case," she said calmly, "that will be another failure for you to remember when you grow old. Now, if you please, I would like to start the lesson."

He sighed, then went to the other side of the court and started lobbing balls onto her racket. She was no better at returning them than she had been the morning before.

When the lesson was over, she said, "Thank you, Mr. Abbott," and walked off the court.

That afternoon he beat Carmen six-love, six-three, maliciously mixing his game with lobs and dropshots to make her run until she was red in the face. She too walked off the court with one curt phrase: "You played like a eunuch." She did not invite him to have a drink with her.

Spain, he thought, as he watched her stride toward the hotel, her blond hair flying, is becoming much less agreeable than it used to be.

———

Wesley took the train from London to Bath, enjoying looking out the window at the neat green countryside of rural England. After the tensions and uncertainties of America, it had been soothing to walk around London, where he knew no one and no one expected anything of him. He had been having lunch standing up at the bar of a pub when the voice of the barmaid had reminded him of the way Kate spoke. Suddenly he realized how much he had missed her. He finished his sandwich and went to the railroad station and took the first train to Bath. She would be surprised to see him. Pleasantly surprised, he hoped.

When he got to Bath, he gave the address to a taxi driver and sat back and stared curiously at the neat streets and graceful buildings of the town, thinking, This sure has Indianapolis beat.

The taxi stopped in front of a narrow small house, painted white, one of a whole row of similar small houses. He paid the taxi driver and rang the doorbell. A moment later the door opened and a short woman with gray hair, wearing an apron, said, "Good afternoon."

"Good afternoon, ma'am," Wesley said. "Is Kate home?"

"Who are you, please?"

"Wesley Jordache, ma'am."

"Well, Good Lord." The woman smiled widely. She put out her hand and he shook it. It was a callused workingwoman's hand. "I've heard all about you. Come in, come in, boy. I'm Kate's mother."

"How do you do, Mrs. Bailey," Wesley said.

The door opened directly on the small living room. On the floor a baby crawled around in a playpen, cooing to itself. "That's your brother, Wesley," Mrs. Bailey said. "Leastwise, your half brother. Tom's his name."

"I know," Wesley said. He eyed the baby with interest. "He seems like a nice, healthy kid, doesn't he?"

"He's a love," Mrs. Bailey said. "Happy all the day long. Can I fix you a cup of tea?"

"No, thank you. I'd like to see Kate if she's home."

"She's at work," Mrs. Bailey said. "You can find her there. It's the King's Arms Pub. It's just a few blocks away. Lord, she'll be glad to see you. Will you be staying for supper?"

"I'll see how things work out with Kate. Hey, Tommy," he said, going over to the playpen, "how're you doing?"

The baby smiled up at him and made a gurgling sound. Wesley leaned over and put his hand out to the baby, one finger outstretched. The baby sat up, then grabbed the finger and stood up, wobbling, as Wesley gently raised his hand. The baby laughed triumphantly. Wesley was surprised at how strong the little hand felt around his finger. "Tommy," he said, "you've got one powerful grip."

The baby laughed again, then let go and flopped back on his behind. Wesley looked down at him, a peculiar emotion, one he had never felt before, seizing him, tender and at the same time obscurely anxious. The baby was happy now. Maybe he himself had been happy at that age, too. He wondered how long it would last for his brother. With Kate as his mother, maybe forever.

"Now," he said to Mrs. Bailey, "if you'll tell me how to find the pub . . ."

"Left as you go out of the house," Mrs. Bailey said, "for three blocks and you'll see it on the corner." She opened the front door for him. She stood next to him, barely coming up to his shoulder, her face sweet and plain. "I must tell you, Wesley," she said soberly, "the time my daughter was with your father was the loveliest. She'll never forget it. And now would it be too much to ask if I said I'd like one big hug?"

Wesley put his arms around her and hugged her and kissed the top of her head. When she stepped back, he saw her eyes were wet, although she was smiling. "You mustn't be a stranger," she said.

"I'll be back," Wesley said. "Somebody'll have to teach him how to play baseball instead of cricket and it might as well be me."

Mrs. Bailey laughed. "You're a good boy," she said. "You're just as Kate said you were."

She stood at the open door watching him as he turned down the sunny street.

The King's Arms was a small pub, paneled in dark wood, with small casks for sherry and port high up behind the bar. It was almost three o'clock, closing time, and there was only one old man seated at a small round table dozing over a pint of bitter. Kate was rinsing glasses and a man in an apron was putting bottles of beer onto shelves as Wesley came in.

He stood at the bar, not saying anything, waiting for Kate to look up from her work. When she did, she said, "What would you like, sir?"

Wesley grinned at her.

"Wesley!" she cried. "How long have you been standing there?"

"Fifteen minutes," he said. "Dying of thirst."

"Would you really like a beer?"

"No. I just want to look at you."

"I'm a mess," she said.

"No, you're not." She looked very much as he had remembered her, not as brown perhaps, and a little fuller in the face and bosom. "You look beautiful."

She looked at him solemnly. "It's not true," she said, "but it's nice to hear."

The clock over the bar struck three and she called, "Time, gentlemen, please." The old man at the table shook himself awake, drained his glass, stood up and went out.

Kate came out from behind the bar and stopped a few feet from Wesley to examine him. "You've become a man," she said.

"Not exactly," Wesley said.

Then she kissed him and held him for a moment. "I'm so glad to see you again. How did you know where to fine me?"

"I went to your house. Your mother told me."

"Did you see the baby?"

"Yes," he said. "Stupendous."

"He's not stupendous, but he'll do." Wesley could see she was pleased. "Let me throw on a coat and we'll go for a nice long walk and you'll tell me everything that's happened to you."

As they went out the door she called to the man behind the bar, "See you at six, Ally."

The man grunted.

"This is a pretty town," Wesley said, as they strolled in the mild sunshine, her hand lightly on his arm. "It looks like a nice place to live."

"Bath." She shrugged. "It's seen better days. The quality used to come here for the season and take the waters and marry off their daughters and gamble. Now it's mostly tourists. It's a little like living in a museum. I don't know where the quality goes these days. Or if there's any quality left."

"Do you miss the Mediterranean?"

She dropped her hand from his arm and stared reflectively ahead of her as she walked. "Some things about the Med, yes. . . ." she said. "Other things not at all. Let's not talk about it, please. Now, tell me what you've been up to."

By the time he had told her about what he'd been doing in America, they had walked over a good part of the small city. She shook her head sadly when he told her about Indianapolis and became pensive when he told her about the people he had talked to about his father and stared at him with a kind of respectful awe when he described his part in Gretchen's movie.

"An actor," she said. "Who would have ever thought? You going to keep it up?"

"Maybe later on," he said. "I have some things I have to attend to in Europe."

"What parts of Europe?" She stared at him suspiciously. "Cannes, for instance?"

"If you must know," he said, "yes. Cannes."

She nodded. "Bunny was afraid that finally you'd come to that."

"Finally," Wesley said.

"I'd like to take revenge on the whole fucking world," she said. "But I serve drinks in a bar. Revenge has to stop somewhere, Wesley."

"Revenge has to *start* somewhere, too," he said.

"And if you get yourself killed, who'll revenge *you?*" Her voice was bitter and harsh.

"Somebody else will have to figure that out."

"I'm not going to argue with you. You're too much like your father. I never could argue him out of anything. If nothing will stop you, I wish you well. Do it smart, at least. And supposing you do it and suppose you get away with it, which is a lot of supposing, what'll you do then?"

"I've been thinking about that, too," Wesley said. "With the money I get from the inheritance and the money I may be able to make in the movies, in a couple of years I might have enough to buy a boat, something like the *Clothilde,* anyway, and charter. . . ."

Kate shook her head impatiently. "You can be your father's son," she said, "but you can't *be* your father. Lead your own life, Wesley."

"It'll be my own life," he said. "I even thought that with the money you're getting from the estate, maybe you'd like to come in with me as a partner and crew the ship with me. By the time we can buy a ship, the kid, Tommy . . ." He stumbled over the name. "He'd be old enough to be safe on board and . . ."

"Dreams," she said. "Old dreams."

They walked in silence for half a block.

"I have to tell you something, Wesley," she said. "My money's gone. I don't have it anymore."

"Gone?" he said incredulously. "The way you live . . ?"

"I know the way I live," she said bitterly. "I live like a fool. There's a man who says he wants to marry me.

He's in business for himself, he owns a small trucking business in Bath. He said he needed what I had to keep from going into bankruptcy."

"And you gave him the dough?"

She nodded. "I thought I was in love with him. You've got to understand something about me. I'm not a woman that can live without a man. I see him just about every afternoon when the pub closes. I was supposed to go to his place this afternoon and he'll be mortal mad when he comes around this evening and I tell him I spent the afternoon with Tom's son. He won't even *look* at the baby when he comes home to take me out."

"And you want to marry a man like that?"

"He wasn't like that until after he lost the money," she said. "He was plain wonderful until then. With me, the baby, my mother . . ." She sighed. "You're young, you think things are black and white. . . . Well, I've got news for you. For a woman my age, my family, working at lousy jobs all my life, not pretty, nothing is easy." She looked at her watch. "It's nearly five o'clock. I make a point of having at least an hour with Tommy before I have to go back to work."

They walked back to her mother's house in silence. There was a car parked in front of the house, with a man at the wheel. "That's him," Kate said. "Waiting and fuming."

The man got out of the car as Kate and Wesley came up to the house. He was a big, heavy man, red-faced and smelling from drink. "Where the fuck you been?" he said loudly. "I been waiting since three o'clock."

"I took a little walk with this young gentleman," Kate said calmly. "Harry, this is Wesley Jordache, he came to visit me. Harry Dawson."

"Took a little walk, did you?" Dawson ignored the

introduction. He slapped her, hard. It happened so suddenly that Wesley had no time to react.

"I'll teach you to take little walks," Dawson shouted and raised his hand again.

"Wait a minute, pal," Wesley said and grabbed the man's arm and pushed him away from Kate, who was standing, bent over, her two hands up to protect her face.

"Let go of me, you fucking Yank," Dawson said, trying to pull his arm free.

"You've done all the hitting you're going to do today, mister." Wesley pushed Dawson farther back with his shoulder. Dawson wrenched his hand free and punched Wesley high on the forehead. Wesley nearly went down from the force of the blow, then grunted and swung. He hit Dawson square in the mouth and Dawson grappled with him and they both fell, tangled, to the pavement. Wesley took two more punches to the head before he could knee the man in the groin and use his hands on the man's face. Dawson went limp and Wesley stood up, over him. He kicked Dawson viciously in the head, twice.

Kate, who had been standing, bent over, without making a sound as the men fought, now ran at him and put her arms around him, pulling him away from the man on the ground. "That's enough now," she cried. "You don't want to kill him, do you?"

"That's just what I want to do," Wesley said, trembling with rage. But he allowed Kate to lead him away.

"Are you hurt?" she asked, still with her arms around him.

"Nah," he said, although his head felt as though he had been hit with a brick. "Nothing much. You can let go of me now. I won't touch your goddamn friend."

"Wesley," Kate said, speaking swiftly, "You have to

get out of here. Go on right back to London. When he gets up . . ."

"He won't do any more harm," Wesley said. "He learned his lesson."

"He'll come back at you," Kate said. "And not alone. And he'll bring some of the men from his yard with him. And they won't come bare-handed. Go, please, go right now. . . ."

"How about you?"

"Don't worry about me," she said. "I'll be all right. Just go."

"I hate to leave you with that miserable, thieving bastard." He looked down at Dawson, who was beginning to move, although his eyes were still closed.

"He won't come near me again," Kate said. "I'm finished with him."

"You just saying that to get me out of here?" Wesley said.

"I swear it's the truth. If he ever tries to come near me again, I'll have the police on him." She kissed Wesley on the mouth. "Good-bye, Tommy."

"Tommy?" Wesley laughed.

Kate laughed, too, putting her hand to her face distractedly. "Too much has happened today. Take care of yourself, Wesley. I'm so sorry you had to get mixed up in this. Now go."

Wesley looked at Dawson, who was trying to sit up and was fumbling blearily at his bloody lips. Wesley knelt on one knee beside Dawson and grabbed him roughly by his necktie. "Listen, you ape," he said, his face close to Dawson's puffed ear, "if I ever hear you touched her again, I'll be back for you. And what you got today will seem like a picnic compared to what you get. Do you understand?"

Dawson blubbered something unintelligible through his cut lips.

Still holding the man's tie, Wesley slapped his face, the noise sharp and loud. He heard Kate gasp as he stood up.

"End of chapter," Wesley said. He kissed Kate on the cheek, then walked down the street without looking back. His head still hurt, but he strode lightly along, feeling better and better, the memory of the fight making him feel wonderfully at peace with the world. He felt wonderful on the train, too, all the way to London.

———

Billy was playing with Carmen, this time without malice, when a young man in blue jeans, with streaked blond hair, a backpack on his shoulders, appeared at the court, stood watching the game for a while, then took off the backpack and sat down on the grass outside the court to watch in comfort. Travelers with backpacks were not a usual sight at El Faro and Billy found himself glancing over at the young man with curiosity. The expression on the young man's face was grave and interested, although he showed no signs of either approval or disapproval when Carmen or Billy made particularly good shots or committed errors.

Carmen, Billy noticed, seemed equally curious and also kept glancing frequently at the spectator sitting on the grass. "Do you know who that boy is?" she asked, as they were changing courts between games.

"Never saw him before," Billy said, as he used the towel to dry off his forehead.

"He's an improvement on that Hitzman woman," Carmen said. Monika had taken to appearing a little after four o'clock, which was the hour at which they started every day, and watching Carmen and Billy play. "There's something peculiar about that woman, as though she's not interested in the tennis, but somehow in *us*. And not in a nice way."

"I give her a lesson every morning," Billy said, remembering that his father had also said there was something peculiar about Monika when he had seen her in Brussels. "Maybe she's decided to become a student of the game."

They started playing once more and Billy ran out the set, using orthodox, non-eunuch shots.

"Thank you," Carmen said, as she put on a sweater. "That was more like it." She didn't ask him to go up to the hotel with her for a drink and smiled at the young man on the grass as she passed him. He didn't smile back, Billy noticed. Billy didn't have any more lessons that afternoon, so he put on his sweater and started off the court. The young man stood up and said, "Mr. Abbott?"

"Yes." He was surprised that the young man knew his name. He certainly didn't look as though he could afford tennis lessons at El Faro.

"I'm your cousin," the young man said, "Wesley Jordache."

"Well, now," Billy said. "I've heard a lot about you." They shook hands. Billy noted that his cousin's hand was a workingman's hand, hard and powerful.

"I've heard considerable about you, too," Wesley said.

"Anything favorable?"

"Not particularly." Wesley grinned. "You play a pretty hot game of tennis."

"Rosewall isn't worried," Billy said, although he was pleased at the compliment.

"That girl, too," Wesley said. "She really can run, can't she?"

"She's in good shape," Billy said.

"In more ways than one," Wesley said. "She sure is beautiful."

"Skin deep," Billy said. Carmen's treatment of him since their argument about the admiral still rankled.

"Deep enough," Wesley said. "That's not a bad job you have, if all the people you get paid to play with look like that."

"They don't. Where're you staying?"

"Noplace. I'm on the road," Wesley said.

"What brings you here?"

"You," Wesley said soberly.

"Oh."

"I thought it would be a good idea finally to see what the other male half of this generation of Jordaches was like."

"What do you think so far?"

"You've got a good service and you're a demon at the net." They both laughed.

"So far, so good," Billy said. "Listen, I'm dying for a beer. Will you join me?"

"You're my man," Wesley said, shouldering his pack.

As they walked toward the hotel, Billy decided he liked the boy, even though he envied him his size and the obvious strength with which he swung his pack onto his shoulders.

"My—*our* Uncle Rudolph told me you knew my father," Wesley said, as they walked in the direction of the hotel.

"I met him only once," Billy said, "when I was a kid. We slept in the same room for a night in our grandmother's house."

"What did you think of him?" Wesley's tone was carefully noncommittal.

"I liked him. He made everybody else I'd known seem soft. He'd lived the sort of life I thought I would like to have—fighting, going to sea, seeing all kinds of faraway places. Then—" Billy smiled. "He didn't sleep in pajamas. Everybody else I ever knew always slept in pajamas. I suppose that became some crazy kind of symbol for me of a freer way of life."

Wesley laughed. "You must have been a weird kid," he said.

"Not weird enough," Billy said as they went into the bar and ordered two beers.

Carmen was there, sitting with her father at a table. She looked up curiously at them, but made no sign of welcome or recognition.

"The way it turned out," Billy said, as they drank their beers, "I never had a fight, I never wandered around, and I always sleep in pajamas." He shrugged. "One other thing impressed me about your father," he said. "He carried a gun. Boy, oh, boy, I thought when I saw it, there's at least one person in the family who has guts. I don't know what he ever did with it."

"Nothing," Wesley said. "It wasn't within reach when he needed it."

They sat in silence for a moment.

"I'm awfully sorry, Wesley," Billy said gently, "about what happened, I mean."

"Yeah," Wesley said.

"What're your plans?" Billy asked. "I mean from here on in."

"I don't have any real plans just yet," Wesley said. "See what comes up."

Billy had the impression that Wesley knew what he wanted to do, but was evading the question. "My mother," Billy said, "writes she thinks you could have a great future as a movie actor."

"I'm open to offers," Wesley said, "but not just yet. I'll wait and see how the picture turns out."

"My mother writes that it's being considered for the festival in Cannes this year."

"That's news to me," Wesley said. "I'm glad for her sake. She's really something, your mother. If you don't

mind my butting in, I think it's about time you were
nice to her. I know if she was my mother, I'd do everything I could for her. Maybe it would be a good idea, if
they are going to show the picture in Cannes, to visit
her there."

"That's a thought," Billy said reflectively. "Would
you be going?"

"Yes. I have some other business in Cannes, too."

"Maybe we could drive up together," Billy said.
"When is it?"

"In May. Toward the end of the month."

"That'd be about six weeks from now. It's a good
season for traveling."

"Can you get away from here?"

Billy grinned. "You ever hear of tennis elbow?"

"Yes."

"I feel a bad case of tennis elbow coming on. A crip-
pling case, which would take at least two weeks of absolute rest to cure. What'd you be doing until then?"

Wesley shrugged. "Don't know. Hang around here
for a while, if it's all the same to you. Maybe take some
tennis lessons from you. Maybe get a few weeks' work
down at the harbor."

"Do you need dough?"

"I'm not down to the bone yet," Wesley said, "but a
little dough would come in handy."

"The guy who works at the pool here—cleaning it
up, putting out the mats, stuff like that, with a little life-
guarding on the side—quit two days ago. Can you
swim?"

"Well enough."

"Want me to ask if the job's still open?"

"That might be fun," Wesley said.

"I have two beds in my room," Billy said. "You
could camp in with me."

"Don't you have a girl?"

"Not at the moment," Billy said. "And nothing, as far as I can tell, on the horizon."

"I don't want to be a nuisance."

"That's what cousins are for," Billy said. "To be nuisances to each other."

The next day, Wesley started working at the pool. At night, under the lights, Billy began teaching him how to play tennis. Wesley was very fast and a natural athlete, and soon he was hitting the ball harder than anybody on the courts. He played with abandon, his face intent, his eyes narrowed, and slugged the ball as though he was disposing of enemies. Although Billy was proud of Wesley's constant improvement under his tutelage, the sober ferocity with which Wesley played made him uneasy and at times he wanted to say, "Remember, it's only a game." He had the disturbing impression that nothing in his young cousin's life was ever a game.

Billy enjoyed having Wesley around and soon discovered that he was an ideal roommate, keeping everything neat and shipshape, which, after Monika's messy housekeeping, was refreshing. The manager of the hotel was pleased with Wesley's work and congratulated Billy for having found him. After Billy had introduced Wesley to Carmen, her attitude changed, too, and she soon was inviting them both to dinner at one of the small restaurants on the port when her father wasn't with her at the hotel. Wesley's manner with Carmen was grave and courteous, and Billy found that Carmen, who had until then not been addicted to swimming, was spending the best part of the hot mornings at the pool. After Billy had told her that his mother had directed Wesley in a movie, Carmen even began to show a moderate respect for Billy and his opinions, and when a movie that she wanted to see was playing in town took them both with her to see it. She was partial to gory films, with sad endings, and liked to come out of the theater with her cheeks streaked with tears.

Best of all, after the second week of her lessons, Monika told him she was discontinuing her daily hours, as she was leaving the next morning. But, she said coldly, as she gave him a generous tip, she would be coming back, although she didn't tell him when. "We look forward to seeing you again," she said, although she didn't tell him who the "we" were.

"Don't you want to hear what happened on the rue du Gros-Caillou?" Billy asked her, as she gathered up her things.

"I know what happened on the rue du Gros-Caillou," she said. "The wrong man got killed. Among several others."

"I tried to call you," he said.

"You didn't leave a forwarding address," she said. "Don't make that mistake again. Do you intend to be a small-time tennis pro in this miserable country all your life?"

"I don't know what I intend," he said.

"How did you meet that boy at the pool?"

"He just wandered in one day," Billy lied. He had told no one that Wesley was his cousin and he didn't want him to get mixed up with a woman like Monika.

"I don't believe you," Monika said calmly.

"I can't help that."

"He has a good face," Monika said. "Strong and passionate. Someday I must have a long talk with him."

"Keep your hands off him."

"I don't take instructions from you," Monika said. "Remember that."

"I remember a lot of things about you," he said. "Some of them delicious. How is your memory these days?"

"Bad," she said, "very bad. Thank you for being so

patient with me on the tennis court, even though it wasn't much help, was it?"

"No," he said. "You're hopeless."

"I hope you have more success with your other pupils. That blond Spanish bitch, for example. How much does she pay you to be her gigolo? Do you have to have a union card for that profession in Spain?"

"I don't have to listen to crap like that from anybody," he said angrily.

"You may have to get used to it, laddy," she said, "after a few years at the game. *Adiós!* Johnny."

He watched her walk away. His hands were shaking as he pocketed the tip Monika had given him and picked up his racket to start the next lesson. With it all, he couldn't help hoping she would turn around and come back and give him the number of her room and ask him to come up after midnight.

Wesley was writing a letter at the desk in their room as Billy dressed for a party two weeks later. It was to be a flamenco party with a group of gypsies hired for the occasion, and the guests had been asked to dress in Spanish clothes. Billy had bought a frilled shirt and borrowed some tight black pants, a bolero jacket and high-heeled boots from one of the musicians in the band. Wesley had been invited, too, but had said he'd rather write some letters. Besides, he said, he'd feel like a fool in a getup like Billy's.

He had received a letter from Gretchen that morning, in which she had written that *Restoration Comedy* had been chosen for a showing at the Cannes Festival and asking him to come there and take a bow and share in the kudos. Rudolph was coming over with her and David Donnelly. Frances Miller, as the star of the picture, was going to try to come for at least three days. It promised to be an interesting two weeks. She was pleased, Gretchen wrote, that he had finally met Billy and that they liked each other and she wondered if he could influence Billy to come to Cannes, too.

"Billy," Wesley said as Billy was struggling into the musician's boots, "I'm writing to your mother. She would like us both to come to Cannes. What should I tell her?"

"Tell her . . ." Billy hesitated, one boot on, the other still off, "tell her . . . Okay, why not?"

"She'll be pleased," Wesley said.

"What the hell," Billy said, getting into the second boot and standing up, "I suppose once every ten years a man can do something to please his mother. How do I look?"

"Ridiculous," Wesley said.

"That's what I thought," Billy said agreeably. "Well, I'm off to the gypsies, tra-la, tra-la." He did a little stamping step and they both laughed.

"Have a good time," Wesley said.

"If I'm not back by morning, you'll know I've been kidnapped. You know how those gypsies are. Don't pay more than thirteen dollars and fifty cents in ransom."

He went out, whistling the toreador song from Carmen.

The gypsies were fine, the guitar and castanets blood-tingling, the music and singing sorrowful, full of wailing passion, the dancing proud and fierce, the wine plentiful. Again, as he had felt when he first crossed the border into Spain, Billy had the feeling he had come to the right country for him.

Why deny it, he thought, as the music boomed around him and the girls with roses in their hair flounced their skirts and advanced erotically toward their partners only to repel them, with a clatter of thick heels, at the last moment, why deny it, the pleasures of

the rich are real pleasures. Carmen sat next to him most
of the evening, resplendent in a dark dress that showed
off her lovely shoulders and full bosom and he could
see her eyes gleaming with excitement. It was a long
way from the proms at the college in Whitby and Billy
was happy that he had put all that distance behind him.

One of the male dancers came over to Carmen and
pulled her up from where she was sitting to join him.
She danced joyously and very well; as well, Billy
thought, as any of the professional dancers, her long
bright hair flying, her face set in traditional proud disdain. Whatever else she felt about Spain, Billy saw, its
music struck some deep, responsive, racial core in her.
The dance finished and the guests applauded loudly,
Billy among them. Instead of sitting down again, Carmen came over to him and pulled him up. To general
laughter and handclapping, Billy began to dance with
her, mimicking the movements of the male dancers. He
was a good dancer and he managed to move almost like
the gypsies, while at the same moment slyly making
fun of his own performance. Carmen caught on to what
he was doing and laughed in the middle of one of her
wildest passages. When the dance was over she kissed
him, although the sweat was streaming down his face.

"I need some air," he said. "Let's go outside for a
minute."

Unobtrusively, they left the room and went out onto
the terrace. The sky was turbulent and dark, with black,
scattered clouds moving across the face of the moon.

"You were wonderful," Carmen said.

He took her in his arms and kissed her. "Later," he
whispered, "I want to come to your room."

She stood still in his arms for a moment, then pushed
him away from her. "I will dance with you," she said
coldly, "and play tennis with you and argue with you.

But I wouldn't dream of making love to you in a thousand years."

"But the way you looked at me . . ."

"That was part of the fun," she said, wiping her mouth contemptuously. "*All* of the fun. No more. If I were going to make love to anyone in this corrupt place it would be with the young man at the pool."

"I see." His voice was hoarse with anger and disappointment. "Do you want me to tell him that?"

"Yes," she said. As baldly as that.

"I'll do just that," he said. "As always, at your service, ma'am."

"My room number is 301. Can you remember that?"

"Till my dying day."

She laughed. The laugh was not pleasant. "I must go back," she said. "People noticed we left together. This is a backward country, as you know, and we put great store on appearances. Are you coming in with me?"

"No," he said. "I have a message to deliver. And then I'm going to sleep."

"Pleasant dreams," she said and turned and went back toward the music.

He walked slowly toward his room, the sweat getting suddenly cold on his body in the night wind and making him shiver. Beware the *señoritas,* his father had written. Good old Dad knew what he was talking about.

Wesley was asleep when he got to the room. He slept restlessly, moving around in sudden jerks, making a tangle of the covers and moaning from time to time, as though at night some ineradicable anguish that he avoided or disguised during the day took hold of him. Billy stood next to the bed, looking down at his new cousin, not knowing whether he pitied him or loved him or hated him.

He nearly started to undress and get into the other bed, leaving Wesley to his sorrowful dreams, but finally he thought, What the hell, it's all in the family, and shook the boy awake.

Wesley sat up with a start. "What is it?" he asked.

"I just came from the party," Billy said, "and I have some news for you. If you go to room 301 you will find a lady waiting for you. Her name is Carmen. She asked me to tell you personally."

Wesley was completely awake now. "You're kidding," he said.

"I was never more serious in my life."

"What in blazes made her say something like that?"

"In your place, I wouldn't ask any questions," Billy said. "You've told me how beautiful she is. If it were me, I'd grab while the grabbing is good."

"I don't love her," Wesley said. He sounded petulant and unhappy, like a small boy being asked to perform a distasteful chore for the first time, making Billy conscious of the seven-year difference in their ages.

"You're playing with the grown-ups now," Billy said. "Love is not always a prime consideration in matters like this. Are you going?"

Wesley swung out of bed and sat on the edge, hunched over. He slept only in pajama bottoms, and the muscles of his torso gleamed in the light of the lamp Billy had turned on when he came into the room. He looks like a beaten fighter, Billy thought, who knows he's going to be knocked out in the next round.

"I don't want to sound like a fool," Wesley said, "but I can't do it. I'm in love with someone else. A great girl. Back in New York. She's going to try to come over to Europe to see me in a few weeks. I don't care what that lady will think of me," he said defiantly, "I'm waiting for my girl."

"You may regret this later," Billy warned him.

"Never. You think she's beautiful, too, you know her a lot better than I do—why don't *you* go?"

"The lady has made it clear," Billy said, "that she would not be pleased to see me in room 301."

"Christ," Wesley said, "who would have thought a lady like that would pick on me?"

"Maybe she likes movie stars."

"This is nothing to joke about," Wesley said severely. "I'm no movie star and she knows it."

"I was just being shitty," Billy said. "Well, I've done my duty. Now I'm going to bed."

"So am I." Wesley looked down at the tangled bedclothes. "What a mess," he said. "Every time I wake up in the morning the bed looks as though I've gone twenty rounds during the night." He straightened the covers a little and lay down under them, his arms raised and his hands under his head. "Someday," he said, as Billy undressed, "maybe I'll figure out just what to do about sex and love and other little things like that."

"Don't count on it," Billy said as he put on his pajamas and got into his bed. "Sleep well, Wesley. You've had a big night and you need your rest."

"Yeah," Wesley said sourly. "Turn off the goddamn light."

Billy reached over and put out the light. He didn't try to close his eyes for a long time, but kept staring up at the dark ceiling. After five minutes he heard Wesley's steady breathing as he slept and an occasional low moan, as his dreams took over once more. Billy lay awake till the light of the dawn filtered into the room. In the distance the throb of the music could still be heard. Spanish hours, he thought, Spanish fucking hours.

———

The next day, promptly at four, Carmen appeared at the court looking rested and serene. They were playing doubles that afternoon and the other players were already there and Carmen greeted them and Billy with the same radiant smile. Although the others were men, they were weaker players than Carmen, so she and Billy were on opposing teams. She played better than Billy had ever seen her play before, agile and accurate, poaching at the net and making Billy and his partner work hard for every point. The score was four all when, after a long rally, she lobbed over Billy's head. He got a glimpse of her ironic smile as he backpedaled at full speed and by leaping into the air, just managed to reach the ball. He hit the overhead viciously, trying to put it at Carmen's feet, but she had charged the net and the ball whistled toward her head. She stumbled a little, and the smash hit her in the eye and bounced crazily off the court as she dropped her racket and bent over with a cry and put her hands to the eye.

Oh, God, Billy thought, as he jumped over the net to her side, that's all I needed.

The doctor was grave. The eye was in danger, he said. Carmen had to go to Barcelona immediately to see a specialist. An operation might be necessary.

"I'm terribly sorry," Billy said as he drove her back from the doctor's office to the hotel.

"Nothing to be sorry about," Carmen said crisply, although he could see she was in great pain. "It wasn't your fault. I had no business being at the net. I was trying to psych you into missing the shot. Don't let anybody make you believe it was your fault."

He leaned over and kissed her cheek. This time she didn't push him away.

But no matter what she or anybody would say, he knew that it was his fault, that if the night before hadn't happened, he would never have hit the ball at her so hard and at such a short distance.

The next afternoon, the manager of the hotel called him into his office. "Young man," he said, "I'm afraid you're in very deep. The father has just called me. The eye will probably be all right, he said; the specialist doesn't think he will have to operate, but the father is furious. As for me, I did not pay you to brutalize the guests. The father insists that I dismiss you, and although the daughter called me, too, and said she would never forgive me if I did, I'm afraid I have to bow to the father's wishes. You'd better pack your bags and leave. The sooner the better for you." The manager took an envelope out of the drawer of his desk and handed it to Billy. "Here's your month's pay. I have deducted nothing."

"Thank you," Billy said numbly.

The manager shook his hand. "I'm sorry to see you go. You were well liked here."

As Billy walked toward the pool to tell Wesley what had happened, he remembered what his father had said about the luck of the Jordaches. It made no difference that his name wasn't Jordache, but Abbott.

———

That same afternoon they were on the road for France, driving in the sunshine in the open Peugeot. Billy had tried to persuade Wesley that it was foolish for him to leave his job, but Wesley had insisted and Billy hadn't pressed too hard. He had grown fond of the boy and the prospect of driving through the springtime countryside of Spain and France with him was a tempting one. They went at a leisurely pace, sight-seeing and having picnic lunches of sausage and rough bread with a bottle of wine on the side of the road, shaded by olive trees or on the edge of vineyards. They had their tennis gear with them and usually were able to find a court in the towns through which they passed and play a few sets almost every day. "If you keep at it," Billy said, "you'll be able to beat me in two years."

As they traveled north Billy realized that he was glad they had quit El Faro, although he would always feel guilty for the way it had come about. He regretted leaving Spain but he didn't regret having to wonder every day if Monika would arrive to chill him with her hopeless tennis and oblique threatening hints of future complications.

Wesley spoke more openly about what he had been doing than he had at El Faro and told him of the people in his father's life he had searched out. He told Billy a little about his visit to Bath, just mentioning Kate and not saying anything about Dawson and the fight, but describing his half-brother lovingly. "Pretty little kid," he said. "Strong as a young bull. I think he's going to turn out like his father—our father. He's a real happy little boy."

"*You* don't seem happy," Billy said. "You're young and strong and good-looking and from what my mother writes with a big career ahead of you if you want it, but you don't act like a happy boy."

"I'm happy enough," Wesley said evasively.

"Not when you sleep you aren't. Do you know that you moan practically all night?"

"Dreams. They don't mean anything."

"That isn't what the psychiatrists say."

"What do *you* say?" Wesley's voice was suddenly harsh.

"I'd say that something is bugging you. Something bad. If you want to talk about it, maybe it would help."

"Maybe I will," said Wesley. "Some other time. Now let's drop the subject."

When they crossed into France, they spent the first night in a small hotel overlooking the sea just across the

border in Port Vendres. "I have a great idea," Billy
said. "We're not due in Cannes for another two
weeks—why don't we tool up to Paris and give ourselves a holiday there?"

Wesley shook his head. "No," he said, "I've got to
get to Cannes. I've been avoiding it and now it's time to
go."

"Why?"

Wesley looked at Billy strangely. "I've got to see
Bunny, he was on the *Clothilde* with me. Actually he's
in Saint-Tropez. He may have some information for me.
Important information. You drive up to Paris. I'll hitchhike east."

"What sort of information?" Billy asked.

Again Wesley looked at him strangely. "I'm looking
for someone and Bunny may know where I can find
him. That's all."

"Can't whoever it is wait a couple of weeks?"

"He's waited too long."

"Who is it?"

"It's the man who's responsible for the way I sleep. I
dream about him every night. I dream that I keep stab-
bing him with a knife, over and over again, and that he
doesn't fall, he just stands there laughing at me. . . .
When I wake up I can still hear him laughing."

"Do you recognize him?" Billy asked. "I mean in the
dream?"

Wesley nodded slowly. "He's the man who had my
father killed."

Billy felt a cold tingle at the base of his neck at the
tone of Wesley's voice. "What are you going to do when
you find him?"

Wesley took a deep breath. "I finally have to tell
someone," he said, "and it might as well be you. I'm
going to kill him."

"Oh, Christ," Billy said.

They sat in silence, looking out at the sea.

"How do you plan to do it?" Billy said finally.

"I don't know," Wesley shrugged. "I'll figure it out when the time comes. A knife, maybe."

"Have you got a gun?"

"No."

"Is *he* likely to have one?"

"Probably."

"You'll get yourself killed."

"I'll try to avoid that," Wesley said grimly.

"And if you do manage to knock him off," Billy said, "you'll be the first one the cops would come looking for, don't you know that?"

"I suppose I do," Wesley admitted.

"You'd be lucky to get off with twenty years in jail. Do you want that?"

"No."

"And still you want to go to Cannes and do it?"

"Yes."

"Listen, Wesley," Billy said, "I can't let you go charging ahead to your doom. You've got to let me help you."

"How?"

"I have a gun with a silencer stashed away in Paris, for openers."

Wesley nodded gravely. "That would be useful."

"I could help you plan it. The . . . the murder." Billy stumbled over the word. "After all, I was trained as a soldier. I speak French a lot better than you do. I know how to handle guns. I'm going to tell you something that you've got to keep absolutely to yourself— while I was in the army I joined a cell of terrorists in Brussels. . . ."

"You?" Wesley said incredulously.

"Yes, me. I was in on a job in Amsterdam on the Spanish tourist office. I know how to put together a bomb. Sonny, you couldn't have found a better partner for the job. I'll tell you what I'll do," he went on. "While you head for Saint-Tropez, I'll go up to Paris and get the gun and I'll meet you in either Saint-Tropez or Cannes, whichever you say. Fair enough?"

Wesley looked at Billy consideringly. "Are you hustling me?"

"Oh, come on now, Wesley," Billy said, sounding aggrieved. "I wouldn't do anything like that. What have you got to lose? I'll be back down south in a few days. With the gun. And enough ammunition so that you can practice using it. Does that sound like a hustle?"

"I guess not," Wesley said, but he sounded reluctant to say it. "Okay. You let me know where you're staying in Paris and I'll call you and tell you where you can find me."

"I think we can use a drink," Billy said.

"I think so, too," said Wesley.

The next day they drove together to Nîmes, where Billy would turn north toward Paris. Billy sat at the wheel in silence under the shade of a poplar while Wesley got his backpack out of the car and slung it over his shoulder. They had agreed that Billy would send him a telegram at Poste Restante in Saint-Tropez to let Wesley know in what hotel he was staying in Paris.

"Well," Wesley said, "take care of yourself."

"You, too," Billy said. "You're not going to do anything foolish while I'm gone, are you?"

"No. I promise." They shook hands. "I'm going to miss the tennis." Billy grinned.

"You'll remember," Billy said, "that they play very little tennis in French jails."

"I'll remember," Wesley said and stepped back.

Billy started the motor and waved as the car, built for holidays and sunshine, spurted onto the road from beneath the shadow of the poplar tree. In the rearview mirror he saw the tall, lean figure start trudging in the direction of Cannes.

———————

When he got to Paris, the first thing Billy did after checking into a hotel on the Left Bank was put in a call to America. When Rudolph came to the phone, Billy said, "Uncle Rudolph, this is Billy Abbott. I'm in Paris at the Hôtel Alembert. I need help. Bad. Something awful is going to happen to Wesley—and maybe to me, too, unless . . ." He stopped.

"Unless what, Billy?" Rudolph said.

"Unless we can stop certain things from happening," Billy said. "I can't tell you over the phone."

"I'll be in Paris tomorrow," Rudolph said.

"God," Billy said, "those're sweet words."

He lay back on the bed wearily and a minute later he was asleep.

# CHAPTER 9

"Now," Rudolph said to Billy as they turned onto the auto route that led from the airport toward Paris, "explain."

"It's Wesley," Billy said, driving carefully. It was raining and the headlights of the late evening traffic glared off the wet surface of the road. "He's down in the south of France now looking for the man he says was behind the murder." He pulled at the wheel to swerve into the right lane because the driver of the car behind him was blinking his lights impatiently at him. The car passed in a whoosh, throwing up a curtain of rain that made the windshield opaque for several seconds. "Bastard," Billy said, grateful to have something else to worry about, even for a moment.

Rudolph pushed his hat back on his head and ran his hand across his forehead, as though relieving pain there. "How do you know all this?" he asked, his voice dull.

"He told me," Billy said. "We became very close in Spain. I was glad we could become such good friends. He shared my room with me. He slept as though he were in a foxhole, with the artillery hitting nearer to him all the time. I could see something was psyching him out and it worried me and I finally asked him and he told me."

"Do you think he's serious?" Rudolph asked.

"Absolutely," Billy said. "There're no jokes in that kid's repertoire. There's even something scary about the way he plays tennis. He's not like any other boy I've every known. Or man, for that matter."

"Is he sane?"

"Except for this," Billy said.

"Do you think a psychiatrist would help?"

Billy thought for a moment. "It wouldn't do any harm," he said. "If you could get him to sit still for it for maybe a year or so. Only you couldn't get him to do it."

Rudolph grunted. "Why didn't you stay with him?" He sounded accusing.

"Well . . ." Billy said uncomfortably. "That's another part of the story. I said I'd help him."

"How?"

Billy shifted uneasily in the bucket seat and changed his grip on the wheel. "I said I'd try to figure some way of our doing the job together," he said, "some way of getting away with it without being caught. What with my training as a soldier and all."

"Are *you* sane?" Rudolph's voice was sharp.

"I've always thought so."

"Did you *mean* what you said?"

"I don't know what I meant, really," Billy said flatly. "If it comes to the sticking point, I guess I mean it now. You don't have to sound like a cop interrogating a prisoner, Rudolph."

Rudolph made an exasperated noise. "Two nuts," he said, "two young nuts off the same tree."

"All in the family," Billy said, offended by Rudolph's

estimate of him. "Welcome to nutsville, European division, Uncle."

"Why're you in Paris while he's down there getting into God knows what kind of idiotic trouble?" Rudolph's voice rose in anger as he spoke.

"I told him I had a gun in Paris with a silencer and that I would bring it to him," Billy said.

"*Do* you have a gun with a silencer?"

"Yes."

"God damn it, Billy," Rudolph said, "what the hell have you been messed up with these last few years?"

Again Billy shifted uneasily in the bucket seat. "I'd rather not say. And it's better for you—and for me—if you don't know."

Rudolph took a deep breath and then sighed. "Are the police after you?"

"No. At least not that I know of." Billy said, glad that he had to keep his eyes on the road so that he couldn't see the expression on his uncle's face.

Rudolph rubbed his face wearily, the gesture making a rasping sound on his unshaven cheek. "You'd better give me that gun," he said.

"I told Wesley I'd bring it down to him in a day or so," Billy said.

"Listen, Billy," Rudolph said, trying to keep his voice even, "you asked me to come over here to help. I took the next plane. Either you're going to do what I say or . . ." He stopped.

"Or what?" Billy asked.

"I don't know. Yet. Something. Just exactly where is Wesley now? Today? This minute?"

"Saint-Tropez. We agreed I'd send him a wire telling him where he could call me in Paris and arrange for where and when we'd meet down south."

"*Did* you send the wire?"

"This morning."

"What was your rush? Why didn't you wait until I got here? Maybe it would be better if he didn't know where to find you."

"He's suspicious enough of me as it is," Billy said, defending himself. "If I don't come through with my half of the bargain, he'll just go off on his own and that will be the end of Wesley Jordache."

"Ah, maybe you're right," Rudolph said. "Maybe. Has he called you yet?"

"No."

"All right," Rudolph said. "When he does call don't tell him I'm in Europe. And tell him it's taking more time than you thought to lay your hands on that goddamn gun."

"What good will that do?"

"It'll give me some extra time to come up with something, that's what it will do," Rudolph said angrily. "And you could use some time to do a little thinking, too. Now don't talk for a while. I'm bushed from the trip and I want to close my eyes for a few minutes and hope that either you or I will be struck by lightning or at least one single useful thought before we get to the hotel."

Just before they said good night Rudolph said, "Remember, I want that gun tomorrow. And one thing is sure—Wesley's never even going to *see* it."

"Then he'll use a knife or a club or maybe his bare hands," Billy said. "You don't know what he's like."

"That's true," said Rudolph. "And I'm sorry I'm finding out now."

"Listen," Billy said, "if you don't really want to get mixed up in this, I'll try to handle it myself. You can always forget what I've told you, you know."

Rudolph looked thoughtfully at Billy, as though he was considering the disadvantages of not forgetting, then shook his head. "Maybe," he said, "I should have been the one to go looking for Mr. Danovic. Long ago. Only it never occurred to me until tonight. No, I don't think forgetting is the answer. Good night, Billy. If you have any good ideas during the night, call me. I don't think I'll be sleeping all that well, anyway."

He wiped his face with his hands again and walked slowly and heavily toward the elevator.

I never thought about how old he is before this, Billy thought, as the elevator door opened and then shut behind his uncle.

---

The next morning they had breakfast together in the hotel dining room. Rudolph looked haggard, with puffs under his eyes, and he ate without speaking, drinking one cup of coffee after another.

"You go get the—the object—this afternoon," he said finally, "and hand it over to me."

"Are you sure you want to . . ." Billy began.

"One thing I'm sure of," Rudolph snapped, "is that I don't want any more arguments from you."

"Okay," Billy said, "you're the boss." He felt relieved to be able to say it, the responsibility for decision no longer only in his hands.

The concierge came into the dining room and approached Billy. "There's a telephone call for you, Mr. Abbott," he said in French. "In the hall booth."

"Thank you." Billy stood up. "It must be him," he said to Rudolph. "Nobody else knows I'm here."

"Be smart about how you talk to him," Rudolph said. "Make everything sound plausible."

"I'll do my best. I'm not guaranteeing anything when it comes to that boy," Billy said and started out of the dining room. The coffee he had drunk suddenly tasted sour in his mouth as he went into the hall and entered the booth and picked up the phone.

"Billy," Wesley said, his voice thin over the wire, "can you talk?"

"Not really."

"I'm at Les Pinèdes in Saint-Tropez. When will you get here?"

"Not for a few days, I'm afraid, Wesley. There've been some complications about getting the stuff." His own voice sounded fake to him as he spoke.

"What sort of complications?" Wesley said harshly.

"I'll tell you when I see you."

"Are you going to get it or aren't you going to get it?"

"I'm going to get it all right. It's just going to take a little time."

"What's a little time?"

"Four, five days."

"If I don't see you in the next five days, I'm going on to Cannes," Wesley said. "Alone. Do you understand what I'm saying?"

"Keep your cool, Wesley. I'm doing the best I can."

"I think you're stalling, Billy."

"I'm not stalling," Billy said. "It's just that certain things have come up."

"I bet," Wesley said and hung up.

Billy walked slowly back into the dining room. "He's at Les Pinèdes in Saint-Tropez," he said as he sat down. "And he's not happy. He gave me five days."

Rudolph nodded. "You didn't tell him I was here, did you?

"No."

"I'll take the train down to Antibes tonight," Rudolph said. "I don't want to go through the check at the airport. I'll be at the Colombe d'Or at Saint-Paul-de-Vence if you want to reach me."

"Did you come up with any ideas during the night?" Billy asked.

"Maybe." Rudolph smiled grimly.

"Do you want to tell me what they are?"

"No. As you said last night, I'd rather not say. And it's better for you and for me if you don't know."

"We're a great family at keeping secrets from one another, aren't we?"

"Up to a certain point." Rudolph stood up. "I'm going to enjoy the city of Paris today. I may even go to the Louvre. I'll meet you back here at five o'clock. Don't do anything foolish until then."

"I'll try not to," Billy said. "Until five o'clock."

After his uncle had gone, Billy took a taxi to the bank on the corner of the rue St. Dominique. He didn't want anyone noticing the convertible Peugeot and perhaps taking down the number on the license plate. He took his tennis bag along with him, and when the attendant in the vault had turned the two keys and had gone back to his desk, Billy slipped the automatic and the extra clips into the bag and what remained of the ten thousand francs and went upstairs and told the clerk he was giving up the *coffre-fort* and handed over his key.

Then, carrying the bag, he took a taxi back to the hotel and put the bag on the bed. He sat there looking at it until five o'clock.

———

Rudolph got off the train into the southern morning sunlight at Antibes. The car he had ordered from Hertz was waiting for him at the station. As he signed for it he kept one leg pressed against his locked bag.

When he drove up to the Colombe d'Or he carried the bag with him to the hotel and after checking in followed the porter who carried the bag.

After the porter had left he telephoned the old lawyer in Antibes and made a date for eleven o'clock in his office. Rudolph shaved and had a bath, in which he drowsed for a long time. It was two o'clock in the morning in New York and his body knew it. He moved lethargically as he put on fresh clothes and ordered a big cup of coffee to be sent to his room. It was the same room he had had before. Jeanne had visited him there and the memory of the times with her stirred old desires. He took out a sheet of paper and wrote, "Dear Jeanne, I'm back at our hotel and wonder if you're free—" He stopped writing and crumpled the sheet of paper. It had been too long ago. Over.

At ten-thirty he locked his bag and went down to the rented car and drove carefully to Antibes.

The old man was waiting for him at the large polished table with the sunny blue sea framed in the big window behind him.

"It's safe to talk in here, isn't it?" Rudolph asked as he sat down.

"Completely," the lawyer said.

"I mean, there are no tape recorders in the desk or anything like that?"

"There is one," the lawyer admitted, "but it is not turned on. I only use it when the client demands it."

"I hope this doesn't offend you, sir," Rudolph said, "but I would like you to put it on the desk so that we both can be sure it is not recording."

The old man wrinkled his face into a frown. "If you wish, sir," he said coldly. He pulled open a drawer and put the little machine on the desk, to one side.

Rudolph stood up to look at it. It was not turned on. "Thank you, sir," he said and sat down again. "I would also appreciate it," he said, "if you didn't take any notes either now or after I've left."

The old man nodded. "No notes," he said.

"The matter I'm here for is a very delicate one," Rudolph said. "It concerns the safety of my nephew, the son of my brother who was killed."

The old man nodded again. "A sad affair," he said. "I trust the wounds have healed somewhat."

"Somewhat," Rudolph said.

"And," the lawyer said, "that the estate was divided with a minimum of—ah—acrimony."

"Maximum," Rudolph said grimly.

"Alas," the old man said. "These family matters."

"My nephew is in the south of France," Rudolph said. "He doesn't know that I'm in the country and I would prefer it if he didn't learn about my presence for the time being."

"Very well."

"He is here to find out where he can reach Mr. Danovic."

"Ah," the old man said gravely.

"He intends to kill the man when he finds him."

The old man coughed, as though something were stuck in his throat. He took out a large white handkerchief and wiped his lips. "Forgive me," he said. "I see what you mean when you say it is a delicate matter."

"I don't want him ever to find Danovic."

"I understand your position," the lawyer said. "What I don't understand is how I can be of any help."

Rudolph took a deep breath. "If Danovic is killed—by other means, let us say—before my nephew learns of his whereabouts, the problem would be solved."

"I see," the old man said thoughtfully. He coughed again and once more produced the handkerchief. "And just how do you believe I can help achieve this desirable result?"

"In your time, sir," said Rudolph, "you must have handled cases that involved members of the *milieu* along this coast. . . ."

The lawyer nodded. "In my time," he said softly, "yes."

"If you would introduce me to a man who knew where Danovic could be found," Rudolph said, "and who could be persuaded to undertake the job, I'd be prepared to pay very well for his—his services."

"I see," the lawyer said.

"Naturally," Rudolph said, "I'd be prepared to deposit a considerable sum in your Swiss account for *your* services."

"Naturally," the lawyer agreed. He sighed. Rudolph could not tell whether it was because of the risks that might have to be run or at the thought of the considerable sum in the Swiss account.

"It would have to be done very soon," Rudolph said. "The boy is impatient and foolish."

The lawyer nodded. "I sympathize with your position, *Monsieur* Jordache," he said, "but as you can imagine, it is not something that can be arranged overnight, if at all. . . ."

"I'm prepared to go as high as twenty thousand dollars," Rudolph said steadily.

Again the lawyer coughed. Again he wiped his mouth with the handkerchief. "I have never smoked in my life," he said, almost petulantly, "and yet this cough pursues me." He swung around in his chair and looked out at the calm sea, as though some fruitful answer could be found there for the questions that were troubling him.

There was silence in the room for a long moment. In the silence Rudolph reflected painfully on what he was doing. He was committing an evil act. All his life he had believed in goodness and morality and he was now committing an evil act. But what was he doing it for? To prevent an even more evil act. Morality can be a trap, he thought, just like a lot of other noble words. The

question is—what comes first, your principles or your
own flesh and blood? Well, he had answered the question, at least for himself. He would suffer for this later,
if he had to.

The silence in the room was broken when, without
turning to face Rudolph, the lawyer said, "I will see
what I can do. At the very best, I can only hope to
communicate with a gentleman who might just possibly
be interested and have him get in touch with you. I
hope you understand that would have to be the beginning and the end of the matter for me."

"I understand," Rudolph said. He stood up. "I am
staying at the Colombe d'Or in Saint-Paul-de-Vence. I
will be waiting for a telephone call."

"I promise nothing, dear *monsieur*," said the lawyer.
He turned around, and with his back to the sea, smiled
wanly at Rudolph. "To be perfectly honest with you, I
would prefer it if you could persuade your nephew to
abandon his rash scheme."

"So would I," Rudolph said. "But I doubt that I
could do so."

The lawyer nodded somberly. "Young men," he said.
"Ah, well, I shall do what I can do."

"Thank you." Rudolph stood up. As he went out of
the room the lawyer was looking out at the sea again.
They had not shaken hands as they said good-bye.

The power of money, Rudolph thought, as he drove
along the port. Would Hamlet have paid Rosencrantz
and Guildenstern to do the job on his uncle, the king, if
he had had the florins?

When he got to the Colombe d'Or, he called the
Hôtel Alembert, in Paris. Luckily, Billy was in. What
Rudolph didn't know was that Billy hadn't left the ho-
tel, except for the one trip to the bank the day before.

"Billy," Rudolph said, "there's a ray of hope. I can't
tell you about it, and don't ask what it is—now—or

ever. But it's there. What we have to do is buy time. What you have to do is keep Wesley pacified. Can you hear me clearly?"

"Too clearly," Billy said. "What am I supposed to do to keep him pacified?"

"Get to Saint-Tropez on the fifth day. Make up some story—any story—you're a clever fellow. . . ."

"That's what they tell me," Billy said bleakly.

"Just hang in there with him," Rudolph said. "I don't want him disappearing into the blue. We've got to know where he is at all times. Got it?"

"Got it," Billy said, without enthusiasm.

"If necessary," Rudolph said, "you can tell him where I am. I'd rather he didn't know, but if that's the only way we can put him off, I'll chip in on the holding process. And keep me posted."

"How long do I have to keep him pacified?" Billy asked.

"As long as it takes."

"That's a nice round figure," Billy said.

"No witticisms, please," Rudolph said severely. "I'm doing my share, you do yours."

"Yes, sir," Billy said. "I'll spend the next couple of days making up a story."

"That's a good boy."

"Making that crazy man believe it is another story," Billy said.

"Get lucky," Rudolph said and hung up.

---

The *Clothilde* was moored not far from the Christ-Craft that Bunny was crewing in the port of Saint-Tropez, and Wesley and Bunny went over to take a look at it. Bunny hadn't wanted him to go. "You've seen enough of that boat," he said.

"Don't worry, Bunny," Wesley said. "I won't break into tears or hit anybody. It was the only home I ever had that I felt good in. I'll just look at it and remember that, how it was when my old man was on it. I've been looking at a lot more depressing things since then. . . ." He had spent the days and nights of waiting for Billy prowling around the ports of Saint-Tropez and Cannes and going in and out of the nightclubs in both places. He couldn't ask Bunny if Danovic was around, because Bunny would start arguing with him. He couldn't ask anyone else, either, about Danovic because he couldn't let Danovic, or eventually the police, know that he was after him, but he could look. He had looked and hadn't found the man, but he was certain that, given enough time, Danovic would surface. Well, he had plenty of time. Surprisingly, being around the ports in the quiet month or so before the season began had calmed him. He even slept more quietly and the violent dreams that had plagued him for so long did not recur.

When they reached the place where the *Clothilde* was tied up, they stood looking at it, without talking. The ship looked old-fashioned and comfortable and Wesley was pleased that it was clean and well-kept. It would have hurt him if the ship was messy or looked neglected.

"They keep it up nice, don't they?" he said to Bunny.

"They're Germans," Bunny said; "you could eat off the deck. You want to go on and take a look around? They put in an automatic pilot."

Wesley shook his head. "No. This is enough. I'm glad I saw it, but it's enough."

They went back to the Chris-Craft, where Wesley had a fish stew going on the range for lunch. There would be three for lunch, because Bunny had taken up with a girl who worked in one of the boutiques on the port and she lunched with him every day. She was a pretty, small, dark-haired girl who spoke fairly good English and Bunny was crazy about her and as far as Wesley could tell, she was crazy about him. She came over to the Chris-Craft after work, too, and sometimes spent the night with Bunny. Bit by bit, Bunny was losing some of his womanish gestures, Wesley noticed. Bunny and she were talking about getting married and signing on as a couple in a bigger ship. Bunny, Wesley noticed, was not only taking on some of the mannerisms of Tom, he was moving consciously or unconsciously toward the sort of life his father and Kate had had together.

Wesley was pleased by that, too—it was a tribute, he recognized, to the value of his father, a tribute from the man who had known him better than anyone else alive. It made up for a lot of the things Wesley had heard about his father from Teddy Boylan and from Schultzy, in the Hebrew Home for the Aged in the Bronx.

The lunch was a good one, with a bottle of cold wine. Wesley had asked Bunny not to tell anybody that he was acting in a picture that was going to be shown in Cannes, but when the girl, whose name was Nadine, asked Wesley what his profession was, Bunny blurted out, "He's a goddamn movie actor. How do you like that—my old shipmate?"

Well, Wesley thought, if it gives Bunny points with his girl, what harm can it do?

"Is that true?" Nadine looked at him incredulously.

"I'm afraid so," Wesley said. "After the picture comes out I may be an ex-movie actor."

"Are you two fellows pulling my leg?" Nadine asked.

"You can see for yourself," Bunny said. "He's the star of a movie they're going to show at the festival."

"Not the star," Wesley protested. "It's just a bit part."

Nadine looked at him closely. "I thought you were too good looking just to be *nobody*."

"A dime a dozen," Wesley said. "I'm really just a seaman at heart."

"There's a girl who works with me," Nadine said, "actually my best friend, she's crazy about the movies, she's awfully cute, why don't I bring her to dinner tonight?"

"I'm just staying in Saint-Tropez a little while," Wesley said uneasily. Remembering Alice's promise to try to come over to Europe for at least two weeks, he didn't want to be tempted by an awfully cute French girl.

"She speaks good English," Nadine said.

"Actually," Wesley said, "I have a date for tonight." It was the fifth day and he wanted to be at the hotel if and when Billy showed up.

"How about tomorrow night?" Nadine persisted.

"I'll probably be in Cannes tomorrow night," Wesley said. "Maybe some other time."

"Are you coming back from Cannes after the festival?" Nadine asked.

"That depends," Wesley said.

"She just broke up with her boyfriend," said Nadine. "You'd be just the thing to cheer her up."

"I'm not much good at cheering people up," Wesley said. "Ask Bunny."

"He's a serious boy," Bunny said. "He can stand some cheering up himself."

"If we come to Cannes," Nadine said, "can you get us tickets to see your film?"

"I guess so. I'll let Bunny know where I'm staying." Christ, Wesley thought, that's all I need, two French girls hanging around my neck just as I bump into that sonofabitch Danovic.

"You won't forget now?" Nadine said, as she prepared to go back to her boutique.

"I won't forget," Wesley lied.

Nadine kissed Bunny, and they both watched her walk swiftly down the quay, a curvy small girl with a swinging walk.

"What do you think of her?" Bunny asked. He had not asked before.

"She's pretty as can be," Wesley said.

"Do you think she's too flighty to make a good wife?" Bunny asked anxiously.

"I think she's fine, Bunny," Wesley said. He didn't want to be responsible in any way for a decision as grave as marriage for Bunny. "I hardly know her."

"I tell you something," Bunny said, "with your looks and what you learned from your father and now, with being a movie actor and all, I bet you know a hundred times more than I do about women. That's never been my strong point and I don't want to kid myself about that." He hesitated. "Did you get the impression she was flirting with you or anything like that?"

"Come on, Bunny." Wesley was honestly shocked.

"I wouldn't want to get hooked up with any woman who made passes at my friends," Bunny said.

"Rest easy, mate," Wesley said. "There wasn't the flicker of an eyelash."

"I'm glad to hear that," Bunny said. "Now—about you—"

"What about me?"

"I got the feeling you didn't come down to the Côte d'Azur just to see your old shipmate or to go to any goddamn movie. . . ."

"You're imagining things. I just . . ."

"I'm not imagining anything," Bunny said. "I have feelings about you. When you're on the level. When you're hiding something. You're hiding something right now. I keep watching you when you don't know I'm looking and I don't like what I see, Wesley."

"Crap," Wesley said roughly. "Stop being an old lady."

"I know one thing," Bunny said. "Your father would hate to see you get into trouble—bad trouble—especially if it's because of that Danovic fellow. Are you listening to me, Wesley?"

"I'm listening."

"He loved you and the thing he wanted most was for you to have a good life. And that goes almost ditto for me. I don't want to have to visit you in prison or in a hospital or in a morgue."

"Don't make me feel sorry I came to see you, Bunny," Wesley said quietly.

"I don't care if you never see me again," Bunny said, "if I can hammer some sense into your head. You've got a great life ahead of you—don't ruin it. Your father's dead and that's that. Respect his memory, is all I'm asking from you."

"I've got to get back to my hotel," Wesley said; "I'm expecting a call."

Bunny was standing at the stern of the Chris-Craft staring coldly at Wesley as Wesley mounted the one-cylinder bicyclette he had rented and chugged off toward his hotel.

———

When Wesley reached the hotel, he saw the open Peugeot standing in the parking lot. He hurried into the hotel. "There's a gentleman waiting for you in the bar," the concierge told him as he gave Wesley his key.

Billy was sitting alone in the empty bar, sipping at a beer and staring out at the inlet of the bay on which the hotel was built. He looked small and disconsolate, slumped in his chair. His clothes were rumpled and he hadn't bothered to comb his hair, which had been whipped by the wind on his journey. The long trip to Paris and back in the open car had made his normally dark complexion two or three shades darker. He looks like a shifty little Arab, Wesley thought as he went up to him. Billy stood up as Wesley approached, and they shook hands.

"Well, Cousin," Wesley said, "it's about time."

"For Christ's sake," Billy said querulously, "are you going to start like that?"

"Let's go to my room," Wesley said, looking over at the barman who was peeling lemons at the other side of the room. "We can talk there."

"You might let me finish my beer," Billy said. "And you look as though you could use one yourself."

"There's a lot of things I could use more," Wesley said. "Drink up."

Billy looked around him. "This is a pretty fancy place," he said. "It must cost a fortune."

"I thought I was only going to be here a couple of days," Wesley said. "I didn't think I'd have to stay here for the whole season. You finished with your beer?"

"I suppose so," Billy said, "but I have to pay."

"Put the gentleman's drink on my bill, please," Wesley called to the bartender at the other end of the room.

"Thanks," Billy said as he followed Wesley out of the bar.

"It's the least I could do," Wesley said sardonically, "for my true-blue cousin."

In his room, Wesley turned on Billy. "Have you got it?" he asked harshly.

"You have to let me explain," Billy said. "The man who was holding it for me is on the lam. He wasn't in Paris and his girlfriend said she didn't know where he is. But she said he would call her and . . ."

"When?" Wesley asked. "When is he going to call her?"

"She couldn't say. Soon, she thinks."

"Soon? The fourth of July? Christmas?"

"Jesus," Billy said aggrievedly, "there's no call for you to talk to me like that. I did my best. It's not like going into a store and buying a box of candy."

"You know what I think, Billy," Wesley said levelly, "I think you're lying to me."

"Don't be so goddamn suspicious. I volunteered, didn't I, for Christ's sake? Nobody put a gun to my head. All I was doing was trying to help."

"Balls," Wesley said. "You know where that gun is— if there ever was a gun . . ."

"There's a gun." Billy said. "I swear it."

"Then you're going to tell me where it is. And you're going to tell me right now." With a sudden, feline motion, Wesley leaped at Billy and began to choke him. Billy struggled, clawing at the hands around his throat and trying to use his knee to Wesley's groin. But Wesley outweighed him by forty pounds. Soundlessly, they struggled around the room. Billy slipped and was on the floor, with Wesley kneeling on him, his face calm, his hands pressing maniacally on Billy's throat. Just before Billy was about to black out, the hands relaxed.

"You going to tell me or not?" Wesley whispered.

"Christ," Billy gasped, "you could have choked me to death."

"Highly possible." Wesley's hands began to press a little harder.

"Rudolph . . ." Billy said brokenly. "He's in Saint-Paul-de-Vence . . . the Hôtel Colombe d'Or. Now will you get off my chest?"

Slowly, Wesley released his grip and stood. He helped Billy up and Billy fell into a chair, feeling his throat with his hands. "You're too fucking strong for your own good," he said.

Wesley stood over him, still threateningly. "How did Uncle Rudolph come into the picture?" he asked. "And no more fairy tales, Billy."

"I called him in New York. I thought if anybody could help you, he could. I did it for you. You don't think I did it for myself, do you?"

"You chickened out," Wesley said contemptuously. "And you called in Santa Claus. I should have known. What the hell would you expect from a tennis player? Go back to your fancy ladies, you bastard. What a royal fucking runaround."

"You go to Saint-Paul-de-Vence, you murdering idiot," Billy said, "and you try to choke your Uncle Rudolph."

"Maybe I'll try just that," Wesley said. "And now you get out of my room. And out of town. If I see you around I might be sorry I ever let up on you."

"The next time I see you," Billy said as he stood up. "I'm going to have a knife on me. I warn you."

"Thanks," Wesley said, "I'll keep that in mind."

At the door, Billy turned. "One last word," he said, "I'm your friend, no matter what you think."

Wesley nodded somberly and Billy opened the door and went out.

When he got downstairs he called Saint-Paul-de-Vence. When Rudolph came to the phone, Billy told him what had happened.

"Oh, Lord," Rudolph said. "He's as bad as that?"

"Worse," said Billy. "Demented. You'd better move to another hotel, if you don't want another choking session in the family."

"I'm not moving anywhere," Rudolph said calmly. "Let him come."

"Just don't see him alone," Billy said, admiring his

uncle's serenity. "With that boy you need plenty of witnesses."

"I'll see him any way he wants."

"Have you come up with anything?"

"Maybe," Rudolph said. "We'll see."

"If I can give you some advice," Billy said, "I'd get
rid of the thing before he gets there. Throw it in the
sea."

"No," Rudolph said thoughtfully, "I don't believe I
want to do that. It may come in handy. In the not too
distant future."

"Good luck," Billy said.

"I'll see you next week in Cannes, at the festival,"
Rudolph said. "I've reserved rooms at the Hôtel Majestic for all of us. I put you in a room with Wesley. Given
the circumstances . . ." He chuckled oddly. "Given
the circumstances, I think I'll put you on another
floor."

"You think of everything, don't you, Rudolph," Billy
said sarcastically.

"Almost everything," Rudolph said.

Billy hung up and went over to the concierge's desk
and said, "Please put the call on Mr. Abbott's bill."

Wesley didn't call that day or the next, but the lawyer
from Antibes did.

"I may have some news," the lawyer said. "The gentleman I have in mind to apply for the position you
spoke to me about the other day is not available for the
moment. He happens to be in prison in Fresnes. But he
is due to get out in two weeks and he is expected at his
home in Marseilles shortly after that. I will be in touch
with him and will tell him where he can reach you."

"I'll be at the Hôtel Majestic in Cannes," Rudolph
said.

"I'm sorry about the delay," the lawyer said.

"It can't be helped," Rudolph said. "Thank you for your trouble. I'll be expecting the call."

It can't be helped, Rudolph thought as he hung up. That would be a good title for the story of my life. It can't be helped.

# CHAPTER 10

The publicity man at the festival for Gretchen's movie had put out a story about the woman whose first picture as a director had been chosen as one of the American entries to be shown in Cannes, so there were photographers at the Nice airport when Gretchen's plane came in. The photographers took pictures of Gretchen getting off the plane and then again as she greeted Billy and Rudolph after going through customs. She was near tears as she kissed Billy and hugged him, hard. "It's been so long," she whispered.

Billy was embarrassed at the show of maternal emotion with the flashbulbs popping off and extricated himself, gently but firmly, from his mother's embrace. "Mother," he said, "why don't we save the reunion scene for later?" He didn't like the idea of a photograph of himself being clutched in a domestic stranglehold appearing in the papers, publicity or no publicity.

As Gretchen stepped back Billy saw her lips set in the cold line that was all too familiar to him. "Billy," she said, her tone formal, "let me introduce you to Mr. Donnelly. He did the sets for our picture."

Billy shook hands with the red-bearded young man. "Glad to meet you, sir," he said. Another one, he thought. She never gives up. He had noticed the possessive, protective way the man had held his mother's arm as they came through the small crowd grouped around the exit from the customs. He had intended to be warm and responsive at this first meeting after so long, but the sight of his mother, as beautiful as ever in her smart blue traveling suit, being squired ostentatiously off the plane by a man who seemed not much older than himself had disturbed him.

Then he felt ashamed for allowing himself to be annoyed. After all, his mother was a big grown woman and what she did on her own time and her taste in partners was none of his business. As he walked beside her toward the chauffeured car that had been sent for her, he squeezed her hand affectionately, to make up for the remark about the reunion scene. She looked at him, surprised, then smiled widely. "We're going to have a great two weeks," she said.

"I hope so," he said. "I can't wait to see the picture."

"The omens are good," she said. "The people who've seen it so far seem to like it a great deal."

A lot more than a great deal," Rudolph said. "People're raving about it. I've already been offered a hundred percent profit on my share of it and I've turned it down."

"Faithful brother," Gretchen said lightly. "He puts his money where his heart is." Then she frowned. "Rudy," she said, "you don't look well. You look as though you haven't slept in weeks. What's the matter?"

Rudolph laughed uneasily. "Nothing. Maybe I've been staying up too late at the casino."

"Have you been winning?"

"As always," Rudolph said.

As the porter and the chauffeur were putting the bags in the car, Gretchen said, "I'm a little disappointed."

"Why?" Rudolph asked.

"I'd hoped that Wesley would come to meet me, too."

Rudolph and Billy exchanged glances.

"Isn't he staying at the hotel with us?" Gretchen asked.

"No," said Rudolph.

"He's in Cannes, isn't he? After the picture's shown, he's going to be mobbed by the papers and TV people for interviews. He's got to *behave* like an actor even if he doesn't think he is one."

"Gretchen," Rudolph said softly, "we don't know where he is. He was in Saint-Tropez the last we knew, but he's disappeared."

"Is there anything wrong?"

"Not that we know of," Rudolph lied. "Don't worry, I'm sure he'll turn up."

"He'd better," Gretchen said, as she and Donnelly got into the car. "Or I'll send out a missing persons alarm."

With all the baggage there was no room in the car for Rudolph. He and Billy went toward where the Peugeot was parked. "We'd better cook up *some* kind of story for her about Wesley," Rudolph said as they got into the Peugeot.

"*You* cook up the story this time," Billy said, as they drove out of the parking lot. "The last story I cooked up nearly got me killed."

"Maybe when he sees Gretchen's picture in the papers, he'll come around," Rudolph said. "He grew very fond of her while they were shooting."

"I know. He told me so. Still, I wouldn't be too hopeful. What he's really fond of these days is finding a certain Yugoslav." He turned his head and peered curiously at Rudolph. "Anything new on your front?"

"I won't know for a few days yet."

"You still don't want to tell me what it might be?"

"No," Rudolph said decisively. "And don't pry."

Billy devoted himself to his driving for a minute or so. He had had the car washed and he had dressed in clean, neat clothes for his mother's arrival. He was sorry that Wesley's absence had cast a shadow over the occasion. "I hope," he said, "that wherever he is or whatever he does, he doesn't spoil my mother's big moment. She seemed in great spirits at the airport."

"Except when you made that snide crack about the reunion," Rudolph said sourly.

"Force of habit."

"Well, break the habit."

"I'll try," Billy said. "Anyway, for your information, I made up for it on the way to the car."

"You think she's tough," Rudolph said. "Well, let me tell you something—she isn't. Certainly not about you."

"I'll try, I said." Billy smiled. "She looks beautiful, doesn't she?"

"Very."

Again, Billy turned his head to peer at Rudolph. "What's there between her and that Donnelly fellow?"

"Nothing that I know of," Rudolph said curtly. "They worked well together and he's now a business associate of mine, too. Don't pry into that, either."

"I was just asking," Billy said. "A son's natural concern for his mother's welfare. What sort of guy is he?"

"One of the best," Rudolph said. "Talented, ambitious, honest, with a drinking problem."

"She ought to be used to that," Billy said, "after her life with my father. The drinking part, I mean."

"She invited your father to come over, too," Rudolph

said. "He said he had a new job and couldn't leave Chicago. Maybe he's taking hold of himself at last."

"I wouldn't bet on that," said Billy. "Well, he's done at least one useful thing for his son."

"What's that?"

"He turned me off drink." Billy chuckled. "Say—I have an idea. Not about my father or my mother—about Wesley."

"What's that?"

"You know, the police pick up those forms you have to fill in when you check into a hotel . . ."

"Yes."

"I don't think Wesley knows anybody he could stay with in Cannes," Billy went on earnestly, "so he's most probably in a hotel in the town. We could go to the police and ask for information. After all, he's in the picture and we could say he's needed for press photographs and interviews, stuff like that."

"We could, but we won't," Rudolph said. "The less interest the police take in Wesley, the better it will be for all of us."

"It was just an idea."

"We'll just have to find him ourselves. Hang around the port, go to the nightclubs, generally keep our eyes open," Rudolph said. "Meanwhile, you can tell your mother that he told you he's shy about any publicity before the picture is shown, he's afraid he's no good in it and that people will laugh at him, he'd rather not be around if that happens . . ."

"Do you think she'll go for that?" Billy said doubtfully.

"Maybe. She knows he's a strange young man. She'll probably say it's just what you could expect from him."

"What I'm surprised at," Billy said, "is that he never called you or came to see you."

"I was almost sure he wouldn't," Rudolph said. "He

knows that he'd never get what he was looking for out of me."

"Have you still got it?" Billy asked. "The gun?"

"Yes."

Billy chuckled again. "I bet you're the only one at this festival with a gun with a silencer in his hotel room."

"It's a distinction I would gladly renounce," Rudolph said bleakly.

When they drove down the Croisette in Cannes, Rudolph saw that among the posters advertising the movies to be shown in the next two weeks there was one for *Restoration Comedy* and that Gretchen's name was prominently displayed.

"She must have gotten a kick seeing that," Rudolph said. "Your mother."

"Now," Billy said, joking, "with all the other things I have to worry about her for, I'll have to figure out how to handle being the son of a famous mother. What do I say if they interview me and ask me how it feels?"

"Say it feels great."

"Next question, Mr. Abbott," Billy said. "Did your mother, in your opinion, neglect you in the interest of her career? Answer—only for ten or fifteen years."

"You can joke like that with me," Rudolph said sharply, "but not with anyone else. You understand that?"

"Yes, sir. Of course I was kidding."

"Anyway," said Rudolph, "she's not famous yet. In a place like this, you can be famous one day and nonfamous the next. It's a tricky emotional time for your mother and we've got to be very careful with her."

"I will be steadfast as an oak in her support," Billy said. "She will not recognize her wayward son and will look at me in amazement."

"You may not drink like your father, Billy," Rudolph

said, "but you seem to have inherited his lack of ability to make anyone believe he ever took anything seriously."

"A protective device," Billy said lightly, "passed on from father to son, to hide the quivering, tender soul hidden beneath."

"Let it show once in a while," Rudolph said. "It won't kill you."

When they went into the lobby of the hotel, Rudolph asked if there were any messages for him. There were no messages.

Gretchen was in a corner of the lobby, surrounded by journalists and photographers. The big guns had not yet arrived in Cannes and the publicity man for *Restoration Comedy* was making the most of it. Rudolph saw that Gretchen was talking smoothly, smiling and at ease.

Gretchen saw them and gestured for them to join her, but Billy shook his head. "I'm going out," he said to Rudolph. "I'll take a swing around the port looking for our lost angel child. Tell my mother I love her but I had an errand to run."

Rudolph went over to Gretchen and she introduced him as her brother and a backer of the film. She didn't inquire where Billy had gone. In a lull in the questioning, when a photographer asked Gretchen to pose with Rudolph, Rudolph asked her where Donnelly was.

"One guess," she said, smiling up at Rudolph for the photograph.

Rudolph went to the bar and saw Donnelly hunched over it gloomily, a glass of whiskey in front of him.

"Enjoying the fun and frolic of the famous festival?" Rudolph asked.

Donnelly scowled at him. "I'll add another f. I shouldn't have fucking come," he said.

"Why not?" Rudolph asked, surprised.

"That kid," Donnelly said. "Her son, Billy. He gave me the old cold eye at the airport."

"You're imagining things."

"I didn't imagine this. I'm afraid he's going to make Gretchen's life miserable on account of me. What is he—jealous?"

"No," Rudolph said. "Maybe he's worried that you're so much younger than she and that she'll get hurt."

"Did he tell you that?"

"No," Rudolph admitted. "He didn't say anything."

"She's told me about him." Donnelly drank what was left in his glass and signaled for another. "He's been a pain in the ass since he was a kid."

"He's turned over a new leaf, he told me."

"He wasn't turning over any new leaves at the Nice airport, I'll tell you that. And where's the other kid—Wesley? The two of them were supposed to drive up together from Spain, according to Gretchen."

"He's around," Rudolph said vaguely.

"Where around?" Donnelly demanded. "He wasn't around when we got in and he damn well should have been, after all Gretchen did for him." He sipped thirstily from the second glass. "I'll bet a dollar against a plugged nickel that son of hers has something to do with it."

"Don't be neurotic about one look at an airport," Rudolph said. "I guarantee that everything will be all right."

"It better be," Donnelly said. "If that kid ruins these next two weeks for his mother, I'll break his back for him. And you can tell him that for me. You can also tell him I've asked his mother to marry me."

"What did she say?"

"She laughed."

"Congratulations."

"I'm just so crazy about her I can't see straight," Donnelly said gloomily.

"You'd see straighter . . ." Rudolph tapped the glass on the bar lightly, "if you laid off this stuff a bit."

"Are *you* going to bitch about it, too?"

"I imagine Gretchen must have mentioned something of that nature in passing."

"So she did. I promised her that if she married me I'd go the wine route only."

"What did she say to that?"

"She laughed."

Rudolph chuckled. "Have a good time in Cannes," he said.

"I will," Donnelly said, "but only if Gretchen does. By the way, the day before we left New York, our lawyer called and said that he thinks there's a good chance we can settle the Connecticut business before the year's out."

"Everything's going our way, lad," Rudolph said. "Stop looking so darkly Irish."

"The Celtic twilight on the Côte d'Azur," Donnelly said, breaking into a smile. "I see demons in the Gallic dusk. Pay it no heed, man."

Rudolph patted Donnelly's arm in a comforting, friendly gesture and left the bar. In the hall he saw that the press conference was over, although the publicity man was still there, assembling papers. The publicity man was an American by the name of Simpson who worked out of Paris for various movie companies.

"How did it go?" Rudolph asked him.

"Fine," the man said. "She knows how to use her charm with those guys. You know, I saw the picture at a screening in Paris and I think we've got a winner there."

Rudolph nodded, although he'd never heard of a publicity man who said he had a loser the first week on the job. "I'd like you to make a special effort," he said, "to get Wesley Jordan's photograph spread around."

"No sweat," the man said. "The word's out already that he's something special. His looks won't hurt, either."

"He's missing in action somewhere in the neighborhood," Rudolph said, "and I want people to recognize him so that we can find him for background stories before the picture's shown."

"Will do," the publicity man said. "I could use some personal stuff on him myself."

"Thanks," Rudolph said and went up to his room. The bag was where he had left it on a chair. He twirled the combination lock and opened it. The automatic was still there. What an ugly piece of furniture, he thought, as he closed and locked the bag again. He found himself going to his room and looking into the bag ten times a day.

He went into the bathroom and took two Miltowns. Ever since he had arrived in Paris he had been jittery and had developed the first tic of his life, a twitching of the right eyelid that he tried to hide when he was with anybody else by rubbing at the eye as though he had something caught in it. The Miltowns helped each time for an hour or two.

The phone was ringing when he went back into the bedroom. He picked it up and heard a woman's voice saying, "Mr. Rudolph Jordache, please."

"Speaking," he said.

"You don't know me," the woman said. "I'm a friend of Wesley's. My name is Alice Larkin."

"Oh, yes," Rudolph said. "Wesley's spoken about you. Where're you calling from?"

"New York," Alice said. "Is Wesley with you?"

"No."

"Do you know where I can reach him?"

"Not at the moment, I'm afraid."

"He was supposed to call me last week," Alice said. "I was trying to get my vacation moved up so that I could come over to Cannes for a few days. I think I can manage it. I'll be told definitely tomorrow and I'd like to know if he still wants me to come."

"I think you'd better wait before making any decision," Rudolph said. "To be honest with you, Wesley's disappeared. If he turns up, I'll tell him to call you."

"Is he in trouble?" Alice asked anxiously.

"Not that I know of." Rudolph spoke carefully. "Although it's hard to tell with him. He's an unpredictable boy."

"You can say that again." Now the girl sounded angry. "Anyway, if you do happen to see him, tell him that I wish him all sorts of success."

"I'll do that," Rudolph said. He put the phone down slowly. He wished the Miltowns would start working quickly. The burden of Wesley's obsession was wearing him down. Maybe, he thought, when I do find him I'll give him the goddamn gun and wash my hands of the whole thing. He went over to the window and looked out at the sea, calm and blue, and the people walking below on the Croisette, enjoying the sunshine, with the flags above their heads snapping festively in the warm breeze. Momentarily he envied each and every stroller on the broad avenue below, just for not being him.

———

Billy got back to his room at dusk. He had patrolled the old port all afternoon, peering at the boats and going into the bars and restaurants. Wesley had not been on any of the boats or in any of the bars or restaurants. He called his mother's room, but the operator said that she was not taking any calls. Probably in the sack, he thought, with that fellow with the beard. Best not to think about it.

He undressed and took a shower. It had been a long hot day and he luxuriated under the needle-sharp cold spray, forgetting everything but the delicious tingling of his skin.

When he got out of the shower he heard a knock on the bedroom door. He wrapped a towel around his waist and, leaving wet footprints on the carpet, he went to the door and opened it. Monika stood there, smiling, in one of the pretty cotton gowns he had seen her wearing in Spain.

"Good Lord," he said.

"I see you're dressed to receive guests," she said. "May I come in?"

He peered past her into the corridor to see if she was alone.

"Don't worry," she said, "this is a social visit. There's nobody with me." She brushed past him and he closed the door. "My," she said, looking around at the large, handsomely furnished room, "we're moving up in the world, aren't we? This beats Brussels by a mile, doesn't it? Capitalism becomes you, laddy."

"How'd you find me?" Billy asked, ignoring what she had said about the improvement over Brussels.

"It was easy," she said. "This time you left a forwarding address."

"I must remember never to do that again," he said. "What do you want?" He felt foolish, standing there soaking wet, with the towel precariously draped around him.

"I just wanted to say hello." She sat down and crossed her legs and smiled up at him. "Do you mind if I smoke?"

"What would you do if I said I *did* mind?"

"I'd smoke." She laughed and took a cigarette out of her bag but didn't light it.

"I'll put some clothes on," he said. "I'm not used to entertaining strange ladies naked." He started past her toward the bathroom, where his pants and shirt were hanging.

She dropped the cigarette and reached out and held his arm. "No need," she said. "I'm not as strange as all that. Besides—the less you're wearing the better you look." She took her hand off his arm and reached around and held him, encircling his legs. She tilted her head and looked up at him. "Give me a kiss."

He pulled against the pressure of her arm, but she held him tight. "What're you up to now?" he said harshly, although he could feel the familiar stirrings in his groin.

She chuckled. "The same old thing," she said.

"It wasn't the same old thing in Spain," he said, cursing the sudden erection that plainly bulked under the towel.

"I had other things on my mind in Spain," she said. "And I wasn't alone then, if you remember. Now I'm alone and on holiday and it's the same old thing. I think I told you once that orgasms are few and far between on the New Left. That hasn't changed." With a swift motion, she reached under the towel and put her hand on his penis. She chuckled again. "I see this hasn't changed, either." She caressed him gently, her hand moving with remembered deftness.

"Oh, Christ," he said, sure that he was finally going to regret what he was saying, "let's get into bed."

"That was my general idea," she said. She stood up and they kissed. "I missed you," she whispered. "Just lie down while I get these clothes off."

He went over to the wide bed and lay down, the towel still draped around him, and watched as she pulled the pretty dress over her head. She wasn't wearing a brassiere and the sight of the lovely small breasts made him ache with pleasure. He closed his eyes. One last time, he thought, what the hell? His mother was probably doing the same thing one floor above. Like mother, like son. A big evening for the family. He heard Monika moving barefooted toward the bed, and the click of a switch as she turned off the light. He threw off the towel. She fell on top of him with a low moan and he put his arms around her.

———

Later, in the warm darkness, he was lying on his back, his arm under her neck, as she snuggled against him, her head on his shoulder, one leg thrown across him. He sighed. "The best," he said, "the very goddamn best. All in favor say, Aye."

"Aye," Monika said. "From now on always remember to leave a forwarding address."

"Aye," he said, although he wasn't sure he meant it. He had been through too much with her and the only place he felt safe with her was in bed. "What's *your* address now?"

"What do you have to know that for?"

"I might just happen to be passing your hotel," he said, "and be suddenly overcome with an irresistible urge."

"I'll see you here," she said, "when *I* happen to be overcome with an irresistible urge. I don't want to be seen with you. You'll see me often enough. But only in this room."

"Dammit." He wriggled his arm free from under her

neck and sat up. "Why do you always have to be the one who calls the signals?"

"Because that's the way I like to operate," she said.

"Operate," he said. "I don't like that word."

"Learn to live with it, laddy," Monika said. She sat up, too, and searched for the pack of cigarettes she had put on the bedside table. She took out a cigarette and lit it, the small flare of the match illuminating her face and eyes.

"I thought you said you were on holiday," Billy said.

"Holidays end."

"If you don't tell me where I can get hold of you, *this* is the end," Billy said angrily.

"I'll see you here," she said, inhaling smoke, "same time tomorrow."

"Bitch."

"I've always been amused by your vocabulary." She got out of bed and began dressing, the glow of her cigarette the only light in the dark room. "By the way, I saw your cousin coming out of a hotel this afternoon. You know, the boy you used to play tennis with."

"You did?" Billy said. "Who told you he was my cousin?"

"I looked him up in *Who's Who.*"

"Funny as usual, aren't you? What hotel was it?"

Monika hesitated. "Isn't he staying here with you?"

"No. What hotel? We have to find him."

"Who's we?"

"What difference does that make to you?" Billy tried to keep his voice down.

"You never can tell what difference it might make to me. Who's we?"

"Forget it."

"Actually," Monika said, "I don't remember the name of the hotel."

"You're lying."

She laughed. "Perhaps. Maybe if you're here, like a good boy, tomorrow evening, I might remember it."

"Did you talk to him?"

"No. I'm interested in another member of the family."

"God," Billy said, "you know how to make sex complicated."

"Sex?" she said. "Once upon a time you used to use the word love."

"Once upon a time," Billy said grimly.

"Have it your own way, laddy," Monika said lightly. "For the moment. One last compliment—you're better in bed than on a tennis court."

"Thanks."

"*Pour rien,* as the French say." She threw away her cigarette and came over to the bed and bent and kissed his cock, briefly. "Good night, laddy," she said, "I have to go now."

As the door closed behind her Billy lay back against the pillows, staring up at the dark ceiling. Another problem. He had to decide whether or not to tell Rudolph that Wesley had been seen coming out of a hotel in Cannes that day, but that he didn't know the name of the hotel, although he might find out tomorrow. But then he'd have to explain how he had heard it and why he had to wait for tomorrow. And he couldn't explain anything, without at least mentioning Monika. And then he'd have to explain something, at least, about Monika. He shook his head irritably against the pillow. Rudolph had enough on his mind without having to worry about Monika.

The phone rang. It was Rudolph to tell him that they would all meet at the bar downstairs in a half hour before going to dinner. After he hung up, Billy went in and took another shower. He didn't want to go to dinner smelling as though he had been in an orgy. He wondered if his mother was upstairs now also taking a shower.

———

# CHAPTER 11

"No," Gretchen was saying, "I don't want any party after the showing. I'm exhausted and all I want to do is fall into bed and sleep for forty-eight hours." She was in the salon of her small suite with Donnelly and Rudolph. It had been Rudolph's suggestion that after the evening performance of *Restoration Comedy* they should celebrate by having a gala supper, inviting the festival judges and some of the representatives of the major distribution companies as well as several of the newspapermen with whom Gretchen and Rudolph had become more or less intimate in the last few days. Gretchen was showing increasing signs of tensions as the date approached. A party might help her unwind.

"If there was anyone else but us three here," Gretchen said, "maybe a party would be called for. But I don't want to be the only one to accept the kudos, if there *are* going to be any kudos to accept, or the only one to see the long faces of all those people if the picture flops. If Frances Miller and Wesley were here, I'd say yes, but that little bitch couldn't take the trouble to

come and you can't find Wesley for me and I'm too old
for parties anyway. . . ."

"Okay," Rudolph said. "No party. We'll have a nice
little foursome for supper—us three and Billy—and
congratulate each other." He looked at his watch. "It's
getting late," he said. "I suggest you go to bed and try
to get some sleep." He kissed Gretchen good night and
started toward the door.

"I'll go along with you," Donnelly said, "I need some
sleep, too. Unless you want me to stay, Gretchen . . . ?"

"No, thanks," Gretchen said. "See you in the morning."

In the corridor, on the way to the elevator, Donnelly
said, "I have to talk to you about her, Rudy. I'm worried. She's taking it too hard. She can't sleep and she's
dosing herself with pills and she has crazy crying fits
when she's alone with me and I don't know how to stop
her."

"I wish I were a woman," Rudolph said. "I'd like to
break down and cry myself."

"I thought you felt fine about the picture." Donnelly
sounded surprised.

"I do," Rudolph said. "It's not that. It has nothing to
do with the picture."

"What then?"

"Some other time," Rudolph said.

"Can I help?"

"Yes," said Rudolph. "Take care of Gretchen."

"Maybe," Donnelly said, "it would be a good idea,
after the showing, if I got into a car with her and took
her on a little sight-seeing trip—get out of this mad-
house for a couple of days."

"I'd be for that," Rudolph said, "if you could convince her."

"I'll try in the morning."

"Good man," Rudolph said, as the elevator door

opened. "Good night, David. Sleep well." Donnelly walked back along the corridor and stopped in front of the door to Gretchen's salon. There was no sound from the room. Donnelly put out his hand to rap on the door, then stopped himself. Tonight, he thought, it's probably better if she sleeps alone. He went back toward the elevator and took it down to the ground floor where he strode into the bar. He hesitated when the bartender asked him what he wanted. He ordered a whiskey and soda. The wine route could wait for another time.

———

The phone was ringing when Rudolph unlocked the door to his room. He hurried over to the phone and picked it up to say hello. *"Monsieur* Jordache . . . ?" It was a man's voice.

"Yes."

*"L'avocat d'Antibes,"* the man said, *"m'a dit que vous voulez me parler . . ."*

"Do you speak English?" Rudolph said. If it was the man he thought it was he had to understand every word he said. He might just barely be able to arrange a murder in English, but never in high-school French.

"A leetle," the man said. He had a hoarse, low voice. "The lawyer of Antibes, he say per'aps we do a leetle business together . . ."

"When can we meet?"

"Now," the man said.

"Where?"

*"A la gare.* Z' station. I stand by z' bar in z' buffet."

"Ten minutes," Rudolph said. "How will I recognize you?"

"I am dressed z' following," the man said. "Blue pantalons, jacket brown, I am small man, w'z grand belly."

"Good," Rudolph said. "Ten minutes." He hung up.

Blue pants, brown jacket, big belly. Well, he wasn't
picking the man for his beauty or his taste in clothing.
He unlocked his bag, peered in. The automatic was still
there. He closed the bag, locked it and went out.

Downstairs, he went into the cashier's room behind
the desk and had his safe-deposit box opened. He had
had ten thousand dollars sent over from his bank in
New York and had converted them into francs. Whatever was going to happen, good or bad, he knew would
cost money. He looked down at the neat bundles of
bills, considered for a moment, then took out five thousand francs. He put the remaining bundles back in the
box and locked it. Then he went out of the hotel and
got into a taxi. *"La gare,"* he said. He tried to think of
nothing on the short trip to the station. He fumbled as
he pulled some ten-franc notes out of his pocket and his
hand was shaking as he took the change and tipped the
driver.

He saw the fat little dark man in the blue pants and
brown jacket standing at the bar, a glass of pastis in
front of him. "Good evening, *monsieur,*" he said as he
went up to the man.

The man turned and looked soberly at him. He was
dark, with a fat face and small, deep-set black eyes. His
lips were thick and wet. An incongruous baby-blue cotton golf hat that was too small for him sat back from his
domed and wrinkled forehead. It was not a prepossess-
ing face or one that in other circumstances Rudolph
would have been inclined to trust. "Per'aps we go for
walk," the man said. He had a strong Provençal accent.
"Z' light here bad for z' eyes."

They went out together and walked away from the
station and along a narrow, dark, deserted street. It
could have been a thousand miles away from the bright,
crowded bustle of the festival.

"I listen proposal," the man said.

"Do you know a man called Danovic?" Rudolph asked. "Yugoslav. Small-time hoodlum."

" 'oodlum?" the man said. "What z' 'oodlum?"

*"Voyou,"* Rudolph said.

"Ah."

"Do you know him?"

The man walked ten paces in silence. Then he shook his head. "Per'aps under different name. Where you t'ink 'e z'?"

"Cannes, most likely," Rudolph said. "Last time he was seen it was in a nightclub here—La Porte Rose."

The man nodded. "Bad place," he said. "Varry bad."

"Yes."

"If I find him, what 'appens?"

"You will get a certain number of francs if you dispose of him."

"Dispose?" the man said.

"Kill." Good God, Rudolph thought, is it me who is saying this?

*"Compris,"* the man said. "Now we talk money. What you mean certain number of francs?"

"Say—fifty thousand," Rudolph said. "About ten thousand dollars, if you want it in dollars."

" 'ow much advance? Now? To find z' man."

"I have five thousand francs on me," Rudolph said. "You can have that."

The man stopped. He put out a pudgy hand. "I take money now."

Rudolph took out his wallet and slipped out the bills. He watched as the man carefully counted them by the dim light of a streetlamp thirty feet away. I wonder what he would say, Rudolph thought, if I asked him for a receipt. He almost laughed aloud at the thought. He was dealing with a world where the only guarantee was vengeance.

The man stuffed the bills into an inside pocket of his

coat. "When I find him," he said, " 'ow much I get?"

"Before or after the . . . the job?"

"Before."

"Twenty thousand," Rudolph said. "That would make half the total."

*"D'accord,"* the man said. "And after, how I make sure I am paid?"

"Any way you want."

The man thought for a moment. "When I say I find him," he said, "you put twenty-five thousand in hands of lawyer. The lawyer read in *Nice-Matin* he is . . . what word you used?"

"Disposed of," Rudolph said.

"Dispose," the man said, "and a friend of me go to lawyer office for rest of money. We shake on deal?"

Rudolph had shaken hands on a variety of deals in the past and had celebrated after. There would be no celebration after this handshake.

"Stay near z' telephone," the man said and turned and walked quickly back in the direction of the station.

Rudolph took a deep breath and started walking slowly toward the Croisette and his hotel. He thought of the two men who had ambushed him in the hallway of the house in New York and who had been so furious that a man who looked as prosperous as he did had only a few dollars on him to reward them for their trouble. If anybody mugged him tonight on the dark streets of Cannes, they'd probably leave him for dead after they'd searched his pockets. He didn't have much more than cab fare left.

———

Billy was awakened by a knocking on his door. He got sleepily out of bed and barefooted and in pajamas

he went over to the door and opened it. Monika was
standing there, smoking a cigarette, a raincoat draped
over her shoulders like a cape. She came in quickly and
he closed the door and switched on a lamp.

"Hello," Billy said, "I was wondering when you
would turn up." It had been four days since her visit.

"Did you miss me?" She threw off her coat and sat
on the rumpled bed, facing him, smiling.

"I'll tell you later," Billy said. "What time is it?"

"Twelve-thirty," Monika said.

"You keep some weird office hours."

"Better late than never," she said. "Wouldn't you
agree?"

"I'll tell you later about that, too," he said. "The fact
is, I like afternoons better."

"How European you've become."

"What the hell do *you* do with your afternoons?"

Monika smiled demurely up at him. "Curiosity killed
the cat," she said.

Billy grunted. "I see this is your night for clichés," he
said. "Did you remember the name yet of the hotel
where you saw my cousin?"

"I am trying hard," Monika said. "Sometimes it
seems to be almost on the tip of my tongue."

"Oh, balls," Billy said.

"What a nice word," she said. She threw her cigarette
to the floor and ground it into the carpet. Billy winced.
Her manner of dressing had improved considerably but
her housewifely instincts were still at the Brussels level.
She stood up and came over to him and put her arms
around him and kissed him, her tongue sliding softly
inside his mouth. His erection was immediate. He tried
to think of other things, whether it was time to have the
oil changed in his car, whether he wanted to play tennis
the next day or not, if he had to get his dinner jacket

pressed for the evening performance of *Restoration Comedy* two nights from then, but it was no good. "Let's get to bed," he muttered.

"I was wondering how long it was going to take you to say that." She chuckled, sure of the hold she had on him.

An hour later she said, "It's not too bad at night, either, is it?"

He kissed her throat. She wriggled out of his arms and slid from the bed and stood up. "I have to go now," she said.

"Why the hell can't you stay the night?" he said, disappointed. "At least once."

"Previous engagements." She began to dress. It didn't take her long. She put on her panties, girlishly plain and white, over her tan, shapely legs and slipped her dress over her head. He watched her, feeling deprived, as she pulled on her ballet slippers and combed her hair in front of the mirror. "By the way," she said, "we decided to call in our debts."

A cold chill went over him and he drew the blankets over him. "What do you mean by that?" he said, trying to keep his voice calm.

"The Paris debt," she said, still combing her hair. "You remember that, I imagine?"

He said nothing and lay absolutely still.

"I'll tell you what you're going to do," she went on, tugging at her tangled hair with the comb. "Two nights from now, you're going to go to a bar called the Voile Vert on the rue d'Antibes at six P.M. There will be a man there waiting for you. He will have two magazines with him, *L'Express* and *Le Nouvel Observateur*. He will be reading *L'Express* and the *Observateur* will be on the table in front of him. You will sit down at the table with him and you will order a glass of wine. He will reach under the table and will pick up a sixteen-millimeter movie camera."

"Only it won't be a sixteen-millimeter movie camera," Billy said bitterly.

"You're learning," Monika said.

"Will you for Christ's sake stop combing your hair?" Billy said.

"You will take the camera and when you go into the Festival Hall that evening you will open it and take out what you find in it and hide it in an inconspicuous place. It will be timed to go off at nine forty-five." Monika finally put the comb down and pushed at her hair with her hands, twisting her body so that she could look at her reflection from the side.

"You must be out of your mind," Billy said, still with the blankets pulled up under his chin. "At nine forty-five they'll be running my mother's picture."

"Exactly," Monika said. "No one will suspect you. There will be dozens of photographers with all sorts of cameras. You can wander all over the building without anyone questioning you. That's why you were chosen for the job. Don't worry. Nobody's going to be hurt."

"You mean it's going to be a nice, harmless, friendly type of bomb?"

"You should know enough by now not to be sarcastic with me." Monika turned away from the mirror and faced him. "The police will be called at nine o'clock and told there is a bomb somewhere in the building. They'll clear the place in five minutes. We're not out to kill anybody. This time."

"What *are* you out to do?" Billy was ashamed of the quaver in his voice.

"A demonstration," Monika said evenly, "a demonstration which will have the greatest kind of publicity, with newspapermen, television crews all over the place and internationally famous people falling all over themselves to get out of there. If anything represents the rot of the whole system better than this disgusting fat circus, we haven't heard of it."

"What if I say no, I won't do it?"

"You will be dealt with," Monika said quietly. "When it is done to our satisfaction, I believe I'll remember what hotel your cousin is at. In the meanwhile I trust *you'll* remember—the Voile Vert, the two magazines, six P.M. Good night, laddy." She picked up her bag, threw her raincoat over her shoulders and went out the door.

———

As Billy went up the steps of the Festival Hall for the morning showing of *Restoration Comedy* with Gretchen and Donnelly and Rudolph, he said, "I think I'd like to sit downstairs in the orchestra with the peasants." The others had reserved seats in the balcony. He kissed his mother and whispered, *"Merde."*

"What's that?" Gretchen asked, surprised.

"It's French show-business for good luck," he said.

Gretchen smiled and gave him another quick kiss. "I hope you like the picture," she said.

"I hope so, too," he said gravely. He showed his ticket to the man at the door and went into the auditorium. It was already crowded, although the picture was not scheduled to start for another ten minutes. An inconspicuous place, he thought, an inconspicuous place. Everywhere he looked seemed like a highly conspicuous place to him. He went to the men's room. At the moment it was empty. There was a trash basket for paper towels. It would be possible, given thirty seconds alone, to open the back of the camera, take out the bomb and hide it. If he could manage thirty seconds alone.

The door to the men's room opened and a man in a flowered shirt came in and went over to the urinals. Billy ostentatiously washed his hands, pulled out a paper towel and dried them. Then he went out and found a seat near the front of the auditorium, where there were still a few vacant places. In the state he was in he didn't know whether or not he would be able to sit through the picture, which was another reason for not sitting beside his mother for the showing. But when the picture started he found himself immediately engrossed and even laughed with the rest of the audience at the humorous scenes. And Wesley's performance astonished him. It was Wesley all right, but a Wesley who had somehow blended someone else's character with his own, to become a boy hidden and besieged, revealing bits and pieces of himself at rare, emotional moments, by a glance, a movement of his head, a mumbled monosyllable, and through it all looking brutally handsome while suggesting sweetness and vulnerable sensitivity, even when the script demanded violence and cynical behavior from him.

After the final fade-out, the applause was loud and sustained, greater than that at any of the other movies Billy had heard about since the festival opened. Then people began turning around and applauding, and he saw that they were applauding his mother, who was standing, smiling tremulously, at the railing of the balcony. Billy, near tears himself, clapped with the heartiest of the people around him. As he filed out of the hall, moved by his mother's accomplishment, he wondered what had driven him to be such a bastard with his mother for all those years.

Outside, on the Croisette, he saw a cluster of young people getting autographs from a man who was standing with his back toward him. Whoever it was, he was almost obscured by a tall, bulky boy in blue jeans. Cu-

riously, Billy went toward the group. Then he stopped.
The man who was autographing programs and notebooks
and scraps of paper was Wesley. Billy grinned. The
ham, he thought, I should have known he couldn't resist seeing himself. He pushed his way, as politely as
possible, through the little crowd around Wesley, who
was bending over, signing a notebook held out to him
by a short girl in a gypsy skirt. "Mr. Jordan," Billy said,
lisping in a high, feminine voice, "will you sign my pro-
gram for me? I think you're just wonderful."

Wesley looked up from the notebook. "Go fuck yourself, Billy, he said. But there was a pleased smile on his
face.

Billy took Wesley's arm firmly. "That's all for the
moment, boys and girls," he said loudly. "Mr. Jordan
has to go upstairs for the press conference. Come with
me, sir." He started off, still holding Wesley's arm.
Wesley held back for a moment, then walked beside
him. "You're just what my mother needs today," Billy
said, "and you can't let her down."

"Yeah," Wesley said. "Jesus, she's a wonder, isn't
she?"

"A wonder," said Billy. "And you're going to tell her
so. You were pretty wonderful yourself in there, too,
you know."

"Not too bad," Wesley said complacently, the smile
now permanently glued on his face.

As they waited for the elevator to take them up to the
conference room, Billy said in a low voice, "Any luck in
finding the man?"

Wesley shook his head.

"Don't you think it's about time you forgot all about
it?"

Finally, Wesley stopped smiling. "No, it's not time."

"Movie stars don't go around murdering people,"
Billy said.

"I'm not a movie star," Wesley said shortly.

"Everybody in Cannes knows your face by now," said Billy. "You won't be by yourself long enough to swat a fly without witnesses, let alone kill a man." Then he had to keep quiet because two other people joined them waiting for the elevator.

Gretchen was just beginning to speak in the conference room, crowded with journalists and cameramen, as Billy and Wesley came in. She saw them immediately and broke off what she was saying. "Ladies and gentlemen," she said, her voice not under full control, "I have just had a most pleasant surprise. One of the most promising young actors I have ever seen has just walked into the room. Wesley, will you come up here, please."

"Oh, Christ," Wesley muttered under his breath.

"Get up there, idiot." Billy pushed him toward the raised platform where Gretchen was standing. Slowly, Wesley made his way through the crowd and stepped onto the platform. Gretchen kissed him and then, addressing the room, said, "I have the honor to introduce Wesley Jordan."

There was hearty applause and flashbulbs going off everywhere and the smile, now a little glassy, reappeared on Wesley's face. Billy slipped out of the room. He could hear the applause continuing as he walked quickly toward the elevators.

Outside, he left the Croisette and went into a café and ordered a beer, took a sip, asked for a token for the telephone, then went downstairs, where the booth was located. He looked in the directory for the *préfecture de police,* found the number and dialed it. A man's voice said, *"Allo."*

"This evening at six o'clock at a café called the Voile Vert, on the rue d'Antibes," Billy said in French, with a harsh Midi accent, which he had only used before to amuse people at parties, "you will find a man sitting at a table with a copy of *L'Express* in his hands and a copy of *Le Nouvel Observateur* on the table in front of him . . ."

"One moment." The policeman's voice was excited and he stumbled over the words. "Who is this? What do you want?"

"On the floor under the table," Billy went on, "you will find a bomb."

"A bomb!" the man shouted. "What are you saying? A bomb for what?"

"It will be timed to go off at nine forty-five tonight," Billy said. "Six this evening, the Voile Vert."

"Wait a minute. I must . . ." the policeman shouted more loudly.

Billy hung up the phone and went up to the bar and finished his beer.

———

They were in Gretchen's salon after the evening showing of the picture, drinking champagne, and Simpson, the publicity man, was saying, "We're going to take home everything—best picture, best actress, best supporting actor. I guarantee it." He was a tall gaunt man, with a mournful, seamed face and he waved his hands as he talked. "I usually have a tendency to look at the worst side of things, but this time . . ." He shook his head wonderingly, as though the immensity of the treasure entrusted to him was beyond his comprehension. "I've been coming to Cannes for fifteen years and I tell you that was one of the most enthusiastic audiences I've ever seen down here. As for you, young man," he turned to Wesley, who was sitting next to Billy on a small sofa, dressed in a dinner jacket that was too tight and too short that the publicity man had borrowed for him for the evening, "as for you, I'd bet my left nut that you're going home with a prize."

Wesley just sat there, a glass of champagne in his hand, the permanent glassy smile on his face. Billy got up and poured himself his fifth glass of champagne. He had sat through the beginning of the picture staring blankly at the screen. The images had made no sense to him and the dialogue had seemed to come out of the actors' mouths in spurts of nonsense syllables. He had kept looking at his watch until nine forty-five and then had slumped in his seat and closed his eyes.

Gretchen looked pale and drawn, nervously pulling a ring on and off her finger. The champagne that Billy had poured for her lay untouched in the glass on the end table beside her. She had said hardly a word all night. From time to time Rudolph, who was sitting next to her on the sofa, reached out and patted her arm soothingly. Donnelly, standing leaning against the fireplace, tugged at his beard and seemed annoyed at the publicity man's effusions.

"Tomorrow," Simpson said, "is going to be a full day for you, Gretchen, and for Wesley. Everybody, but *everybody,* will be wanting to talk to you and take photos. I'll give you the schedule at nine in the morning and . . ."

Rudolph and Donnelly exchanged glances and Rudolph stood up and broke in on Simpson. "If it's going to be a big day I think Gretchen had better get some rest. We all ought to leave her alone now."

"I think that's a good idea," Donnelly said.

"Of course," said Simpson. "It's just that I'm so excited with what we have here that . . ."

"We understand, old man," Rudolph said. He bent and kissed Gretchen. "Good night, Sister," he said.

She smiled wanly up at him. As they all prepared to

leave she stood up and went over to Donnelly and took
his hand. "David," she said, "could you stay on for a
little while?"

"Of course," Donnelly said. He stared sternly at
Billy.

Billy tried to smile, then kissed Gretchen's cheek.
"Thanks, Mother," he said, "for a marvelous day."

Gretchen gripped his arm, briefly, then broke into a
sob. "Forgive me," she said. "It's just that it's—well—
it's all too much for me. I'll be all right in the morning."
Wesley opened the door and was about to go out when
Gretchen called to him. "Wesley, you're not going to
disappear again, are you?"

"No, ma'am," Wesley said. "I'm just two floors down
if you need me." Rudolph had tried to put him in the
same room with Billy, but Billy had said he was afraid
of sleeping in the bed next to Wesley's, there was no
telling what that crazy boy might do, even on a night
like this. He hadn't told Rudolph what he really was
afraid of and with any luck Rudolph would never find
out.

As the door closed behind the four men and they
went down the corridor, Rudolph said, "I'm not sleepy.
I have a bottle of champagne in my room, too. Would
you like to help me with it?"

"I have some people to see about tomorrow," Simpson said, "but you boys drink hearty." He stood against
the back of the elevator wall, gaunt and mournful,
doomed to praise other people and never himself all his
life, as he raised an eloquent hand in a parting salute to
the uncle and two nephews who were going to continue
the evening's celebration with a bottle of champagne
while he prepared the morning.

As Rudolph wrestled with the cork of the champagne
bottle, he noticed Wesley eyeing the locked bag on the
chair near the window. "I bet," Wesley said, as the cork

popped and Rudolph began to pour, "I bet it's right in there."

"What's right in there?" Rudolph said.

"You know what I'm talking about," Wesley said.

"Drink your champagne." Rudolph raised his glass.

Wesley put his glass down deliberately and reached into the pocket of the borrowed dinner jacket and brought out a small pistol. "I don't need it anymore," he said evenly. "Keep it as a souvenir."

"Crazy as ever," Billy said.

"I'll drink to that," Wesley said.

They drank.

Wesley put the pistol back in his pocket.

"So," Rudolph said, "you were sitting there in the hall watching yourself act and taking bows with that thing on you all night."

"Yep," Wesley said. "You never know when a target might show up."

Rudolph paced around the room, frowning. "Wesley," he said, "what if I told you that the matter will be taken care of without your having to do anything about it?"

"What does that mean? Taken care of?"

"It means that right now, as we drink champagne in this room, a professional killer is looking for your man."

"I'd say I don't want anybody to do the job for me," Wesley said coldly, "and I don't want any more gifts from you or anyone else."

"I intend to stay here in Cannes until the end of the festival," Rudolph said. "That's only ten days. If the job isn't done by then, I'm going home and calling it quits. All I want from you is a promise that you won't do anything until then. After that, you're on your own."

"I'm not promising anything," Wesley said.

"Wesley . . ." Billy said.

Wesley turned on him sharply. "You keep out of this. You've meddled enough already."

"Calm down," Rudolph said. "Both of you. Another thing, Wesley. Your friend Miss Larkin called the other day. You owe her a lot, too."

"More than you know," Wesley said. "What did she have to say?"

"She wants to come over here. She thinks she can get leave from the magazine for two weeks. She's waiting for a call from you."

Wesley finished his glass of wine. "Let her wait," he said.

"She said you knew she might come over. That you wanted her to come."

"I thought the whole thing would be over by now," Wesley said. "Well, it isn't over. I'll see her some other time."

"Ah, the hell with it," Rudolph said. "I'm not going to play Cupid with all the other things I'm doing. Let's finish the bottle. I'm going to get some sleep."

"What're you going to do now?" Billy asked Wesley when they were alone in front of the hotel.

"Night patrol," Wesley said. "Want to come along?"

"No."

Wesley looked quizzically at Billy. "What do you think of all this?" he asked.

"I'm scared shitless," Billy said. "For all of us."

Wesley nodded solemnly.

"I'll walk with you as far as the parking lot," Billy said. "I forgot to put the top up on the car and it looks as though it might rain."

Wesley helped as they put the top up and Billy rolled up the windows. "Wesley," Billy said, "it still would be a nice idea if we two drove up to Paris, with a few stops for tennis and feasts along the way. You could ask your girl to meet you there. They'll drive you bats down here in the next ten days. How much harm can another ten days do after all this time?"

"I'll play tennis all right with you, Billy," Wesley said. "Down here. Good night, pal."

Billy watched the tall figure in the dark suit with the little bulge in the pocket stride off. He shook his head and walked back to the hotel. In his room he double-locked the door.

The next morning he awoke early and sent down for the newspapers. Along with the special sheets put out for the festival, the bellboy brought a copy of *Nice-Matin*. On the front page there was a photograph of a man who looked familiar. The man was wearing dark glasses in the photograph and he was between two policemen. It was Monika's frozen-food friend from Düsseldorf. In the accompanying story, Billy read that he had been arrested on an anonymous tip over the telephone and that he had been caught with a bomb in his possession hidden in a motion picture camera case. The man who had phoned in the tip, the article continued, had spoken in a pronounced Midi accent.

Billy smiled as he read that. Wesley, he thought, was not the only actor in the family.

———

They played tennis the next morning, driving over to a quiet club in Juan-les-Pins in the little open car, Wesley, in blue jeans and faded cotton shirt and a tweed jacket with frayed cuffs, not looking so much like an actor who had been acclaimed in the press as a man with an exciting career ahead of him. Billy had touched the little bulge in the pocket with distaste and had said, "Can't you leave that damn thing at home even when you play tennis? It gives me the willies. I have the feel-

ing you'll take it out and shoot me if I ace you once too
often."

Wesley smiled benignly. "Where I go, it goes," he
said. And when they went out to the court he wore the
jacket over his tennis clothes and before they started to
play laid it carefully over a bench near the net, where
he could see it at all times.

The first day Wesley played with the same old wild
abandon, hitting the ball savagely, more often than not
into the net or to the backstop. After two hours of that
Billy said, "That's enough for today. If you *acted* like
that they wouldn't let you as much as *see* a movie even
if you paid for the ticket."

Wesley grinned. "Youthful high spirits," he said, putting on the tweed coat over his soaked shirt. "I promise
to reform."

"Starting when?"

"Starting tomorrow," Wesley promised.

When they went in to take their showers, although
there was nobody else in the locker room, Wesley insisted that Billy stay in the room and watch his jacket
while he took the first shower.

"I've done some foolish things in my time," Billy complained, "but this is the first time I've hired out as a coat
watcher." He sat down on the bench in front of the
lockers as Wesley stripped, the big muscles of his back
standing out clearly, the long legs heavy, but perfectly
proportioned. "If I had a build like yours," Billy said,
"I'd be in the finals at Wimbledon."

"You can't have everything," Wesley said. "You
have brains."

"And you?"

"None to brag about."

"You'll go far in your chosen profession," Billy said.

"If I choose it," Wesley said, as he went into the
shower room.

A moment later, Billy heard, over the splash of the water, Wesley's voice, singing, "Raindrops keep falling on my head . . ." He had a strong, true voice and an accurate talent for phrasing on the lyrics. That, too, Billy thought, along with everything else he has. There was one sure thing, Billy thought, if anyone came into the locker room and saw and heard him, as though he hadn't a care in the world, they'd never guess in a million years that he carried a pistol around with him day and night.

As they went to where the car was parked behind the clubhouse in the shadow of the trees there, Billy said, "If you piss it all away, my mother will never forgive you. Nor will I."

Wesley didn't say anything, but just plumped himself down in the bucket seat, whistling a melody from the score of his picture.

The next day Wesley kept his promise and played more calmly. Suddenly, he seemed to have found a sense of the tactics of the game and mixed up his shots, playing the percentages and not trying to kill every ball. At the end of the two hours Billy was exhausted, even though he had won all four sets. Wesley wasn't even breathing hard, although he had run twice as much as Billy. And once again, he made Billy watch his coat while he took his shower.

The third day they could only play an hour because Billy had promised to get back early so that Donnelly and Gretchen could have the car to drive to Mougins for a quiet lunch. Since the running of the picture there was no chance of even a quiet fifteen minutes in Cannes for Gretchen, and she was showing the strain.

It took the whole hour just to play one set and Billy had to fight for every point, even though he won six-three. "Whew," he said as they walked toward the locker room, "I'm beginning to feel sorry I asked you to calm down. You'll wear me down to the bone if you keep this up."

"Child's play," Wesley said complacently.

They were dressing after their showers when they heard the explosion outside.

"What the hell was that?" Billy asked.

Wesley shrugged. "Maybe a gas main," he said.

"That wasn't any gas main," Billy said. He felt shaky and had to sit down for a moment. He was sitting there shirtless when the manager of the club came running into the locker room. *"Monsieur* Abbott," he said, babbling, his voice high and frightened, "you'd better come quick. It was your car. . . . It's horrible."

"I'll be right there," Billy said, but didn't move for a moment. In the distance, there was the sound of a police siren approaching. Billy put on his shirt and meticulously and slowly began to button it as Wesley rushed into his jeans. "Wesley," Billy said, "don't you go out there."

"What do you mean, don't go out there?"

"You heard me. The police'll be there in a few seconds," Billy spoke swiftly, biting out his words. "You'll be all over the papers. Just stay right here. And hide that fucking pistol of yours. In an inconspicuous place. And if anybody asks you anything, you don't know anything."

"But I don't know anything . . ." Wesley said.

"Good," said Billy. "Stay that way. Now I have to go and see what happened." He finished buttoning his shirt and walked, without hurrying, out of the locker room.

People from the nearby apartment buildings had begun to stream toward the trees behind the clubhouse where the car had been parked. A small police car, its siren wailing, sped through the club gates and squealed to a halt on the driveway. Two policemen got out and ran toward the car. As Billy approached he saw that the car was torn apart, its front wheels blown off and the hood lying some feet from the body of the car. Billy's view of the scene was blocked by the people standing around it, but he could see and hear a woman gesticulating wildly and screaming at the policemen that she had been walking past the gates and had seen a man bending over the front of the car with the hood up and then a few seconds later, after she had passed the gate, had heard the explosion.

In the high babble of excited conversation, Billy could hear one of the policemen asking the manager of the tennis club who owned the car and the manager answering and turning to point at Billy. Billy pushed through the crowd and only then saw the body of a man lying facedown, mangled and bloody, next to what had been the radiator of the Peugeot.

*"Messieurs,"* Billy said, "it is my car." If the manager, who knew he spoke French, had not been there, he would have pretended he only spoke English.

As the two policemen started to turn the dead man's body over, Billy turned his head. The people in the crowd recoiled and there was a woman's scream.

*"Monsieur,"* one of the policemen said to Billy, "do you recognize this man?"

"I prefer not to look," Billy said, with his head still turned away.

"Please, *monsieur,*" the policeman said. He was young and he was pale with fright and horror. "You must tell us if you know this man. If you don't look now you will be forced to come to the morgue later and look then."

The second policeman was kneeling over the dead man, searching what remained of his pockets. The policeman shook his head and rose. "No papers," he said.

"Please, *monsieur,*" the young policeman pleaded.

Finally, turning his head slowly, conscious first of looking at the stricken faces of the onlookers, of the tops of trees, of the blue of the sky, Billy made himself look down. There was a gaping red hole where the chest had been and the face was torn and there was a crooked grimace that bared broken teeth between charred lips, but Billy still could recognize the face. It was the man he had known as George in Brussels.

Billy shook his head. "I'm sorry, *messieurs*," he said, "I've never seen this man before."

# VOLUME

---

# FOUR

# CHAPTER 1

Billy was sitting at his desk in the almost deserted city room, staring at his typewriter. It was late at night and he had done his work for the day and he was free to go home. But home was a nasty little one-room studio near the university and there was no one there to greet him. This was by choice. Since Juan-les-Pins he had avoided company of all kinds.

On his desk, there was a bulky letter from his Uncle Rudolph, from Cannes. It had been on his desk, unopened, for three days. His uncle wrote too many letters, with tempting descriptions of the fascinating life at high pay for bright young men in Washington, where Rudolph now spent a good part of his time, doing some sort of unpaid but seemingly important work for the Democratic Party. At least his name had begun to appear in the newspaper stories from Washington, linked sometimes with that of Helen Morison and that of the senator from Connecticut with whom he traveled on missions to Europe.

Billy was reaching for his uncle's letter when the telephone on his desk rang. He picked it up and said, "Abbott speaking."

"Billy, this is Rhoda Flynn." It was a woman's voice, with the sound of music and conversation in the background.

"Hello, Rhoda," he said. She was a cub reporter on the paper, a pretty girl who was doing a lot better than he was, who already had a by-line and who tried to flirt with him whenever they bumped into each other in the office.

"We've having a little party over at my house," the girl said, "and we could use some extra men. I thought, if you weren't doing anything . . ."

"Sorry, Rhoda," Billy said. "I'm still working. Some other time, maybe."

"Some other time." She sounded disappointed. "Don't work too hard. I know what they're paying you and you shouldn't spoil them."

"Thanks for the advice," he said. "Although there're no visible signs that they think I'm spoiling them. Have a good time."

After he had put down the phone he stared at his typewriter, only the clatter of a distant teletype machine breaking the silence, the sounds of gaiety and companionship he had heard on the telephone still echoing in his ears. He would have liked to go to the party, talk freely to a pretty girl, but what he really wanted to say he couldn't say.

What the hell, if I can't talk to anybody else, I can still talk to myself.

He put a sheet of paper in the typewriter and began to tap on it.

This is for the 1972 notebook. For various reasons I haven't done anything on it since Spain and I'm alone and

anonymous and afraid in the city of
Chicago and I think there are some
things that should be said by a man of
my generation and my peculiar career
that might eventually be read with
interest in the future by other young
men. As the Colonel said in Brussels,
"We're on the firing line of
civilization," which if it was true of
Brussels, must be equally true of
Chicago. Messages from such an important
position should be left where survivors,
if there are any, might be able to find
them.

He paused, reread what he had written, remembered
that he had heard that the Colonel had been passed
over for his star and had retired to Arizona, where he
could play tennis all year. Then he began to type, very
fast.

I am getting neurotic. Or maybe not. I
think that I am being constantly
followed. I think I see men and women
whom I have never seen before staring
intently at me in restaurants, I have
gotten into the habit of turning
unexpectedly around when I walk in the
street, I have moved four times in six
months. Up to now, I have not caught
anybody in the act. Perhaps my mind is
prescient and is warning me of my
future. Maybe time is a circle and not a
spiral and somebody is on the circle,
coming the other way. William Abbott,
Jr.'s, neurosis, heretofore
unrecognized by science.
If I am killed or die in a curious
way, the person who will be responsible

is a woman who called herself Monika
Wolner when she worked at NATO as an
interpreter while I was in the army in
Brussels, and Monika Hitzman when I saw
her later at the El Faro Club near
Malaga in Spain. She was, and I suppose
still is, a member of a terrorist
organization which operated and probably
still operates all over Europe, with
connections, perhaps, with similar
organizations in America.

The man who was found dead after
accidentally blowing himself up while
placing a bomb in my car in Juan-les-
Pins, France, was a man known to me only
as George and was the leader of the cell
to which Monika Wolner-Hitzman belonged.
He was an expert with small arms and
until the accident which caused his
death, was considered an expert in the
manufacture of explosive devices.

I am writing this in the city room of
the Chicago Tribune, where I have been
employed for the last six months, as a
result of the friendship of my father
with one of the editors. My father will
know where to find this quite lengthy
notebook. Along with some books and
papers and old clothes and various
pieces of junk I have accumulated in my
travels, I keep my notebook in a foot
locker in the basement of his apartment,
as there's no space for it in my tiny
room. He knows that in the footlocker
I have some stuff I've written, but he
hasn't read any of it. I have led him
to believe that it is an outline for the
novel which he is constantly encouraging
me to write.

Since I left Cannes, where I underwent
a quite rigorous interrogation by the
French police, who rightly suspected
some sort of connection between the man
I knew as George and myself, but who
could prove nothing, I have not seen any
members of my family, more out of fear
of what could happen to them in my
company than any lack of affection. The
thought that just some twenty minutes
after the bomb went off I was to lend
the car to my mother and her friend for
a luncheon date haunts me, although this
is the first time I have been able to
bring myself to write about what
happened on the Cote d'Azur.

Once again he stopped typing and remembered the
hours with the two detectives who had interrogated him,
first politely and sympathetically and then harshly and
with open hostility. They had threatened to arrest him
but he knew they were bluffing and had held out, saying over and over again, "I can only repeat, in answer
to your questions, that I am here in Cannes only to see
my mother's movie and I never saw the man before and
I have no enemies that I know of. I can only guess that
the man made some sort of tragic mistake."

Finally, they had broken off and let him go, with a
last warning that the case was not closed and that there
was an extradition treaty between France and the
United States.

Rudolph had looked at him queerly, but that was to
be expected, after the business with the gun and silencer.

"You're a lucky man," Rudolph had said at the airport the next day, just before he boarded the plane to
New York. "Just keep it that way."

"Never fear," he had said.

Wesley, who was with them and who had lost his smile, shook his hand soberly, but had said nothing.

Gretchen had not been able to come. When she had heard about the bombing—there was no way of keeping it from her—she had collapsed and gone to bed. The doctor they had called for her had discovered that she had a raging fever, although he couldn't diagnose her ailment. He had ordered her to stay in bed for at least five days.

When Billy had gone to her room to say good-bye to her he was shocked at her appearance. Her face was a bluish-white and she had seemed to diminish in the space of a few hours and her voice was almost inaudible when she said, "Billy, please—for my sake—take care of yourself."

"I will," he said and leaned over and kissed the hot forehead as she lay propped up against the pillows of the bed.

Billy shook his head at the flood of memories, then started typing again.

```
     If I could have told the whole truth
to the cops, they might have given me
the Legion of Honor. After all, I was
instrumental in breaking up or at least
depleting a gang of assassins that was
terrorizing all Europe. Of course I did
it by accident, but accidents count,
too, maybe more than anything else. The
entire history of the family is one of
accidents, good and bad. Maybe of all
families.
     Despite the fact that I seem to be
avoiding any meetings with my relatives,
they write me often and keep me abreast
of their affairs. I write cheerful and
```

chatty letters in return, pretending
that my father is sober most of the time
and that I am doing splendidly on the
paper. Since I cover police headquarters
and small crimes in the local courts,
this is hardly the case. While I do not
pretend to my father that the novel I am
theoretically outlining will be another
War and Peace or even The Great
American Novel, I confide to him that I
beleve it is shaping up to my
satisfaction.

My Uncle Rudolph, who is the cement,
the saviour, the conscience and
ministering angel of the family, even
though he now, in his eternal search for
good deeds to be done, commutes between
Long Island, Connecticut, Washington and
the capitals of Europe, finds time to
send out long letters of admonition and
advice, which none of us follow. He
is the most ardent of letter writers and
it is through him that I hear of the
various activities of himself, my
mother, who is now Mrs. Donnelly, and
my Cousin Wesley, who has remained in
Cannes, having found himself a job as a
deckhand on a yacht. Uncle Rudolph finds
the time to visit Wesley in Cannes, in
connection with an affair that . . .

He stopped typing, stood up and walked around the
desk. Then he sat down again, stared at the sheet of
paper in the machine and began to type again, more
slowly than before.

Even now, I think it would be wiser
not to go into the subject of Wesley's
obsession. All of us, my mother, my

uncle and myself, have tried to get
Wesley away from the Cote D'Azur. None
of us have happy memories of the place,
to put it mildly. Even the festival
turned out to be a disappointment.
Contrary to what the publicity man on
the picture predicted, nobody was voted
anything by the jury and it's lucky for
Mr. Simpson that nobody took him up on
the bet of his left nut that Wesley
would go home with a prize. According to
my mother, who is about to start
shooting her second picture, Wesley has
refused her offer of a part, with a lot
of money attached to it, as well as
offers of important roles by other
companies. As of now, Wesley is
undoubtedly potentially the richest
deckhand on the Mediterranean. In his
last letter to me, Wesley wrote me that
when he gets through with that I still
have to call his affair on the Cote,
he will do enough work in the movies to
save up for a boat and set himself up,
as his father did, as a charter captain.
He sounds cheerful enough in his
letters, but he may be lying, as I do,
when I write to the family. Still, he's
got something that I haven't got to be
cheerful about. At eighteen he came into
about thirty thousand dollars minus a
big bite for the tax people, and his
girl wangled herself a job in the Paris
bureau of _Time_ and flies down to Cannes
to see him as often as possible. He
also writes that he gets in a lot of
tennis, except for the summer months,
and believes he could swamp me if he

played me now. I haven't touched a
racket since Juan-les-Pins.

The police never did find out what
George's real name was or where he came
from. I can't get over the feeling that
one day I will look up from my desk and
see Monika standing there. I dream about
her constantly and the dreams are erotic
and happy and leave me desperate when
I wake up.

---

Billy stopped typing, frowned. "Oh, hell," he said
aloud. He took the sheet of paper out of the machine
and put it with the other two sheets of paper into a large
envelope to take home with him. He stood up and put
on his jacket and was about to leave when he glanced
down and saw the bulky envelope his uncle had sent
him from Cannes. Might as well, he thought. I'll have to
read it *sometime.* He tore open the envelope. There was
a note clipped to a page of newsprint that had been
folded many times. There was a second note clipped to
the back of the newspaper page. "Read the item circled
in red," was written in his uncle's handwriting, "and
then read the note on the other side."

Billy shook his head annoyedly. Games, he thought.
It wasn't like Rudolph. Curious, he sat down so that he
could put the newspaper page under the light. At the
top left-hand corner of the page MARSEILLES was
printed in block letters and in smaller letters, *Page
Deux.* The column headed *Faits Divers* was circled in
red crayon.

*Mort d'un Voyou,* he read, his French still service-
able. Then the story:

Last night, the body of a man, later identified
by the police as that of Janos Danovic, a Yugoslav
national, was found on a pier in the Vieux Port.
He had been shot twice through the head. He was
known to belong to the *milieu* along the Côte
d'Azur and in Marseilles and was arrested several
times for pimping and armed robbery, although he
was never convicted of the crimes. Police believe
that it was another incident in the settling of accounts that has been keeping them occupied in
Marseilles in recent weeks.

Billy slowly put the paper down. Christ, he thought,
Rudolph must be crazy to send something like this
through the mails. If it had gone astray or if it had been
opened accidentally, some curious bastard would have
wondered why an adviser to an American senator
would be interested in the murder of a small-time murderer in Marseilles, and started to make unpleasant inquiries. He was about to tear the page into small pieces
when he remembered the note on the back.

He turned the page over and slipped the note out of
the clip. "Look at the date on the newspaper," his uncle
had written. Billy looked at the top of the page. It was
page one of *Le Meridional* and it was dated Samedi, 24
Octobre, 1970.

1970. Danovic had been dead over six months before
Wesley had gone back to Europe. Billy leaned over his
desk, his elbows on it, and put his head in his hands. He
began to laugh. The laughter grew hysterical. When he
finally could make himself stop, he picked up the phone
and asked the night operator for Rhoda Flynn's phone
number. When she answered the phone, he said, "Hi,
Rhoda, is the party still on?"

"If you can make it," Rhoda said, "yes."

"I'm on my way," he said. "What's the address?"

She told him the address and he said, "Ten minutes. Make me a stiff drink. I need it tonight."

As he walked out of the Tribune Building and went along Michigan Avenue, looking for a taxicab, he had the feeling he was being followed. He turned around and looked, but there were just two couples half a block behind him.

Maybe, he thought, it would be a good idea if I asked Rudolph if he still has that gun. It might come in handy.

Then he saw a taxi and hailed it and got in and went to the party.